# THE MILITARY HEROES COLLECTION

They've put their lives on the line to protect others
without a second thought to their own safety.
They are heroes. And it will take very special
women to capture the hearts of these brave men.

This classic 2-in-1 collection is dedicated
to those courageous, loyal and rugged men
who face danger on a regular basis…and are
willing to risk it all for a chance at love.

Whether they're secret agents,
brave soldiers or fearless pilots, these men
will have us all wishing for our own heroes!

D0835197

## RACHEL LEE

was hooked on writing by the age of twelve, and practiced her craft as she moved from place to place all over the United States. This *New York Times* bestselling author now resides in Florida and has the joy of writing full-time. Her bestselling Conard County series (see www.conardcounty.com for more information) has won the hearts of readers worldwide, and it's no wonder, given her own approach to life and love. As she says: "Life is the biggest romantic adventure of all—and if you're open and aware, the most marvelous things are just waiting to be discovered."

*New York Times* Bestselling Author

# RACHEL LEE

*A Soldier's Homecoming*

and

*A Soldier's Redemption*

**H HARLEQUIN®**
™ MILITARY HEROES COLLECTION

Recycling programs
for this product may
not exist in your area.

ISBN-13: 978-0-373-60622-1

A SOLDIER'S HOMECOMING AND A SOLDIER'S REDEMPTION

Copyright © 2014 by Harlequin Books S.A.

The publisher acknowledges the copyright holders
of the individual works as follows:

A SOLDIER'S HOMECOMING
Copyright © 2008 by Susan Civil-Brown and Cristian Brown

A SOLDIER'S REDEMPTION
Copyright © 2010 by Susan Civil-Brown

This edition published by arrangement with Harlequin Books S.A.

For questions and comments about the quality of this book,
please contact us at CustomerService@Harlequin.com.

® and TM are trademarks of the publisher. Trademarks indicated with ® are registered in the United States Patent and Trademark Office, the Canadian Trade Marks Office and in other countries.

**Printed in U.S.A.**

# CONTENTS

# A SOLDIER'S
# HOMECOMING

To Mom, who got me started.
I will always miss you.

# CHAPTER ONE

DEPUTY CONSTANCE HALLORAN drove along the U.S. highway toward Conard City, taking her time, keeping an eye on traffic, glad her shift was almost over.

Spring had settled over the county, greening it with recent rains, filling the air with the fragrance of wildflowers and the scent she thought of as *green*. With her window rolled down, the aroma wafted into her car, earth's special perfume.

Today had been a lazy day, an easy shift. She'd had only one call about a minor theft at one of the ranches; then she'd spent most of the day patrolling her sector. She hadn't written any speeding tickets, which was unusual. Even the traffic seemed to be enjoying a case of spring fever.

Maybe she would light the barbecue tonight and make some hamburgers. Sophie, her seven-year-old daughter, loved grilled hamburgers beyond everything, and loved the opportunity to eat outside at their porch table almost as much. Of course, the evenings could still get chilly, but a sweater would do.

The idea pleased her, and she began to hum a lilting melody. A semi passed her from the opposite direction and flashed his lights in a friendly manner. Connie flashed back, her smile broadening. Some days it felt good just to be alive.

Another mile down the road, she spotted a man standing on the shoulder, thumb out. At once she put on her roof lights, gave one whoop of her siren and pulled over until he was square in the view of her dash camera. He dropped his arm and waited for her.

A couple of cars passed as she radioed dispatch with her position and the reason for her stop.

"Got it, Connie," Velma said, her smoke-frogged voice cracking. "You be careful, hear?"

"I always am."

Glancing over to make sure she wouldn't be opening her door into traffic, Connie climbed out and approached the man.

As she drew closer, she realized he looked scruffy and exotic all at once. Native American, she registered instantly. Long black hair with a streak of gray fell to his shoulders. He also had a beard, unusually thick for someone of his genetic background. Dark eyes looked back at her. The thousand-yard stare. She'd seen it before.

For an instant she wondered if he was mentally ill; then her mind pieced together the conglomeration of clothing he wore, and she identified him as a soldier, or maybe a veteran. His pants were made of the new digitized camouflage fabric, but his jacket was the old olive drab. As she approached, he let a backpack slip from his shoulder to the ground, revealing the collar of his cammie shirt, and she saw the black oak leaf of a major.

At once some of her tension eased. "I'm sorry, sir," she said courteously, "but hitchhiking is illegal."

He nodded, his gaze leaving her and scanning the surrounding countryside. "Sorry, I forgot. Been out of the country."

"I guessed that. Whereabouts?"

His inky gaze returned to her. "Afghanistan. I'll just keep walking."

"No," she said impulsively, breaking all the rules in

an instant. "I'll drive you to town. How come you don't have a car?"

Something like amusement, just a hint, flickered swiftly across his face. "I need to be home a while longer before I'll be comfortable behind the wheel."

She let that go, sensing the story behind it wasn't something he was about to share. "Well, hop in. I'm going off shift, so unless something happens, I'll have you in town in twenty minutes."

"Thanks."

He hefted his backpack and followed her to the car. Breaking more rules, she let him sit in front with her, rather than in the safer backseat cage. Even in the large SUVs the department preferred, he seemed too big. Over six feet, easily, and sturdily built.

She reached for her microphone and called the dispatcher. "I'm back on the road, Velma, on my way in. I'm giving someone a ride."

Velma tutted loudly. "You know you shouldn't."

"It's a special case."

"Whatever." Velma sounded disgusted in the way of a woman used to having her good advice ignored.

Connie signed off and smiled at her passenger. "Velma is the department's mother."

He nodded, saying nothing. A few seconds later they were back on the road, heading down the highway toward town. They passed a herd of cattle on a gentle slope, grazing amicably alongside a group of deer. In places the barbed-wire fences were totally hidden in a tangle of tumbleweed. Indian paintbrush dotted the roadside with scarlet and orange, as if the colors had been scattered by a giant hand.

"It's beautiful country," Connie remarked. "Are you staying or just passing through?"

"A bit of both."

"You have friends here?"

"Sort of. Some folks I want to see, anyway."

She opened her mouth to ask who, then swallowed the words. He didn't seem to want to talk much—maybe with good reason, considering where he'd been. She thought of Billy Joe Yuma, her cousin Wendy's husband, and the problems he still suffered sometimes from Vietnam. This guy's wounds had to be fresher.

When she spoke again, it was to ask something less invasive. "Ever been here before?"

"No."

Well, that gambit wasn't going to work. Stifling a sigh, she gave her attention back to the road and tried to ignore the man beside her. If he stayed in town for more than twenty-four hours, someone would learn something about him and word would pass faster than wildfire. The county had grown quite a bit in the past fifteen years, but it hadn't grown much. People still knew everything about their neighbors, and strangers still attracted a lot of curiosity and speculation.

However, it went against the grain for her to treat a stranger with silence. Around here, folks generally made strangers feel welcome.

"I can take you to a motel if you want."

"Sheriff's office is fine."

"Okay." A scattering of houses near the road announced that Conard City now lay less than ten miles ahead. "My uncle used to be sheriff here," she said by way of keeping a friendly conversation going.

"Yeah?"

At last a sign of curiosity. "He retired a couple of years ago," she explained. "He and my aunt are in South America and are later going on a cruise to Antarctica. It blows my mind to even think of it."

That elicited a chuckle. "It wouldn't be my choice."

"Mine, either, right now. Maybe when I retire I'll see things differently."

"You never know."

She tossed him another glance and saw that he appeared a bit more relaxed.

"So," he said after a moment, "you followed in your uncle's footsteps?"

"Eventually. I grew up in Laramie. Then I moved to Denver."

"How'd that work out?"

"Well, I got my degree, got married, got divorced, decided I didn't like the big bad world all that much and came back to be a deputy."

"What's that like?"

"I love it." She glanced at him again, wondering what had suddenly unlocked the key to his mouth. But he seemed to have gone away again, looking out the windows, watching intently. So on guard. Expecting trouble at any instant.

And there were no magic words to cure that. Nothing but time would do that, if even that could succeed.

"I worked as a cop in the city," she said after a moment. "It's better here."

"Why?"

"Less crime. More helping people."

"I can see that."

She reckoned he could.

"So do you like your new sheriff?"

"Gage Dalton," she supplied. "Yeah. He can be hard to get to know, but once you do, he's great. He used to be

DEA, then he came here and my dad hired him as a crimi-
nologist. We never had one before."

"That is small-town."

She smiled. "Yeah. It's great."

They reached the edge of town, and soon were driving along Main Street toward the courthouse square and
the storefront sheriff's office. On the way, she pointed out
the City Diner.

"Eat there if you want rib-sticking food. Despite the
sign out front, everyone calls it Maude's diner. You won't
find high-class service, but if you're not worried about
cholesterol, sugar or salt, there's no better place to get a
meal or a piece of pie."

"I'll remember that."

She pulled into her slot in front of the office and turned
off the ignition. Before he climbed out, she turned in her
seat to face him directly. "I'm Connie Halloran," she said.

"Ethan. Thanks for the ride."

Then he slipped out of the vehicle with his backpack and
began to stride toward the diner. She watched him until
he disappeared inside, then shook her head and climbed
out, locking the car behind her.

Inside the office, Velma arched thin brows at her.
"You're still alive, I see."

"I'm not totally stupid."

"Just save the excuses until your uncle gets back."

Connie shook her head and hung her keys from the rack
near Velma's dispatch station. "I'm all grown up, Velma."

"That won't matter a flea dropping on a compost heap
if anything happens to you. I don't want to be the one explaining to Nate what you did."

Connie leaned over the counter, grinning at the older
woman. "I'm armed and dangerous, Velma."

All that earned was a snort. "Damn near everyone

around here is armed. It don't keep bad things from happening."

"Nothing bad happened. Now I'm going to sign out and go home to grill burgers for my daughter and my mother."

But Velma stopped her. "Who'd you give a ride to?"

"Some guy named Ethan. He says he has some friends around here."

"And you believe that?"

Connie sighed. "Why wouldn't I? He's wearing a major's oak leaf on his shirt collar, and he says he just got back from Afghanistan. Not your ordinary bad-guy disguise."

Velma's expression soured. "For somebody who patrolled the streets in Denver, you're awfully trusting."

"No, I just know how well I can take care of myself."

Velma's snort followed her out the door.

# CHAPTER TWO

GAGE DALTON, CONARD County's new sheriff—for three years now, which he guessed meant he would always be the new sheriff—sat at his desk reviewing reports, his scarred face smiling faintly as he remembered how Nate Tate used to complain about the paperwork. Nate had been sheriff for thirty-five years, a long time to complain about paperwork. As for Gage, he would count himself lucky if twenty years from now he was still the new sheriff and still doing paperwork.

Not that folks gave him a hard time or anything. It was, he supposed, just their way of distinguishing him from Nate. He signed another report and added it to the stack of completed work.

Not much happened in this county on a routine basis. Cattle disappeared or were killed under strange circumstances. That whole cattle-mutilation thing still hovered around, leaving questions whose answers never entirely satisfied the ranchers.

Break-ins, vandalism—more of that over the past few years as the county grew and bored youngsters got ideas from movies, television and gangsta rap. Although, to his way of thinking, the growing size of the younger population probably meant that, percentage-wise, there was no more crime than ever.

There were new jobs, though. When he'd first moved here fifteen years ago, the county had been losing many of its young folks to brighter city lights. Then the lights here had grown a bit brighter when a semiconductor plant was set up outside town. Easier work than ranching. Good wages. Folks had moved in, and more kids stayed, especially now that they had a local college, too.

Small changes with outsize impact. Nothing threatened the old way of life here yet, but it sure was odd to see kids wearing saggy, beltless, shapeless pants, as if the whole world wanted to see their underwear, instead of boot-cut jeans and ropers. Among the younger set, the cowboy hat had been completely replaced by the ball cap. Sometimes Gage grinned, because it was all familiar to him from the days before he moved here. It had just taken longer to arrive than he had, that was all.

Velma buzzed him on the intercom. "Sheriff? There's a man here looking for Micah."

Gage didn't hesitate. "Send him back."

Maybe he remained overly cautious from his DEA days, but Gage was protective of his deputies, their addresses and their whereabouts. Velma's description had spoken volumes. She hadn't given the visitor a name, which meant he wasn't local. Gage went instantly on guard.

A half minute later, a tall dark man appeared in Gage's doorway. Gage experienced an instant of recognition so fleeting it was gone before he could nail it down.

"Come in," he said to the stranger, rising to offer his hand.

The man took it and shook firmly, giving Gage a chance to study him. His first guess was Native American, but the thick beard threw him off. Coppery skin tone, but that could be from the sun. Chambray shirt and jeans.

"Gage Dalton," he said. "Have we met before?"

The man shook his head. "Major Ethan Parish."

At once Gage stilled. He studied the man even more

closely, and now the instant of recognition made sense. "You look a bit like him. Related?"

Ethan nodded.

"Well, take a seat."

The two men sat facing each other across the expanse of the old wood desk with its stacks of papers.

"Does Micah know you're here?" Gage asked.

"No."

"I see." Gage drummed his fingers on the desk for just a moment. He recognized the look in Ethan Parish's eyes. Micah still showed it on occasion, as did Billy Joe Yuma, the county's rescue pilot. He had also seen the look on the faces of his fellow DEA agents when they'd been on the streets too long. Sometimes he saw it in his own mirror.

"Look," he said after a moment. "If Micah doesn't know you're here, I don't feel I should be telling you how to find him. Maybe you should call him."

"This isn't something I want to do on the phone."

"Why not?"

Ethan Parish hesitated, looking past Gage as if debating how much to tell.

"Tell you what," Gage said after a few moments. "Tell me who you are. Something about yourself."

"Marine recon, special operations. One tour in Iraq, two in Afghanistan. Other things I can't tell you about. I won't be going back. Medical discharge."

"You were wounded?"

"More than once."

Gage nodded. "I'm sorry."

Ethan Parish merely looked at him. "I'm better off than many."

Gage nodded again. "Still walking."

Ethan nodded once. "And talking. Anyway, I'll be officially discharged within the next six months."

"Need a job?"

"If I stay here."

Gage rubbed his chin and settled back in his chair. "How's Micah fit in the picture?"

Ethan's mouth tightened.

"Look, you know about protecting your men. I'm no different."

That seemed to cause a shift in the man facing him. At last Ethan relaxed a hair. "This can't get out."

"Believe me, I know how to keep a secret. I was undercover DEA before I came here."

That did the trick. "Micah Parish doesn't know it, but he's my father."

Gage froze. "Oh, hell," he said finally. "This could raise a real storm."

"That's why I don't want it getting out until I talk to him."

"I can sure understand that." Gage paused to think again. "Okay," he said finally. "Tell you what I'll do. Micah's on his day off, so I'll drive you out to his ranch. But you better not tell his wife who you are before you get a chance to talk to him in private."

"That's how I was hoping to handle it."

"Then we see eye-to-eye. Come on, let's go. You can think up a cover story while we drive."


THAT AFTERNOON, CONNIE'S world blew up. It happened the way such things do, utterly without warning, and in an instant that was otherwise utterly benign.

On her day off, she always had plenty to do. Her mother, disabled by a severe fall several years ago, helped as much as she could, but being stuck in a wheelchair severely limited her activities. In many ways she created extra work for Connie, but it was work she didn't mind, because she didn't know how she would have been able to hold a job and care for Sophie properly at the same time without her mother there.

Sophie had reached the amazing age of seven, when girls start to act like little mothers, developing a streak of independence and becoming downright bossy. So far, Sophie's imitation of motherhood had proved more amusing than anything else, although Connie suspected that at some point they would need to have a discussion before the girl alienated all her friends by bossing them around.

"Perfectly normal," Connie's mother said. "All girls do it. It'd be worse if she had a brother."

"I suppose."

Connie climbed down from the ladder where she'd been spackling a small crack in the ceiling. Some major problems had begun to brew in the old house, but she couldn't afford to deal with them yet. "Want some coffee, Mom?"

"I'll never pass up a cup of coffee," Julia answered. "You know that. You don't even have to ask."

"Sophie should be home soon," Connie remarked as she washed both her hands and the spackling knife at the sink. "She'd better hurry. It looks like we might get a storm."

Julia turned her wheelchair so she could look out the tall window over the sink. "So it does. I wanted to ask you something."

Connie grabbed a towel to dry her hands and turned, leaning back against the counter. She raised her eyebrows. "I always hate it when you say that."

"Why?"

"Because it always means it's not an ordinary question."

Julia laughed. "Well, you're too old for me to send to your room, so I think you're safe."

Connie laughed, too. Just at the edge of hearing, she heard a rumble of thunder. "What is it?"

"I want to get Sophie a dog."

"Oh. Is that all?" Connie draped the towel on the rack by the sink.

Julia cocked her head to one side. "I don't know how to take that."

"Well, take it that I'm listening. Why do you want to get her a dog?"

"She's been asking for one. And Pru's dachshund just had a litter."

"A little dog, huh?"

"Well…" Julia drew the word out.

"Well, what?"

"Pru's not sure who the father is. And some of the pups have pretty big feet."

Connie couldn't help the laugh that escaped her. "Do you know what an image that is? A dachshund with those short, short legs and huge feet?"

Julia laughed, too.

"Sort of like a basset hound," Connie remarked. "Long, low and short. It's okay if she gets a dog, Mom. But she's got to take care of it."

"I was thinking it would be a chance to use her mothering urges on something besides her friends."

"Every little bit helps. Just be sure you're comfortable with the idea, because you know Sophie is going to forget at times."

"I'm a great reminder."

"Nag, Mom. The word is nag."

They were still laughing together when Sophie burst into the room with her best friend, Jody, out of breath and looking scared.

"Mom! Mom! A man tried to talk to us when we were walking home! He chased us!"

## CHAPTER THREE

As GAGE's SUV drove up the rutted drive to Micah's house, neither man said a word. Then a two-story house with a gabled roof came into view, a barn not far away. A woman was visible outside the house, hanging laundry. She was small and blonde, looking as delicate as a flower petal.

"That's his wife, Faith. The school bus won't bring their kids home for another half hour, at least. I'll wait for you unless you tell me otherwise."

Ethan nodded. His face felt chiseled from stone. Gage wheeled into the large yard, waving at Faith as he did so. She waved back, one hand holding a shapeless piece of laundry.

"There you go," Gage said. His hands were tight on the wheel as he stopped.

Ethan paused for a moment, then climbed out.

He had no idea what to expect. Faith froze like a frightened deer when she saw him. Statuelike, she watched him approach. He did so slowly, not wanting to frighten her more, wondering why she was frightened at all when Gage was here.

But then, in an instant, she dropped the laundry she held and gasped, "You look just like Micah when he was younger."

Ethan paused awkwardly. "We're related."

"I thought so." Then she astonished him by hurrying

toward him and wrapping him in a hug. "This is wonderful," she said. "Absolutely wonderful!"

A moment later she stepped back, holding his arms as she looked up at him. Her smile was wide and welcoming, and then perplexity entered her eyes, followed by the wavering of her smile.

"I'm sorry I shocked you," Ethan said quickly.

Faith shook her head. Biting her lower lip, she continued to search his face. "You look so much like him. You're not just a cousin, are you?"

She said it more like a statement than a question. Ethan hesitated, not sure whether to lie, and that hesitation apparently gave him away.

"You're...you're his son, aren't you?"

Slowly Ethan nodded. He hadn't expected to feel gut-punched, hadn't expected to feel his stomach quiver nervously. He had thought very little could fill him with fear any longer. But he felt fear now, as if everything rested on this small woman's decision.

There was an instant, just an instant, when she seemed to gather herself; then her smile steadied again. "That's wonderful. I'm surprised he never mentioned you."

"He doesn't know."

She nodded, almost a rocking movement. "I see. Well, then, this will certainly be a great day for him."

"I wish I were sure of that."

A little laugh escaped her. "I am."

"You're not upset?"

She tilted her head to one side. "Micah was forty-two when I met him. I'd have to be a foolish woman indeed to think I was his first and only love."

Tension seeped out of Ethan, allowing him to smile at last. "Thank you."

"Come inside. He's in the upper pasture checking on

the sheep, but he'll be back soon." She turned and gestured to Gage to join them.

"I'm just the transportation," Gage called. "Don't let me get in the way."

"You're never in the way. But if you want to go home to Emma, we can take care of him."

"You're sure?"

"Absolutely."

Gage waved and drove back down the long ranch road, trailing a cloud of dust in his wake.

Leaving the laundry, Faith took Ethan's hand and gently urged him toward the door. "This is remarkable," she said. "Absolutely remarkable."

He thought the only truly remarkable thing was that this woman, who had never seen him before, was so ready to accept him and take him in.

Inside, she motioned him to the kitchen table. "Coffee?"

"I'd love some."

She put a pot on the stove to brew, then sat facing him, her eyes drinking in every detail. "It's strange, but I feel like it's fifteen years ago and I'm meeting Micah for the first time."

"I didn't know I looked so much like him."

"Except for the beard." She nodded, her fingers twisting together. "So tell me about yourself, about your mother. Or you can wait for Micah, so you don't have to do it twice."

"I…" He hesitated. Then he said frankly, "I'm not used to talking about myself much."

"Then let me tell you about us." She seemed comfortable with that, and he was grateful. "We met and married about fifteen years ago. I have a daughter by a previous marriage, and together we have two daughters, twins. Micah saved my life." Her eyes darkened with memory, but he didn't ask, allowing her to tell her story in her own way.

She shook herself a bit, then smiled. "You also have an uncle here. He and his family live on a ranch a few miles from here."

"An uncle?"

"Micah's brother, Gideon. They didn't grow up together, but you'd never guess it now. You'll like him, I'm sure. He's a born horse whisperer, and he mainly trains and breeds horses these days. His wife is also a deputy, Sara Ironheart."

"Interesting family."

"To put it mildly." Faith smiled. "And now we have you. I'm the only ordinary person in the lot."

"Ordinary?"

She shrugged. "I've never done anything special. Everyone else has."

"I don't consider anything I've done special."

"Really?" She didn't look as if she quite believed him. "There's something about you that makes me think otherwise. Something like Micah. You've had a hard life."

"Everyone has."

"Not like that." She reached out unexpectedly and patted the back of his hand. "You can talk to Micah about it. He's the most understanding man in the world."

CONNIE SAT BOTH girls at the table while her mother set about making some hot chocolate to soothe them. But Connie wasn't about to be soothed.

Jody was crying, and Connie gave her a tissue. "I'll call your mom, Jody, then I'll drive you home, okay?"

The little girl nodded and sniffled.

After calling Jody's mother, telling her nothing but that Jody was going to be with Sophie for a bit, she joined them at the table.

"Now tell me everything. Every single thing you remember," Connie said gently. But she wasn't feeling gentle at all. At that moment she felt as close to murder as she ever had, even when her ex-husband had beaten her.

"It was a man in an old car," Sophie said. She was scared, but not as scared as Jody, for some reason.

"He followed us," Jody said, hiccupping.

"Followed you? How?"

"He drove real slow," Sophie said. "We kinda noticed it, so we looked."

Connie's heart slammed. "And then?"

Jody sniffled again. "He saw us looking at him, and he called out for Sophie."

"By name?"

"Yeah," Sophie said. "But I remembered what you said about strangers. So we started to run away from the car, and he yelled he just wanted to talk to me." Her eyes seemed to fill her face. "We got really scared when he started to drive after us, so me and Jody cut across the backyards."

For an instant, terror struck Connie so hard she felt light-headed. Her mind raced at top speed, trying to deal with dread and speculations, all of them enough to make her nearly sick.

Connie's mother spoke. "Come get your hot chocolate, girls. It's ready."

Connie grabbed for the phone receiver on the wall and dialed the emergency number. Velma's familiar voice became an anchor.

"What's up, honey?"

"A stranger went after my daughter and her friend. I need someone at my house right now."

Velma disconnected without another word. Slowly Connie hung up the phone and attempted to gather herself.

When she felt composed enough, she turned back to the girls.

"What did he look like?" she asked as the girls politely took mugs from Julia, who then began to put cookies on a plate for them.

"Ugly," Sophie answered. "He had a dirty beard. His clothes were old."

Connie's thoughts immediately flew to the stranger she'd driven into town just yesterday. Ethan, that was his name. But his beard hadn't been dirty. Nor had he been wearing old clothes. But who knew what he might be wearing today?

"Did he say anything else?"

"No," Sophie said, returning to the table. "We ran away."

"Can you tell me anything about his car?"

Jody sniffed away the last of her tears and came back to the table with her mug. Julia put the plate of cookies in front of the girls.

"Brown," Sophie announced. "But not dark like a crayon."

"Was it big or small?"

"Not as big as a sheriff car, but bigger than our car."

That was quite a range. "Anything else you can remember?"

Both girls shook their heads.

"Okay, you enjoy your cookies and cocoa while we wait for a deputy."

By that point, both girls were more interested in their cookies than in what had scared them. Ah, for the resilience of the young, she thought.

Because she was still angry and terrified. She wanted to grab her gun and go hunting for this man who had scared her daughter. She wanted to make sure he never again frightened a child.

Which was precisely why she joined them at the table and tried to smile, tried to cover all the protective, angry feelings inside her.

"It's going to be okay. Another deputy is coming to help, and we'll find him."

God willing.

## CHAPTER FOUR

GAGE WAS HALFWAY back to the office when he got the radio call from Velma.

"Connie's all upset. I'm sending Sara over there."

"What happened?"

"Some stranger approached her daughter."

"I'm on my way."

"Uh, boss?"

At least Velma didn't refer to him as the new boss. "What?"

"Those kids are already terrified."

"Meaning?" He thought instantly of his scarred face, of the shiny skin where the bomb that had killed his family had burned his cheek. There had been a time when he'd thought he ought to wear a mask like the phantom in *Phantom of the Opera*, so he wouldn't scare children, but surprisingly few, if any, kids were scared of him. Certainly not around here.

"Well, I was just thinking," Velma said, "too many cops all at once…"

"Might make them feel safer," Gage finished. "I'm on my way." With that he switched on his light bar and hit the accelerator hard. If some creep was hanging around, the sooner they got him, the better.

MICAH GOT HOME before Ethan had finished half a cup of coffee. He walked in the door, hat in hand, and froze almost as soon as he was inside. His dark gaze flicked from his wife to Ethan, then back.

Ethan rose to his feet and stared at the man he had been told was his father. There was an instant when he felt almost as if he were looking in a mirror, but only an instant, for almost at once he saw the differences. His face was weathered, but Micah's was substantially more so. His own jaw was a little squarer, and he was the taller by almost an inch. Less muscular, though. Running around the Afghan mountains on very little food had made him leaner, rangier.

But then gaze met gaze, and there was an instant of almost preternatural recognition that pinned them both to the spot.

"Micah," Faith said. "Micah?" Her husband looked at her. "This is Ethan Parish."

Micah's gaze shot back to the younger man. "Parish?"

"My mother was Ella Birdsong."

"Ella…" Micah repeated the name slowly, almost doubtfully. Then his face darkened. "She left me when I was ordered overseas on an extended op. I never knew where she went."

"She told me."

"She never said…"

"That she was pregnant," Ethan finished. "I know. She told me that, too. There's no blame here."

After a moment, Micah nodded. Then he advanced farther into the kitchen and reached out to shake Ethan's hand. "Good to meet you," he said, as he might have said to any stranger.

"Sit down, love," Faith said. "I'll get you some coffee. The kids will be home from school soon."

Micah nodded again, put his hat on a peg, then sat at the table. His gaze remained fixed on Ethan. "How's your mother?"

"She died three years ago."

"I'm sorry."

Ethan nodded. "I am, too. She was a good woman. I don't know why she never told you. She just said it was for the best."

"I know she wasn't happy about me being special ops."

"Then maybe that's all it was."

Micah thanked Faith for the coffee and took a sip, still studying his son. "What have you been doing?"

Ethan almost heard the unspoken question, *Why didn't you come sooner?* But he chose to take his father's words at face value. "Marine recon," he said.

"Iraq? Afghanistan?"

"Both." Ethan hesitated. "I just got out of Walter Reed. I'll be discharged soon. Medical."

Micah's face tightened. "I'm sorry."

"I'm better off than most."

"I can see that."

Faith stirred. "Why don't I go out to meet the kids at the bus? So you two can have some time. Ethan, you're welcome to stay with us."

He looked at her. "No, thank you, ma'am. I don't think I'm ready for that."

"If you ever change your mind, the invitation will be open." Then she grabbed a sweater off the peg beside Micah's hat and slipped out through the screen door. It slapped closed behind her.

The two men stared at one another, tied by blood, separated by a gulf of years.

"I probably should have called first," Ethan said finally.

Micah shook his head. "It's a surprise any way you want to announce it."

"I suppose it is."

"Well, hell." Micah stood up from the table and walked

once around the kitchen before going to stand at the screen door, looking out. "I knew," he said finally.

"Knew what?"

"I knew you were out there."

"What? She told you?"

"No." He turned slowly and looked at Ethan. "I just had a feeling. Like a piece of me was out there somewhere. I always wondered if it would turn up."

Ethan turned his chair so that he could look straight at his father. He crossed his legs. "My mother said you weirded her out sometimes."

At that Micah chuckled. "She didn't like the shaman in me."

"She didn't like it in me, either."

Understanding suddenly crackled in the air between them, like lightning, a feeling almost strong enough to make hair stand on end.

"You're my son," Micah said. His tone brooked no doubt.

"I am."

Micah returned to the table. "Then we've got a lot of time to make up for."

Connie stood outside with Gage, her arms wrapped tightly around herself. Cops were cruising all over town and the surrounding countryside, looking for the stranger who had accosted the girls.

"Bigger than your car and smaller than mine isn't much of a description," Gage remarked.

"No. But a beard. I thought immediately of the guy I gave a ride to yesterday."

Gage faced her directly. "Who was that?"

"I thought he was a major. He had the rank on his shirt collar. Native American, but with a beard."

Gage shook his head. "Not him."

"How do you know?" Her voice held an edge.

"Because while Sophie and Jody were being approached by this stranger, I was driving Ethan Parish out to Micah's place."

"Ethan *Parish?*"

Gage nodded. "Big guy, kinda lean, back from Afghanistan."

Reluctantly Connie nodded. "So it's not going to be that easy."

"Afraid not."

"What do we do now?"

"You know the drill," Gage said quietly. "You escort Sophie to and from school. I'll make sure you have time to do it. And if it's not you, it'll be me or one of the others, okay?"

"And Jody?"

"She doesn't seem to have been the target, but I'll tell her folks they need to watch her, too. And I'm going to double the in-town patrols so we can keep an eye on all the kids as they walk to and from school."

"Good idea. Maybe he just happened to know Sophie's name."

"Maybe." Gage looked past her, scanning the area. "If we don't find him, all this activity will probably scare him on his way."

"Probably." But Connie still couldn't relax. "All the parents need to know."

"Of course. The school is already taking care of that."

"Good." Connie sighed. "Gage, I'm scared to death."

"I don't blame you. But this isn't New York or Chicago, Connie. There aren't a lot of places to hide."

"In town, anyway." She suppressed a shudder. "I promised Jody's mother I'd bring her home."

"I'll do it. You just stay here with Sophie. I'll leave Sarah here, too. The rest of us will keep searching."

"Thanks, Gage."

He surprised her with a quick hug, then gave her a straight stare. "You know this whole town is going to be watching now. Sophie will be safe."

"Yes. Yes." But something in her couldn't quite believe that. The unthinkable had happened. And it had happened to her daughter.

She stayed outside in the gathering dusk while Gage retrieved Jody and put her in his car. Only then did she go back inside the brightly lit kitchen, where her daughter, mother and Deputy Sarah Ironheart were sitting.

She tried to smile brightly for Sophie's sake. "I was going to grill burgers again tonight," she said, "but I don't feel like it anymore. How about we try ordering from that new Italian place? They deliver."

Sophie was over her fear now, and the idea of pizza thrilled her. So easy, sometimes, to be a child.

Not so easy to be a mother. Connie didn't sleep a wink that night.

# CHAPTER FIVE

EVERYONE IN THE county knew about Sophie's encounter by
morning. Even Ethan could tell something was going on
as he walked into town from the motel to get breakfast at
Maude's. He noted that he was getting a lot of suspicious
looks he hadn't received even the day before, and by the
time he sat down at a table in the diner, he knew he was
under surveillance.

His skin crawled with it. He waited for Maude to come
to his table, pretending not to notice, but every nerve end-
ing in his body was wound tighter than a spring. Hyperalert, on guard, half expecting a bomb or a gunshot.

What he got, instead, was a menu, and a few minutes
later Gage Dalton entered the restaurant. Gage stood looking around the room and announced easily, "This man is
*not* the man who approached Sophie Halloran yesterday.
Leave him alone."

The eyes shifted away, conversation resumed, and in
seconds Ethan had heard enough to understand the basics
of what had the whole town acting as if it was under attack.

Gage joined him at the table, and Maude returned for
their orders.

"Steak and eggs, over easy," Gage said to Maude.

She snorted. "Like you have to tell me that." Then she
looked at Ethan.

"Same here," he said.

"So what's your name?" Maude demanded. "I don't like to call people 'hey, you.'"

He rustled up a smile. "Ethan."

Maude nodded. "You want coffee with that?"

"Always."

Another nod, then she grabbed the menu and stomped away.

"Our Maude," said Gage, "has great charm. It does take some getting used to."

"She's harmless enough," Ethan said.

"Depends on your point of comparison."

"So what exactly happened yesterday? I was half-sure I'd get shot while I was walking into town this morning."

"Remember the deputy who gave you a ride the other day? Connie Halloran?"

"Yeah."

"Some stranger approached her daughter in a car and called her over by name."

"I gathered that somebody had tried to abduct a kid, but I didn't know it was *her* kid."

Gage shook his head. "The rumor mill is in high gear. No abduction attempt, though. At least, not overtly. The guy wanted to talk to the girl."

"That's creepy enough."

Gage leaned forward, lowering his voice. "When Micah came in this morning, he suggested I take you on."

Ethan was startled. "Take me on?"

"As a deputy. At least temporarily."

"But why?"

"He seems to feel you're fresher at dealing with threats than the rest of us." Gage grinned. "He's right, you know. Whatever we used to be, we're all small-town cops now."

Ethan nodded slowly, turning the idea over in his head.

He, too, kept his voice low. "You want me to protect the girl?"

"Sort of."

Ethan waited patiently. He was good at that from years of sitting in out-of-the-way places waiting, waiting, waiting for his target. For information. For whatever.

"The thing is, what if this guy isn't really a stranger?"

Ethan's brow creased. "What do you mean?"

"Sophie didn't recognize the guy, but she's only seven. Anyway, everyone has it fixed in their heads that this guy is someone from outside the county. What if he's not? They'll dismiss anyone they know, even if he does something suspicious."

"I see what you mean."

"Now maybe Sophie's his target. Or maybe he just happens to like little blonde girls and goes for another one. Whichever way, if Farmer Sam sees Rancher Jesse talking to a little girl, he's not going to get suspicious. Because they're neighbors."

"I read you."

Gage smiled. "Micah said you'd help."

"He did, did he?"

Gage's smile broadened. "I always wanted another Micah Parish on my staff." He laughed and leaned back to let Maude pour their coffee, then put their plates in front of them. After she moved away, he leaned in again, keeping his voice well below the level of surrounding conversation. "We'll go over to the office after breakfast. It's time to plan."

"I didn't say I'd do it."

Gage's smile faded as he studied the younger man. After a bit he said, "You'll do it. You're not the kind to walk away."

ETHAN WALKED BACK to the sheriff's office with Gage. Throughout breakfast, only a few more words had passed between them, either because neither man was much of a talker or because too many ears were listening.

Ethan had come this way looking for something of himself, something that wasn't connected to the years in Afghanistan and Iraq. Whoever, whatever he'd been before was gone. Now, about to return to civilian life, he needed new anchors. Experience had taught him to deal with events that came out of the blue, often hectic, usually unstoppable and always initially confusing. It took a lot to throw him offstride.

But right now he felt very much offstride. He wasn't exactly sure what he'd expected coming out here, but this sure as hell wasn't it. He hadn't expected events to rise around him like quicksand again.

Protect a little girl? How could he say no?

"Velma," Gage said as they passed the dispatcher's desk, "Ethan here is going to be working with us. And I don't want anyone outside the department to know that for a while."

She snorted and blew smoke through her nostrils. A cigarette dangled from her left hand, ash hanging precariously. "Like that's gonna happen."

"You heard me. I know you can keep a secret."

They were already turning into Gage's office as Velma called after them, "It won't be me who lets the cat out."

Gage half smiled. "That woman is such an icon at that desk that if she ever passes on, we're going to have to put a statue of her there."

Ethan returned the half smile and settled into the chair he'd occupied only the day before. Gage rounded the desk, running his fingers through his prematurely gray hair, and sat.

"Help me here," he said. "We need to run surveillance. Keep an eye on Sophie in a way that doesn't overly restrict her. Keep an eye on the other kids. Because what we don't know here is whether she was a specific target or a target of opportunity. He could know the names of dozens of kids."

"Certainly possible if he's a local."

"The schools will be on lockdown all day. No students will be allowed out. Parents are being advised to pick up their kids at school or at bus stops. But that still leaves after school."

Ethan nodded. "My bet is that if the guy hasn't moved on, he's not going to try anything until the heat lessens. Just walking from the motel to the diner, I could tell you're on high alert."

"Are you saying we should stop?"

"I'm saying you need to be less visible." Ethan leaned forward. "If the guy hasn't moved on, you need to surveil in a way that will give him the guts to make a move. Otherwise, once things have been quiet for a week or so, you're going back to your normal routine and he's coming out of the woodwork."

"I was thinking that, too." Gage rubbed his chin. "But if we're facing a local, then all my deputies are well-known. It won't matter if they're in or out of uniform."

Ethan nodded slowly. "In Iraq and Afghanistan, I never removed my uniform. I knew I was walking around with a target painted on me."

"Which means?"

"You still have to be there. Just gradually lessen your patrols so it looks like you're going back to normal. But make sure everyone in the department knows you're not. That they have to leave what look like gaps, but only briefly. Sort of like fanning out but making sure you can always manage crossfire, if you follow."

Gage nodded. "And nobody gets in and out of town without being noted."

"Yes. So basically, you widen your perimeter, let it become porous, but not so porous you can't close it up fast."

"Makes sense. It'll take a little time to put it into practice."

"Yeah, it will," Ethan agreed, "but you don't want to relax your patrols too quickly, anyway. Never signal the enemy that you're laying a trap."

Gage rose and poured two cups of coffee from the drip coffeemaker on a rickety side table. He passed one to Ethan.

"I've got one more thing," he said as he resumed his seat. "It involves you directly."

Ethan arched a brow, waiting.

"Nobody in town knows who you are yet, especially since you registered at the hotel under the name Birdsong. So, I called Micah about this, and he agrees. He and Faith won't say anything about you. And I want you to move in with Connie."

Ethan stiffened. "Hold on there."

Gage shook his head. "It will work. You're an old friend of Connie's from Denver. She decided to ask you to stay with her."

A million alarm bells sounded in Ethan's head. "What good will that do? The guy isn't going to try to steal the little girl out of her bed."

"No, but it will make it easier for you to keep an eye on her, and nobody would know you were working for me. So if you happen to be seen around Sophie, you have a cover story. Otherwise…"

Otherwise pretend he was back in the mountains, on recon. Passing like a ghost through all kinds of danger. Except the danger here wasn't directed at him.

Things inside him that had just begun to loosen once again clenched like fists. He was painted, man. He was always painted.

He put his coffee down. "You better make sure the lady is okay with this. Because I'm not sure I am."

"She will be," Gage said confidently, his face darkening as if with memory. "Parents tend to be willing to do anything to keep their children safe."

Anything, Ethan agreed silently. Anything. He'd sure as hell seen enough of what that meant.

But all too often it resulted in horror that could sear the soul.

# CHAPTER SIX

CONNIE COULDN'T BELIEVE she was standing in a store getting a cell phone for her seven-year-old daughter. It seemed surreal. She'd never wanted one for herself, even after the technology arrived in the county, complete with two different carriers to choose from. Of course, she was hooked up by radio to the department, so a cell phone had struck her as just another intrusion.

Not anymore. Now it meant safety. Safety for Sophie. Her daughter would now have an immediate means of calling her mother or calling the sheriff. As Connie scanned the various plans, she started to choose the cheapest one with a minimum of minutes until she realized the obvious: Sophie was bound to use the phone to call friends, at least until the novelty wore off. Like parents everywhere, she gave up the fight before it began and protected herself against sky-high charges by purchasing a plan with more minutes than she thought Sophie could possibly use.

She bought a case to protect the phone, one that would loop fully around Sophie's belt, not just clip there. Then she got a phone for herself.

She walked out of the store with her plastic bag, feeling that somehow time had slipped its moorings. Conard City—all of Conard County—had always been a safe place for children, as safe as any place could be. She had the strangest feeling that she had switched centuries, that time had warped and carried her into a frightening new world.

Ridiculous, of course. Her time in Denver had exposed her to all this. But Conard County had in many ways escaped the worst of current times.

Climbing back into her cruiser, she gave herself a mental kick in the butt. How many times had she heard someone say on the TV news, "These things just don't happen in this town"?

They happened everywhere. She knew it then, and she knew it now. The difference, of course, was that her daughter would be the subject of the news story if things didn't work out.

Her radio crackled even before she pulled out of the parking place.

"Get on back to the office, sweetie," Velma said. "Gage needs you. Nothing bad."

A good thing Velma had added that, Connie thought, as she wheeled away from the curb and headed back to the office. Her heart had been caught in mid-slam. *Nothing bad.*

Five minutes later she was sitting in Gage's office with the sheriff and Ethan Parish. Ethan's presence made her uncomfortable in some way. Not fear or anything. Just a sense of discomfort.

"Ethan's joining the department," Gage said.

Connie looked at him. "Congratulations."

He nodded but said nothing.

"I figure it this way," Gage said. "Nobody knows Ethan yet, so nobody's gonna know he's a deputy. So we're going to put the story out that he's an old friend of yours from Denver."

Connie blinked. "Why?"

"Because then he can move into your house and help keep an eye on Sophie."

Connie's chest tightened as if it had suddenly been grabbed and squeezed. Her vision narrowed, and the next thing she knew she was leaning forward, gripping the edge of Gage's desk, panting for air.

She felt, rather than saw, Gage reach her side, felt him grip her shoulders.

"Connie. Connie?"

It was as if she'd been holding it all back, refusing to truly face the reality of the threat to Sophie until this very instant. She'd been scared, she'd been worried, she'd lain awake, but she'd managed to maintain some distance, some control.

In an instant, all that shattered. Reality came home with heart-stopping, mind-pounding force.

"Connie? Do you need medical help?"

She managed a shake of her head. Her voice came out thin, as if she couldn't get any air into it. "Somebody tried to kidnap my daughter."

Gage seemed to understand. He squatted beside her, rubbing her shoulder. "Delayed reaction," he said. "He didn't succeed, Connie. And we're not going to let him succeed. That's why Ethan is going to stay with you. His skills aren't dulled yet by living here. He's in peak form. He'll smell danger before it gets anywhere near Sophie."

She managed a nod, closed her eyes and fought for control. She wouldn't be any good to Sophie like this. She had to stay cool. Keep her wits. Finally she began to breathe again and was able to sit up.

The first thing she did was look at Ethan. "Will you?" she asked. "Do you mind?"

His was a face that didn't smile easily, she could tell, but he gave her a small one now. "Not at all. It's been a while since I felt useful."

"Take the rest of the day, Connie," Gage said, returning to his seat. "Get Ethan settled however you want, get Sophie from school, do whatever you need to so you can cope." For an instant his gaze grew distant. "I know what it's like."

He did, Connie thought. He certainly did.

TOGETHER SHE AND Ethan stopped by the motel to pick up his gear; then they drove to her house. Julia's eyes widened when Connie walked into the kitchen with Ethan in tow.

"What's this?" she asked.

"This is Ethan, Mom," Connie answered. "An old friend. He's going to stay with us for a while."

Julia's eyes narrowed. "I can smell a fib from fifty feet."

Ethan surprised Connie by pulling out a chair from the kitchen table so that he and Julia were near eye level. "The truth is, ma'am, I'm here to keep an eye on Sophie. I'm a deputy."

"A new one." Julia's eyes narrowed. "Looks like you've seen some grief."

Ethan shrugged. "The point is, I've been hired as personal protection for your granddaughter. Good enough?"

"Better than nothing."

"Mom!"

Julia looked at her, then back at Ethan. "She hates it when I'm truthful."

"Well," said Ethan, "that wasn't exactly truthful."

"Why not?"

"Because Connie is protection, too. She's not nothing."

At that, Julia cracked a smile. "Okay, then. Go get settled."

"I have a spare bedroom where—" Connie began, but Ethan interrupted her.

"No bedroom," he said. "I'll camp out in the living room. I want to be able to watch the doors."

"Okay." At that point, Connie didn't care. He could

perch on the roof if he wanted to, as long as he kept Sophie safe. He tossed his backpack into a corner, out of the way.

"Is it okay if I look around?"

"Help yourself." Connie dropped her plastic bag on the armchair. "I'm going to have to figure out how to use a cell phone by tomorrow morning."

"Why is that?"

"I got one for Sophie."

He nodded. "Good idea."

"It's not something I ever thought I'd do for a seven-year-old."

"Seems smart to me." Then he gave another small smile. "But don't look to me for lessons. I've never had a cell. I'm a radio kind of guy."

"I was a radio kind of girl until yesterday."

She walked him through the house, not that there was much to see. She'd converted the downstairs dining room into a bedroom for her mother. Upstairs, there were three small bedrooms, two with dormers. She used one of those and Sophie the other. The third room, at the back of the house, was cramped, with a low sloping ceiling, but adequate for a twin bed and dresser, if little more.

The house's only bathroom was downstairs, behind the kitchen. The house had all the earmarks of a place that had been built a bit at a time, the mudroom tacked on like an afterthought next to the kitchen. When the weather was bad, it was the way to enter. Otherwise Connie preferred the side door, between the kitchen and the driveway.

By the time they finished the tour, Julia had a pot of coffee brewing and invited Ethan to join her. He seemed willing enough, so Connie sat with them. She could barely hold still, though. Her eyes kept straying to the clock, counting the minutes until she went to pick up Sophie. Counting the minutes until she could hug her daughter and assure herself that everything was all right.

"What time do we pick her up?" Ethan asked.

"Two-thirty."

"Okay. When I finish this wonderful coffee—" Julia beamed "—I'll walk down to the school and scope things out from cover. After I get back, I think we ought to walk back down together to pick her up."

"Why not take the car?"

"Because if anyone's watching your daughter, I want to know it."

"All right." She wondered how he could be so sure, then decided he'd probably developed a sixth sense for such things where he'd been. It was probably the reason he had survived.

"All right," she said again. "What if I take a ball and we stop at the park on the way back? Let her get some exercise."

He nodded. "Soccer ball?"

"I have one, yes."

"Good. Bring it." He smiled then, a real smile. "Soccer is an international language. It was a great way to break the ice in Afghanistan. All I had to do was take out my ball and start kicking it around, and pretty soon I'd have a dozen or more kids with me, everyone having a great time. Some of my best memories are of kicking a ball around in that dirt and dust."

Connie felt herself smiling with him. She could see the pleasure the memories gave him, and she felt relieved to finally see a softer side to him.

But then her eyes strayed to the clock again. The minutes couldn't possibly move any slower.

ETHAN AND CONNIE left early to pick up Sophie at the school. Ethan carried the soccer ball under his arm, and they strolled along as if they had all the time in the world.

Ethan wanted it to look exactly that way. His eyes moved restlessly, noting every detail of the streets, the cars, the houses that lined them. Connie found herself doing pretty much the same thing, seeking anything that seemed out of place.

Ethan spoke. "It must be hard, being a single mother."

"Easier than being married to an abusive jerk. Safer for Sophie and me both."

"I'm sorry. What happened?" He paused. "I guess it's none of my business."

"I don't mind discussing it. I've given some courses in anger management, and I've used my personal experience to illustrate. My ex beat me. As in most cases, at first he was just controlling. It didn't seem too bad. Then he started to object to my friends. Classic. Cut me off from my support network."

Ethan nodded.

"But even though I was a cop, I couldn't see what was happening to me. It's odd, isn't it, how you can see something happen to someone else but not see the same thing happening to you?"

"I think that's pretty much normal."

"Maybe. Anyway, he undermined my self-confidence, made me feel responsible for everything that went wrong. Then he hit me a couple of times. He always apologized and swore it would never happen again. I was too ashamed to tell anyone. Cop as abused wife. Sheesh. Talk about humiliating."

"So what got you out?"

"When he knocked me down and started kicking me. I was pregnant. That's standard, too. It's like they resent the intrusion, the loss of control. Regardless, I had someone to think about besides myself. That time I didn't take it."

"Good for you."

She shook her head and sighed. "It wasn't pretty. After I managed to get to my feet, I knocked him down and got my gun. After that it was a restraining order and divorce. I never saw him again."

"He couldn't stand up to the gun, huh?"

"I don't know. I mean, it was a dangerous time. Thank God for my buddies on the force. They got me out of the house and into a shelter, and for a long time I never went anywhere alone." She looked over at him. "That's the time when most women get killed. After they stand up to their abuser and decide to get out. I'll forever be grateful to my fellow officers."

"That's the way it should be. If we don't take care of each other, who will?"

She figured he was thinking about his own unit and a very different set of circumstances. Sometimes one's own scars ached in response to similar scars in others. It was as if like recognized like.

"You're a strong woman," he remarked.

"Sure. That's why I'm coming apart. Sophie needs me, and I'm coming apart."

He touched her arm tentatively, as if afraid of her reaction. "You have to allow those feelings," he said. "The important thing is that you allow them when it's safe to have them. That's what you did in the office this morning. Sophie was safe at school, you were in a safe place, and it hit you. Good timing, actually."

"Yeah." She gave a short, mirthless laugh. "There's this level I was operating at, where I was in control and focused on doing what I needed to. Then, *bam,* I lost it."

"That's okay. Now you're back in control."

She glanced at him. "I guess you know about this stuff."

"Too much about it."

Surprising herself, she took his hand, feeling its strength, size and power. It was a toughened hand, callused and firm. She squeezed it gently. "Thanks, Ethan."

He didn't pull away. "Nothing to thank me for. There have been times when I wanted to beat my head against a wall until it hurt so bad I couldn't feel anything else. I never gave in, but I think you know what I mean."

"Yeah, I think I do."

All of a sudden she felt a whole lot better about things. She had an ally. An ally who understood. "So Micah is… your father?"

"Yeah."

"I'm sorry, but I never heard about you before."

"He didn't know about me."

"I'm so sorry."

"Can't say that I am." He shrugged. "I never knew him, so I never knew what I was missing. A few times when I was a kid I got angry at my mother for never giving us a chance, but I finally understood. She was scared."

"Scared?"

"Micah was in special ops. He'd go away suddenly, without warning, and she never knew when or if he'd come back. She couldn't handle the strain."

"I guess I can see that."

"Eventually so did I. She explained to me that she just couldn't see raising a kid that way. That *she* couldn't live that way."

"Did you have a stepfather?"

"That was the interesting thing. She'd date once in a while, but she never married. I don't know why."

They were talking about some very painful things, Connie realized, and both of them were acting as if they meant nothing. Just chatting casually about things that had at one time or another nearly cut them in two emotionally.

When she thought about her marriage, which was rare, she thought of it as being behind a glass wall. She could see it, remember it, but it no longer had the power to touch her. She wondered if Ethan had learned to do the same thing.

Unfortunately, the feelings, the pain, were still there and could escape at any time to inflict emotional mayhem.

Growing uncomfortable, she withdrew her hand from Ethan's and tried to slow her suddenly racing heart.

After a moment she said through a constricted throat, "I just realized something."

"What's that?"

"When the unthinkable has happened in your life, you live in constant fear of the worst."

He fell silent as they continued walking. They reached the corner, then continued to the right. The school was only two blocks away.

"Yeah," he said finally. "You do."

It was then that she noticed he wasn't looking around in the same way she was. She scanned things at street level exclusively, seeking shadows behind shrubs, people sitting in cars, danger in alleyways.

He scanned the ground level, too, but spent much less time on it. He looked higher, as well, to rooftops and upper-story windows. His perception of possible threat seemed significantly greater than hers.

But of course it would be, she realized. Nothing in her life could compare to war.

All of a sudden she felt as if she'd been whining. He'd seen things she couldn't even imagine, had probably lost friends in the ugliest ways imaginable.

But Sophie... Sophie was precious, too. Incalculably

precious. To her. Ethan seemed to understand that or he wouldn't be here with her right now.

Nor had he given her any sense at all that he didn't consider her feelings and her daughter to be as important as anything he had ever dealt with.

She felt a warm flutter toward him, and a burst of gratitude. "Thanks so much for helping me with this."

"What kind of man would I be if I didn't?"

She glanced at him before returning her attention to the street. "Trust me, there are men who wouldn't."

"Well, I'm not one of them. If there's one thing I've learned, it's that every single life is precious."

She believed him. And in believing him, she understood the horror of the life he'd led. By choice or by mandate, he had sundered his soul.

They reached the school. Around it, everything was dead quiet, so they took the time to walk the perimeter. Nothing caught their attention, but by the time they reached the front of the school again, busses were pulling into the circular drive, and cars were pulling into the parking lot.

Connie looked at her watch. "Five minutes till the bell."

He nodded. "I'm going to stand back a little and watch while you collect Sophie."

She understood. Only one of them should be looking for Sophie, the other should be keeping a lookout. "Don't stand too far away," she said. "You don't want to look suspicious yourself."

He nodded acknowledgment and stepped back only a couple of feet. In his chambray shirt and jeans, he looked pretty much like anyone else around here who was over thirty, except perhaps for the heritage writ plain on his face. He received more than one look from arriving parents, but no one approached him, perhaps because he stood in a way that indicated he was with Connie.

A group of teachers and administrators emerged from the building, smiling and saying hello to everyone, but taking no time to pause in conversation. They looked around as uneasily as anyone.

Shortly after, the bell rang over speakers inside and out. Within fifteen seconds kids began erupting through the doors, headed for buses or parents.

Sophie arrived within a couple of minutes. She ran over and threw her arms around Connie's waist, hugging her tightly but giggling at the same time.

"Jeremy has green hair!" she exclaimed.

"How did he get green hair?" Connie asked, squatting to eye level with her daughter.

"He painted it in art class. Mrs. Belgia tried to wash it out, but it stained. His mom is gonna be *sooo* mad."

"Maybe." Although if Connie knew Jeremy's mother as well as she thought, she figured the woman was going to laugh herself silly. Far better than getting angry, in her experience. And Jeremy would have to live with the hair.

Connie stroked her daughter's blond curls. "I'm glad you didn't decide to paint yours. I like it the way it is."

"Me, too." Sophie beamed.

Connie straightened, taking her daughter's hand. "I want you to meet a friend of mine. He's going to be staying with us for a little while. Ethan, this is my daughter, Sophie. Sophie, this is Mr. Ethan."

Sophie looked up, then up farther, her eyes widening. "You're an Indian!" she blurted.

For an instant Connie wished she could stuff cotton in Sophie's mouth.

But Ethan only smiled and squatted, the soccer ball

still under his arm. "I am," he said. "You've seen Indians before, right?"

"Yeah." Sophie grinned. "I think they're cool. I wish I was Pocohantas."

"Like in the movie?"

"Yeah. She's beautiful."

"Not as beautiful as you."

Sophie's brow creased. "Why not?"

"Cuz she's not seven years old, plus she's only a cartoon."

Sophie giggled. "I *know* that. What's the ball for?"

"I thought we could kick it around a little at the park."

"Cool." Sophie tugged her mother's hand. "Let's go."

With Sophie skipping and holding her hand, Connie started walking toward the park. Ethan was on her other side.

Part of her felt relieved that Sophie didn't seem afraid, but another part worried about Sophie's ready acceptance of Ethan. Of course, she'd introduced him to Sophie herself, but still…

"Maybe," she said quietly as Sophie sang cheerfully about the wheels on the bus as they passed the long line of waiting vehicles, "a little shyness would do her some good."

"Naw," said Ethan, just as quietly. "I didn't mind what she said, and you don't want to change her because of this thing."

"No." She looked at him. "That really worries me. That this *could* change her."

"Then don't let it."

"Easier said than done, I fear."

Sophie waved to friends, skipping along tirelessly, eager to get to the park. Connie kept scanning for anything the least bit suspicious but saw nothing. Everyone who was there should have been there. Nobody lurked or seemed out of place.

And the farther they got from the school, the thinner the crowds became, until they were nearly by themselves.

"Where's Jody?" Connie asked Sophie. "I didn't see her. I thought the two of you were stuck together like bubblegum."

Sophie giggled again and downshifted from skip to walk. "She didn't come to school today. I think maybe she was sick."

Connie's heart slammed. "I'll call and check on her." What if something had happened to Jody? But then she reminded herself that Jody's mother had been the first to learn of what had happened, apart from the police. So maybe she had just kept Jody at home today.

"I got a surprise for you," she told Sophie.

"Yeah? What?"

"A cell phone."

"Oh, boy!" Sophie let out a shriek of delight. "I get my own cell phone!"

"I got one for me, too, so when we get home, we'll figure out how to work them, and then I'm going to give you some rules."

Sophie's face scrunched up. "Everything has rules."

"Everything," Connie agreed.

Sophie peered around at Ethan. "Do you have rules, too?"

"Lots of them," he said. "More than you do, I bet."

"How come?"

"Because I was a soldier."

"Oh."

"Lots of rules for soldiers."

Sophie shook her head. "Not as many as my mom makes."

Ethan laughed. "We'll see about that."

They reached the park without seeing anything unusual, which contradictorily both eased Connie's mind and heightened her fear. No threat right now, but what if the threat was merely hiding and waiting?

She shook her head, trying to clear it of such thoughts. No good to think that way. Utterly useless worrying.

No one else was at the park. Not a single swing moved. Connie would have expected to see at least a few children, preschoolers out with their mothers, if nothing else. Cold winters made spring days welcome and cherished, but apparently everyone had hunkered down.

Ethan chose an open patch of ground between the swings and the baseball diamond, and set the ball down. "We're just going to practice kicking it around, okay? Because there's no one else here yet to play with."

Sophie nodded and dropped her backpack on the ground. "Everyone's scared because of that man yesterday."

"Are you scared?"

"A little. But I'm not alone."

"Right." Ethan smiled. "Have you ever kicked a soccer ball before?"

"Once in gym class. I wasn't very good."

"Then we'll work on making you the best kicker in your class."

Sophie nodded. "Yeah. The best."

"That's what we'll shoot for."

Connie stepped back, giving them room and pretending to absently look around, although there was nothing absentminded in her surveillance of the area.

She listened while Ethan showed Sophie how to kick with the side of her foot, not her toe. Pretty soon she got the hang of it and was kicking the ball where she wanted it to go. Both Connie and Ethan applauded her efforts.

A few minutes later, Sophie and Ethan were kicking the ball back and forth, even running with it a bit, every move accompanied by Sophie's cries of delight.

Connie would have bet Ethan hadn't a thought to spare for anything except the little game he and Sophie were playing. But then, in one dreadful moment, she learned otherwise.

"Let's go," Ethan said. His tone was level. Connie's gaze snapped to his face. He was looking at something behind her. Instinctively she whirled around, but she saw nothing.

"I don't wanna go," Sophie argued. "This is fun."

"We'll play more later," Ethan said. "Connie, take Sophie home. She needs a drink of water."

"But—"

Connie took her daughter's hand. "Let's go, sweetie." She hoped her voice didn't betray the sudden terror and tension she was feeling. "We've got cell phones to learn how to use, remember?"

Apparently that didn't seem important, because Sophie continued to pout as she left with her mother.

Ethan dashed away, soccer ball abandoned on the field.

## CHAPTER SEVEN

CONNIE PACED, TRYING to ease the tension in every muscle of her body. Julia kept telling her daughter to calm down and have some coffee, but Connie hardly heard her. All she could think of was the way Ethan had looked—and the way he had suddenly run off.

He'd seen something. Someone had been watching them, she was sure of it. For the hundredth time, she went upstairs and checked on Sophie, who was already in command of her cell phone and calling friends on it.

"Jody's mom didn't have the car today," she told Connie on one of her trips through the house.

"I know. I called."

"Okay."

"How'd you figure out how to use the phone so fast?"

Sophie rolled her eyes. "It's *easy,* Mom."

"I guess you'll have to show me."

"Sure."

"Later."

"Okay." Sophie went back to her giggling conversation with Jody. At least Connie presumed it was Jody.

Connie walked around the house yet again, looking out all the windows, then went back downstairs, checking the perimeter from inside.

"You're going to drive me crazy, girl," Julia said. "Sit."

This time Connie obeyed, even though her entire body felt electrified with the urge to move.

"You don't know that he saw a threat," Julia reminded her. "Remember, he doesn't know folks around here. He could be mistaken."

"Yeah. Of course."

Julia pushed a cup of coffee over to her. "Now listen to me, Connie. You'll be of no earthly use to anyone if you wear yourself out over nothing. Which is exactly what you're doing."

Connie snapped. "Don't you get it, Mom? Some stranger knows Sophie's *name*."

"I get it, all right. I also get that everyone in this county is on high alert right now, and if some stranger approaches *any* child, he's apt to be shot before he's questioned."

It was true, Connie knew. Maybe not the shooting part, but nobody around here was going to turn a blind eye to anything now. Not anything.

"Your neighbors are watching out for Sophie. For all the kids," Julia said. "You know that."

Connie drew a deep breath and tried to release some of the tension. "You're right," she said.

"Of course I'm right. I'm always right."

Connie managed a wan smile. "Very true."

Julia patted her hand. "Just hang in there. If the guy isn't gone, he'll get caught. In the meantime, everything possible is being done."

Also true.

But it still wasn't *enough*.

Just then, just as Connie was struggling with a desire to crawl out of her own skin as she tried to sit calmly at the table, Ethan entered through the kitchen door.

"Wild-goose chase," he said succinctly.

"What did you see?"

"I thought I saw someone lurking in the bushes. If he

was there, I sure as hell couldn't find any evidence of it. Sorry I scared you."

"Sit down," Julia said, "and have some coffee with us. Thank you for trying to protect Sophie."

Thank you? Connie thought. *Thank you for scaring me out of my wits,* she wanted to scream. But she knew that wasn't fair even as she thought it, so she bit the words back. Instead, she filled her mouth with bitter coffee.

"How's Sophie?" Ethan asked. He poured his own coffee and joined them.

"Oh, Sophie," Connie said, trying not to let the tension seep into her words. "She's so excited about having a cell phone, I doubt she noticed anything."

"Good." He sat across from her, studying her from dark eyes that seemed to see through her. The feeling was discomfiting, and she wanted to look away, but she couldn't. "At least there's one person I didn't scare."

Connie bit her lip, guilt edging into anger's place. "Sorry," she said. "I've been worried to death."

"Of course," he answered. "You can yell at me if you want."

His words acted like a pin, puncturing the last of her tension. A sigh escaped her as she rested her forehead on her hand. "You didn't find anything at all?"

"No."

The word hung on the air, bald and uncompromising, but its very brevity seemed to say something. Connie lifted her head. "There *was* someone there."

His face took on that carved look again, as if it had turned to stone.

"What did you find?" she demanded.

"Nothing." He shook his head. "I don't usually hallucinate. My life depends on seeing what's really there. I thought I saw something. I don't like being wrong."

That was a whole mouthful, Connie thought. A butterfly returned to her stomach.

Julia apparently missed the subtext, however, because she said kindly, "We all make mistakes, Ethan. God never made a perfect man or woman."

"No," he agreed. "Thank God."

LATER, MUCH LATER, after Julia and Sophie had gone to bed and to sleep, Connie found Ethan sitting up in the darkened living room. He hadn't even spread out the blankets and sheets she'd given him earlier.

"Are you going to stay up all night?" she asked. "You need some sleep."

"You're one to talk." He turned in the darkness, and she caught the glimmer of his eyes. In the faint misty light that came through the sheer curtains, he became a figure of myth, a tall man with long hair, lacking only a shield and a sword to complete the image. Deep down inside, sensations began to stir, sensations she had banished to hell years ago.

Instinctively, she pulled her robe tighter and held it closed over her breasts.

"I can sleep while Sophie's in school tomorrow," he said. Apparently he sensed the awkwardness in the silence, too.

"Coffee?" she asked. "I thought it was just going to be me, so I planned on making tea, but since you're a night owl, too, we might as well make coffee."

"That would be great."

Much to her relief, he didn't follow. She made the coffee in the dark, waiting patiently for it to perk, thinking it was high time she got a drip coffeemaker. In short, anything that didn't involve thinking about Sophie and the threat.

Or the man in her living room.

Some kind of preternatural shiver passed through her, focusing her mind on how Ethan had looked standing in the dark. Some psychic part of her clamored that she had business with him, though she couldn't imagine what.

Oh, hell, yes she could. It didn't take that big a leap to realize he drew her in some elemental way. Worrying about Sophie had kept her from recognizing other feelings, but here in the dark, they surged to the surface.

She could have turned on the lights, but she didn't. She didn't want to rupture the spell. It provided a much needed distraction right now, this yearning and need. This aching hunger that had grown unseen until it sprang from the jungle of her subconscious.

He would be safe, she realized. He would go away and take all the complications with him.

At once shock filled her. She didn't think that way. She had never thought that way.

The aroma of the coffee filled her nostrils, speaking of hot, delightful, yet bitter flavors. Turning, she switched off the flame beneath the burner and filled two mugs. Strong and black.

Ethan still stood in the living room, looking out through the sheers at the street. She went to stand beside him and passed him a mug when he glanced at her.

"Thanks," he said.

She didn't reply. The spell locked her voice in her throat. An aura surrounded him. Holding her mug in both hands, closing her eyes, she sensed an emanation of power, strength and something far greater. For a moment she knew with certainty that if she opened her eyes, she would see him surrounded by rainbows. Crazy.

He spoke, his voice like night, all black velvet. "My people," he said slowly, "believe that everything is alive, even the rocks."

"Yes?"

"Yes. My mother was Cheyenne. She taught me some of the old ways and had her brother give me some training in what I suppose could be called the occult."

She faced him then, forgetting everything else. "Shamanic tradition?"

"Yes."

"Wow." She barely breathed the word.

"Of course, it didn't fit with most of what I was learning elsewhere or with my friends, so I took it all with a large grain of salt."

"But now?"

"But now…" He shook his head. "I've felt the rocks cry out in protest at the blood spilled on them. I have heard the thunder speak. The ways of my mother's people are as valid as your ways."

Connie nodded. He *did* have an aura, she thought. She couldn't see it, but she sure as hell could feel it, humming around him.

Almost in answer to what he had just said, a crack of thunder rent the night.

Connie bit her lip, waiting. The air around them crackled.

"I'll protect your daughter," he said. "But know this."

She waited, her heart freezing.

"The danger is still there. I sense it. And it's closing in."

She wanted to scream at him that he was just trying to scare her, but deep in her very soul his words resonated with truth.

"Are you psychic?" she asked finally.

"Not really. If I were, many of my friends would still be walking this earth. But I *am* a mystic. I will admit that."

"And you sense things."

He looked at her, his eyes glimmering. "I sense things."

Turning, she put her coffee on an end table and wrapped her arms tightly around herself. "I can't stand this."

He astonished her, opening his arms and drawing her close, holding her snugly and comfortingly. Her head rested on his hard chest, and she could hear his heartbeat, a steady thud.

Tension, a tight spring inside her, began to loosen, as if his touch held soothing magic. His embrace seemed like a safe haven, an experience she had never known.

Then his fingers found their way into her hair, stroking and massaging gently.

He didn't offer any false promises, merely the sense that she wouldn't be alone. A ridiculous feeling, when the whole county shared her concern. But this felt closer and more intimate, more real.

They stood together for a long time, coffee forgotten, everything forgotten. Another crack of thunder, this one even louder, drove them apart.

Connie jumped back. Then, embarrassed, she reached for her coffee and retreated to an armchair. He, too, picked up his mug, then turned to face the window again, watching the flickers of lightning brighten the night.

Eventually she found her voice again. "What do you mean when you say you've heard the thunder speak?"

He turned slightly in her direction. "Just that. If you listen, it can speak to you. Not that I'm going to say it happens all the time. You're a Christian, right?"

"Yes."

"Have you ever heard God's voice in your heart?"

"A few times."

"Well, it's the same. Sometimes I hear the thunder in my heart. It speaks to me."

"And the stones?"

"The stones are alive. Everything is alive, Connie.

That's where we make our biggest mistake, I think, believing that some things aren't. Or maybe a better word would be *aware*. Everything is aware. That's why my uncle taught me to give thanks for even the smallest things. Give thanks to the tree before you cut it, things like that."

"I happen to think that's a beautiful way of looking at the world."

"It could be."

He returned his attention to the street. Lightning flashed brightly again, followed by a boom of thunder. "Give thanks to the rain, to the food you eat. To the mountains that shelter you. It's not exactly pantheistic, at least not the way my uncle taught me. But it does recognize the importance of everything in our world."

Intuition made her say, "You haven't thought about this for a long time, have you."

Another flicker of lightning limned his figure against the curtains, and she saw echoes of ancient warriors in the afterimage.

"No, I haven't. For years now, I haven't really had time to think about that part of myself except in a general way. I've been too focused on external reality. On trying to survive and keep my fellows alive. Not much room for anything else."

"I wouldn't think so. But now you have time."

"I do." He bent, retrieving his mug and sipping. "You make great coffee."

"Thanks."

The voice of thunder spoke again, a deep rolling rumble. Yet no rain fell.

"What I saw earlier today…" He hesitated.

"Go on. At this point I would believe you if you told me that you saw a leprechaun all dressed in green."

A chuckle escaped him, a sound not unlike the thunder. "No leprechauns. Something else."

She leaned forward, resting her elbows on her knees. "Tell me."

"What I saw wasn't there. It wasn't a man. But I didn't hallucinate, either."

"Meaning?"

"I didn't see with the eyes in my head."

Shock slammed her chest like a semi running out of control. She couldn't breathe; no air remained in the room. Finally, sucking in something that posed as air, she managed to say, "I don't understand. Why did you run after it if it wasn't real?"

"It *was* real," he said with certainty. "I hoped to learn more, but I failed. All I can tell you is that the threat has not gone."

"He's still here?"

"And looking for your daughter."

THAT PUT PAID to any possibility of sleep for Connie. She drained her coffee mug, then went to refill it. When she returned to the living room, Ethan was sitting on the couch, holding his own mug. He was turned to the side so he could continue to look out the front window.

Lightning flashed, thunder boomed hollowly, and the fury seemed to be trying creep indoors.

Connie spoke. "You can't know that."

"Perhaps not."

He didn't seem to mean it, and she didn't believe him, anyway. She considered herself a practical, prosaic person, but she also knew that was a bit of self-delusion. She'd had premonitions in her life. She'd had moments of absolute knowing that couldn't be explained any other way. Not many, but enough to give her respect for Ethan's intuition.

"Sorry," she said after a moment. Her hand shook so badly she put her coffee down. "I'm trying to find denial here."

He nodded. "I can understand that. But even if you do manage it, you won't stay in denial long. You're not the type."

"Maybe not anymore. I used to be pretty good at it."

"During your marriage."

"Yes."

That time the lightning flash blinded her, washing out the room with its glare. Then a crack of thunder threatened to rend the world. A cry from upstairs brought Connie from her chair and toward the stairway as if springs had ejected her.

Even so, Ethan beat her to it. He reached the top of the stairs when she was still only two-thirds of the way up.

She heard the bedroom door open, saw the light spill on as he flipped the switch. A couple of seconds later she was looking into her daughter's bedroom. Sophie, pale-faced, was sitting upright in bed. "I'm scared," she said.

Connie moved toward her. "That was sure loud, honey," she agreed. She sat on the edge of her daughter's bed and pulled the girl into a hug. "It made me jump, too."

"I wanna come downstairs."

"Fair enough," Connie agreed. "Hot milk?"

"Hot chocolate."

"Hmmm." Connie pretended to think about it, hoping Sophie couldn't hear how hard her heart was hammering. "Well, okay…"

A wan smile formed on Sophie's mouth, but her eyes remained pinched.

It was too much for her, Connie thought. First the attempted abduction, and now this storm. *Straw, camel, back,* she thought. "Okay, let's go downstairs. Hot chocolate sounds wonderful."

Another crack of thunder shook the house to its foundations. Sophie looked up, clearly trying to be brave. "This is a nasty storm."

"It sure is. Bad, bad, bad storm," Connie added, as if scolding the weather.

Sophie's smile grew more natural. Connie helped her daughter into her slippers and robe, and took her hand so they could walk down to the kitchen together.

Only as they moved toward the door did she realize that Ethan had vanished.

Gone like a ghost.

IN THE KITCHEN, with the lights all on, Connie began to warm milk. The storm had reached a peak of rage, shooting bullets of rain at the windows. Every growl of thunder made the house tremble. Long before the milk began to simmer, Julia appeared in her wheelchair.

"Goodness!" she said. "Only the dead could sleep through this."

"Maybe they're not," Connie remarked.

"Yeah," Sophie said. "Maybe they're sitting on their tombstones and wishing it would quiet down."

Julia and Connie both laughed.

"Where's Deputy Ethan?" Sophie asked.

"I don't know," Connie answered truthfully. "Mom, will you watch the milk while I get him?"

"As if you need to ask."

Connie didn't exactly want Ethan to join the family circle; he'd already breached too many of her defensive barriers, leaving her exposed. But if it made Sophie feel more secure…

He had returned to the living room, to his guardian position.

"Sophie wants you to join us," she said.

"Not necessary," he replied quietly.

"I didn't say it was. You've been invited."

She clearly saw him hesitate in the glare of another lightning flash from outside, but then he turned to follow her. "Thank you," he said.

The kitchen, the heart of this family, which ordinarily welcomed her with warmth, felt odd tonight. Alien. And it wasn't Ethan who made it feel that way. It was something about the storm, Connie thought. Something had leached away the comfort she usually found here.

As they drank, Sophie announced, "I don't want to go to school tomorrow."

Connie hesitated. Part of her wanted to wrap Sophie up and keep her right here beside her until the threat vanished, but another part of her of understood that would be a bad way to handle the situation. It would teach Sophie all the wrong lessons about dealing with fear.

Her hesitation gave Julia time to enter the breach. "Don't you feel well, dear?"

Sophie shook her head. "My stomach hurts."

Another boom of thunder caused the table to shake and their mugs to slide a bit. *Wisdom,* Connie thought. *Grant me wisdom. How do I deal with this?*

Julia knew no such qualms. "We'll see how you feel in the morning."

Ethan spoke. "It's all right to be afraid, Sophie."

"Do you get afraid?"

"All the time. I used to be a soldier. I was afraid every day."

"What did you do?"

"I did my job anyway."

Sophie nodded, her young face serious. Maybe too serious. "That's what you're supposed to do," she agreed. "Mom says fear is like a warning signal, and all it means is to be careful and think first."

"That's very wise," Ethan agreed.

"But my stomach still hurts. I wanna puke."

"Then don't drink that chocolate, child," Julia said. "Heavens, that's the worst thing when you feel that way. Let me get you a little ginger ale."

Sophie screwed up her face. "No. I don't want anything."

Watching her daughter, listening to her, Connie felt capable of murder. If she ever got her hands on the man who had frightened Sophie, he might never see the light of another day. Her hands gripped her mug so tightly her knuckles turned white.

She looked from Sophie to Ethan and saw a wealth of understanding in his dark gaze.

"Tell you what," Julia said. "You can sleep in my bed with me. It's close to the bathroom, in case you get sick."

"I *am* sick," Sophie said. She shivered. Then she leaped up from her chair and ran to the bathroom. Connie followed to find her daughter being sick in the toilet.

She grabbed a washcloth, wet it with cold water and pressed it to the back of her daughter's neck, speaking soothing words about nothing, rubbing Sophie's back until the dry heaves stopped.

When Sophie at last caught her breath and straightened, she looked white as a ghost.

"Well, that settles it," Connie said as she gently wiped her daughter's face, then helped her rinse her mouth. "You're staying home tomorrow."

"I *said* I was sick."

"So you did. And you certainly proved it."

RACHEL LEE71

Sophie looked grumpy. "You just thought I was scared, like a little kid."

"Sometimes it happens."

"But I don't wanna sleep upstairs until the storm is gone."

"No, of course not. This is the worst storm I can remember in a long time. I don't want to sleep upstairs, either."

"I'll sleep with Grandma."

So it was settled. A little while later, Julia and Sophie were tucked into Julia's bed, with a light on. Connie went back to the kitchen and found that Ethan had once again disappeared. The man had a way of doing that.

She made more coffee and poured herself a cup, listening to the storm, wondering if they might get a tornado. It sounded violent enough.

Then, as if drawn by an invisible wire, she returned to the living room.

Ethan was still there, standing at his chosen post. Connie sank into the armchair. "I don't think this is fair to you."

He turned to look at her. "Why not?"

"Well, you came here to see your father, and instead, you're living in my house, protecting my daughter, and your father's at the other end of the county."

He sat facing her, stretching his legs out before him. "It's good to be useful. As for Micah and me...we have no history to speak of. There's a silence between us. It may take years to cross it."

"But you can hardly do that while you're stuck here."

"Do you want me to go?"

Part of her did, but most of her didn't. "No. No. That's not what I meant. What kind of silence are you talking about?"

"It's hard to explain."

"So many things are."

"They seem to be," he agreed. In another flash of light from outside, she saw him rub his bearded chin. "There's a time," he said, "when silence speaks best. A time when just being with someone gradually creates a knowing. This is one of those times. He only just learned about me, and I never knew anything about him at all, really. It's not as if we can simply sit down and share the last thirty-some years in a burst of words."

"I can understand that." But she thought how odd it must be. It would be like that for Sophie, she realized, if that son of a gun ever returned. She prayed every night he never would, because with hindsight she could see that he'd never had a thing to recommend him, and she certainly had no reason to think he'd changed. "Has it been hard?" The devil made her ask as she thought of her daughter.

"Not knowing him? Not really. I understood why my mother chose as she did, and I respect that. There were a few times when I felt a little resentful that I didn't have a father the way other kids did. But not often."

Connie sighed. "Sometimes I worry about that with Sophie."

"You couldn't have raised her with that man."

"Absolutely not! But how old will she have to be to understand that?"

"Maybe not very old at all. Like I said, *I* understood, and my mother's reasons were very different from yours. Micah never abused her. She just didn't want to live the lifestyle. Her choice was purely selfish, and yet I understood it."

Connie tipped her head to one side. "Are you so sure it was purely selfish? Maybe she was thinking about trying to raise a child in those circumstances."

"It wouldn't have been easy," he agreed. "But I don't

think she really loved him, either. It was, as the song says, just one of those things."

"Perhaps. You're very philosophical about it."

"I've had time to think."

She nodded and transferred her gaze to the window as the wind took a sudden turn at battering the house. "This is going to go on all night."

"Seems like."

"So everything went well when you met Micah?" she asked, quickly changing tack.

"Better than I expected. Faith wanted me to move in."

At that, Connie chuckled. "She'd mother the whole world if she could. They make a truly interesting pair."

"What do you mean?"

"Well, you wouldn't ordinarily think of the two of them together, they're so different in so many ways. Yet she seems to touch a place in him, and he in her, that welds them. When they're together, you feel the sense of magic."

"I noticed that." He crossed his legs at the ankle. "Some families seem to make a circle around themselves, like a spell. They have that."

Connie nodded. "Exactly."

"So do you, with Sophie and your mother."

Connie smiled. "Thanks. I like to think so."

"I can feel it. It's good." He rose without warning and went to the window. He didn't speak, and Connie found herself holding her breath, waiting. The rain had stopped, but the wind still rushed.

"I'm going outside," he said.

"Why?"

"I just want to walk around the house."

"God, you're creeping me out! Did you see something?"

"No. No. It's just my training."

"What training?"

"A storm is good cover for an approach. It doesn't mean anything except that I won't be able to relax until I check."

She watched him stride out, thinking that his life had marked him deeply. Very deeply.

Most people carried scars from the past, but his wounds remained deep and fresh.

Would he ever let down his guard?

## CHAPTER EIGHT

OVER THE NEXT several days, life began to return to normal. Children again played in the park after school, the school itself resumed regular recesses, and while kids still walked in groups, as advised, parents no longer hovered over them every instant.

Even the police presence seemed to have lightened, although Connie knew that was far from true. Most everyone else assumed the creep had moved on. Not Connie. That creep had known her daughter's name.

Even so, she had to allow Sophie to return to some semblance of normalcy, walking home with her friends again, laughing and playing. She couldn't keep her daughter under constant lock and key.

But she remained watchful, and she was sure Ethan did, as well, even though he sometimes appeared to be invisible.

For her part, Gage assigned her to an in-town beat during the days, which meant she was available for Sophie at any time. Ordinarily she disliked working in town, preferring to cover the county's wide-open spaces and deal with the ranchers' families. Working in town usually bored her.

Not right now.

Her third day on the shift, Micah Parish shared the car with her. She wondered what Gage had been thinking, if there was some particular reason.

Apparently so. Micah, usually a quiet man, opened a

conversation several hours into the shift. "How's it going with Ethan?"

"Fine," she admitted. "He's not a problem, if that's what you mean."

"Not exactly."

"Oh." She waited, knowing from experience that pressing Micah often led directly to a stone wall.

"I was just wondering what you think of him."

"He seems like a pretty nice guy. For some odd reason he reminds me of you."

Micah laughed. "Faith said exactly the same thing."

"You're not getting much of a chance to know him."

"That'll come."

Connie hesitated. "It must have been a shock when he showed up."

"Not exactly. Somehow, at some level, I almost expected it."

"As if you knew?"

"As if I knew."

"Maybe you should come over to my place after school gets out. You could spend some time with him."

"He's not ready yet."

She glanced at Micah, then took the risk. "How can you know that?"

She expected the stone wall of silence, but he surprised her. "I just do. He knows where to find me."

Connie managed to stifle a sigh of exasperation. Ethan had come all this way, to the virtual middle of nowhere, to find his father, and now he wasn't ready to talk to the man? Why did she find that so hard to believe?

Yet Ethan had said much the same thing. Something about needing the silence first.

She was still thinking about that near shift's end, and she positioned herself strategically to keep an eye out for

Sophie as she pulled up near the school and Micah got out. He walked up the street, as if checking the cars parked along the curb.

Even with the cover of routine patrol and Micah checking cars for parking violations, he was still too visible, Connie thought. Still too visible to someone trying to avoid them. This wasn't exactly the porous surveillance Nathan had recommended. Yet how far could she let the risk run?

Life was all about risk. She knew that. Complete safety existed only in a padded cell, and perhaps not even there. But while she could risk herself, she found it impossible to risk her daughter.

She scanned the street again and noted that Micah had vanished from sight. Like father, like son. Ghost men.

She let out the brake and resumed cruising, circling the general area where the kids would walk as they left school, but trying not to get too close. Micah was surely out there somewhere, watching, as was Ethan. She could afford to create the appearance of space.

She stopped at one point to put a warning on a car with a broken taillight. She waved to the crossing guards who began to appear on corners. She knew every one of them as a neighbor. That was the wonderful thing about Conard County. Even with the recent growth, she could still get to know nearly everyone.

It was also the reason she had always felt safe here. But all of that now lay shattered like a broken mirror, reflecting scattered, distorted images.

Had it ever been safe here? Or was that an illusion?

She watched the schoolchildren as they scattered toward their homes. As usual, she enjoyed watching them and their sheer exuberance. It reminded her of the days when getting out of school for the afternoon had been enough to fill her with elation.

Unfortunately, it seemed to take a lot more to excite her these days. It occurred to her that the human race would probably be a lot healthier if they could hang on to some of that joy, wonder and exuberance later in life.

Or maybe that was just a lousy perspective to take. Maybe adults crushed themselves.

Then, once again, her thoughts wandered to Ethan. They kept doing that. Her mind, she thought wryly, had a mind of its own. Here she was, prowling the streets looking for a potential criminal, and she was thinking of Ethan.

And her thoughts, heaven help her, reeked of sexual attraction and desire. Funny thing, that. It always sprang up when you least wanted it. And, as she'd learned, often for the wrong person. After her ex, she just plain didn't trust her judgment of men that way. Now Ethan, a man she hardly knew, was turning the key in the locked box of her desires.

She'd tested the secure power of his arms, the hard muscles of his chest, in that single comforting embrace. But she hadn't felt his skin, and she found herself wanting to know in the worst way what his skin felt like. Warm and smooth? Rough?

*Damn!*

At that moment, she spied Sophie coming around a corner from an unexpected direction. Worse, she was alone.

Connie's heart accelerated along with her patrol car as she zoomed over to her daughter. Sophie looked over and smiled.

"Hi, Mom."

"Where are Jody and your other friends?"

Sophie shrugged. "I dunno."

"Climb in and I'll take you home."

Sophie did as she was told, climbing into the passenger seat, sitting with her book bag on her lap.

"Sweetie, you know you're not supposed to walk home alone."

"I guess I missed the others."

"How come?"

"I dunno."

When she paused at a stop sign, Connie looked over at Sophie. "What aren't you telling me?"

Sophie's lower lip stuck out. "Nothing."

For the first time in a long time, Connie didn't believe her daughter. "Honey, you know there's nothing that makes me madder than a lie."

"I'm not lying!"

"Okay." Connie thought about that, admitting that *I dunno* was the kids' equivalent of *I don't recall* under oath. "You're going to be a great lawyer someday."

Sophie looked at her. "Huh?"

"Never mind. Look, there's Micah. I need to stop for him, because we're supposed to be working together today."

"Okay."

Micah stood on the sidewalk, watching her approach, and when she pulled up and rolled down her window, he bent to look in. "I see you found Little Miss Lost."

"Lost?" Connie turned her head to look at Sophie. "Sophie, where did you go?"

"Nowhere," Sophie said. "I told you. I dunno where the other kids went."

Connie looked at Micah. "Later," he said. "Take her on home. Ethan and I are going to stop for a coffee and a chat. Gage said for you to take the rest of the day."

Connie nodded, her teeth clenched, sure Micah wasn't telling her everything. One certainty leaped out at her, however: Gage hadn't told them to take the rest of the day over nothing.

"Later," Micah said again. "Ethan and I will be over shortly, if you don't mind."

"I'll put the coffee on."

"Thanks."

She met Micah's obsidian gaze and saw reassurance there. Forcing herself to relax, she lifted her foot from the brake and drove toward her house.

ETHAN AND MICAH met at Maude's diner. Midafternoon, the place was quiet, with only Maude about to handle things. She poured their coffee, then disappeared into the back. The banging that carried through the kitchen door indicated that she might be involved in dinner preparation.

The two men, so alike yet so different, looked at one another across the table. The words, it seemed, still weren't there.

Finally Ethan broke the silence. "This thing with Sophie Halloran… I don't like it."

"Me, neither." Micah sipped his coffee. "Connie tell you about her marriage?"

"A bit. As if it were the distant past."

Micah nodded. "Faith went through something similar. When I met her, she was running from her husband, and a couple of weeks after she got here, he found her and tried to kill her."

Ethan's eyes narrowed. "And?"

Micah shrugged. "I was a deputy. I got there in time. He's gone."

Ethan nodded, as if approving. "Are you suggesting that Connie might be facing the same threat?"

"Not directly." Micah looked down at his mug and suddenly smiled. "You'll never know how many of the problems of life Faith and I solved over a cup of coffee."

Ethan answered with a similar smile. "Good time to talk."

"Especially when winter is howling outside. But back to Connie. She talks like it's all in the past and she's long over it. But I can tell you from my experience with Faith, she's *not* over it. She's buried it. That woman hasn't dated in all the time she's been here. Tells you something, because there are plenty of men around here who have asked."

Ethan nodded. "I got the feeling her rendition was more cover than fact."

"It is. When we did her background check before hiring her, I discovered the story was a lot uglier than the way she tells it. She sort of does the outline thing, like she's reading from a list of all the abused-spouse indicators. It doesn't get personal. But trust me, Ethan, it was personal. Very personal and very ugly."

"Kid gloves, then."

"That would be my advice." Micah leaned back and sighed heavily.

"You think this has something to do with Sophie?"

"It might. You know what evil men are capable of. You don't need me to draw you a picture. They say hell hath no fury like a woman scorned, but I can tell you, men are worse. Far worse. And if this guy is still p.o.'d that Connie got away, there's no telling what he might do to get even."

"But why wait seven years?"

"Didn't she tell you?"

"Tell me what?"

"He went to prison for what he did. And the judge really slammed him, because she was a police officer."

Ethan lowered his head a moment. "When did he get out?"

"About seven months ago."

"Does Connie know that?"

"I don't know. Probably. We got a routine notice through the office, because she lives here now."

"She never mentioned it. She doesn't even seem worried about that."

"Then maybe she *doesn't* know. Or maybe she thinks she covered her tracks well enough. She changed her last name, for one thing, after she got here. The post office has long since stopped making forwarding addresses available to the general public because of the danger. It may not have entered her head that after all this time he might come after her."

"And maybe he hasn't."

Micah nodded. "Maybe he hasn't. But I'll tell you, Ethan, I don't like that this guy knew Sophie's name. And I don't like that she disappeared today."

"Just briefly."

"Briefly is too long, under the circumstances."

Ethan sipped his coffee, thinking, reordering the pieces of the puzzle he'd been working with. "Okay. That helps."

"Maybe." Micah straightened and sipped his own coffee. "So tell me."

"Tell you what?"

"Where you've been and what you've been doing."

The question couldn't have been unexpected. Indeed, it wasn't. But Ethan had learned to compartmentalize his life in units he could handle. After a minute or so, he replied, "I think you know."

Micah waited, then nodded. "I guess I do. The hard part is figuring out how to forgive yourself."

Those words struck a chord in Ethan, seeming to crystallize a whole bunch of emotional and mental baggage. "Yeah. Have you?"

"There comes a point," Micah said slowly, "where you realize that the past is past. I'm not saying all of it was right, or even that any of it was right—or, for that matter, wrong—but it's the past, and you can't change it. So what you do, what you *have* to do, is understand that all that matters now is how you live today. If you're looking for atonement, that's the only kind you'll find. And the only way to get rid of nightmares is to build new dreams." Then he said, "I'm glad you came looking for me, son."

At that, Ethan smiled. "So am I."

# CHAPTER NINE

IT WAS FRIDAY evening, so one of Julia's friends picked her up for their usual "girls' night." Julia and her friends would dine at one or another's house, then go to a movie or play cards. Connie found it hard now to believe that once she had worried that her mother's confinement to a wheelchair would turn her into a shut-in.

Ethan and Micah made their appearance rather later than she expected. Sophie and she had already dined, and Sophie had vanished into her room with her cell phone. The ticker in Connie's head was already making her wonder if she'd bought enough minutes on her cell plan.

But all that faded to insignificance when the two men arrived.

"Sorry we're late," Micah said. "We went to do a little nosing around."

"Did you find anything?

"Unfortunately, no."

They gravitated to the kitchen table with their coffee, as far out of Sophie's hearing as they could get.

Connie, her nerves already shredded by Sophie's behavior after school, asked, "What did you mean by 'Little Miss Lost'?"

The men exchanged glances.

"I lost sight of her," Ethan said. "I was watching the kids come out of school, waiting for her. She came out with her friends. I moved farther down the street, trying not to be too obvious, and the next thing I knew, she wasn't there."

Connie bit out a word she rarely used.

"Exactly," said Ethan. "So I started looking. I found Micah, and we fanned out. She couldn't have been out of sight more than a minute or two, Connie. Honestly. Then I saw her walking alone along a different street toward home. I followed at a distance until she ran into you."

Connie nodded, aware that she was about to begin shaking. "She lied to me. She said she didn't know where her friends went."

"A kid's lie," Micah said. "Whatever happened in those couple of minutes, she probably did lose sight of her friends. You know, it might be nothing at all. She might have chased a squirrel, seen a dog." He shook his head. "It's obvious nothing happened to her."

"Except she's not telling me something."

"Maybe she's embarrassed because she didn't follow instructions, even scared because she lost sight of her friends."

Connie put her face in her hands, weary, worried and unsure. "I wish I could believe that."

A hand settled on her shoulder. Ethan's. The touch zapped her like electricity, almost painful in its intensity. Then the hand lifted, and she was once again alone in her own miserable little universe.

She raised her head, looking at them. "I'll make sure she doesn't do this again. Thank God it's the weekend."

Micah spoke. "Raising kids is the hardest thing I've ever done. Somehow you have to protect them without being overprotective. You need to warn them about dangers without making them scared of their own shadows. Connie, Sophie was just being a kid. They feel safer than they probably should, but you shouldn't want to take that away from them."

"I don't want to. It's just that…a few days ago she came through that door terrified because some stranger had tried to talk to her and called her by name. And then today…"

"Today the threat is in the past," Ethan said.

"Yeah," Micah agreed. "Eons ago in her mind. A week is a long time when you're seven. The whole world changes. So maybe what she did today was just some healthy hijinks. Kicking up the traces a bit. The point is, she's okay, and we'll watch more closely."

Connie nodded and managed a smile. "Sorry, guys. I'm not usually such a mess."

"You're not usually worried about your daughter." Micah stood, stretching a bit. "I need to get back to my family. You'll be okay with Ethan, Connie."

"I know."

Micah smiled. "Even bad things can sometimes bring about good."

And with that enigmatic statement, he walked out of the house.

Connie looked at Ethan. "Would you mind moving to the living room? I can hear Sophie better from there."

"Not a problem."

Just then the girl's voice trailed down the stairway as she giggled on the phone.

Golden evening light filled the room, so Connie didn't turn on any lamps. She sat on the sofa, and to her surprise, Ethan did, too. There was still plenty of room between them, but it felt more intimate than before. And she liked it.

That liking frightened her, raising images from the grave of her past. Leo hitting her, then apologizing and wanting to make love. Always, always, like some sick twisted game. How many times had she fallen for that?

Too many.

She began curling in on herself, as if in anticipation of an attack. She could feel it in every muscle and struggled to let go of it.

"Am I too close?" Ethan suddenly asked.

She nearly jumped as she looked at him. "What do you mean?"

"I seem to be making you uncomfortable."

"It's not you."

He nodded. Then, after the briefest pause, he said, "Why don't you tell me about it?"

"Why? I show you my scars and you show me yours?" The words sounded so bitter that shock shook Connie. "I'm sorry..."

"It's okay," he said, and everything in his tone said it was. "It's okay. I'm still reacting to threats that aren't there. I know what it's like."

"Yeah. I guess you do."

"It's like your brain gets rewired."

She nodded, still watching him in the golden glow.

"It's hard to turn it back around. When I came back on leave from Iraq, I couldn't drive. I absolutely panicked for a while, thinking every oncoming or parked car might be a bomb."

"That must have been awful."

"It was crazy. I knew it wasn't true, but I couldn't restrain the learned response." He shook his head a little, as if trying to drive away an exasperating bug. "I guess everything in life changes you somehow."

"So it seems."

"I still can't drive." He said it flatly, but even that tone spoke volumes to her. "Well, I can if I have to, but it's an awful lot of effort. More than it's worth most of the time. That's why you caught me hitchhiking."

"I can understand that." And she could. Maybe not in his precise terms, but in her own… Yeah, she could understand.

But the curling inward wouldn't stop, and finally words burst out of her. "Sophie is the best thing in my life," she said, tears starting to run down her cheeks. "My God, if something happened to her…"

He moved closer, drawing her into a gentle embrace, rocking her as if he knew how soothing that motion could be. "Nothing's going to happen," he murmured. "We'll take care of her."

The tears flowed silently, as if she couldn't release the pain and terror enough to sob. Water seeping over a dam that held back the huge lake of terrible things that had never ceased to haunt her.

She felt guilty. The man holding her had been through far worse. Endured far worse. That thing about not being able to drive a car was only the tip of his iceberg, and she knew it. Yet he had the strength to try to protect her daughter. To hold her and offer comfort.

In the midst of it all, she realized what a crabbed soul she had become.

"My God," she said, pulling away and hunting for the box of tissues she always kept on the end table. Finding it by feel, she pulled out a wad and scrubbed her face.

"What?" he asked.

"Sophie… She's never known her father. It's like with you. I took her away from him and made sure he couldn't even see her on supervised visitation. What if she's not as understanding as you? What if she grows up to hate me for that?"

Several heartbeats passed before he answered. He seemed to be choosing his words with care. "Do you think," he asked slowly, "that it would have been good for her to visit her father in prison? Good for her to ask questions about it at such a young age?"

"God! How did you know about Leo going to prison?"

"Micah." He touched her shoulder briefly. Then he moved back to his end of the couch, giving her space.

She needed that space, and she hated needing it. She wanted the comfort he offered, yet it terrified her. Finally she asked the most dreaded question. "Did you ever hate your mother for what she did? Ever? Did you ever resent your father for not knowing?"

"I'm human," he said. "I felt some ugly things, sure. Mostly when I was younger. As I grew older, I understood better. My mother used to have a saying. It helps."

"And that was?"

"The secret to happiness is wanting what you have, not what you wish you had."

Connie nodded, wiping her face again. "That's good advice."

"Not always easy to follow, but it's a good guidepost." He fell silent and thoughtful as the golden light began to fade from the living room. When he spoke again, it was to express volumes in a few words. "Sometimes it's impossible to want what you have."

She drew a sharp breath, sensing the anguish those calm words covered. The urge to try to soothe him in some way nearly overwhelmed her, but she didn't have a clue what to do or say.

"I guess," he said after a moment, "the thing you need to keep in mind is that even the worst things pass eventually. Everything passes."

She suspected he might know more about that than most, given what he'd done and where he'd been. Impulsively, she reached out and took his hand. He didn't pull away but let her squeeze his fingers gently.

At that exact instant, Sophie bounded into the room, waving her cell phone and nearly hopping up and down. Connie swiftly released Ethan's hand.

"Mom, Mom, Jody wants me to come over to spend the night tonight! Can I, please?"

Everything inside Connie shrieked *no!* but she held her tongue, trying to deal with the terror that swamped her and respond rationally. "I don't know…"

"Aww, Mom, I'll be safe there, and we'll have so much fun."

Connie fought the battle that every parent faces sooner or later, though in this case the threat was real, not imagined. In the end, after nearly biting a hole in her lip, she said, "Okay. But I'm driving you over there and picking you up in the morning, and under no circumstances are you to go anywhere without Jody's mom."

Sophie let out a shriek of delight and began babbling to Jody on the phone that she'd be over as soon as she got her pajamas and sleeping bag. A second later she was running up the stairs.

"That was brave," Ethan remarked.

"Or foolish." Connie shook her head. "I'm overreacting. She'll be okay with Jody's family."

"Of course she will. One thing you can say about creeps like this is that as a general rule they prefer their victims to be alone and unprotected. She'll be neither."

Gratitude warmed Connie. "Thanks."

"Don't thank me. You're doing the hard job."

"I just hope I'm doing it right. I guess you get the night off. Want me to take you up to see Micah?"

He shook his head. "We talked some this afternoon. Some things just take time, Connie. We're taking our time."

"All right, then. Help yourself to anything you want."

She rose. "It'll only take me ten minutes to run Sophie over there."

He nodded. "I'll be fine. You just go."

She thought about inviting him to ride along, then realized that would mean getting into a car, and she suspected that being a passenger probably was only marginally more comfortable for him than driving, despite all his hitch-hiking. As a passenger, if he had a flashback at least he couldn't be in control of the vehicle.

Sophie came bouncing down the stairs with her sleeping bag and backpack. "I'm ready!"

Ethan smiled. "I guess so."

Connie looked at Sophie and started smiling, too. This child was so precious, so full of life. Her heart swelled with love. "Let's go, sweetie."

Behind her, Ethan sat staring into the darkening living room.

# CHAPTER TEN

WHILE CONNIE WAS gone, Ethan stepped outside to walk around the house again. His training had built a restlessness into him, and he still struggled to realize that war no longer surrounded him. The thing with Sophie was keeping him on his toes, which he supposed was delaying his readjustment a bit.

Not that he blamed anyone for that. He actually felt good about having something useful to do, something he'd been lacking since he'd been shipped home on a stretcher from Afghanistan. He didn't remember much about being wounded, and the pain that plagued him had become a background noise to his days.

He still didn't fully understand why he was receiving a discharge. People with worse injuries returned to combat or took support positions of some kind. But somehow, because of the decision of some review board, he was out.

He struggled with that. He worried about his unit all the time. A sense of failure pervaded his every waking moment, just as nightmares haunted his dreams. He didn't *feel* as if he had a problem of that magnitude, but apparently others thought differently.

*You have inoperable shrapnel embedded near your spine.* It hadn't affected him yet, other than to cause pain, but one of the doctors had said that it would be years, if ever, before the body's protective mechanisms immobilized it or even ejected it. Until then, the wrong move could paralyze him.

And maybe that was all it was. Maybe they felt he could endanger his unit. One wrong move and he could become an instant paraplegic. Yeah, that could be a problem, all right, but no more of a problem than if it happened because of a wound on the spot.

He paused, looking up at the stars, noting that here in town he couldn't see very many. Not nearly as many as he had seen at night in Afghanistan. Most people in this country probably had almost no idea anymore of how many stars were up there, how many could be seen in the inky blackness of true night. He knew he'd been amazed when he'd looked up from the mountains of Afghanistan the first few times.

Sighing, he continued his perimeter check. He wondered if the good memories would ever begin to replace the bad. These days, his brain functioned like a bad TV show, with almost subliminal flashes of people being torn apart, buddies dying, and all the rest of it. It was as if no matter what he was doing or thinking about, some nasty director would flash up an image so fast he almost didn't catch it.

Except he knew what they were. He didn't have to wonder what had just zipped past his mind's eye. Some things were burned too deeply into memory to escape awareness that easily.

*Time,* they said. It would just take time, and maybe some therapy. He'd tried the therapy while he recuperated but found it pointless. The guy he had talked to didn't have any direct experience. Oh, he tried, even offering medication, but how could you discuss something worse than the worst horror movie with someone who hadn't even seen *The Exorcist?*

Smiling grimly, he finished his circumnavigation of the

house, aware that if this were his post, he would be ripping out a lot of concealing shrubbery and cutting down a few trees that came way too close to the roof.

But this wasn't a military post, and he wasn't preparing for a Taliban incursion. Drawing that distinction seemed to be getting a little easier, and for that he gave thanks.

Inside again, he glanced at his watch. Connie had been gone more than ten minutes. A man who had learned that tardiness could be a sign of catastrophe found it hard to remember that she had probably just stopped to talk with Jody's mother for a few minutes.

God, this living in two worlds was going to drive him nuts.

The phone rang, and he hesitated only a moment before answering it.

"Hi, Ethan, this is Julia. Is my daughter there?"

He felt a smile tug at the corners of his mouth as he heard laughter in the background. "Sorry, ma'am, she took Sophie over to spend the night at Jody's. She should be back any minute. Do you want her to call?"

"Oh, that's not necessary. Just tell her I won't be home tonight. The girls have decided to have an old-fashioned pajama party."

"Hey, that's great," he said with as much warmth as he could muster. "Have fun."

"I will. Sally will bring me home in the morning." Then Julia paused, her voice taking on a different note. "Take care of my girls for me, Ethan. Please."

"I intend to."

When he hung up, he felt oddly revitalized. As if he had his orders now and knew what to do.

He heard Connie pull into the driveway and come through the kitchen door. He heard the lock click behind her; then she returned to the darkened living room.

"Ethan?"

"I just realized something," he said without preamble.

"What's that?"

"That someone else has been organizing my life for so long, I don't know how to get on without orders."

She came farther into the room but didn't switch on a light. "That must stink."

"In a way it does. In another way it's good."

"How so?"

He turned toward her. "It's another challenge. I need challenge."

"I see." Leaning over, she switched on a light at the end of the sofa. It wasn't terribly bright, but it blocked all view of the world beyond the windows and revealed them to one another.

"Your mother called. She said she and her friends are going to have a pajama party. She'll be back in the morning."

At that Connie laughed. "Those women. They're in their second childhood. It's so neat."

"Yeah."

Her eyes came back to him, searching his face. "Didn't you have decisions to make in the service?"

"Plenty. But they were always directed at completing my assignment. My orders."

She nodded. "I hadn't thought of that. And you've been feeling at loose ends without an assignment."

"Basically, yes."

He made a conscious effort to relax and sat on the couch again. "That's probably part of the reason I feel so out of it. I've lived one lifestyle since I was eighteen, and now it's gone."

"That's gotta be tough, Ethan."

"No. I just needed to understand what was happening. Part of it, at least."

"Is that why you were so ready to step in and help with Sophie?"

"Partly. But most of it is that nothing makes me madder than a guy who wants to hurt children." His hands clenched on his lap, and he let them. "But don't think this is some kind of therapy for me."

"I didn't think it was. If anything, I thought it might make your reentry more difficult."

That surprised him. He looked at her and felt an unexpected surge of something so primal and elemental that it shocked him. Urges he hadn't had time or room for since the war began, not even when he came home on leave, because even then he was too busy just coping with what now seemed like an alternative universe.

Despite his preference for silence, for dealing with things in the privacy of his own mind, he started talking.

"Coming home doesn't feel like coming home anymore."

She nodded encouragingly.

"I don't know if you can understand, but I walk around feeling naked because I don't have an M-16 in my arms. It's as if I'm exposed to every danger in the world, and I don't even have a knife to pull."

"Oh, Ethan…"

He made a slight gesture, asking her to just let him continue.

"I know it's wrong. I know it's a kind of mental instability, but there it is. I come home, and I feel adrift. Purposeless. Naked. Being at home…it's like visiting another planet. I felt less out of place the first time I was shipped overseas."

"They say that Peace Corps volunteers adjust to their

new countries more easily than they adjust to their return here. There must be a reason for it."

He sighed. "Sorry, I'm dumping."

"Dump away."

He rose and began pacing the living room slowly. He paused just once to draw the heavy curtains closed over the sheers. "It's like I know things other people can't understand. Some folks I know think that makes them better. Hell, I know a SEAL who's so full of his own superiority because he's been through life-and-death situations, because he knows things…he scorns civilians."

"Do *you*?"

"No. That's the thing. I took on this job because I had the stupid idea that I'd be protecting other people from having to know, not because it would make me special. But now I can't come home."

He hated showing his weakness the instant the words escaped him. He wanted to snatch them back and rip them to shreds with his bare hands, because he had no business whining about this shit. No business at all.

But before self-disgust could conquer him, he had a warm, soft woman in his arms, holding him tightly as if she wanted to anchor him in the storm.

"Oh, Ethan… Ethan…"

Her voice seemed to call to him from across an abyss, the abyss that separated him from his current reality. The yawning abyss of places he had been, horrors he had seen, evils he had done.

*I'm not worthy.*

The words had been rattling around in his head for a long time, but now they rang loud with a truth he couldn't ignore. He'd bloodied his hands, whether for good or ill he no longer knew. How could he know? Clausewitz had written that war was politics by other means. He couldn't judge the politics. And after he got to Afghanistan, he couldn't even tell any longer if the cost of chasing the Taliban and al Qaeda was worth it. Because he saw the cost day in and day out. The cost in innocent lives, which hadn't stopped on 9/11.

His job over there had been to win hearts and minds while pushing back the forces of darkness. He wished he could be sure that was all he had done.

But in a war without uniforms, how could you always tell?

You couldn't. So you had to live with the stain and wonder forever.

His hands weren't clean, might never be clean, but he wrapped them around Connie and held her as tight as he would a lifeline. He needed the affirmation as much as he'd ever needed anything.

Odd, he'd wanted it from Micah, but he found, instead, that it mattered more coming from this woman, an innocent who had never sullied herself. It didn't make logical sense, but emotionally he felt as if she was offering forgiveness.

He just didn't know if he could accept it. Didn't know if he deserved it.

Soon, even that question began to slip away, replaced by deepening awareness of the body pressed against his. Sexual desire, long held at bay by the need for survival that could be lost in a moment's inattention, began to pace within him like too-long-caged wolf.

Nor was it simply desire for any woman. No. He desired *this* woman and no other. *Her* warmth, *her* curves, awakened him. It would have been so easy just to give in and carry her to the floor, but conscience rose, reminding him of her vulnerability.

Just as he would have released her, she lifted her head

and her lips found his. The brush of a butterfly wing, so light he barely felt it, but it sent an electric jolt to the farthest cells of his body.

He almost swore. Like Frankenstein's monster, lightning was bringing him to life. She deserved so much better.

But the thought never fully formed, because she moved against him, just a little, a soft murmur escaping her as she sought deeper contact with his mouth.

He couldn't resist. He needed this kiss more than he had needed anything in his life. He lowered his head, pressing his mouth to hers, gently at first, then more deeply, as she welcomed him.

His groin throbbed with forgotten longing as his body woke to new possibilities that seemed to offer salvation of some kind.

He ached deeply, needing...needing...

"Ethan..."

His name sounded like a prayer as she whispered it. Buried parts of his very being burst free of their bonds, reminding him that he was a living, breathing man like any other.

It would have been less painful to rip off his own skin, but he pulled away, conscience piercing him like a dagger.

She looked at him from sleepy, worried eyes. "Ethan?"

"I don't want to hurt you, and I'm afraid I might. I can't even trust *myself,* Connie. How can I ask anyone else to trust me?"

A wounded look pinched her eyes, and finally she nodded. "You're right," she said thickly. "I can't trust myself, either. I've been avoiding men since Leo because I know I'm not a decent judge, and..." She turned and fled.

He listened to her feet pound as she ran upstairs to her bedroom, and he hated himself.

Not hurt her? He just had.

# CHAPTER ELEVEN

ALTHOUGH IT WAS still early evening, Connie got ready for bed. She went through the motions automatically, trying to fight down feelings of hurt and despair that really had nothing to do with Ethan. All he had done was remind her of Leo. That wasn't his fault.

In fact, she told herself as she brushed her teeth, he had been kind enough to protect her from herself.

So why did she feel so bad?

A quick shower washed off the day's grit but not the day's worries. Nothing could wash those away, and she seemed to nurture them sometimes. Oh, not her concern about Sophie. That was as real as a worry could be. But other stuff. Her past. Her constant tension, as if she feared being beaten again. As she knew only too well, not even packing a gun could protect her from that, not when she loved someone. Or thought she did.

Some old country song floated into her mind as she climbed into a cotton nightshirt. Something about it not really being love if it tore you apart.

Great line. But as someone who had been there, she knew the other side of that one. Leo had never loved her in the true sense of the word, but she had sure as hell loved him. At least until fear pushed out the love.

She flopped onto the bed and reached for the TV remote on her night table, then hunted for something that would occupy her mind enough to keep her from thinking. She'd been thinking for too many years as it was, but tonight she doubted she would be able to even manage to read a book. Everything about her felt scattered to the four winds.

No crime shows, too close to her job. No romances, too painful. Ghosts? Didn't she already have enough of her own? Comedy didn't seem very funny tonight. News? No, there might be something there to remind her of the very things she was trying to forget.

Finally she settled on a lightweight British police procedural. Amusing, devoid of ugliness, very different from the real thing.

She switched off the light and settled in, hoping the eccentric British characters would suffice to distract her.

Unfortunately, her body wasn't quite ready to quiet down. She wondered if Leo had ever aroused her the way Ethan just had. If he ever had, she couldn't remember now.

Somehow she doubted it. Something about Ethan was magical, tormented soul though he was. A pang seized her heart as she remembered what he'd shared with her. Awful. Absolutely awful. He needed a magic wand, but the universe didn't hand those out to anyone.

Somehow you just had to keep muddling through, trying to mend yourself or put the bad stuff behind you. All a therapist could do, she had learned through experience, was give you the tools to do one or the other. Maybe that was the hardest thing of all: learning you had to be your own healer.

She rolled over on the bed, her body restless with hunger she couldn't erase, hunger so strong it almost hurt. Her loins ached with it. Her breasts had become exquisitely sensitive to every movement of her nightgown across her nipples.

She didn't want this. She had a child to think of, and

her mother, in addition to herself, and the agenda didn't include playing with fire.

But she burned anyway, television forgotten.

Could just one night be that dangerous? Why couldn't she scratch the itch and move on? Other people did.

Why, she wondered almost angrily, couldn't she enjoy the most basic human contact? Did she feel she had to punish herself for one major mistake? What made her so different from anyone else? Who said she could never trust herself again?

*She did.*

She had devised all the rules for her current life, maybe in reaction to her complete lack of control in her relationship with Leo. Maybe now she felt she had to control *everything*.

Talk about an impossibility! Apparently she couldn't even protect her own daughter.

The phone beside her bed rang, and she reached for it, expecting to hear Sophie's voice bubbling over with giggles about how much fun they were having.

Instead, she heard a chilling voice.

"She's a beautiful child, Connie."

Her veins turned to ice as she slammed the phone down on the cradle. No! *No!*

Then she screamed.

"Ethan!"

ETHAN BOUNDED UP the stairs three at a time and burst into Connie's room. In the flickering light from her television, she was pulling frantically at the phone cord, trying to yank it out of the wall.

"Connie?"

"It was him," she sobbed. "It was *him!*"

"Who?"

"The man who wants Sophie. He said she's a beautiful child. Oh, God, oh, God, oh, God…"

Ethan crossed the room and took her into his arms, at once confining her gently and supporting her. "Shh… Shh…"

"He called. Oh, God, he called! Sophie…" She began shoving against Ethan, trying to escape. "I have to call and see if she's all right. Sophie… Oh, my God…"

"Shh," he said more sharply. "I'm here, and I'll help. Is the phone still plugged in?"

"I don't know. Oh, God…"

He lifted the receiver and heard the dial tone. "What's the number?"

She managed to gasp it out, then grabbed the receiver as he dialed for her.

"Hi," said the cheerful voice of Jody's mom, Enid.

"Enid, this is Connie. A man just called. Is Sophie okay?"

"She's okay, Connie. My God, she's okay. She's right here with the other girls, eating popcorn and watching *The Little Mermaid.* Are you sure it was the guy?"

At that, Connie collapsed onto the edge of her bed and began sobbing. "He talked about Sophie. He said she was beautiful."

"Oh, sweetie," Enid said, her voice taut with concern and an echo of Connie's fear. "I won't let her out of my sight. John's here, too, and he's keeping an eye on them. And between you and me, he's loaded for bear. But…would you feel better if you took her home?"

"No!" Somehow the idea of bringing Sophie here right after that man had called was even more terrifying. "No. She's probably safer there. I'll call Gage and let him know what happened. Don't be surprised if you see a deputy out front."

"Good. That was my next suggestion. Now, you're sure you're okay if she stays here?"

Connie forced herself to breathe. "I'm okay with it. He called here. Maybe he doesn't know she's there."

"No reason he should, unless he has a better intelligence network than the CIA. Which probably isn't saying much. We're not letting the girls out of the house, and John has already said he's staying up all night to keep an eye on them. Not that I expect either of us will sleep, anyway. The girls are having too much fun."

"Okay," Connie said shakily. "Okay. I just had to be sure."

"Of course you did," Enid said comfortingly. "My God, I've been scared to death ever since the guy talked to the girls. I just sound like I'm calm. Look, I'll call you again in an hour or so if you want. I can keep you posted all night."

"Oh, Enid, that's too much!"

"No, it isn't," Enid said firmly. "I know how I'd be feeling in your shoes. I'll give you updates. But don't get worried if I'm a little late, because these girls are keeping me busy. Now they want brownies. Good thing I like to bake."

Connie managed a choked little laugh. "You're a good woman, Enid. An angel."

"Nah. I'm just a mom. You hang in there. John and I are on guard."

"Thank you. Thank you so much."

"You'd do the same for me. Now relax and try not to climb the walls."

Connie's hand shook as she replaced the receiver. Ethan stood not a foot away, waiting. "Everything's okay," she said.

"Good." He squatted to her eye level, an exotic, mysterious-looking man with eyes nearly as dark as midnight, yet strangely comforting. "Tell me everything he said."

"That was all. He said Sophie was a beautiful child."

"Okay, then let's think about why he would call."

She realized he was trying to get her to think like a police officer, instead of a mother. And he was right. She needed all her wits about her. "To scare me. To let me know the threat is still there."

"That would be my guess. So what does that mean? It sure won't make it any easier for him to get to Sophie, will it?"

Her eyes felt full of glue, hot and burning, as she met his gaze. "No," she whispered. "It'll make it harder."

"So maybe we need to think about what *that* means."

She nodded slowly. "I've got to call Gage."

He waited while she did, and Gage promised to dispatch some officers to Enid and John's house to keep an eye out. He also wanted to place one at Connie's, but she told him no. "Just watch the kids, Gage. I'm a deputy, too, remember. I'll take care of myself."

When she hung up, Ethan still stood there. Then he asked, "Want to come downstairs for coffee or something? Or are you better here?"

"I need to move."

"Let's go, then."

He led the way downstairs. She carried a robe with her, but it was too warm to put on. Nor did she care in the least that she was in a nightshirt. Trivialities no longer existed for her.

Surprisingly, the homey scent of coffee brewing helped pull her back from the precipice of a breakdown. Rationality began to reassert itself. Gradually her breathing slowed and her heart calmed. Ethan sat beside her, close enough to reach for her if she needed comforting, but far enough not to crowd her. No reason that should surprise her. He'd probably dealt with more terror and horror in a few years than most people did in a lifetime.

"He's after me," she said presently.

"In what way?" The question, however, seemed to suggest that he had an idea.

"He wants me scared. He's trying to get to me."

"I agree. Right now it seems that way. Can you handle it?"

"Him scaring me? Only if Sophie isn't at risk."

Ethan nodded "You're a strong woman. If we could be certain he intends Sophie no harm, that would be the end of it."

"But there's no way to know!"

"That's the devil of it. I won't kid you, Connie. This is the worst-possible kind of threat."

"What do you mean?"

"Well, in Afghanistan, we might meet a group of village chieftains who claimed to be all gung-ho for getting rid of al Qaeda and the Taliban, then the next day we'd drive into their village to provide medical care or help rebuild a school, and get attacked. When you don't know where the threat is coming from, or exactly what it's going to be, your options are a mess."

"Yeah." She stared down at the oilcloth-covered table, her hands knotting together until they hurt. "I don't know how to handle this."

"That's what I meant. Is Sophie the target? Are you the target? Are you both the target? What do we most need to guard against?"

"I wish I knew."

"What did this guy sound like?"

"Distant, almost. But there was something else in his tone. I can't put my finger on it."

"Anything familiar? Any recognition?"

"Maybe. Maybe so." But every ounce of her being recoiled at the thought that she might know this creep. She didn't want to believe it possible that someone like that could have crawled into the most distant periphery of her life.

"Okay." He rose and went to get them both coffee.

Connie cradled her mug, but made no attempt to drink. She felt cold, so very cold. The kind of cold no amount of heat could dissipate.

As if he sensed it, Ethan reached for the robe she'd thrown over the back of a chair and draped it over her shoulders. It actually helped a little.

"Connie, who might want to get at you both?"

Everything inside her turned glacial: cold, hard and ready to crack. She whispered, "Leo."

He remained silent, waiting.

Slowly she turned her head to look at him. "Ethan, he got out of jail several months back. But I've changed my name. There's no reason he should have found me."

"Did he know about your uncle living here?"

"God…" She tipped her head back, closing her eyes, loosing a long, despairing sigh. "I didn't think so. I mean, Uncle Nate and I were never that close until I moved here. Leo knew I had family in Wyoming, but I'm pretty sure I never mentioned Nate or Conard County. Leo wasn't the kind of guy to be interested in that stuff, and my maiden name was different. It never occurred to me that he could make a link." She shook her head almost violently. "Damn, I'm stupid. I guess I need to pack up and leave again."

"Not so hasty, there. First of all, you're surrounded by people who want to protect you here. Second, you've got to face the bastard and deal with him."

"I dealt with him once before! Do you know how hard

it was to go into a courtroom and describe what he did to me? What I *let* him do to me?"

"You know better than that. You weren't responsible for what he did for you. I don't need to be a shrink to understand how domestic violence works, to understand how helpless and vulnerable it leaves a woman. He tried to blame you for it, but you know better than that, Connie. Or you should. It wasn't your fault."

"That's what everyone says. But I still have to live with the fact that I didn't leave sooner. That I let it go on so long."

"If it were easy to get out of those situations, they wouldn't exist. You get undermined before you know it. And those bastards are really good at making you feel responsible for what they do."

She looked at him. "How do you know so much?"

"Because I've seen it happen. Because I've talked about it with other guys. The military has a lot of domestic-abuse counselors. One of them was a friend of mine. He explained it all to me."

"Okay, so you know the mechanics. But then there are the feelings."

"Trust me, I know about those, too. Maybe you aren't ready to make peace with the fact that you were skillfully manipulated and brainwashed. I can understand that. I'm having problems of my own. But that doesn't change the fact that *he* was responsible, not you." He leaned toward her, his eyes burning. "And you are *not* responsible for what is happening now."

"I *feel* responsible!"

"So? That doesn't make it true. You didn't ask for this. You did everything you could to avoid it. Now it's here, and we're going to deal with it so you can have the life you deserve."

Something in his expression made her shiver. "You wouldn't..."

"Yeah, I'm a trained killer," he said bitterly. "But generally I don't kill unless I have to. I don't just get up on Saturday morning and decide it would be a good day for a murder."

"I didn't mean that!"

"Maybe not."

"You know damn well I didn't. And frankly, if it's Leo terrorizing me and my daughter, I might kill him before you get a chance!"

They glared at each other across twelve inches of space, nerves and wounds so raw in both of them that it didn't matter if they were reacting rationally.

Right then and there everything hurt too much to make sense of it.

Then, without warning, something inside Connie shifted. All of a sudden she felt the hysterical urge to giggle. The laugh started bubbling out of her, totally random, totally without reason, and then, only God knew why, she said, "Make love not war."

His jaw dropped a half inch and his eyes widened; then, just as helplessly, he started laughing, too.

"Where did that come from?" he asked, breathless.

"I don't know!" She couldn't stop laughing. "Where did any of this come from?"

Laughter existed only a millimeter from tears, just as hate was the flip side of love. The strongest emotions occupied the same realms, basic and primal, entangled beyond extrication.

Tears began to stream down Connie's cheeks, and she felt the crash coming. A pit yawned before her, and she didn't know how to step back from it.

But Ethan knew his way around these emotional pitfalls, maybe because he'd survived so many, presenting a stony facade to the world when everything inside him began to crack.

He reached for her, pulling her onto his lap, wrapping her in his strength, pressing her face to his shoulder. She fit as if the space had been created for her.

Staring over her head at the ordinary sights of a kitchen, he saw, instead, distant landscapes, horrible anguish and suffering.

Life could be such a bitch.

But he knew one thing for certain: if he never did another thing with his life, he was going to make this woman and her child safe from this creep.

It was as solemn a vow as any he'd ever taken, filling his heart, touching his soul, giving back purpose and meaning where they had been stripped away.

No matter what it took.

## CHAPTER TWELVE

CONNIE'S LAUGHTER HAD given way to tears, but copious though they were, they fell silently, as if her body were too exhausted to do more than weep. The shoulder of his shirt grew damp, then sopping, as Ethan continued to hold her.

Calm returned slowly, finding its way back one quiet step at a time. Finally Connie lifted a hand and wiped her cheeks. "Sorry."

"No need." He didn't want to let go of her. He wanted to keep her right where she was, as if it were the only way he could protect her. And maybe himself.

Nor did she seem eager to escape his embrace. She rested against him, within the circle of his arms, as if she had found a measure of peace at last.

That wouldn't remain. It never did. But for now, neither of them risked disturbing it.

Reality had its own rules, however, and at last, with a sigh, Connie slid from his lap and back into her own chair. She reached for her coffee, found it cold and went to get a fresh cup.

"Thank you," she said quietly.

"If you can't hunker down with your friends in a fire-fight, when can you?"

"That's an interesting analogy." She returned to her seat and sipped the coffee.

"This situation qualifies."

"I guess it does." She shook her head, as if trying to

wipe away a thought, then looked at him with a pallid smile. "I usually cope better."

"With something like this? I suppose you have a whole lot of experience with this kind of thing?"

At that, her smile broadened a shade. "No, I guess I don't. If Sophie weren't involved... But why even think about it? She *is* involved. That's what's killing me."

"Of course it is. Most of us worry less about ourselves than we do about those we care for."

"You're right." A shiver passed through her—a release of tension, he guessed. "Time to stop being hysterical and start thinking."

He nodded when she looked at him, waiting to hear what she had to say.

"I'm going to start by calling Enid and telling her she doesn't have to call me on and off all night as long as everything is okay. Because I'm damned if I'm going to answer the phone again."

"I could answer for you."

"No. I don't want to give the creep the satisfaction." Rising, she went to the wall phone and dialed Enid's number. In the background, mayhem still reigned.

"Okay," Enid said. "If you're sure. These girls are so wound up, I can guarantee you they won't crash before dawn. And the cops keep prowling around. I think *they're* making me more nervous."

"I appreciate everything, Enid. I really do. But I need to start focusing on why this guy called me and what I should do about it, and honestly, I'd rather not be answering the phone tonight."

"I can see why, honey. Don't give the crud the satisfaction. And if you get concerned, just call. Like I said, we're going to be up all night."

When Connie hung up, she returned to her seat and her coffee. "It's got to be Leo," she announced.

"That's my guess."

"No one else would want to scare both Sophie and me."

"You think he just wants to scare you?"

"Him? I don't know. In the end, guys like him often turn out to be bullies who can't stand up against any show of strength."

Ethan nodded. "Did he say anything threatening at all?"

"No. Just that Sophie was a beautiful child."

"Could he have any other motive?"

"Why would he? He kicked me in the stomach when I was pregnant. Does that sound like a man who wants his child?"

"That sounds like a man who feels threatened."

"Exactly. And maybe now he's angry because I sent him to prison. But I'm not the woman he used to kick around."

"I'm sure you're not."

She looked at Ethan, determination in every line of her. "If it's Leo, we could put his photo out there. At least among the deputies."

"How sure are you?"

She paused thoughtfully. Finally she said, "I'm not a hundred percent sure, but close to it. He only said one thing, which didn't give me much to go on, considering how shocked I was. It was like I lost all sense for a few minutes there."

"Hardly surprising."

"Yeah." Then she astonished him by taking his hand and holding it. "You're a godsend, Ethan."

"No. Just a guy who happened to be in the right place when needed."

Her smile was pinched. "I think you have a worse self-image than I do. And it's not right. I can tell what a good man you are. Yeah, you did some awful things, but you didn't do them alone. You did them because I and every other person in this country asked them of you."

"I don't—"

"Shh," she said gently. "It's true. You were in the service. You got your orders from this country, and you went. If there's any guilt in what you did, we all share it. All of us. We can't claim lily-white hands because we didn't put on a uniform. Not in this country."

He didn't respond, seeming to lack the words.

"You know it's true, Ethan. You do the dirty work we ask you to do. Whatever gloss we put on it, however high we hold the flag and however loud we cry the justifications, you and your fellow soldiers are just carrying out our will. Sometimes you'll be sure it was absolutely right. But I suspect that in all wars the people on the front lines often wind up wondering what they've done and what it makes them."

"Connie—"

"Listen to me. Just remember, when you walk down a street, that you didn't do a damn thing all the rest of us walking those same streets didn't ask of you. Didn't send you there to do."

Her grip on his hand had grown vise tight, and he squeezed back. Finally he gave a short, mirthless laugh and said, "I guess this is a night for therapy."

"Or a night for putting things into perspective. You tried to help me see I wasn't responsible for what Leo did. Well, you need to understand that just because you were the tip of the spear doesn't make you any more responsible than the rest of us, the spear throwers."

For a few moments he seemed about to argue with her, but then tension seeped from him. Before she knew what to expect, she was swept up into his arms and being carried up the stairs as if she weighed nothing at all.

She didn't make a sound, didn't offer a protest. How could she? Nothing had ever felt so right as being in his arms.

He carried her into her darkened bedroom, where the TV still flickered, and laid her on her bed. Then he stretched out beside her, fully clothed, and pulled her close, as if he wanted their bodies to melt together. She managed to wrap one arm around him, feeling the breadth and strength of his back. Feeling the wonder of him in every cell of her being.

"This'll sound crazy," he said huskily.

"Tell me."

"You just said something to me that made more sense than anything anyone's said in a long time—except for something Micah said the other day."

"What did he say?"

"He told me the past was past, that if I wanted atonement, I had to find it in today. And that if I had nightmares, I had to build new dreams."

She drew a sharp breath. "That's so true! So beautiful. Oh, Ethan, I need to remember that, too."

"I know. We're not so very different, in some ways."

"No, we're not." She tightened her hold on him. "When was the last time someone told you how beautiful you are?"

"Me?" He gave an embarrassed laugh.

"You," she repeated. "Not just the way you look, although you probably have no idea what a handsome man you are, but in other ways. The first night you spent here, I felt something about you, something in the air around you. You were saying something about having studied shamanism and being a bit of a mystic. I don't remember exactly. I just know I could feel it all around you, as if you're a special spirit."

"Not me. I'm an ordinary man."

"No, you're more than that." She sighed and shifted so that her head was cradled comfortably on his shoulder. "I used to think we were beings of light unwillingly tethered to the ground."

"And now?"

"I still think we're beings of light, but we aren't tethered unwillingly."

"No?"

She tilted her head so she could see his face. "No," she repeated. "We came here for this. For something beautiful we can experience no other way. Holding and being held. Comforting and being comforted. Skin touching skin across the abyss of seeming separateness."

He closed his eyes as if absorbing her words. "You should try poetry."

"Not me. It's just what I feel sometimes. Transcendence through our very limitations. Tell me you haven't felt it."

He nodded slowly. "Rarely," he said presently. "Too rarely. But yes, I've felt it."

"These are the moments we exist for, Ethan."

He cradled her even closer, if that was possible, and rocked her gently. The motion was soothing, seeming to lift her to another level.

This wasn't possible, she warned herself, but the warning seemed distant and faint. She knew she would never trust fully again, and she knew that Ethan would undoubtedly move on until he found a life that suited him. They were too wounded to build anything between them.

So if she gave in to the longings building in her, it would be for a night. A single night. There would be no future in it.

Oddly, that seemed to free her. It banished all the fears from her marriage that had been holding her back. There was nothing to fear here, because this wouldn't be a commitment. Nothing to upset her carefully established balance.

In Ethan's arms, she felt herself grow weightless, as if she were rising to the heavens, above it all, safe from it all. Magic surrounded her, sheltered her, filled her.

She hardly felt herself move as she turned her face up, seeking his kiss.

When it came, gentleness came with it, a tender touching of lips that spoke not of hunger but a different kind of need, a more important one.

She responded in kind, shedding her shell, reveling in the freedom to just experience and share. Savoring the deep sense of safety that must have been coming from him, because it surely didn't come from her.

He began to stoke her back, firmly but gently, shoulder to small of back, over and over until she understood why cats purr. A soft moan escaped her, saying all that words couldn't.

Slowly his hand slipped lower, pressing her rounded bottom and bringing her into the cradle of his hips. Now she could feel his need, too, as well as her own, and the feeling was so good, so good…

She had never known a man could be so hard all over, nor that his hardness against her softness could be so enticing. Every inch of Ethan had been honed for action, and awareness of that carried her to some elemental place inside her where nothing existed except man and woman, woman and man. Identity slipped away, succumbing to urges as old as time.

They fit together as if they had been created for this. His kiss grew deeper, and her hips rocked in response, trying to get closer to him, trying to find the answer to her growing ache.

His mouth left hers, tracing a path lower, along the slender column of her neck, awakening new nerve endings, sending a shiver through her. Warm, soft lips, hard body, heat…passing chill, all of it descending through her to her very center, where it fed the growing, hardening ache inside.

The cotton of her nightgown provided no barrier as he moved lower, tracing her collarbone with his tongue, slipping straps away to bare her shoulders to his chase.

He rolled her gently onto her back, as if sensing she was utterly open to him. First his lips, then his tongue, found the stiffened buds of her nipples through the thin cotton, causing her to give a soft cry of delight and need.

He teased her, light brushes and kisses while the cotton grew damp, until she writhed in helpless thrall to the hunger he drew from her. Only then did he close his mouth over her, drawing her in, sucking gently in a rhythm that caused an echoing tightening between her legs.

His hand slipped up the outside of her leg, drawing her nightgown with it, exposing her to the cool air and, wonderfully, to his touch. The first brush of his fingers at the apex of her thighs was a mere hint, barely stirring the nest, yet causing her to shudder breathlessly.

Yes, that was what she wanted. More of that. Harder. She lifted her hips to find what she needed, but he pulled his hand away, denying her. Tormenting her in the most beautiful way imaginable.

"Ethan…" A sharp whisper, and she reached for his powerful shoulders, trying to draw him closer, but he resisted. His mouth moved to her other breast, drawing her desire out like a taut string ready to be plucked to create the most perfect note.

The realms she visited then were places she had never imagined could exist. Her entire body became his instrument, played for both her pleasure and his.

Then, almost without her realizing it, her nightgown vanished over her head. Naked, exposed, vulnerable…

And enthralled with the beauty of it all.

"Ethan," she said on a sigh, letting him have whatever he chose to take, because every taking was a giving beyond any but the rawest comprehension.

He lifted her to the mountain peaks, and she soared willingly with him.

A dark moment came, a moment when he vanished. She struggled against the web of heat and wonder that held her to try to find him, but then he returned, and when he did, she felt his smooth, hot skin along her side.

"Oh, Ethan…" She turned toward him then, wrapping her arms around his shoulders, surrendering herself to him.

She belonged completely to him.

## CHAPTER THIRTEEN

IT HAD BEEN too long. Ethan had buried this part of himself for the last four years, using his stateside rotations to try to sort himself out, not wanting to turn to easy women, absolutely refusing to draw a better woman into the mess of his life.

Now here he was with a good, decent woman, feeling a hunger for her that took him by surprise in its strength. There was no way he could have pulled back now. All that he had tried to spare himself and others turned to dust.

He needed this beyond all reason and caution, although at some point he had realized that Connie wanted this just as much. Just these beautiful, glorious moments of man meeting woman in the most basic way, the way the human race had always dissolved its aloneness.

He had been alone for a long time now. Intense as friendships could be in battle, this was a kind of union that could be replaced by no other. It reached out to fill places nothing else could.

He felt her shiver and tremble against him, felt her vulnerability as a blessing, felt her hunger and need meet and match his own, validating him at his deepest levels, way below thought.

The magic that bound her surrounded him, as well. He felt as if rainbows danced along his arms and zinged through his nerves. The voice of thunder roared through him.

Each shiver or sigh he drew from her was a gift that

tightened his throat. When her nails dug into his shoulders, trying to pull him closer, he knew joy and triumph that he could give such a gift.

And when at last he levered himself over her and slowly sank into her welcoming heat, he knew a kind of salvation.

Then everything vanished as they rode the wave higher and higher, until they exploded together in a place beyond the stars.

THEY LAY TOGETHER in a hot, damp heap, limbs sprawled across each other, breaths slowing, heartbeats steadying. The TV still flickered, but the sound was too low to penetrate their cocoon of satisfaction and wonder.

She trailed her fingers lightly along his arm, as if reassuring herself of his reality. He held her hips close, as if he couldn't bear for her to move away.

A long, shuddering sigh escaped her, and she pressed a kiss to his chest, near one small nipple. A shiver passed through him in response.

The hunger, fulfilled, had not vanished but merely simmered.

"Are you okay?" he asked. His voice rumbled deep in his chest.

She kissed him again. "I never knew it was possible to feel this wonderful."

"Me, neither." Sad to say, yet true. Something special had just happened here, but he wasn't ready to think about that.

Maybe he was even *reluctant* to think about it. Better to accept some things rather than analyze them.

Cooling now, he reached with one arm for the sheet and pulled it up. She settled more comfortably against him, displaying no desire to end these moments. That relieved him. He could have understood it if she had wanted to run.

They had crossed lines he suspected neither of them had ever intended to.

Yet here they were, and he wanted it to end no more than she did. Comfort, he thought, could be such a rare thing, yet he'd found it here in this woman's arms. He hoped she had found it in his.

MIDNIGHT WAS CREEPING close on stealthy feet when Connie asked, "Are you hungry? I am."

"I guess I am, but only a little."

"Do you want real food, or will dessert do you?"

He smiled into her fragrant hair. "Dessert sounds fabulous."

She pushed him playfully. "Food first, then me."

He laughed and followed her out of the bed, pulling on his T-shirt and shorts while she knotted her robe around herself.

As he followed her down the stairs, he noted how small and fragile she appeared, in direct contrast to the iron strength of her spirit and will. A powerful urge to wipe the sorrows from her life rose in him.

When she bent to look in the refrigerator, he noted the perfect curves of her bottom, and his hands remembered the way her flesh had felt.

"We have strawberry pie," she said.

"What's that?"

"My mother's concoction." She pulled out a pie plate with a plastic lid. "Trust me, it's good. Strawberry gelatin full of real strawberries on a graham-cracker crust. Topped with whipped cream and more strawberries."

"That does sound good." It sounded like heaven, in fact. "I'm sure I've never had anything like it."

She flashed a grin and cut him a generous portion of the pie. "It's not as high in sugar or fat as you'd expect, not with all the strawberries. And she's gentle with the whipped cream."

Given the life he'd been living, such concerns were pretty much foreign to him. Flavor was everything, and he'd had little enough of that for a while. A surprising number of soldiers in the field had to be reminded to eat, despite their heightened need for calories. Even so, most lost twenty or thirty pounds on a tour.

When he sank his teeth into his first bite of pie, he closed his eyes in sheer bliss, shutting out anything that might distract him from the taste. Fresh strawberries, perfectly balancing the sweetness all around them. When he finally allowed himself to swallow, he said, "Tell Julia I want to marry her."

"You can tell her yourself. But," she added coquettishly, "I know how to make this, too."

"Then I'll marry both of you. You have no idea how long it's been since I tasted something like this."

"I can guess. And there's plenty more."

He smiled and raised another forkful to his mouth. "Over there," he said before he put it in his mouth, "we don't get anything even a tenth as tasty as this. MREs, of course. Food we cook at our firebase, but none of us is a great chef, including the chef."

She giggled a little at that.

"Well, he doesn't have a lot to work with. We have to bring in all the food, so everything's pretty much dried or canned. Eating is more a duty than a pleasure most of the time."

"I'm sorry."

He shrugged. "Most of the world is in the same straits. In fact, we're better off than most, even if it's all in cans and boxes. More variety."

She nodded. "I can't imagine the hardship those people suffer."

"Most people can't. It's beyond imagining. You have to see it, live it. Yet the wonderful thing, the truly wonderful thing, is how few of them feel they're living in hardship, except in terms of the war." He paused, then shook his head.

"They must consider you a striking figure," she remarked.

At that his mouth twisted wryly. "I've been mistaken for bin Laden a few times. Despite my uniform."

"Oh, that must be something."

"Oh, yeah. Never for more than a few seconds. We favor different headwear, of course, and we really don't look alike. In all honesty, I don't know why it happened."

"I don't see a resemblance. Maybe some people have never seen his photo, just heard how tall he is."

"That's the only thing that would explain it."

He savored another mouthful of pie. "Damn, this is good."

She pulled the pie pan closer and sliced another piece, sliding it onto his plate.

"Whoa," he said.

She shook her head. "My guess is you're beneath your fighting weight, and anyway, Julia will be thrilled you like it. The best compliment to the cook is eating."

She turned her head, a mistake, because all of a sudden she became uneasily aware of the lurking night, held at bay only by the thin glass of the windows. Ordinarily she loved the night, but not now. Not when a threat was hovering over her daughter.

"Excuse me," she said. "I need to check on Sophie."

He nodded, his gaze following her as she went to the phone and dialed.

"Hi, Enid, it's Connie."

"Hi, kiddo. Well, we're into *Cinderella,* the girls ate all the brownies, if you can believe it, and now there are rumblings about popcorn. It's all good, Connie. Honestly."

"Thanks, Enid. Is it okay if I check again later?"

"Any time, Connie. Like I said, this is going to be an all-nighter. The later it gets, the more awake they seem."

Connie replaced the receiver and found Ethan watching her. "Everything's all right."

He nodded, saying nothing, returning his attention to his plate as if wishing to give her a moment of privacy, one she seemed to need.

Looking at her hands, she realized she was shaking. Not good. She stuffed them in the pockets of her robe and returned to the table, trying to act as if everything hadn't all just come crashing back.

"I'm sorry," she said.

"Nothing to be sorry for."

She bit her lip. "I just realized something."

"What's that?"

"Leo made me feel as if I needed to apologize for everything. I'm still doing it."

He nodded, pushing his plate to one side. Hardly a crumb remained. "That's a damn shame, because I can't see anything you need to apologize for. Not one thing."

"I've been working on that," she admitted. "My mother hates it when I keep on apologizing."

"I don't hate it," he replied, "but I think it's sad you feel that way."

"Maybe it's more habit than anything."

"Maybe."

She watched as he rose and took care of the dishes, washing them and putting them in the rack. Then he put the pie away and wiped the table down. She supposed it was his military training, but she liked it. Leo had never done anything like that in the whole time she'd lived with him.

Together they climbed the stairs and returned to her bedroom, where they lay in the dark, embracing. The sexual fever had passed for now, replaced by an equally urgent need for comfort and closeness.

"I've been alone for too long," he said quietly. She could feel his voice rumble deep in his chest.

"Even with your buddies?"

"That's different. That's an intense community. We depend on each other for our very lives. But it's different."

She gave him a little squeeze and waited for him to continue.

"There's a special bond," he continued slowly, then cleared his throat, as if he were finding it difficult to speak. "You know your buddies always have your back. You know you always have theirs. I don't know if I can really explain it. But it's like many have said, when you're in the foxhole, you're not fighting for principles, country or any such abstract thing, you're fighting for the guy next to you."

"I can understand that," she murmured.

"But there's something more. We were dedicated to something, Connie. Something bigger than us. Something we were willing to die for. And it wasn't just the guy beside us who depended on us. It was—this is going to sound nuts, given all that's happened—we were dedicated to helping those people in every way we could. We didn't want to abandon them to the darkness again. We wanted to save lives, improve lives, make sure little girls could go to school, and that babies didn't die needlessly of treatable diseases. We wanted to get rid of all the threats."

"Yes."

"The horrible thing about it is, no matter how much

good you try to do, you create more ugliness at the same time."

"That must be awful."

"It is. It was better in Afghanistan, actually. In Iraq, everything was all blurred. But when I got to Afghanistan, it was clearer, believe it or not."

"I can believe it. Iraq turned into such a mess."

"Yeah. It's horrifying. There wasn't anybody in uniform who didn't want to make life better for those people. Not a one of us. But it turned out to be like opening Pandora's box.

"In Afghanistan, though, it's clearer. A lot of people just want us to go away. But a lot want us to put an end to the Taliban. I don't think they care much one way or another about al Qaeda, but the Taliban…there's still a lot of anger against them. And every time they raid a village and destroy a girls' school, it's amazing to watch the village elders get together to rebuild it."

"Do they ask you for help?"

"Sometimes. We're still occupiers."

"It's sad."

"What?"

She tried to see his face in the dark but couldn't. "It's sad that trying to help has hurt so many."

"I know. And I don't blame the locals for having mixed feelings about us. How could I? Most of us understand how *we'd* feel if a firebase run by some other country was up the road from us."

She sighed and moved closer. "I'm sorry."

"Don't be. I volunteered. And I learned a lot."

"But now you're cut off from your mission and your buddies."

"That hits the nail on the head."

"Basically, you have to start all over."

"Yeah." He sighed. "You did it, though, didn't you?"

"Yes. But it wasn't exactly the same."

"Emotionally it's exactly the same. You gave up all your buddies in the Denver police, all your friends, and vanished into a different world to protect your daughter. The only differences between us are in degree and the idea of choice. I didn't choose to leave."

"I'm not sure I did, either." She shook her head and pressed her face into his chest. "I had no choice, not once I felt my baby was threatened."

He squeezed her. "We'll take care of her, Connie, I swear. Nothing's going to happen to her."

All of sudden she couldn't hold still. She pulled away and left the bed, throwing on her robe against the deepening chill and pacing.

"What could he want with her, Ethan? What could he possibly want with her after all this time?"

The words emerged as a cry from the abyss of fear inside her.

"I don't know," he said heavily. "I wish to God I did."

# CHAPTER FOURTEEN

THEY PICKED UP Sophie from Jody's house around eight. Connie had the day off, because Gage always gave her weekends off to be with her daughter. It was one of the perks of being on a small force; personal needs could be taken into account.

Sophie looked at them sleepily from puffy eyes. Enid said the girls hadn't fallen asleep until nearly six. But when Ethan suggested they go to Maude's for breakfast, Sophie perked up. She liked steak and eggs, and didn't get them often, usually because Connie needed to watch her budget.

A crowd filled Maude's, as it usually did on Saturday mornings. Lots of folks came in from surrounding ranches to take care of business in town, and the City Diner usually topped the list of places to go. Still, they found a booth near the back, and Sophie surprised Connie by squeezing onto the bench beside Ethan, instead of sitting next to her.

One of those unexpected pangs hit Connie as she wondered how much Sophie missed having a father figure in her life. Probably a whole lot. And while Leo could never have been a decent one, not given his violent nature, that didn't mean Sophie didn't need a dad.

But dads didn't grow on trees. She couldn't just go out and pluck one from a branch somewhere and bring him home. Nor could she risk bringing home the wrong man.

There it was again, her fear of making another bad character judgment.

Somewhere in the midst of steak, eggs and English muffins with jam, the bomb dropped.

Sophie looked at her mother and asked, "Where's my daddy?"

All of sudden Connie felt light-headed and faint. Her mind seemed to have flung itself somewhere far away, divorcing itself from her body, leaving her with tunnel vision. Distantly, she knew that Sophie was still staring at her, waiting.

Now she understood why Sophie had chosen to sit beside Ethan and not her. Her heart slammed, dragging her back to the table and out of complete shock.

"I'm not sure where your father is," she said finally, hoping her voice sounded steadier to Sophie than it did to her.

"Why not?"

"Because I haven't seen him in a long time."

"Why?"

So that was the way it was going to be. Connie drew a long breath. "This isn't a good place to discuss this, Sophie. Can you wait until we go home after breakfast?"

Sophie's lower lip began to tighten, then relaxed. She looked down at her plate and shrugged. "Sure."

Connie looked from her daughter to Ethan, feeling helpless, and saw sympathy in his gaze. He probably understood Sophie's side of this better than hers. God!

Her appetite gone, Connie had to force herself to eat as if nothing was wrong. Maude's ordinarily wonderful cooking tasted like sawdust and stuck in her throat.

When they got home, Sophie took Ethan's hand as they walked into the house. A message if ever there was one. Then she sat at the kitchen table and simply looked at her mother.

Ethan started the coffeepot. "Should I go to another room?"

"No," said Sophie and Connie simultaneously.

Ethan looked from one of them to the other, then shrugged and turned back to the coffeepot.

"Maybe you can help," Connie said. "You've been in Sophie's shoes."

"Only if she wants my help."

Sophie, meanwhile, had returned her attention to her mother. "Where's my daddy?"

"I told you I don't know. Why are you asking all of a sudden? You never wondered about it before."

Sophie's lower lip trembled. "Because last night at Jody's we were playing a game with her mom and dad. All my friends have dads. All of them. But not me. Why not?"

"Some of your friends' moms and dads are divorced," Connie pointed out.

"But they know them! They visit them. Is my dad dead?"

Connie, her stomach knotting until it hurt, wished she could answer with a lie. For the very first time in her life, she wanted to out-and-out lie to Sophie. "No," she said finally. "We're divorced."

"So why don't I ever get to visit him? Other kids do."

She'd already said she didn't know where Leo was. Apparently that wasn't going to suffice. She barely nodded when Ethan put a cup of coffee in front of her. His hand touched her shoulder, offering silent comfort.

"Mommy?"

Connie sighed, looking down at the table, seeking words that would satisfy without causing harm. She couldn't seem to find any.

"Your father," she said finally, "was bad to me."

"Bad how?"

"Sophie…" But the girl's stubborn expression said she wasn't going to settle for that. When and how did a seven-year-old become so mature? "Okay," Connie said carefully. "He hit me. A lot. I ran away."

Sophie frowned. "That's bad."

"Yes, it was very bad. And when I knew you were coming, I realized I couldn't stay there anymore. I didn't want you to grow up that way."

"But why couldn't *I* see him?"

Connie stared at the child, aching, wondering how she could answer that, short of telling Sophie that her father had tried to kill her even before she was born. Sophie should never know that, should never feel that her father hadn't wanted her, had resented her presence in Connie's womb so much that he had kicked her there over and over. Only a miracle had prevented a miscarriage or damage to Sophie.

She couldn't possibly share that with her daughter. On that score, her lips had to remain sealed unto death.

Ethan sat at the table, looking from daughter to mother. "Excuse my butting in, Connie, but the truth is always best. Sophie can handle more than you think."

"But…" Even as she started to protest, Connie realized that he was right. Lies would only come between them later. But she could limit the truth for now. She *had* to.

"Okay," she said finally, looking straight at Sophie. "I ran away from him because it wasn't good for you. I went to a special home they have for women who have been hit by their husbands. A shelter."

Sophie nodded, her sleep-puffy eyes wide and attentive.

"But after they helped me get set up in a different home, a place that was supposed to be secret, he followed me home from work one day. Even though the court ordered him to stay away from me. And he hit me so hard I had to go to the hospital."

"I'm sorry, Mom." Sophie's lips were trembling.

"Is that enough, honey? Because the story is ugly."

"That's why we came here?"

"Yes. To hide even better."

"What happened to him? Did he get in trouble for hurting you?"

Connie drew a deep breath, then let it go. "He went to jail."

"For a long time?"

"Six years."

Sophie nodded. "But…do you think he would hit me, too?"

"Honey, I wish I knew. I just can't take the chance."

Sophie nodded again. Then she said, "I'm tired. I'm going to bed."

"Hug?"

Sophie came around the table and hugged her mother tight. Then, without a backward look, she disappeared up the stairs to her bedroom.

"God," Connie breathed. She put her head down on the table and battled an overwhelming urge to cry. "Did you see?" she whispered. "Did you see the look in her eyes? Like something had died."

Two powerful hands gripped her shoulders from behind, kneading gently. "She'll be okay," Ethan said reassuringly. "You'll see. Kids are resilient. But she needed to know the truth, Connie. Especially if it *is* Leo going after her."

"I know, I know." Every terrible fear that had haunted her for years seemed to be coming to fruition in this horrifying week. Fear that Leo would hurt Sophie, fear that the truth would hurt Sophie, fear that lacking a father would hurt Sophie…

And fear that she would lose Sophie. Always, always that terrible fear.

She lifted her head, unaware that tears trembled on her lower lashes. "I've been so afraid I would lose her. I've never stopped being afraid of that."

"I can tell."

"I guess, until this past week, I never faced the fact that I'd never stopped being afraid of that. Of Leo."

"Some ghosts just won't go away." He stopped kneading her shoulders and sat beside her, drawing her close, as if to protect her.

"I thought it had." She dashed the tears away. "This is ridiculous. I can't go on being a prisoner of fear. I've got to stand up to it."

"Isn't that what you're doing?"

"Not enough. Not nearly enough." She clenched her hands, then released them. "I've got to find this guy. If it's Leo, I'm going to teach him a lesson."

"Be careful what kind."

She looked at him angrily. "What do you mean?"

"Just be careful. There are lots of ways to teach a lesson, some not so good."

"I'm not an idiot!"

"But you carry a gun. Just—" He broke off, then shrugged. "Sorry. You don't need me telling you things you already know."

A shudder ripped through her. "No, you're right. I'm not sure I'm fully rational right now. It's as if...as if a great big gaping wound has been torn open. I'm hurting so bad, and I'm so worried about Sophie. And you're right, I'm armed. If someone threatened her..."

"If someone threatens her, that's different. You know it. You're a police officer. If you need to apply reasonable force, you can and you will."

"But can I trust myself not to be *un*reasonable? Right now, I don't know. Right now, I'm afraid I might not be able to."

"Right now, you have time to think about what's going on inside you. To deal with it. You'll calm down."

"Sure. Yeah." She gave a bitter laugh. "I thought for years I was calm. Apparently I was hiding from myself, too."

"You wouldn't be the first person to do that."

"Did you see how she looked when she walked out of here, Ethan? Did you see her eyes?"

"She's tired," he said soothingly. "She's a little kid, and she's been up all night. Sure, what you told her was probably difficult to swallow, and it'll take time for her to wrap her mind around it, but most of what you saw was pure fatigue."

"How can you know that? How can you possibly know that? What if she hates me now? I sent her father to jail!"

He shook his head and caught her chin in his hand, forcing her to look at him. "Listen, Connie. Please listen. She understood that he hurt you bad enough to put you in the hospital. You underestimate her love for you if you think she's going to turn on you because Leo broke the law and went to jail."

"What if she doesn't see it that way?"

"With a mom who's a cop, I'm pretty sure she understands that. Besides, she's seven, not three. Bad people go to jail. She knows that."

"Yeah. Yeah. But other bad people aren't her dad."

His expression grew gentle. "She doesn't know the man, Connie. Her only emotional attachment to him is an attachment to an idea. He's not real. He hasn't been with her all these years. He hasn't taken care of her. Give her a chance to think about it and absorb it. She'll be okay."

"You're so sure."

"I had less reason to understand, but I did."

She couldn't deny the truth of his words. Maybe she really wasn't expecting too much of a seven-year-old. The questions had arisen, and needed to be answered. If Sophie was wondering, she deserved to know. Connie had always followed the rule that if the child asks, the child is ready to know at least something. She hadn't dumped gory details on the girl, just a general outline.

"Maybe," she said finally. "Maybe."

"Trust your daughter's love."

Surprising what a tall order that suddenly seemed to her. Yet she knew that Ethan was right. She would just have to prepare herself for an emotional reaction from Sophie. Because there was bound to be one.

There was always a price, it seemed. Even for the truth.

## CHAPTER FIFTEEN

JULIA ARRIVED HOME just before noon. She took one look at Connie and demanded to know what was wrong.

"Sophie asked about her father."

"Well, you knew that was coming." Julia wheeled over to the stove and poured herself a cup of coffee. Ethan rose and started to leave the kitchen, but Julia waved him back. "Stay, Ethan," she said. "You're practically part of this family now, and I suppose you were here when Sophie asked."

He nodded and resumed his chair. Julia's knowing eyes moved between them, as if she sensed the change in their relationship. But she said nothing.

"So how did she take it?"

"I don't know," Connie answered frankly. "She seemed to accept what I said, but then she went straight upstairs to bed. She was up all night, but—"

"Shh," Julia said, interrupting her. "Don't make this bigger than it needs to be. The child was probably just exhausted."

"I'm still worried," Connie told her. "How can I not be worried? And another thing, I'm wondering why this came up now. She said it was because she and the other girls played games last night with Jody's mom and dad, but that's nothing new."

Julia put her mug on the table and rearranged her chair

so she was sitting comfortably facing them. "Maybe it has to do with this stranger."

Connie, thinking of last night's phone call, a call she didn't want to mention to her mother, felt a sickening jolt. "What do you mean?"

"Maybe," Julia said, "she's feeling a need for protection."

"She won't get it from that quarter," Connie said bitterly.

"She probably realizes that now," Julia agreed. "Assuming you told her something about why you had to leave him."

"I made it as sketchy as I could, but yes."

"Poor thing." Julia sighed. "For everything this mess has put *us* through this week, in her own way she's been through just as much. Maybe we haven't given enough thought to how scared she's been. Oh, I know she's acting as if it's all okay, but maybe she's trying to be strong for you, Connie. I wouldn't put it past her."

"Great." Connie closed her eyes briefly. "Here I've been assuming that she was okay, that as long as we surrounded her with protection and she knew it was there, she'd feel safe. God, I feel like a dunce."

"Well, she's not exactly acting as if she's scared of her own shadow. If she doesn't want you to know, how are you supposed to?"

"Because I'm supposed to be her mother and read between the lines. She's only seven."

"And a lot of seven-year-olds would have put that stranger behind them by now. They don't dwell on things unnecessarily, the way we adults do."

"Usually." Connie rose. "I'm going to look in on her."

She climbed the stairs with leaden feet, full of old fears and now new ones. She had honestly believed that Sophie was getting back to normal after her scare. Apparently not.

Why else all the questions about her father?

She opened the door quietly and looked in. Sophie lay in a tangle of blankets, wrapped around her favorite stuffed dog. Maybe, when this was over, she *should* let her mother get Sophie that dog. On the other hand, dogs, as wonderful as they were, meant more bills, bills that might strain an already tight budget.

She started to back out, but stopped when she heard Sophie's sleepy voice. "Mom?"

"Yes, honey?" At once she went to sit on the edge of Sophie's bed and laid a hand on her shoulder.

"It's going to be okay, right?"

"Of course it is. Are you still scared of that man?"

"Not really." Sophie rolled onto her back and looked at her. "I heard Grandma come home."

"Yes, she's in the kitchen with Ethan, having coffee."

"I like Ethan."

"So do I."

"I wish I had a dad like *him,* instead of the other kind."

Connie didn't need to ask what kind her daughter meant. "I'm sorry. I made a big mistake when I married your father."

Sophie surprised her with an impish smile. "But if you didn't marry him, you wouldn't have me."

Connie managed a little laugh. "I don't know about that. I think God always meant for me to have you. The angels saved you specially."

Sophie laughed. "I'm not that good."

"Oh, yes, you are."

Sophie's smile faded. "The man's still there."

A fist punched Connie in the chest. "Have you seen him?"

"Yeah."

"Where?"

"After school yesterday. That's why I went a different way home."

Connie didn't know what to say. For several long seconds she hung in the balance between terror and anguish. Calm, when it came, had a price. But for Sophie's sake, she *had* to remain calm. Finally she cleared her throat. "You would have been safer staying with your friends."

Sophie shrugged. "I was safe. I'm here."

Connie didn't know how to argue with that. She didn't want to scare the child more. Yet Sophie needed to be cautious. "Honey..."

"I know. Don't trust strangers and stay with my friends." Sophie rolled over on her side again and took her mother's hand. "I'll be okay, Mommy. Don't worry."

"Just stay close, honey. Just stay close." Leaning over, Connie wrapped her daughter in a tight hug and felt those warm little arms wrap around her in return. "I love you so much."

"I love you, too, Mommy."

"Now sleep a little longer. You were up all night, Enid said."

Sophie smiled brilliantly. "It was fun."

"I bet it was. Later we'll play some games or something, okay? But get a little more sleep first."

Sophie's eyelids, still puffy with sleepiness, were already sagging to half-mast. "I really like Ethan," she said again. Then she fell sound asleep.

Connie envied her daughter's ability to drop off so quickly. These days, finding sleep herself could be a struggle. And after Sophie's little bomb, she wondered if she would ever sleep again. As if in response to an emotional overload, a kind of numbness settled over her.

She sat with Sophie for a while longer, until the little

girl's breathing deepened; then, after dropping a kiss on her daughter's forehead, Connie tiptoed from the room.

Downstairs, still wearing her numbness like a cloak, she found Julia and Ethan shuffling cards. "What's going on?"

Julia grinned. "Ethan's going to teach me how to play Texas hold 'em. Don't we have chips somewhere?"

"Maybe. I seem to remember getting them for some project."

"Well, go find them, girl," Julia said. "This man wants a chance to clean me out."

Ethan's chuckle followed Connie as she went to look in the living-room credenza.

The box was still there, after all this time. She carried the chips back to the kitchen, but her mind wasn't on poker. While Ethan started divvying up the plastic chips, she said, "Sophie saw him again."

Ethan's hands froze. Julia's smile faded.

"After school yesterday. She said that's why she took a different way home."

Ethan swore softly.

Julia's face sagged. "Why didn't she tell us this yesterday?"

"I don't know." Connie, who had maintained a calm facade until this moment, couldn't hold it together any longer. Her voice stretched thin, became thready, and the panic that had been clawing at her all week grabbed her fully in its jaws.

"He's still here," she repeated. "He's still here, and Sophie saw him. How can we make her safe if he can get to her without our knowing it? How can we protect her?"

Her voice had grown shrill, and she bit back further words, knowing that she was only feeding her own panic and sense of helplessness.

But, dear God, how could she remain calm in the face

of this? A stranger, maybe Leo, maybe not, was stalking her little girl. She pushed back from the table, ignoring it when the chair fell over. Like a terrified horse, she wanted to race from one end of her corral to the other and beat down the bars that held her in.

Before she could dash from the room, Ethan caught her. His strong arms surrounded her, restrained her, held her close. Surrounded her with security.

"Shh," he whispered, and stroked her hair. "Shh. She's safe upstairs right now. I swear to you, Connie, I'll be right beside her every time she leaves this house. I'll walk with her everywhere. I'll watch her when she plays. Nobody's going to hurt that child as long as I have breath in me."

Connie wanted to believe him. She desperately needed to believe him.

"It's gone past trying to keep a loose watch on her," Ethan said. "With a second encounter, we have to tighten up. Sophie may not like it, but that's the way it has to be until we catch this guy."

Connie leaned back and looked up at him. "What if it isn't Leo?" she whispered. Much as she feared Leo's violence and that it might spill over onto Sophie, there were other things to be feared more. Like real strangers. Horrible, terrible sick men who would do the unthinkable.

Not even when she had faced an armed burglar had she felt this much gut-wrenching, sickening fear. Fear for Sophie. Fear of all the monsters that could walk into her innocent daughter's life.

A shudder ripped through her, then another. Flying apart seemed like a valid option right now. Shattering into a million pieces.

But for these few moments, Ethan's arms held her together. His strength seemed to infuse her with something she desperately needed. Little by little, her shudders eased, until finally she sagged against him. He continued to hold her, seeming to understand that the strength needed to return to her muscles.

Something else began to shift within her. All of a sudden she remembered the dreams she'd had before Leo, dreams of a man who would support her and protect her and care for her, not one who would use her. Abuse her.

All those dreams had died at the end of Leo's fist, at the toe of his boot. Or so she had thought. Maybe they had only gone into hibernation.

Ethan had suddenly awakened them, but even as she realized that, she feared the cost of allowing them to reappear. Ethan wasn't here for the long haul. He'd merely come to town to meet Micah, and once he'd established whatever kind of relationship he wanted there, he would move on. Besides, he had problems of his own, and she doubted she was the solution to any of them.

There was danger here, emotional danger, but she couldn't bring herself to step away. Not yet. She needed these moments with near desperation.

Later, she thought. Later she could tear out the roots of what was trying to grow in her. Right now she needed any port in the storm. And she was sure he understood that.

When at last she regained her strength, she backed away. He let her go immediately, which she was sure was a message. No involvement, beyond protecting Sophie. Last night had been an aberration, a fulfillment of a need they both felt as solitary souls. But it had made no promises and offered no answers.

Their wounds couldn't be so easily healed, she thought, as she returned to the table. They would always be there. Healing had to come from within, and it couldn't happen if the scars kept reopening.

Julia was still sitting at the table, staring at the cards

as if they could tell her the future, carefully not watching Connie and Ethan.

Then there was a knock on the side door. Connie jumped, turned and saw Micah through the glass panes. At once she leaped up to invite him in.

He was smiling, and he greeted her with a hug, Julia with a peck on the cheek and his son with a bear hug. "I thought I'd get a progress report," he said. Connie got him a cup of coffee and waved him to a chair as she resumed her seat.

"Do you have ESP?" she asked.

His face darkened. For an instant, except for Ethan's beard, father and son looked like clones of the same Cherokee ancestor.

"What happened?"

Ethan answered. "When Sophie wandered off yesterday after school? It was because she had seen the man again."

"Well, hell. I guess we need to tighten the guard."

"I'm going to be with her every minute she's out of the house and not in school."

Micah nodded. Then he looked at Connie. "How do you feel about that?"

"Better." Because if it was Leo, she didn't know how or even if she would be able to handle it.

Ethan must have noticed her glaring omission of the phone call in her recounting of events to her mother earlier, Connie thought, because he didn't mention it to Micah.

"I can't handle this," Julia said. She couldn't have been paler if every drop of blood had been sucked from her. "I'm going to my room. You'll plan better without me here gnashing my teeth and second-guessing everything because I'm a scared old woman."

Feeling a sharp pang, Connie started to rise. "Do you need help?"

"Just to get into my own bed? I think not."

The three of them listened as Julia's chair squeaked across the linoleum, then onto the wooden floor of the hall. A few moments later, her bedroom door closed.

"Okay," Micah said, leaning forward to rest his arms on the table, "what did you leave out?"

Connie looked at Ethan, wondering if he had told Micah, or if Micah just had some kind of ESP. Shaman, she thought. They both were shaman, crazy idea or not. Then she realized she would have to tell this part herself, if for no other reason than that she had been the one who answered the phone.

"I got a call last night," she said. "A man said, 'You have a beautiful daughter, Connie,' and then I hung up."

"That must have freaked you out."

"Pretty much."

The two men's faces had grown as dark and heavy as thunderclouds before a tornado.

"Your ex," Micah said.

Ethan nodded. "That's what we're thinking."

"But we can't be sure," Connie said.

"I agree it would help if we knew something certain," Micah said slowly, "but we don't. We should definitely be keeping an eye out for Leo. I'll see about getting his picture out to the deputies. But at this point, I'm not sure it would be wise to put it out to the public."

Ethan shook his head. "If it *is* Leo, we don't want to push him too hard. If he flees, it won't help us settle this matter. Besides, he's already proved violent."

"My thinking exactly." Micah looked at Connie, silently requesting her input.

"I don't think I'm a reliable judge of anything right now," she answered. "This is way too close to home. Ethan can tell you, I'm barely holding it together."

"Under the circumstances," Ethan said, "you're holding it together damn well. You won't hear any criticism from me."

"Me, neither," Micah said.

Connie smiled wanly. "I think I'll go lie down. You two can arrange everything with Gage. I'm worn out. In fact, I'm useless with worry."

"Don't stay up there if all you're doing is worrying yourself sick," Ethan said.

But that wasn't it at all. She needed to check on Sophie. She needed to be closer to her daughter. She needed some space to find at least a piece of her center to rely on. The worst way to fail Sophie right now would be by falling apart even more than she already had.

Calm. She had to find calm. Real calm. The kind of calm that would allow her to think.

Before it was too late.

## CHAPTER SIXTEEN

AFTER THE CALL to Gage had been made, Ethan and Micah continued to sit at the table, father and son separated by years if no longer by distance. Yet Ethan felt a recognition somewhere deep inside him, as if part of him had always known Micah. Perhaps it was just that part of him was Micah.

"Are you willing to stay around?" Micah asked.

"Stay around?"

"Here. In this county. You have a permanent job if you want it. Gage said so. And I'd like the time with you. Right or wrong, we've both been cheated out of something."

Ethan nodded slowly, turning inward, testing instincts and long-denied feelings. "I'd like the opportunity."

"Good. When this mess with Sophie and Connie is taken care of, Faith wants you to come stay with us for a while. She wants to get to know you, too, and she wants you to know your sisters."

Ethan nodded, feeling a small lightening in his heart. "I'd like that."

"Good." Micah drummed his fingers on the table for a moment. "I know where you've been, son. I spent twenty years doing what you did. So what happened? You're on disability?"

"IED," Ethan said succinctly. "I've got shrapnel lodged near my spine."

"Well, hell." Micah's frown deepened. "I figured it had to be bad. They aren't letting many out right now."

"No."

"So you're in danger?"

"Could be. Mostly it's just pain. But yeah, they're worried a wrong move could paralyze me."

"How are you handling that?"

Ethan shrugged. "I'm luckier than a lot of guys."

"Yeah, I know that feeling, too. Problem comes in the dead of night, when you start to think some of *them* were luckier."

A look of complete understanding passed between them.

"It gets better," Micah said. "It does. I won't say it ever completely goes away, but eventually you can look forward more than you look back."

"I hope so. Sometimes I just wish the enemy still wore uniforms."

Micah nodded. "I carry some of that with me, too."

"I'm sure you do."

Micah sighed and sipped his coffee. "I don't regret serving my country. I hope you don't."

"No. Never."

Micah nodded. "Good. You shouldn't. Some of us have to."

"I know. I'm proud that I went."

Micah reached out and clasped his son's forearm. "I'm proud of you. War creates atrocities by its very nature. But until we all learn to live in peace, some of us are going to bear that burden. I've had a lot of time to think about this, so I'll just tell you, once again, what I've learned. It's time to look to today. Today is the seed of tomorrow. And from what I can see, you're planting some mighty good seeds right now."

Ethan arched a brow.

Micah smiled faintly. "Sophie."

"Oh."

"And Connie. A man could do a lot worse than Connie."

"I don't think…"

"Not yet, maybe. But she's a good woman, through and through. Almost as good as my Faith. You'll see." He drained his mug and rose to carry it to the sink. "I'm going to get to the office, make sure that picture of Leo gets out to the force. I think we got us a snake in the corn, son, and it ain't no stranger."

Ethan watched his father leave, feeling as if an important connection had just been made. His father was no longer a stranger. He was becoming a friend.

For the first time in a long time, he smiled just because he felt like it.

In the distance he heard a rumble of thunder. Rising, he went to the front of the house to look out and see the clouds. Billowing upward, limned in white so bright it seemed to shine, and black below. Another bad one. A big one, the kind that could build up over miles of open space.

He closed his eyes as thunder rumbled again, feeling it deep inside himself. Thunder spoke, and he listened.

He had been chosen. Somehow, in some way, he had been chosen. The shaman in him rose to accept the task, whatever it might be. As thunder rumbled again, speaking in a tongue only his heart could understand, he gave thanks for the rain, for the lightning, for their cleansing, nourishing powers.

And he gave thanks that he had been brought here at this moment in time, a moment when he was needed.

Because what good was any man if he didn't serve a need?

CONNIE COULDN'T SLEEP. Of course, she hadn't expected to. She looked in on Sophie several times, then lay on her bed listening to the building storm. The storm, she thought, would drive Leo or whoever it was to ground. She could relax, at least for a little while.

But anxiety, her constant companion now, wouldn't let go.

She heard Ethan's footsteps on the stairs. He moved almost silently, as usual, but no matter how light his tread, he couldn't avoid all the creaky steps, even though he missed most of them.

Straining to listen, she heard him open Sophie's door, then close it. A moment later her own door opened, just as a bolt of lightning brightened the darkening afternoon. For an instant he looked as if he were stepping out of another world, a mythic being come briefly to earth. Then the lightning faded and he was Ethan again.

"You okay?" he asked.

"Can't sleep."

"Hardly surprising. Sophie's out like a light." He came into the room and lay down beside her, pulling her close with gentle hands, cradling her head on his shoulder. A shaky sigh escaped her as she relaxed against him, feeling his fingers in her hair, stroking gently.

"You know," she said presently, "I've been totally self-absorbed this week."

"You're worried about Sophie. I'm surprised you can think about anything else at all."

"But what about *you?*" she asked. "How are you doing? Are you hurting? Are you getting on with Micah? I feel so selfish."

"You're not being selfish. Micah and I are hitting it off better than I hoped. He wants me to come stay with

him and Faith for a while after we take care of the threat
to Sophie."

"That's a good idea." But, selfishly, she didn't think it
was a good idea at all. She wanted him to stay here. For
the first time in her life she had someone she could really
lean on. Someone who seemed to have shoulders broad
enough to bear the burdens of life with her. And she didn't
want to let him go.

Which was purely selfish. Ethan hadn't come here to
take care of her. He'd come here to find a missing part of
his life. Only a shrew would deny him that.

But here, right now, she had found a peace so deep that
she hated the thought of losing it, even briefly. When he
kissed her forehead, it felt like a blessing. From his lips, a
warm relaxation spread throughout the rest of her.

He didn't say anything. It seemed as if holding her was
enough for him, too.

"What about pain?" she asked. "I've seen how you move
sometimes. You hurt, don't you?"

He sighed. "Most of the time," he admitted. "They say
it'll get better eventually."

"How do you stand it?"

"Do I have a choice?"

"Did they give you anything for it?"

"Of course. I can have all the painkillers I want. Thing
is, I don't want them."

"Why not?"

"Because I like a clear head, and because I don't want
to become an addict."

"But if it gets really bad…"

"If it gets bad enough that I can't move, I might consider them. But only then. Discomfort is a state of mind
to a large extent."

"Pain is a little more than discomfort."

"Same thing, different degree. A lot depends on how you look at it. It's not a fatal disease, it's an injury. Lots of people live with that."

"You're right." She sighed again and unconsciously snuggled closer. "Was it hard being raised by a single parent?"

"I suppose there were disadvantages, but none I really noticed. My mother made sure I knew her people."

"Her people?"

"Her family. Her father's side was Cherokee, which is how my uncle came to train me. Her mother's side was…" All of sudden he gave a deep chuckle. "You're not going to believe this."

"What?"

"Philadelphia mainline."

"What?" She nearly giggled. *"Mayflower?"*

"They didn't get here quite that early. But you can imagine. They weren't rich. That pretty much went away in the Great Depression, but they were still part of that crowd. And they didn't quite know what to make of me."

"Perplexing indeed."

He chuckled again. "Quite a combination. So I got exposed to two very different worlds, but mostly to her father's side. They didn't seem to care that I was half-blood."

"But the Philadelphia crowd did?"

"I don't know exactly what it was. I mean, you can see how Cherokee I look. So it wasn't as if they could ignore it. But they loved my mother, and I came with her, so they tried. Maybe they were just embarrassed that she had never married. It might have been more that than me. But my uncle…he took me to his heart. So in that sense I didn't miss out on much."

"What made you decide to go into the service?"

"That's simple. I was brought up to be patriotic, to feel

that service is essential. Many Native Americans enlist for that reason. My uncle nurtured that in me, along with my more mystical side, and I guess I felt a natural urge to follow in my father's footsteps, even if I didn't know him."

"I can understand that." She hesitated. "Do you ever wonder if your mother's background and family were part of the reason she never told Micah about you?"

"Yeah, it's crossed my mind. They were a somewhat hidebound bunch. Maybe that entered into her decision. I don't know. But she never hesitated to take *me* with her when she went to visit, so I doubt she ever hid her relationship with Micah."

"Interesting."

He gave her a little squeeze. "Some questions never get answered, not in any fully meaningful way. We keep hunting for those answers, but they stay just out of reach. Thing is, I think hunting for the answers is generally more important than finding them."

"So is knowing when to stop looking," she said, thinking of Leo. "Some questions are only going to drive you crazy. Like why Leo beat me. He made me feel responsible for it. Maybe I was, in some way. But why he did it… I don't think I'll ever understand, even though I've heard all the psychobabble about it."

"Maybe he was just plain mean."

"There's that possibility, too. But you still want to ask why."

"Not necessarily. Some folks are just born with something missing."

"Also true. God knows, I saw enough of it on the streets in Denver. But the thing is, in a particular case, you never know."

"Rarely," he agreed. "But there's another thing my uncle taught me."

"What's that?"

"That no matter what we are when we're born, whether we're missing a leg or missing something else, as long as we have a working brain, we make choices. Those choices define us."

Another crack of thunder rent the afternoon, loud, as if it was right overhead. Moments later a voice called from the doorway, "Mommy, I'm scared."

Before Connie could even sit up, Sophie had catapulted herself into the bed beside her. Connie at once turned her back to Ethan and hugged her daughter. "It's loud, all right."

"It's a bad storm." Sophie snuggled in, seeming not at all fazed that Ethan was there. Seconds ticked by like heartbeats, and thunder cracked again, this time almost at exactly the same moment that lightning bleached the room.

Not long after that, Ethan wrapped his arms around both of them and pulled them close.

Throughout the storm, he sheltered them.

# CHAPTER SEVENTEEN

THE STORM CONTINUED to rage throughout the afternoon.
Around three, Connie, Ethan and Sophie went downstairs
to start dinner.

"I think we should have something special tonight,"
Connie said.

"Yay!" Sophie clapped her hands.

"It has to be something I already have," Connie cautioned her. "I'm not going out in this storm."

Sophie immediately ran to check the refrigerator. Apparently she had something in mind, because in no time
at all she'd pulled out a quart of her mother's frozen spaghetti sauce, grated parmesan and a large container of
ricotta cheese, then ran to get a box of lasagna noodles
from the cupboard.

"Well, that's pretty clear," Connie said, watching with
a smile. "Make sure I have mozzarella."

A ball of same emerged from the cheese drawer in the
fridge and joined the other ingredients on the table.

"We seem to have everything essential," Connie said.

Sophie clapped her hands again.

Connie looked at Ethan. "I hope you like lasagna."

"I love it."

Connie nodded and looked at Sophie. "So what do we
do first?"

"Thaw the sauce."

"Right. You know how."

Sophie retrieved a saucepan from a lower cupboard, filled it half full with water and put in on the stove over a low flame. Then she placed the container of spaghetti sauce in it to thaw.

"Good job," Connie said. "Let's mix the filling, then put it in the fridge until we're ready to use it."

Ethan volunteered to grate the parmesan and mozarella, saving Connie's and Sophie's knuckles. Connie and Sophie mixed the ricotta with seasonings and the mozzarella, and soon the bowl was in the fridge, covered by a plate. Then there was nothing to do but wait for the sauce to thaw.

Sophie saw the cards and chips stacked neatly on the table. "Were you going to play a game?"

Connie hesitated. "Well, it was a grown-up game."

"Oh." Sophie didn't appear at all deterred. "What kind of grown-up game?"

Connie nearly sighed. Sophie could be insistent about getting answers. "Poker," she said. "Not for kids."

"Why not, if you don't play for real money?" Sophie asked, depriving her of speech.

Connie looked at Ethan and realized he was trying not to bust a gut laughing. His face, carved as always, nevertheless seemed to be battling to remain impassive.

Julia chose that moment to roll into the room. "The girl's right," she said. "What's wrong with it, if you're just playing for worthless chips?"

"It's gambling," Connie said.

"Most things in life are," Julia retorted. "The chips are just a method of counting."

Connie didn't have an answer for that, although she tried to think up a good one. Then it struck her. "In most games you don't risk your points. You keep them."

"True," Julia agreed. "But poker has lessons of its own. Like not risking things you don't want to lose. Like making decisions and living with the outcome. Like reading other people."

Connie stared at her mother. She'd never seen this side of her before, and she wasn't sure what to make of it.

"And," Julia wound up, "there's not a thing to be lost at this table except some worthless plastic chips. In real life, when you make decisions, you have a lot more on the line."

Sophie spoke. "Don't get mad at Mommy, Grandma."

"I'm not mad at her, child." Julia smiled. "Not in the least. I just think her reaction to this game is more instinctive than valid."

Sophie's brow creased as she tried to figure that one out.

Julia looked at her daughter. "And it's the very risk that makes some things look so attractive."

Connie felt it then. An emotional blow. A comment on her marriage to Leo, maybe even on her choice of jobs. Was she drawn to risk? Had that been the factor that had gotten her into so much trouble?

Bad boy Leo. *Admit it,* she told herself. *Admit it for once and for all.* He hadn't seemed like an angel. Far from it. She'd been drawn to the bad boy and had paid dearly for the attraction. The thrill of running a risk. The stupid, stupid idea that her love would change him.

She looked down at the table without seeing it. Seeing instead her past from this new angle. And knowing, in her heart of hearts, that Julia was right. She'd been drawn to the thrill and the risk, drawn to the very challenge of possessing Leo. Then, before she really knew what was happening, she'd been ground under the heel of his boot.

All love was a gamble, of course, but some kinds of risk-taking were foolhardy. And maybe it wouldn't hurt Sophie to learn that in a game where the only risk was a few plastic chips.

She lifted her head and looked at her mother. "In that case, I think Ethan is going to teach us Texas hold 'em."

Julia smiled. "Time to learn how to gauge worthwhile risks."

Ethan proved to be a patient teacher, especially with Sophie, but by the time they'd played for an hour, Sophie not only understood the relative values of the cards, but she also grasped that she needed to be careful or lose her chips.

Ethan probably folded to Sophie more than he needed to, but not so much that it was obvious. Besides, as Julia had pointed out, this game was about learning when to take risks and how much of a risk you were willing to take. Even the bluffing became a lesson, as Sophie learned she could be lied to by having large sums of chips dangled in front of her as a temptation.

By the time they stopped to make the lasagna, Sophie was beginning to understand the nuances. Connie hoped her mother was right, that Sophie could learn something about life from playing this game, even the most unsettling fact of all: that even when you did everything right, you could still lose sometimes.

Sophie enjoyed herself, regardless, and Connie found herself looking at her own life and decisions in a very different way than she had in the past. It was one thing to acknowledge that she'd chosen poorly with Leo. It was another to face up to the temptation that had sucked her in. The challenge. The risk. The notion, idiotic though it seemed to her now, that there would be a great payoff eventually.

She also noted something else, something she pondered quietly as she and Sophie layered the lasagna together: that just because you went bust on one risk, that didn't mean you couldn't take another and win. In fact, if you were ever going to win, you had to take another. The necessary element was balancing risk against the likelihood of winning.

It was something she'd never really thought about before in quite that way.

Lessons, it seemed, could sometimes be found in the unlikeliest of places.

AFTER DINNER AND washing up, a general vote was held to watch *Shrek*. Sophie loved the movie, and for the first time ever, Connie watched it without feeling cynical. The ogre remained the ogre throughout, never changing. It was the princess who learned where true beauty lay.

No kissing of frogs to turn them into princes. Quite the contrary. A very different fairy tale. One that seemed strikingly apropos, all of a sudden.

Outside, the storm continued to rumble and growl, a beast at bay. She noted that sometimes Ethan would tilt his head and listen to it, as if he could hear things in that grumbling. A little shiver snaked through her as she once again had the feeling that there was something very, very special about Ethan Parish. Something beyond the ordinary.

She tried to tell herself that he was just a man like any other, that she was just being fanciful, but for some reason she couldn't shake the feeling that the man sitting on the couch on the other side of Sophie was special in some very important way. Like an old soul.

Sophie certainly liked and trusted him. In all honesty, Connie couldn't remember Sophie ever warming up this quickly to a man. But right now she was leaning against his side, and he had an arm around her shoulders, as if she belonged there.

Connie's throat tightened, and she had to blink back burning tears. She hoped nobody noticed.

But Julia did notice. Sitting in her wheelchair, inches

away from Connie, she reached out and squeezed her daughter's hand. "It'll be okay," she murmured. "I promise you, Connie. It's going to be okay."

Looking at her daughter and the stranger who had come into their lives only a week ago, Connie wondered, though.

Thanks to two strangers, their lives had changed dramatically. Maybe things would be okay, but they would certainly never be the same again.

And maybe, just maybe, she wanted something more than "okay" for her life.

She caught herself, appalled by her own greediness. For now, the only thing that mattered was protecting Sophie. Only a fool would ask for more. In that snug little living room, a haven against the storm without, Connie gave thanks for the moment. *This* moment.

Sophie wanted to stay up late and watch another movie.

"We have church in the morning," Connie reminded her.

Something odd passed over Sophie's face, then fled so quickly that Connie doubted she'd seen anything.

"How come I never get to stay up late," Sophie muttered as she started up the stairs.

In that instant, blessed normalcy returned and Connie laughed with genuine ease for the first time in days.

"Cuz you're seven, kiddo," she replied.

"That's your answer to everything."

Not everything, Connie thought as she followed her daughter up the stairs. Not everything.

Life should only be so easy.

## CHAPTER EIGHTEEN

THE STORM DIED sometime during the night. Connie slept restlessly, never imagining her bed could have felt so empty. But Ethan remained downstairs.

Probably having second thoughts. Every time she awoke during the night, she wished he was beside her, and every time, she reminded herself that he had plenty of reasons not to pursue matters any further. At least as many reasons as she had.

Then she would roll over and fall into a restless dream that never quite became a nightmare, but always seemed to feature something dangerous lurking just out of sight.

Finally, when the first light of dawn peeped beneath the curtains, she climbed out of bed, dressed in warm jeans, a sweatshirt and socks, and crept as quietly as possible downstairs to the kitchen. She forced herself not to glance in the direction of the living room to see if Ethan was still sleeping.

In the kitchen, she started the coffee. It was way too early to start breakfast for the family, so she popped a slice of bread into the toaster and brought out some blueberry jam. After a night of tossing and turning, her stomach felt as if someone had filled it with acid.

Just as the coffee started to perk, Ethan appeared. He wore jeans and nothing else, causing her heart to skitter a bit at the sight of his broad, smooth chest. He was a beautiful man, she thought. She wished she could see the face behind the beard.

Then she noticed the scars. How had she missed them before? She must have been too transported when they made love to notice the multitude of white scars, some small and thin, a few larger and longer, that marked one side of his torso.

"Morning," he said. He saw where she was looking and asked, "Should I get a shirt?"

"No. No! It's just that... I guess it was really bad."

"I don't remember much of it. A blessing."

"I'm glad you're alive," she told him, meaning it as much as anything she'd ever in her life said.

"Me, too." He gave her a crooked smile. "About time I was able to say that. Sorry I fell asleep."

"It's not like you were on guard duty," she reminded him. "And you have to sleep sometimes. Besides, the house is locked, and one of us would have heard if someone tried to get in."

"Very true."

"Have a seat. I'm making toast. Would you like some?"

"Just some coffee when it's ready, thanks. I haven't been up long enough to feel hungry. You look exhausted."

She shrugged and pulled her slice of toast from the toaster. "I had a restless night. One of those where you feel like you keep waking up, but you almost never wake up enough to actually do anything about it. You know, like turn on a light and read or something. In and out like a swinging door all night."

"I'm sorry."

"It happens. In a strange way, it almost felt like when I was in the hospital." She sat at the table and began spreading jam on her toast. "When they had me drugged. I wasn't really sleeping, I had the oddest dreams, and I kept waking up but couldn't *really* wake up. Weird."

"Yeah. Been there."

She laughed quietly. "Can't blame the drugs this time. Maybe too much coffee, but not drugs."

He grinned. "Leading the clean life, eh?"

"Oh, yeah. I donate blood as often as I can, and when I go in, they have these forms. Same questions every time. I tease them that I've led a very dull life. Last time the nurse asked me if I'd ever received money for sex, I said, 'I wish.' I thought she was never going to stop laughing."

His smile broadened.

"But you know," she added more thoughtfully, "I find there are lots of questions I answer negatively that I ought to be able to answer affirmatively."

"Such as?"

"'Have you been out of the country in the last three years?' Heck, I haven't even taken a real vacation locally. So I go in and answer the questions and start thinking about taking a cruise, or visiting another country, or..."

"You'll do it someday."

She let go of her wistfulness and smiled. "Yeah, I will. Someday."

"I can't donate blood at all anymore. Been overseas too often and too much."

"That's okay. I think you've given enough, anyway."

He shook his head. "Wrong way to look at it."

"You think so?"

"You can never give enough."

As she considered his words, she nodded. "You're right. There's always a need to be met somewhere."

"Maybe I *will* have that toast," he said. When she started to rise, he waved her back. "I can make it for myself. You just rest."

"Bread's in the bread box. If you want butter…"

"I know." He smiled. "The refrigerator."

She laughed then. "Something about being a mother changes you forever. You start assuming that people need explanations for the simplest stuff."

"Looking after others is never a bad habit."

His words warmed her, and she sipped her coffee, savoring its richness, trying not to stare at the scars on his back. There were probably more she had missed, and somehow she felt embarrassed not to have noticed them. Even in the throes of their incredible lovemaking.

He popped a couple of slices of bread in the toaster, said, "Be right back," and disappeared from the kitchen. He returned before the toast was ready, wearing a sweatshirt of his own.

"Are the mornings always so chilly here?" he asked.

"Most of the year," she admitted. "At the height of summer it can get really hot in the daytime, but the nights cool down fast. I've never yet had a night when I didn't need a blanket."

"That's the best way to sleep."

They sat together for a while, sipping coffee, eating toast, no conversation necessary. They had reached that exquisite point where neither of them felt pressed to fill a silence. Connie savored that comfort. To her, that had always been a mark of a truly good relationship, when there could be companionable silence.

Eventually she glanced at the clock. "I guess we may as well go to the early service, if I can get Sophie and my mother up."

He nodded.

"Do you want to come?"

"Sure. Dress up?"

She shook her head, smiling. "Times have changed. Jeans will do."

"Nobody complains?"

"Why should they?" She shrugged. "I've often felt that God couldn't care less what we're wearing when we pray. Clothes are for other people, not for him."

"I like the way you think, Connie." Standing, he astonished her with a kiss. "I'll go wash up real quick while you wake the others."

Julia awoke quickly, with a smile, and agreed she would like to go to the early service. "Much more peaceful," she said. "Not so many folks stirring around and coughing."

Connie laughed. "Then up and at 'em. I'm going to get Sophie."

She climbed the stairs feeling better than she had in a week. Somehow Ethan's presence this morning had managed to batter back the night's vague fears, and the sunlight pouring in every window seemed to fill the world with a crisp, clean glow. The sky, she thought, would be almost unbearably clear and blue this morning.

She knocked on Sophie's door, then opened it. For an instant she didn't register what she was seeing. For an endless, eternal instant, she couldn't put the pieces together.

"Sophie?"

No answer.

"Sophie?" She turned from the bedroom and ran to the hall bathroom, finding it empty.

Then she screamed. *"Sophie!"*

Only silence answered her.

## CHAPTER NINETEEN

FIVE SHERIFF'S CARS filled the tree-lined street. Gage and Micah were there, along with her other friends. Other cars were already out on the streets and ranging the country-side, searching. Every one of them had Leo's arrest photo.

Connie had pulled on her own uniform and gun, ready to get going. But Gage wouldn't let her, not just yet.

"The doors were locked," she kept saying.

Gage looked at Ethan. "You'd have heard her."

"If she'd come downstairs, yes," he said. "I know myself well enough that even when I sleep, I'm still alert if I need to be. And those stairs creak."

"So that leaves…" Gage's scarred face frowned at the dormer of Sophie's room.

"Exactly," Ethan said. "It wouldn't have been hard for her to get down."

"Or someone to get in," Connie said.

Ethan shook his head. "A normal-size man would have made too much noise. This room's right over the living room."

She turned on him. "Are you saying Sophie left on her own?"

He didn't answer, but his dark eyes said everything.

"Why would she do that, Ethan? *Why?*"

"She said she saw him on Friday. Maybe she talked to him. If it's Leo…"

Connie bit her lip. "You think he could have talked her into meeting him?"

"Remember her questions?"

Connie nodded slowly. It was all starting to make sense, and she hated the sense it was making. She looked from Gage to Ethan. Her voice came out as little more than a terrified whisper. "He won't hurt her. Will he?"

Nobody could truthfully answer.

"Why the hell couldn't he just knock on the door like an ordinary person?" she demanded.

Gage pulled no punches. "I know you're upset, Connie. Hell, I'm upset, too. But if he'd knocked on the door, would you have let him meet Sophie?"

Despair swamped her. "No."

"That's probably why, then."

"But what if he takes her away? What if he kidnapped her?"

That was the ugly possibility. The one they all feared.

"We're working on it," Gage assured her. "I'm assuming she didn't leave until the storm let up, so she's only got a few hours lead on us. Everyone's looking, Connie, and I've notified the neighboring counties. He won't get past us."

Given the wide-open spaces that made up so much of this part of the state, Connie had her doubts. Doubts she didn't want to think about right now.

"Okay," Gage said. "We're all fanning out. Julia, you stay here to wait for Sophie. She might just come skipping home. Micah, see that Julia has a radio, so she can call us directly."

Micah nodded and went to get a spare from his car.

Gage turned to Ethan and Connie. "You two stay together. I know I can't keep you from looking, Connie. But don't do something you'll live to regret. Something Sophie will live to regret."

She knew exactly what he meant, because right now, in the midst of her terror, she could have killed Leo without a second thought.

"She won't," Ethan said, speaking for her. Taking responsibility for her. "She won't."

Gage clasped Connie's shoulder. "Word's getting out, Connie. At the church, at Maude's. Everyone in town is going to be looking very soon."

She nodded, trying to take heart from that, but she couldn't. What if someone angered Leo or scared him into doing something awful? But she knew as well as anyone that when this county went on alert, there was no way anyone could keep her neighbors from taking a hand. That was the way they'd always lived. Today they would beat the bushes, and if they found any kind of information about where Sophie had gone, they would gather and form a search party faster than you could say lickety-split.

Cars began to peel away as directions were given, but Connie and Ethan remained. He kept looking at the dormer and the cottonwood that nearly brushed the roof.

Connie spoke. "You think she climbed down that tree."

"That or one of the others. Weird, but the first time I walked around the house, I saw those trees as a security risk. I had to remind myself I wasn't in Afghanistan."

"You'd have cut them down?"

"Back there, yeah."

She nodded, trying to focus on the problem in the now, not on her fears. Fear could only inhibit clear thinking, and she needed her mind as clear as it had ever been.

Okay, she told herself. It was probably Leo. The only reason she could think of for him to develop this interest in Sophie was to get at her. The terrifying question, of course, was what kind of punishment did he want to inflict on her?

But another possibility existed, a slim one. Maybe during his years in prison he'd learned something. Maybe…

No, she couldn't allow herself to think he might be a changed man. Without proof, that could only be a vain hope.

Ethan started toward the side of the house, to the tree nearest the dormer. Connie's heart rose to her throat at the thought of Sophie crawling across the wet roof to grab on to that tree and climb down. Had her daughter lost her mind?

No, of course she hadn't. Sophie wanted something she felt her mother had denied her. Talk about a knife in the heart.

Near the base of the tree, Ethan paused and pointed. "There? You see?"

She did indeed see. Someone had walked on the wet grass, although with all the rain they'd had, the grass had bent, not broken.

"Small footprints."

Connie nodded. It was then that Micah joined them. "Julia has a radio," he said. "Am I seeing what I think?"

Ethan looked at him. "I think she went toward the park."

"That general direction." Father and son locked eyes. Micah spoke. "I'll follow in the car."

Ethan nodded. "Connie, why don't you ride with Micah?"

"Ethan…"

"I can track better if I'm not disturbed."

Feeling almost as if she'd been slapped, she finally gave a short nod and went to join Micah in the car.

"It's nothing personal," Micah said to her as he began to ease down the street behind Ethan. "A tracker can't afford to be disturbed."

"I get it." But her voice came out tight from her huge number of warring emotions. The only things she *didn't* feel right now were happiness and peace. All the rest of it was there, though. All the ugly, terrifying emotions people associated with their less civilized parts.

Ethan was walking along the sidewalk now, looking from side to side, apparently trying to see if footprints left the pavement at any point.

Finally they reached the park, and Ethan squatted.

"What's he doing?" Connie asked.

"The rain we had is actually a help for this. When he gets down like that, he can see anywhere there's been a disturbance in the moisture pattern."

"But it could be anybody."

"At this hour on a Sunday morning, it's not likely to be."

She couldn't argue with that. Why should she? Besides, what other method did they honestly have, other than a wide search net?

"If anything happens to her..." Connie didn't finish the thought. She couldn't. Her hands clenched into fists so tight that her short nails bit into her palms. "Micah..."

"I know." His tone was grim. "I know. I killed once to protect Faith from her ex. I've got kids of my own. Trust me, Connie, you won't get to your gun fast enough."

She believed him. One look at his face, and she believed him.

And there was Ethan, moving now along the edge of the park. His face looked every bit as grim and determined as his father's. In her heart, she understood that these two men were as dedicated to finding Sophie safe and alive as she was. Gage, too, she thought, remembering his face. He'd lost his whole family to a car bomb many years ago. He knew what she was facing.

The support from those three was enough to light a flame of courage in her heart. They would get Sophie back. Soon.

BACK AT THE sheriff's office, a command post was building. Velma ran off copies of Leo's photo and handed them out to the locals. Pretty soon every road in the county had a patrol on it, even the muddiest back roads, where ranchers and their hired hands patrolled with shotguns, looking behind every bush and tree. In town, residents combed every street, alleyway and backyard. With cell phones and CBs, contact was maintained. Airwaves crackled with calls as people reported nothing on one road and announced their intention to move to another. Others mounted their horses to go places vehicles couldn't on the muddy ground.

Micah and Connie heard a great deal over the car's radio. "That bastard is gonna need a hole in the ground," Micah remarked.

They were now following Ethan down a quiet side street. He strode now, as if he knew exactly where he was going. Micah picked up the radio. "What's going on, Ethan?"

"She was picked up by a car at the park. I can just about see the tire tracks heading this way."

Micah looked at Connie. "He's good. Trust him."

"He's all I can trust," Connie said.

"I meant something else, but I guess now's not the time. You can trust all your neighbors, Connie. That's one thing I've learned living here. When the chips are down, these folks get together."

"I know. God, I wonder…" She trailed off.

"Wonder what?"

"Oh, last night we played some poker. Julia thought it

would be a good lesson for Sophie in risk-taking and calculating risks versus benefits."

"And you're wondering if that had something to do with Sophie's decision to climb out her window."

"Yes. What if I helped her to take this risk?"

Micah fell silent for a bit as they followed Ethan. They were getting closer and closer to one of the least-used county roads, one that had no destination other than the mountains. Then he spoke. "You can't blame yourself. I doubt she made up her mind based on a poker game."

"She's seven. Anything could have been enough to influence her."

"Exactly. That's the point, Connie. She's *seven*. She must have been thinking about doing this since Friday, when she saw him. It was probably planned then. I don't think a card game had anything to do with it, any more than playing Candyland would have. Regardless of what your mother might have said, Sophie's very young. I doubt she was extrapolating the lessons of poker to life."

"Except for what my mother said."

"Julia was talking over Sophie's head. Maybe in time she could have learned something valuable from the game, but from playing for an hour or two? Too abstract."

"I hope you're right."

"I've been raising my own. At that age, they're pretty damn literal."

She nodded, shoving down another wave of guilt and fear that she had somehow pushed Sophie into this craziness.

She should have tried to establish a relationship between Sophie and Leo, she thought now. Maybe if her daughter had seen him in prison often enough, she wouldn't now have the kind of curiosity and need that made her want to climb out a second-story window.

If it *was* Leo.

That thought terrified her. A total stranger scared her more than Leo. At least he was a known quantity. His violence, ugly as it was, hadn't been directed at children in some sick way. So why would he want to kill Sophie? To punish Connie? Somehow that didn't add up in her mind.

The problem was, nothing was adding up quite right. Fear and terror rode her shoulders, whispered in her ears and interfered with rational thinking.

They reached the county road. Ethan squatted, looking both ways, then came back to the car. He climbed in the backseat.

"Drive slow," he said. "They headed west. What's out there?"

"Nothing," Micah said. "Mountains. He could have come back into town."

"Drive up to the western edge, then I'll check for turn-offs."

Connie felt an absolute wave of certainty come over her. "He didn't come back into town. He had to know everyone would be looking for him. He took her to the old mining camp."

For several moments the car was filled with a silence interrupted only by the quiet hum of the engine and the whine of tires on wet pavement.

All of sudden Micah floored it. "You're right," he said grimly. "And that place is probably as dangerous as he is. Maybe more so."

Connie nodded, feeling the blood drain from her face. Unstable ground, old shafts ready to cave in, buildings standing merely from the pressure of memory. Even without Leo, Sophie could get killed up there just by taking one wrong step. And Connie doubted Leo had any idea just how dangerous the place was.

"Hurry," she said. "Oh, God, hurry!"

# CHAPTER TWENTY

THE CLOSER THEY drew to the mountains, the worse the road grew. Past the last ranch, it was mainly used in the autumn by hunters, and sometimes in summer by people who wanted to hike. After the winter, it desperately needed grading again, but as muddy and rutted as it was, good drainage kept them from bogging down. Better still, they could see the fresh tire tracks made since the night's rain.

Micah spared no speed, sometimes skidding in the mud, but going as fast as he possibly could.

As they began the climb, trees closed in around them.

"I've gotta slow down, Connie. We can't risk driving past him."

"I know. I understand." And she did. But she hated it. She peered intently into the shadows beneath the evergreens, feeling the air grow steadily cooler as they climbed. Ethan gripped her shoulder and squeezed comfortingly.

"I'm looking out the left side," he said. "You concentrate on the right."

"Thanks."

Finally they rounded the last curve before the old mining camp, and Connie gasped as she saw the vehicle, a battered old pickup, muddy and almost colorless, parked near the warning sign that advised would-be explorers of the many dangers.

She wanted to jump out before Micah had fully stopped

their SUV, but Ethan held her back, his fingers tightening. "Just wait," he said. "You don't want to break a leg."

"How could he take her in there, with all those signs?"

Nobody had an answer for that. Nor did anybody want to say that Sophie might not even be there.

"We'll split up and circle," Ethan said. "Around the outside. Maybe he didn't take her in there, but if we circle, we'll hear or see something if he did. And if he didn't, they can't be far away."

"He had to have heard our car coming," Connie said. Her heart beat a rapid tattoo, and she began to breathe heavily.

"I know," Ethan said. "So we've got to approach carefully."

"I'm no good at tracking," Connie said. "You two do the perimeter. I'm going in there."

The two men hesitated, but finally nodded. "All right," Micah said.

"I'll disable his vehicle," Ethan added. He slipped out of the car and within a minute had removed the distributor cap from beneath the truck's hood. He shoved it into a pocket.

Then, speaking not a word, he and Micah signed to each other and headed out in opposite directions. Connie stood at the sign, looking into the camp, her mind trying to chart the most dangerous places. Once, this had been a small town, but now collapsing cabins and mine shafts could be found all over the mountainside. Most of the shaft openings had been boarded over, many marked with the radiation-hazard trefoil. Radon gas built up in the shafts, and some shafts had exposed uranium deposits.

And the ass had brought her daughter *here*.

Anger resurged, more helpful than the fear that had

dogged her. Unsnapping her holster guard, she walked into the camp.

The rains had made the place even more treacherous. Running in rivers, pooling in potholes, undoubtedly pouring down shafts. Eroding support everywhere. The old miners had been good builders, but not even they could prevent the ravages of time. Timber rotted. Water carried away supporting ground and rock.

Almost all the tailing mounds had been carted away years ago by the Environment Protection Agency. The stuff the miners didn't want contained all kinds of toxic elements that the rain swept into rivers. Even today, where tailings remained, nothing grew.

The work done here had created a scar on the landscape that not even more than a century had repaired. Trees had not returned, and even scrub still didn't grow in most places.

She walked cautiously, pausing often to listen and look around. If there were any cracks in the ground to give her warning, the rain had filled them in, making this place more dangerous than ever. She tried to remember from times past where the firmest ground lay, but it had been so long...

Then she heard it. *Sophie's voice.*

She turned immediately to the left, looking. She couldn't see a damn thing other than tumbled buildings and rusting equipment. She bit back an urge to call her daughter's name, for fear she might precipitate something.

Then she heard it again. A child's piping voice, speaking quietly, but sounding normal. Not sounding hurt or frightened.

*Thank God!*

Trying not to let eagerness overwhelm caution, she

moved as lightly and quickly as she could, listening intently and scanning the ground for dangers.

To the left again. Along what had once been a narrow street lined by small dwellings. Rotting, sagging, windows gaping without glass or other coverings except for a faded scrap that might once have been a curtain. Boarded-up doors to discourage explorers. More warning signs, posted in just the past couple of years after a hiker was injured by a collapsing building.

Then, oh, God, then...

Sophie's voice again, coming from just behind one of the buildings. Quiet. As if she was trying not to be heard. Then another voice, this one even quieter, low, a man's voice.

Pulling her gun, Connie held it in both hands and slowly worked her way around the weatherbeaten remains of some long-dead person's dreams.

Her heart stopped, and she rounded the back corner. There was Sophie, clad in jeans, sweatshirt and a pink raincoat, sitting on a camp stool. On the muddy ground in front of her sat a man. Connie could see only his back, covered by a denim jacket. His hair was long, graying. She didn't recognize him at all.

Slowly raising her gun, she pointed it straight at the man's back.

"Sophie," she said, keeping her voice calm, "move away from him."

"But, Mommy, it's Daddy."

The man turned his head, and with a slam, Connie recognized him. Leo, aged by his time in prison, looking seedy and too thin.

"Sophie," she said, keeping her gun leveled. "Come here. Now."

"Mommy, don't shoot him."

"I won't shoot him if you come here."

Scowling, Sophie slid off the camp stool and walked toward her mother. Connie, tensed in expectation that Leo might reach for Sophie to use her as a hostage, was relieved when he let their daughter pass him without even twitching a muscle.

As soon as Sophie reached her side, Connie wrapped one arm around her, gun still pointed at Leo.

"You kidnapped her," she said.

"No. She came to me."

"I did, Mommy."

"The minute you put her in the car with you, you kidnapped her." She keyed her shoulder mike. "Micah? Ethan? I've got her. Leo's here. I'm behind a building one block from the town center, uphill."

They rogered her simultaneously over the crackling radios.

"Don't you read the signs, Leo? You could have gotten her killed!"

"I checked the place out. I've been here a while."

"Why? *Why?*"

"Can I get up?"

"You just stay where you are." No way was she going to let him move until she had backup.

He sighed and shook his head. "I was a bastard, Connie. I've had plenty of time to face that fact."

"Yeah, rehabilitated by prison. Next you'll be thumping the Bible at me."

To her amazement, his face actually saddened. "Yeah," he said quietly. "I found God. About time."

She hesitated, holding Sophie even tighter. "I'm supposed to believe that—when you kidnapped my daughter?"

"She's *my* daughter, too! I figured that one out, finally."

"You never cared before."

"I never did a lot of things before that I should have. Instead, I did a lot of things I *shouldn't* have. I had this cell mate in prison. He was in for dealing. He spent the whole damn time whining about how much he missed his kids. At first it pissed me off. But then I began to realize something."

"Yeah?"

"Yeah. I realized I'd thrown away the only good things in my life. The only things that mattered."

"Amazing conversion."

He shook his head. "I don't expect you to believe me. But I'd never hurt a hair on Sophie's head."

"Then why the hell didn't you just knock on my door, instead of putting her and me through hell for a week?"

"Because I knew you'd never let me see her. I tried to talk to you on the phone, but you hung up before I could say anything more than that you have a beautiful daughter."

That was true. The truth of it pierced her. But not enough to make her trust this man.

Ethan appeared, his own gun unholstered, and took up position to one side. "Sophie, are you okay?"

"I'm fine," the girl said. "Why is everyone pointing guns at my daddy?"

Connie answered. "Because he did a bad thing when he brought you up here."

"No, he didn't. I wanted to talk to him. He's my daddy!"

Slowly, without permission, Leo rose and put his hands in the air. "So send me back to prison," he said. "It doesn't matter. I got to see her. And I'll be gone in a couple of months, anyway."

Connie's hand wavered, and she lowered her pistol. "What kind of crap is that?"

"No crap," Leo said. "You can check. Remember how

you always said I should quit smoking? You were right. I got lung cancer. Nothing they can do."

That explained why he looked so worn and way too thin. And now, as she stared at him, she could see lines of pain around his eyes and mouth.

Micah had appeared to one side, and now he spoke. "This isn't a good place to talk. Let's go back into town, where it's safe and dry. We can sort it out there."

Connie slipped her pistol back into its holster and snapped the guard strap into place, then turned to squat and hug Sophie as tightly as she could. "Do you know how scared I was? Do you have any idea?"

"I'm sorry."

"Next time, talk to me first. *Please.*"

Sophie nodded, but she was watching Micah and Ethan walk her father away. "You won't put him in jail, will you?"

Connie hesitated, but as she looked into her daughter's eyes, she realized there could be a worse crime than the scare she'd had this morning. The seeds of it were already in her daughter's clear blue eyes.

"Not if he's been telling the truth. Fair enough?"

That seemed to satisfy Sophie, for now at least. Taking her mother's hand, she followed her back to the SUV.

## CHAPTER TWENTY-ONE

CONNIE SAT ON the edge of Sophie's bed, holding her hand. She'd never felt so tired in her life, but the strain was mostly gone. The threat to her daughter had been eliminated. All the adrenaline that had been keeping her going seeped away like gas from a punctured balloon.

"I know he was bad to you," Sophie said. "But he was nice to me."

"And I promised you could see him here, in this house, if his story checks out."

"I know. People can get better, Mommy."

Connie had her doubts, but she wasn't about to share them with Sophie. People *could* change, she supposed. After all, that was the basis of her religion. The fact that it didn't often happen didn't mean it never could.

The thought of Leo dying… Well, despite everything, that disturbed her. Saddened her. She didn't have a lot of feelings about him one way or another anymore, but she could still be saddened by the news. As she would be for anyone.

She only cared that he treated Sophie well. It would have been kinder if he'd stayed away, so Sophie wouldn't have to suffer through his death, but that had become moot. In the meantime, she could only hope that Sophie garnered some good memories to make up for not having a father all this time.

"Where's Ethan?" Sophie asked.

"Downstairs, I think."

"I want a good-night hug."

"I'll call him." She wished she knew if this growing attachment was a good thing. Ethan had proved himself to be a good and caring man, but if he moved on, and he most likely would, Sophie would suffer another loss. But she could no longer prevent that. Too late. Amazing how much had suddenly become too late, even as the pressure of the threat lifted.

But life brought loss to everyone sooner or later. She couldn't shield Sophie from everything forever. She'd learned that the hard way this week.

Ethan came up in answer to her call and bent over the bed to give Sophie a warm hug. "No more shinnying out the window, Missie, or I'll handcuff you to your bed at night."

Sophie giggled, the happiest she'd sounded all day. "I won't, I promise."

"Sleep tight," he said, and dropped a kiss on her forehead.

Connie waited with Sophie until she slipped into sleep. Then, feeling as if she could barely lift her legs, she went to her own room. She stopped just inside the doorway, surprised to see Ethan there, standing by the window, looking out.

She hesitated on the threshold, then entered and closed the door. "I suppose you'll be moving in with Faith and Micah soon." And then moving even farther away. Her heart plummeted at the thought.

He turned from the window to face her. "Actually," he said slowly, "I was hoping you would let me stay here."

"Here? On the couch?"

He took a step toward her. "No. Here. With you."

She caught her breath, feeling her fatigue drain away. A flicker of wild hope ignited. "Ethan?"

He seemed to glow with some inner strength and fire before her very eyes. His very presence pulled her, as if by magical force.

"I wasn't looking for this," he said. "I never expected to find it, frankly. I was just going to pass through, get a few questions answered and drift on until I found…something. I had no idea what it would be."

"But?"

"But here it is. Right here. With you and Sophie. I was on a quest, and it ended right here. If I have to leave you, I won't go farther than Micah's place. And I'll keep beating on your door and bringing you roses until you say yes. Because I love you, and I want to spend the rest of my life with you."

For an instant Connie doubted her own ears. Then her whole body lightened as she realized she had finally let go of her own self-doubts and wariness, at least with this man. Then, as if carried on angel wings, she flew across the room to land in Ethan's strong arms.

"I don't want you to go. I never want you to go!"

He laughed and lifted her right off her feet. "I take it that's a yes?"

"Yes, yes, yes, and I love you, too!"

He smiled down at her, his face warmer than she had ever seen it. "Will you marry me?"

She pressed her face to his shoulder, overwhelmed by joyful tears. Her prayers had been answered, including one she had barely acknowledged. Sophie was safe, and Ethan wanted her. Her heart swelled until she ached with gratitude. "Yes, Ethan. Oh, yes!"

"Do you think Sophie will be okay with it?"

"Let's go ask her right now."

A minute later the quiet house was filled with a little girl's voice crying, "All *right!*"

The stranger had brought peace, and it settled gently over the house as happy voices talked well into the night.

Even bad things could bring some good, Connie thought much later, as she lay in Ethan's arms, snug and safe.

And this was as good as it could get.

\* \* \* \* \*

# A SOLDIER'S
# REDEMPTION

For my dad, who taught me that a person
is measured by their dedication to honor, duty
and loyalty. You lived those values, Dad.
And they live on in me.

# *CHAPTER ONE*

THE KNOCK ON the door, as always, caused Corinne Farland's heart to skip a beat. Some lessons, once learned, could never be unlearned.

But after a year in Conard County, she found it a little easier to go to the front of the house. As always, she twitched the curtain aside at the front window by the door and looked out. She recognized Gage Dalton instantly, with his scarred face and his sheriff's uniform. Gage was her main protector these days.

She hurried to disengage the alarm system, then opened the door and smiled, an expression that sometimes still felt awkward on her face. "Hi, Gage."

He smiled back, a crooked expression as the burn scar on one side of his face caused one side of his mouth to hitch oddly. "Hi, Cory. Got a minute?"

"For you, always." She let him in and asked if he'd like some coffee.

"I'm coffeed out," he said, still smiling. "Too many cups of Velma's brew and my stomach starts reminding me I'm mortal." Velma was the dispatcher at the sheriff's office, a woman of indeterminate age who made coffee so strong few people could finish a single cup. The deputies, however, sucked it down by the pot.

She invited him into her small living room, and he perched on the edge of her battered recliner, his tan Stetson in his hands.

"How are things?" he asked.

"Okay." Not entirely true, maybe never true again, but the bleak desert of her heart and soul were not things she trotted out. Not for anyone.

"Emma mentioned something to me." Emma was his wife, the county librarian, a woman Cory admired and liked. "She said you were a bit tight financially."

Cory felt her cheeks heat. "That wasn't for distribution."

Gage smiled. "Husband-and-wife privilege. It doesn't go any further, okay?"

She tried to smile back and hoped she succeeded. Things were indeed tight. Her salary as a grocery-store clerk had been tight from the beginning, but now because times were hard, they'd asked everyone to take a cut in hours. Her cut had pushed her to the brink, where canned soup often became her only meal of the day.

Gage shook his head. "I'll never in a million years understand how they work this witness protection program."

Cory bit her lip. She didn't like to discuss that part, the part where her husband, a federal prosecutor, had become the target of a drug gang he was going after. The part where a man had burst into her house one night and killed him. The part where the feds had said that for her own protection she had to change her identity and move far away from everything and everyone she knew and loved.

"They do the best they can," she said finally.

"Not enough. It's not enough to buy you a house, give you a few bucks, get you a job and then leave you to manage. Not after what you've been through."

"There was some insurance." Almost gone now, though, and she was clinging to the remains in case of an emergency. She'd already had a few of those with this house they'd given her, and it had eaten into what little she had. "And they did do more for me than most." Like a minor plastic surgery to change her nose, which caused an amazing transformation to her face, and the high-tech alarm system that protected her day and night.

"Well," he said, "I'd like to make a suggestion."

"Yes?"

"A friend of a friend just arrived in town. He's looking for a place to stay awhile that's not a motel, but he's not ready to rent an apartment. Do you think you could consider taking a roomer? You don't have to feed him, just give him your extra bedroom."

She thought about that. There was a bedroom upstairs, untouched and unused. It had a single bed, a dresser and a chair, here when she had moved in. Her own bedroom was downstairs, so she wouldn't have this guy next door to her at all times.

But there were other things, darker fears. "Gage…"

"I know. It's hard to trust after where you've been. But I checked him out. Twenty years in the navy, all documented. Enough medals to paper a wall. You've met Nate Tate, haven't you?"

"Of course." She'd met the former sheriff. He might have retired, but apparently he still made it his job to know everyone in the county. She'd even had dinner with him and his wife a few times at their house. "Of course."

"Well, this guy is a friend of his son's. I don't know if you've met Seth Hardin."

She shook her head.

"Well, that's a story for another day. But Seth is a good sort, and he suggested this guy come here for a while to decompress."

"Decompress?" She didn't know if she liked the sound of that. "I don't know…"

"I'm not asking you to babysit." Gage smiled again. "This guy is quite capable of looking after himself. He just needs some time away. A change of scene. And he's not a talker. I doubt you'll know he's in the house most of the time."

"I'll think about it." But she had to admit, she trusted Gage, and she needed the money.

"How about I bring him inside and introduce you?"

Fear jammed into her throat. Every new person represented risk. Every single one. Hiding had become her raison d'être, and each time she had to meet someone new, the experience resurrected old fears.

"Let me get him," Gage said before she could argue. "He's in my car."

She wanted to scream for him not to do this, but she sat frozen, her fingers instinctively going to her side where the scar from the bullet still sometimes hurt. Where was her will? Her ability to say no? She seemed to have lost that on one dark night a year ago. Ever since, she had moved through her days like an automaton. Doing what was expected, pretending she cared. The truth was that the only thing she ever really felt anymore was fear. And grief. Sometimes fury.

She heard Gage limp back onto the porch, and with him came a considerably heavier tread. She rose, an instinct these days, not out of courtesy, but out of a need to be able to flee if necessary.

First she saw Gage, but forgot him instantly as she looked at one of the biggest men she had ever seen. He must have been at least five inches over six feet, and even wrapped in a chambray shirt and jeans, he looked to be built out of concrete. Powerful. Strong. Overwhelming.

Scariest of all was the absolute lack of expression on his face. It was a hard face and appeared as if it would yield to nothing at all. His eyes were as black as chips of obsidian, and so was his short hair. She couldn't begin to guess a thing about him, not even his age.

Inside she quailed, helplessly, feeling like a mouse staring down a hawk.

But then he spoke, in a voice as deep as the rumble of thunder. "Ms. Farland. I'm Wade Kendrick." He didn't offer his hand.

The words sounded reluctant. As if he were no happier about putting her out than she was about taking this risk.

And his reluctance somehow eased her fear. "Hi," she said. "Have a seat."

He looked around as if deciding which chair might hold him. He finally took one end of the sofa. Cory sat on the Boston rocker, and Gage eased into the recliner again. The sheriff clearly suffered constant pain, but he never spoke of it.

"Okay," Gage said, since no one else seemed to be willing to talk. "Wade here needs a room indefinitely. Don't know how long, which is why he can't rent an apartment just yet. He's willing to pay monthly for a room. No food."

"I'll eat out," Wade said. "I don't want to get underfoot."

She appreciated that at the same time she wondered at it. He didn't look like a man who gave a damn about such things. "It's not…much of a room," she said hesitantly.

"I don't need much."

Nor did he volunteer much. Of course, she wasn't volunteering anything, either.

"I guess, if you think it's worth it," she finally said. "I've never done this before."

"Ma'am, it's worth it to have a place to lay my head."

She needed the money, and she trusted Gage. Battering down the fear that never entirely left her, not even in her dreams, she said, "Go take a look at the room. It's upstairs. There's a bath up there, too, and it'll be all yours because I have one down here."

The man rose and without another word headed up the stairs at the rear of the living room. Cory glanced at Gage, feeling her heart flutter a little. Panic? Fear? She couldn't tell anymore, since the only feelings she had left were bad ones.

"It'll be all right, Cory," Gage said kindly as they listened to the heavy footsteps overhead. "Sometimes we all need a bolt-hole. That's all he wants."

She could understand that. She was living her entire life in a bolt-hole now.

She stiffened as she heard boots start down the stairway. She didn't want to turn and look, afraid of the impact this huge stranger had on her. But she couldn't evade looking at him for long, because he came to stand in front of her.

"It's just what I need," he said. He pulled out his wallet and handed her six hundred-dollar bills, crisp from the bank. "I'll go get my stuff."

Then he walked out and Cory sat staring at the money in her hand. She was used to seeing money at work, but not holding so much and knowing it was her own. Her hand shook a little.

"That's too much," she almost whispered. It was as much as she made in a month.

Gage shook his head. "He offered it, Cory. It's what he thinks the room is worth."

A minute later, Wade returned carrying a large heavy duffel bag. And that was it. In a matter of less than half an hour, she had gained a roomer, a roomer who carried his entire life, it seemed, in a bag.

How apt was that?

AFTER GAGE LEFT, she had to deal with the uneasiness of hearing someone above her head for the first time since she had lived here. She could tell what he was doing by the sounds the rumbled through the floor: unpacking and putting things in the battered dresser.

She needed to give him a key, she realized, and felt her heart lurch at the thought. Her safety not only lay behind a new identity, but also behind locks that were always fastened, and an alarm system the feds had installed. The idea of giving a stranger both a key and the alarm code very nearly caused her a panic attack.

But then she remembered how easily those men had gotten to her and her husband, and knew that no lock or alarm in the world would protect her if she opened her door at the wrong time.

*God,* she thought, *stop this, Cory!* The whole reason she was here in out-of-the-way Conard County, Wyoming, the whole reason she was working as a grocery clerk instead of a teacher, with all the public documents that would require, was so that she didn't have to look over her shoulder for the rest of her life.

Nothing about her life now in any way resembled her life before. Not even her work. Not even her face. That was where her safety lay, not in locks and alarm systems.

She heard Wade come down the stairs. This time she made herself look at him. He hadn't changed, but she felt a shiver of fear anyway. This was still the man Gage had felt safe bringing into her life, and he might be big and appear ready to kill with his bare hands, but Gage trusted him. And she trusted Gage.

"I need to give you a key and show you the alarm code, Mr. Kendrick," she said. Her voice sounded weak, but at least it was steady.

He stood at the foot of the stairs, looking at her. "You comfortable with that?" he asked.

How had he guessed? Was her terror written all over

her face? "I...you live here now. You need to be able to come and go when I work."

"No."

"No?" What kind of answer was that?

"I can manage."

She felt a bit stunned by his response. He could manage? He was paying what she considered to be an exorbitant rent to use that lousy bed and bath upstairs for a month, but he was willing to be locked out when she was gone? Had he read her fear so clearly? Or did she stink of it?

Probably the latter, she thought miserably. How would she know? She'd been afraid for so long.

"I'm going out to get sheets, towels, a few other things," he said after a moment. "Which direction should I head?"

Another thought struck her. "Do you have a car?"

"I can walk."

"I could walk, too," she said, feeling a smidgen of her old self spring to life. The resurrection was almost as painful as the death, but at least it was only a small thing, and thus a small pain she could endure. "But if you need a bunch of things, then you might need an extra arm."

"I'll manage."

"Yeah. You'll manage." Sighing, she stood up. "I'll drive you. I need some food anyway." And because of him she now had the money to buy it. Guilt, if nothing else, goaded her.

She went to get her purse. Before they stepped out, however, she insisted on giving him her spare key, and showing him the code for the alarm. If he thought it was odd there was such an advanced alarm system in such a ramshackle house, he didn't indicate it by word or look.

Instead he asked just one question. "Motion detectors?"

"Down here at night. I turn them on separately. Same code. Did you see the keypads upstairs in your bedroom?"

"Yes."

"Well, if you need to come down here at night, you can turn off the entire system from up there, too. To turn off the motion detectors, use the small keypad beside the big one. The rest of the system is on the big pad." She made herself look at him then. Another shiver passed through her as she realized this man could probably snap her in two if he wanted to. Once she had never had those kinds of thoughts. Now she had them all the time. "If you leave, for any reason, and I'm not here or awake, please turn on the entire system."

He nodded. Nothing in his face said he thought that was strange.

She explained the panic buttons, which would direct a call instantly to police, fire or ambulance. Their mere existence reminded her of all that had happened.

And none of it would have done her a damn bit of good fifteen months ago.

Then she set the alarm. It gave them only forty-five seconds to get out the front door and close it. It was long enough.

The U.S. Marshals had also given her a car along with the house. It wasn't a standout that might draw attention. In fact, it was practically a tank, four years old already, guzzling gas in a way that pained her conscience, but her protectors had insisted. The engine was new, as of a year ago, and was a full V-8 with more power than she would ever need.

Because if they came after her, they wouldn't give her a chance to get in a car and get away. She was sure of that. Someday soon, she promised herself, as soon as she could find a way, she would try to trade it in for a smaller but reliable car. She didn't need this steel cocoon.

If she could say nothing else for the Suburban, it gave

Wade Kendrick plenty of room. She doubted he could even squeeze into the subcompact she hoped to have someday.

He didn't say another word until she dropped him off in front of the department store. Then it was just, "Thanks."

"When should I pick you up?"

He shrugged. "I won't take long. I'm not picky. Whenever is good for you."

Well, her needs were essentially meager, too. Not even with the extra money could she afford to be reckless. Cooking for one just depressed her, but she made herself buy something more nutritious, like vegetables, and salad fixings, and some chicken. She could shop for more after her next shift, but right now she was off for three days.

Three whole days, and now with a stranger in her house.

Evenings were long here in the summer, the sun not even hitting the horizon until after nine. But as it sank lower in the west, the dry air failed to hold the heat, and the early evening was starting to cool down by the time she emerged from the market with her two cotton bags of groceries. She drove back to the department store, and found Wade already outside on the curb. Apparently he'd bought more than one or two items, to judge by the number of bags, and she was glad she hadn't let him walk. She suspected that if she had, he'd have made several trips because of bulky pillows and blankets as well as sheets and towels.

And he probably wouldn't have said a thing about it. Gage had been seriously guilty of understatement when he said the guy didn't talk much.

She waited while he put his purchases in the back next to her groceries, then he climbed up front beside her.

"Thanks," he said again.

"You're welcome."

And not another sound from him. It was almost as if

he were trying to be invisible in every way. Out of sight, out of hearing, out of mind.

If he'd been one of her students, she would have concluded that silence came from secrets, terrible secrets, because nothing about him indicated shyness. But he wasn't a student, he was a grown man, and maybe the same metrics didn't apply.

They reached the house and she pulled into the short driveway and parked. She never used the garage because it provided hiding places over which she had little control.

As soon as she put the car in Park, Wade climbed out. "I'll get your groceries, too," he said.

Part of her wanted to argue that she could manage, but she recognized it for what it was: a desire to exert some control, any control, over her life again. The man offered a simple courtesy, and maybe it was his way of expressing his gratitude for the ride. She knew better than to prevent people from offering such little acts of kindness, especially when they had just received one.

Ah, hell, she thought. She didn't ordinarily swear, but this day was beginning to make her want to. Needing to take someone into her sanctuary to pay the bills was bad enough. But finding that the teacher in her still existed, lived and breathed even though it was now forbidden to her, actually hurt.

She felt surprised that it still hurt. After the last year she had thought she was incapable of feeling any lack except the lack of her husband. God, she missed Jim with an ache that would probably never quit.

Head down, she climbed the front porch steps, going through her key ring for the house key. She had keys from the store, keys for the car, a key for the garage…so many keys for such a narrow life.

Just as she twisted the key, she heard the phone ring. It

was probably work, she thought, needing her to come in to cover for someone who was sick. Eager for those hours, she left the door open behind her for Wade, punched in the alarm code as fast as she could, and ran for the cordless set in the living room.

She picked it up, punched the talk button and said, "Hello?" Let it be more than a couple of hours. Make it a couple of days. God, she needed the hours.

A muffled voice said, "I know where you are." Then nothing but a dial tone.

The phone dropped from her hands and her knees gave way.

They'd found her.

# CHAPTER TWO

"WHAT'S WRONG?"

She looked up from the floor, at the huge man who had entered her life barely two hours ago. He stood in the doorway, his arms full of bags. She tried to breathe, but panic had locked her throat. Speech was impossible, and she couldn't answer that question anyway. Not to a stranger.

Finally she managed to gasp in some air. The instant she recovered her breath, even that little bit, tears started to run. And then she wanted to run. To get in her car and drive as far as she could on what little money she had left, which wouldn't be far at all in that damn Suburban.

And then she realized that if they'd found her, even stepping out her front door could cost her her life.

"Ma'am?"

The giant dropped the bags, and crossed the short distance between them. He squatted beside her. "Put your head down. All the way down."

Somehow, with hands that seemed too gentle for someone she had already identified as threatening, he eased her down onto the floor, then lifted her legs onto the couch. Treating her for shock, she realized dimly as the wings of panic hammered at her.

"What happened?" he asked again.

The adrenaline had her panting. Who should she call? The Marshals? She knew what they'd do, and God help her, she didn't want to do that again.

"The sheriff. I need to talk to Gage."

At least he didn't question her again. Instead he reached for the phone she had dropped and pressed it into her hand.

"Need me to leave?" he asked. "I'll just go unload the car…"

He shouldn't hear this, but around his dark eyes she saw something like genuine concern. Something that said he'd do whatever was best for her, regardless of what it might be.

Her throat tightened. So few people in her life who would care if she lived or died anymore. Even the Marshals would probably just consider her a statistic on their chart of successes and failures.

"I…" She hesitated, knowing she wasn't supposed to share her true situation with anyone. Not anyone. But what did she have to say that he couldn't hear? She didn't have to mention anything about the witness protection program or her real identity because Gage already knew.

"It's okay," he said. "Just don't get up yet. I'll get the rest of the stuff from the car."

Amazing. He rose and went back to unloading as if she hadn't just done the weirdest thing in the world: collapse and then demand to call the sheriff.

Amazing.

But she realized she didn't want her car left unattended and unlocked with bags in it. Bags in which someone could put something. And she didn't want her front door open indefinitely, or the alarm off. Her life had become consumed by such concerns.

Muttering a nasty word she almost never used, she brought up Gage's private cell phone on her auto dialer. He answered immediately.

"Cory Farland," she said, aware that her voice trembled.

"Cory? Did something happen?"

"Gage I…I got a phone call. All the guy said was, 'I know where you are.'"

Gage swore softly. "Okay," he said. "Okay. Most likely it was just a prank. You know how kids are when they have time on their hands. Stupid phone calls are the least of it."

"I know, but…"

"I know," he said. "Trust me, I know. I'm not going to ignore it, okay? Stay inside. Don't go out at all, and keep that alarm on. Do you have caller ID?"

"No, I can't afford it."

Another oath, muffled. "I'm going to remedy that as soon as possible. But Cory, try not to get too wound up. It's probably a prank."

Yeah. She knew kids. Probably a prank, like Prince Albert in the can. Yeah. A prank. "Okay."

Gage spoke again. "Think about it, Cory. If they'd really found you, why would they warn you?"

Good question. "You're right." She couldn't quite believe it, but he was right. She drew another shaky breath, and felt her heart start to slow into a more normal rhythm.

"I'm not dismissing it, Cory," Gage said. "Don't misunderstand me. But I'm ninety-nine-point-nine percent certain it's some kind of prank."

"Of course." She said goodbye and disconnected, then lay staring at her ceiling. It was an old ceiling, and watermarks made strange patterns, some like faces she could almost identify. Like the face of the man who had killed Jim and almost killed her.

She heard the front door close, the lock turn, the sound of the alarm being turned on. The tone pierced what suddenly seemed like too much silence, too much emptiness.

She heard footsteps and turned her head to see Wade. Still impassive, he looked down at her. "How are you feeling?" he asked.

"I'm fine. I'm fine." Life's biggest lie, and it rose automatically to her lips.

"Your color is a bit better. Need help getting up?"

"I can do it, thanks." Yeah, she could do it. Get up, go to the kitchen, put her groceries away and resume the pretense of normalcy. Because there was no other option. All her options had been stolen over a year ago.

Sighing, she pulled her feet off the couch and rolled to her side to get up. A steadying hand was there to grip her elbow, surprising her. She looked into the rigid, unrevealing face of Wade Kendrick and wondered if he were some kind of instinctive caretaker.

She should have protested the touch. But all of a sudden, after a year of avoiding contact with other people, she needed it, even just that little bit of a steadying hand offered out of courtesy.

"Thanks," she said when she was on her feet. "I need to put groceries away."

One corner of his mouth hitched up just the tiniest bit. His version of a smile? "I think," he said slowly, "it might be best if you sit for a bit. I can put your groceries away, and you can supervise."

She should have argued. The independence thing had become of supreme importance to her since circumstances beyond her control had gutted her entire life. But she didn't feel like arguing at all. No, with her knees still feeling rubbery, and perishables like frozen food and milk in her two shopping bags, the task needed to be done soon, and she honestly wasn't sure she could manage it.

Adrenaline jolts had a high price when they wore off. So she led the way into the kitchen, her knees shaking, and sat at the chipped plastic-topped table while he emptied her two bags and then asked where each item went.

He went about it with utter efficiency: economy of words and economy of movement both.

And she felt very awkward, unable to engage in conversation. She'd lost most of her conversational ability over the past year because she didn't have a past, at least not one she could talk about, and lying had never come easy. So she had become limited to the most useless of topics: the weather, work, a recent film. No depth or breadth of any kind.

And when faced by a man like this, one who seemed disinclined to talk, all she could do was sit in her chair and squirm.

"There," he said when the last item was put away. Then he faced her. "If you're okay now, I'll take my stuff upstairs."

She should have said thank-you and left it at that. That's what she should have done. But all of a sudden, maybe because of the phone call, being alone was the last thing she wanted. Solitude had been her fortress for a long time, so why she should want to breach the walls now, she couldn't understand. But she did anyway.

"If I make coffee," she said, "would you like some?"

One eyebrow seemed to lift, but she couldn't be quite sure. This was a man who seemed to have lost use of his face. Either that, or he had trained himself to reveal absolutely nothing. And the question about coffee seemed to give him pause. He treated it as if it needed real consideration.

"That would be nice," he finally said.

Only then did she realize she was almost holding her breath. Maybe she feared rejection of some kind. How could she possibly consider a no over a cup of coffee to be rejection? God, was she beginning to lose her mind?

It was, of course, entirely possible. In the past year she'd come perilously close to living in solitary confinement with only her memories.

"Okay." She tried a smile and it seemed to work, because he nodded.

"I'll just take my stuff up and be back down in a minute," he said.

She watched him walk out of the room and noticed his broad shoulders and narrow hips. The ease with which he moved in his body, like an athlete. Yes, she was definitely slipping a cog somewhere. She hadn't noticed a man that way in a long time, hadn't felt the sexual siren song of masculinity, except with Jim, and since Jim not at all.

She didn't need or want to feel it now.

Shaking her head, she rose and found that her strength seemed to have returned. Making the coffee was an easy, automatic task, one that kept her hands busy while her mind raced.

Surely Gage had been right. The killers wouldn't warn her they were coming. So it must have been kids pulling a prank. When she thought about it, her own reaction to the call disappointed her. There'd been a time when she would have reached the same conclusion as Gage without needing to consult anyone at all. A time when she hadn't been a frightened mouse who couldn't think things through for herself.

She needed to get that woman back if she was to survive, because much more of what she'd gone through the past year would kill her as surely as a bullet.

Piece by piece, she felt her personality disassembling. Piece by piece she was turning into a shadow of the woman she had once been. She might as well have lopped off parts of her own brain and personality.

How long would she let this continue? Because if it went on much longer, she'd be nothing but a robot, an empty husk of a human being. Somehow, somewhere inside her, she had to find purpose again. And a way to connect with the world.

As one of the Marshals had said when she argued she didn't want to do this, "How many people in this world would give just about anything to have a chance to start completely fresh?"

At the time the comment had seemed a little heartless, but as it echoed inside her head right now, she knew he'd had a point. She hadn't liked it then, didn't like it now, but there was a certain truth in it.

A fresh start. No real reason to fear. Not anymore. If they were going to find her, certainly they'd have done so long since.

Wade returned to the kitchen just as the drip coffee-maker finished its task. "How do you like it?" she asked.

"Black as night."

She carried the carafe to the table, along with two mugs and filled them, then set the pot on a pad in the center of the table. She always liked a touch of milk in hers, one of the things she hadn't had to give up in this transition. She could still eat the foods she preferred, drink her coffee with a little milk and enjoy the same kinds of movies and books.

Maybe it was time to start thinking about what she hadn't lost, rather than all she had.

Brave words.

She sat across the table from Wade, trying not to look at him because she didn't want to make him feel like a bug under a microscope. But time and again her gaze tracked toward him, and each time she found him staring at her.

Finally she had to ask. "Is something wrong? You keep staring at me."

"You're a puzzle."

She blinked, surprised. "You don't even know me."

"Probably part of what makes you a puzzle," he said easily enough. His deep voice, which had earlier sounded like thunder, now struck her as black velvet, dark and rich.

"Only part?" she asked, even though she sensed she might be getting into dangerous territory here.

"Well, there is another part."

"Which is?"

He set his mug down. "It seems odd to find a woman so terrified in a place like this."

She gasped and drew back. His gaze never left her face, and he didn't wait for a denial or even any response at all.

"I know terror," he continued. "I've seen it, smelled it, tasted it. You reek of it."

She felt her jaw drop, but she couldn't think of one damn thing to say, because he was right. Right.

"Sorry," he said after a moment. "I suppose I have no business saying things like that."

Damn straight, she thought, wishing she'd never asked him if he wanted coffee. Wishing she'd never agreed to share a house with him. Those dark eyes of his saw too much. Way too much.

He'd stripped her bare. Anger rose in her and she glared at him. How dare he? But then, hadn't she all but asked for it?

He looked down at his mug, giving her a break from his stare, from his acute perception.

She thought about getting up and walking into her bedroom and locking the door. Hiding, always hiding. The thought stiffened her somehow, and instead of fleeing she held her ground. "Is it that obvious?"

He shook his head. "Probably not to anyone who hasn't been where I've been. Except for when you got that call, you put on a pretty good act."

"My entire life is an act," she heard herself snap.

He nodded, and when he looked at her again something in his gaze tugged at her, something that reached toward her and tried to pull her in. She looked quickly away. None of that. She didn't dare risk that.

"Look," he said finally, "I don't mean to upset you. I just want you to know..." He trailed off.

She waited, but when he didn't continue, she finally prodded him. "Want me to know what?"

"I'm not useless. Far from it. So if...if you need help, well, I'm here." Then he poured a little more coffee in his mug and rose, carrying the mug away with him.

She listened to him climb the creaky stairs and wondered what the hell had just happened.

WADE MADE UP his bed with the skill of long years of practice in the navy. Perfectly square corners, the blanket tight enough to bounce a quarter off. His drawers were just as neat, everything was folded to fit a locker though, so the items didn't exactly match the drawers, but the stacks were square.

Old habits die hard, and six months of retirement hadn't killed any of them.

He sat on the wood chair in the corner of the room, and focused his mind like a searchlight on the present, because looking back got him nowhere, and the future seemed impossible to conceive.

That woman downstairs was as scared as any green combat troop he'd ever seen. As scared as the women and kids he'd seen in situations he didn't want to remember.

He hadn't expected to find that here. Hadn't bargained on the feelings it would resurrect. He'd come to this damn county in the middle of nowhere because Seth Hardin had promised he'd find peace and solitude, and that everything here was as far from his past as he could possibly get.

Right.

Apparently Seth hadn't known about this woman. Corinne Farland. Cory. Regardless, who the hell would have thought that he'd find this mess through the simple act of renting a room?

He leaned over and lifted the coffee mug from the top of the dresser, draining half of it in one gulp. Good coffee.

The back of his neck prickled a little as he thought about the situation, and he never ignored it when the back of his neck prickled. That sensation had saved his skin more than once, or someone else's skin.

But he couldn't figure out why the hell Gage Dalton had brought him to this particular woman. There must be other rooms for rent in this county. Surely.

Well, maybe not. The place didn't exactly look huge. So it could just have been coincidence. But he didn't believe much in coincidence. At some level, conscious or otherwise, Gage had thought of this woman, her terror and her room.

And there was a reason for that, a reason that made the skin on the back of his neck crawl. Cory's level of fear suggested a long-term, ongoing threat.

And here he was, smack in the middle of a place he thought he'd left behind. A place he wanted to leave behind.

He needed to normalize, to stop being a SEAL and start being a reasonably ordinary member of society again. He needed to stop sleeping with one eye always open, constantly ready for death to lunge out of any shadow or hole. He needed to let his reflexes slow again, at least to the point where someone wouldn't risk death simply by trying to wake him from sleep, or by moving too fast in the corner of his eye. That's what he needed, and that had just skittered out the door of his immediate future.

Because downstairs there was one hell of a scared woman, and she shouldn't feel that way. And a phone call, a simple phone call, had caused her to collapse.

From what he'd seen of Conard County and Conard City so far, he would have called the place bucolic.

Well, that was a hell of a reaction for a bucolic place.

It wasn't normal. It didn't fit.

Apparently he would have to keep sleeping with one eye open.

He could leave, of course, but that didn't even truly appear on his menu of options. He couldn't walk away from her terror.

Someone that terrified needed protecting.

For a change, he decided, he'd like to provide the protection, rather than the terror.

A bitter smile twisted his mouth. That, at least, would be a change. A much-needed change.

And wasn't that what he'd come here for?

THE PHONE DIDN'T ring again, thank God. Cory ate a small salad for dinner, then tried to settle in with the TV. She didn't think she could focus on one of the library books stacked on the small table beside the rocking chair, because her mind seemed to have turned into a flea, insisting on hopping from one thing to another, all totally unrelated. Even the sharpness of fear didn't seem able to get her full attention.

So it was easier to turn the TV on, for the noise, for the visual distraction, for the occasional moments in which she could actually tune into the program, whatever it was.

She noted that her roomer upstairs had grown quiet, utterly quiet. Probably sleeping, but with her senses on high alert, the inability to guess what he was about made her uneasy. Solitude was her friend, her fortress, her constant companion.

But she'd invited in an invader, and his silence was worse than the noise he'd made while settling in.

She flipped quickly to the weather station, but too late, because the image of a crime-scene team entering a home where a man lay dead, just a reenactment, was enough to set off a string of memories she tried never to visit.

Jim lying there, bleeding from multiple wounds. Trying to crawl to him despite the wound in her own side, gasping his name, knowing somehow as she crawled that he was lost to her forever.

She squeezed her eyes shut as if that could erase the images that sprang to mind. Gentle, determined Jim, a man with a huge smile, a huge heart and a belief in making the world a better place. A man who could talk to her with such kindness and understanding, then in a courtroom or deposition turn into a circling shark, coming in for the kill.

A gifted man. An admirable man.

The man she had loved with every cell of her being.

Their last dinner together. Jim had taken her to one of the best restaurants in Tampa to celebrate a positive pregnancy test that very morning. They'd laughed, coming up with silly names they would never in a million years give their child.

And shortly after midnight, everything that mattered in her life vanished. At least she didn't mourn the pregnancy as much as she might if she had had time to get accustomed to the idea. That little mark on the stick had scarcely been real to her yet when the gunshot ended it all.

But Jim…Jim had been everything. Jim and her students. The life they had barely begun to build together after only two years.

RACHEL LEE                                    213

Now she drew a shaky breath, trying to steady herself, trying to prevent the gasping sobs she had managed to avoid for months now.

But awake, or asleep, she still heard the banging on the door. Banging that had sounded like the police. Jim had laughed drowsily as he climbed from bed to answer it.

"Somebody probably just tried to steal my car," he had said. His car was also a joke between them, a beater he'd gotten in law school. It was certainly not worthy of stealing, but the very expensive stereo he'd put in it was.

She had heard him open the door then...

Her mind balked. Her eyes snapped open. No, she couldn't do this to herself again. No way. It was done, the nightmares permanently engraved on her heart and mind, but that didn't mean she had to let them surface.

Sometimes she even scolded herself for it, because while grief was natural, and the fear she felt equally so, every time she indulged herself in grief or fear, she knew she was giving that man even more power over her than he had already stolen from her.

And he had already stolen everything that mattered.

The phone rang, jarring her. This time she didn't jump for it, this time she didn't think it was work calling. Part of her wanted to let it ring unanswered, but she didn't even have an answering machine, and what if it was Gage?

Slowly, reluctantly, she reached for it, coiling as tight as a spring. So tight some of her nerves actually objected.

"Hello?"

"Cory, it's Gage. I just wanted you to know a few other women have reported similar calls, so it was probably just a prank, okay?"

Her breath escaped her lungs in a gasp of relief. "Thanks," she said. "Thanks."

"And I'm getting caller ID put on your service. The

phone company says you should have it within a few days. And don't worry about the cost. The department will pay for it."

"Oh, Gage…" Words deserted her yet again. Of all the places on this earth the Marshals could have put her, she was grateful they had put her in a town with Gage Dalton.

"Hey," he said kindly. "We take care of our own around here. It's not a problem."

Before she could thank him again, he was gone.

"Is everything all right?"

Startled, she nearly cried out, and turned to see Wade Kendrick at the foot of the stairs. How had he come down so silently? Earlier his tread had been heavy. Or maybe she'd just been so distracted. She drew a few deep breaths, trying to steady her pulse.

"I'm sorry," he said quietly. "I didn't mean to startle you. I heard the phone ring, and after the way you reacted earlier…"

"Of course. Of course." She closed her eyes and consciously tried to relax, at least a bit. It didn't happen easily anymore, that whole relaxing thing. "Everything's okay. Gage…called." But what could she tell him about the call? Even a few words might be too much.

He waited, and it was clear to her that he wasn't satisfied. But he didn't ask, he just waited. And somehow his willingness to wait reassured her. She couldn't even understand it herself.

"I got a nasty phone call earlier," she said slowly.

He nodded. "I didn't think it was a funny one."

"No." Of course not. And now she was sounding like an idiot, she supposed. She gathered herself, trying to organize her words carefully. "Gage just wanted me to know that several other women received similar calls."

One of his eyebrows lifted. "Really."

"Probably just kids."

"Maybe."

His response didn't seem to make sense. "Maybe?"

"Well, that would depend, wouldn't it?"

"On what?"

"On what has you so scared, and who else received the calls."

"What in the world do you mean?"

He shrugged. "Life has made me suspicious."

"Oh." She bit her lower lip, realizing that nothing in her life had prepared her for dealing with a man like this. He seemed to come at things from a unique direction, unlike anything she was familiar with.

He started to turn away. "Well, as long as you're okay…"

He didn't ask a single question. She found that intriguing, given what little he had figured out about her in the short time since he moved in. Any other person would have been asking dozens of questions, but this man just seemed to accept that she was afraid, she must have good reason for it and that it was none of his business.

In that moment she thought it possible that she might come to like him.

"Wade?"

He stopped and turned back to her. He didn't say a word, simply looked at her.

"I, uh…" How could she say that she didn't want to be alone? That she was tired of being locked in the prison of her own thoughts? That even though solitude had provided her only safety for a year now, she was sick of it, and sick of her own company. Tired enough of it all to feel an impulse toward risk. Just a small risk.

"Should I make coffee?" he asked.

He had understood, though how she couldn't imagine.

She might have been about to ask him anything, tell him anything.

All she said was, "Thanks." Because there was nothing else she could say.

She switched the TV off so she could listen to his movements in the kitchen. Everything he needed was beside the drip coffeemaker, so he wouldn't have trouble finding it. And finally she could afford to have more than one cup each day. Imagine that, being reduced to one cup of coffee and a can of soup each day.

Sure, there were plenty of people in the world who had less, but her life had never before been restricted in such a way. She'd always been luckier than that. Always. Until recently.

Wade returned finally with two mugs, hers with exactly the right milkiness. The man missed nothing. Nothing.

He sat across from her on the easy chair, sipping his own coffee, watchful but silent. Maybe this wasn't going to work at all. How did you converse with a block of stone? But she needed something, anything, to break the cycle of her own thoughts.

Man, she didn't even know how to start a conversation anymore! Once it had come as naturally as breathing to her, but now, after a year of guarding every word that issued from her mouth, she had lost the ability it seemed.

Wade sipped his coffee again. He, at least, seemed comfortable with silence. After a couple of awkward minutes, however, he surprised her by speaking.

"Do you know Seth Hardin?"

She shook her head. "I know his father, but I've never met Seth."

"He's a great guy. I worked with him a lot over the years. He's the one who recommended I come here."

Positively voluble all of a sudden. "Why?"

He gave a small shrug. "He thought it would be peaceful for me."

At that a laugh escaped her, almost hysterical, and she broke it off sharply. "Sorry. Then you walk into this, a crazy widow who collapses over a prank phone call. Some peace."

His obsidian eyes regarded her steadily, but not judgmentally. "Fear like yours doesn't happen without a good reason."

It could have been a question, but clearly it was not. This man wouldn't push her in any way. Not even one so obvious and natural. She sought for a way to continue. "Gage said you were in the navy."

He nodded. "For more than half my life."

"Wow." She couldn't think of anything else to say.

"Yeah." Short, brief. After another moment he stirred. "You need to talk."

She tensed immediately. Was he trying to get her to explain? But then he spoke again, easing her concern.

"I'm not a talker." Another small shrug. "Never was. Making conversation is one of the many things I'm not good at."

"Me, either, anymore. I wasn't always that way."

He nodded. "Some things in life make it harder. I'm not sure I ever had the gift."

"Maybe it's not a gift," she said impulsively. "Maybe most of what we say is pointless, just background noise."

"Maybe. Or maybe it's how we start making connections. I stopped making them a long time ago."

"Why?"

He looked down into his mug, and she waited while he decided what he wanted to say, and probably what he didn't.

"Connections," he said finally, "can have a high price."

Man, didn't she know that. Maybe that was part of the reason she'd kept so much to herself over the past year, not simply because she was afraid of saying the wrong thing. Maybe it was because she feared caring ever again.

"I can understand that," she agreed, her lips feeling oddly numb. As if she were falling away again, from now into memory. But her memory had become a Pandora's box, and she struggled to cling to the moment. To now.

The phone rang again. She jumped and stared at it. Gage had already called. Work? Maybe. Maybe not.

Wade spoke. "Want me to answer it?"

A kind offer, but one that wouldn't help her deal with reality. She'd been protected almost into nonexistence, she realized. Protected and frightened. At some point she had to start living again, not just existing.

So she reached for the phone, even as her heart hammered and her hand shook. "Hello?"

"Cory!" A familiar woman's voice filled her ear. "It's Marsha." Marsha from work, a woman she occasionally spent a little time with because they had some similarities, some points of connection they could talk about. But they'd never really gotten to the point of random, friendly phone calls.

"Hi, Marsha. What's up?" Her heart slowed, her hand steadied.

"I got a phone call. I think Jack has found me!"

Cory drew a sharp breath. While she hadn't shared her story with Marsha, she'd learned a lot of Marsha's story over the past year. "What makes you think that?"

"The person said he knew where I was!"

"Oh. Marsha, I got one of those calls, too. Did you report it to the sheriff?"

"A phone call like that?" Marsha laughed, but there was an edge to it. "Why would he even listen to me?"

"Because I got one of those calls. And a few other women did, too."

Marsha fell silent. Then hopefully, "Others got the same call?"

"Gage thinks it was a prank. I reported it and so did some others."

In the silence on the line, Cory could hear Marsha start calming herself. She waited patiently until she could no longer hear Marsha's rapid breathing. Then she asked, "Do you want to come over?" She'd never asked that before, even though she'd gone to Marsha's a few times. Explaining expensive alarm systems could get…messy, and involve lying.

"No. No. I guess not. If Gage thinks it's a prank, and I'm not the only one to get a call, I must be okay."

"So it would seem."

"But I'm going to get a dog," Marsha said with sudden determination. "Tomorrow, I'm getting a dog. A big one that barks." Then she gave a tinny laugh.

"If it helps you to feel safer."

"It'll help. And if I'm this nervous after all this time, I guess I need the help. Want to do coffee in the morning?"

That meant going out, and Gage had told her not to. But that had been before he decided the calls were a prank. Cory hesitated, then said, "Let me call you about that in the morning."

"Okay. Maybe you can help me pick out a dog."

As if she knew anything about dogs. "I'll call around nine, okay?"

"Okay. Thanks, Cory. I feel a lot better now."

When Cory hung up, she found Wade sipping his coffee, quietly attentive. After a moment's hesitation, she decided to explain.

"My friend Marsha. She got one of those calls, too."

"Why did it frighten her?"

"Her ex was abusive. Very abusive. She's afraid he might find her."

He nodded slowly. "So she's hiding here, too?"

"Too?" She didn't want to think about what his use of that word meant, how much he must have figured out about her.

He said nothing, just took another sip of coffee. Then, at last, "What did the caller say?"

"Just 'I know where you are.'"

Another nod. "That would be scary to someone who doesn't want to be found."

And she'd just revealed a whole hell of a lot. She ought to panic, but somehow the panic wouldn't come. Maybe because having listened to Marsha, some steely chord in her had been plucked, one long forgotten. Prank call or not, at least two women were going to have trouble sleeping tonight, and that made her mad.

"Why would some idiot do this?" she demanded. "I don't care if it was kids. This isn't funny. Not at all."

"I agree."

His agreement, far from settling her, pushed her into a rare contrarian mood. She knew kids, after all, had taught them for years. "They don't think," she said. "They probably got the idea from some movie and are having a grand old time laughing that they might have scared someone."

"Maybe."

"They wouldn't realize that some people might really have something to fear."

"Maybe."

She looked at him in frustration. "Can you manage more than a few syllables?"

At that he almost smiled. She could see the crack in his

stone facade. "Occasionally," he said. "How many syllables do you want?"

"Just tell me why you keep saying maybe."

"I told you, I'm suspicious by nature. Tell me more
about your friend Marsha."

"Why? What? I told you her story, basically."

He set his cup on the end table and leaned toward her,
resting his elbows on his knees and clasping his hands.
"Try this. Have you both always lived here or did you
move here? Are you about the same age? Any similarities
in appearance?"

Just as she started to think he had gone over some kind
of edge, something else struck her. For a few seconds she
couldn't find breath to speak, and when she did it was
a mere whisper. "You think someone could be trying to
find one of us?"

"I don't know." The words came out bluntly. "A sam-
ple of two hardly proves anything. But I'm still curious.
Will you tell me?"

She hesitated, then finally nodded. "Marsha and I are
sort of friends because we…share a few things. We both
moved here within a couple of weeks of each other, almost
a year ago. We work together at the grocery."

"Your ages? And your appearance?"

"We don't look like twins."

"I didn't think you did. But otherwise?"

"I think we're as different as night and day." Indeed
they were. Marsha had short red hair, a square chin, green
eyes and a bust a lot of women would have paid a fortune
for. Cory, on the other hand, now had chin-length auburn
hair—which she hated because she had to keep it colored
herself to hide her natural dark blond—and brown eyes
that had looked good when she was blonde but now seemed
to vanish compared to her hair. The Marshals had given

her a slight nose job, though, replacing her button nose with something a little longer and straighter. They hadn't messed with her bust, though. That was still average.

"Are those differences that could be easily manipulated?"

She didn't like where he was going with this, didn't like it at all. "You are suspicious." But then, so was she. All of a sudden Gage's phone call seemed a lot less reassuring. "Marsha and I don't look at all alike." But how sure was she of that?

"Then I'm overly suspicious." He leaned back, picking up his coffee again. "Way too much so."

"Why?"

"Because I've lived my life in the shadows. Suspicion is part of my creed. I never take anything at face value." He shrugged. "Best to ignore me, I suppose."

It might have been except for her past. Had she an ordinary life behind her, it would have been easy to dismiss him as a nut. But she couldn't quite do that.

"Why," she asked finally, "would he call so many? If someone was after either of us, a whole bunch of phone calls wouldn't make sense, would it?"

He shrugged. "Like I said, just ignore me."

Easier said than done, especially when he seemed to have been following some train of thought of his own. But he said nothing more, and she really couldn't imagine any reason he should be suspicious.

But of one thing she was reasonably certain: the man who would want her dead wouldn't need to call a bunch of women to scare them. In fact, it would be the last thing he would do. Because calling her would warn her, and if she got scared enough to call the Marshals, they'd move her.

Even though moving her would take time, it would certainly make killing her more difficult while she was under constant surveillance once again, as she had been in the three months between the shooting and her eventual re-location.

So it had to be a prank. Surely. She clung to that like a straw in a hurricane.

Because it was all she could do.

# CHAPTER THREE

IN THE MORNING, Cory decided to go for coffee with Marsha after all. She had a little money to spare because of Wade, and a cup of coffee at Maude's didn't cost that much, especially if she avoided the fancier drinks that Maude had begun to introduce, taking her cue from the major coffee chains. So far Cory didn't think there was a huge market for "mocha decaf lattes" here, even though she loved lattes herself, but they were now available if anyone wanted them.

Marsha expressed huge gratitude for the call. In her voice, Cory heard a stress that matched her own. She hadn't slept well at all last night, tossing and turning, one nightmare following another.

When she finally gave up trying to sleep, it was only five-thirty in the morning. She'd grabbed a book from the table beside her bed and had attempted to read for a couple of hours. In the end, though, the words might as well have been random letters, none of the story penetrated, and she thought she might have dozed a bit.

Wade must still be asleep, she thought when at last she reset the house alarm and slipped out the door. She'd been the only one to change the alarm settings since she awoke—she'd have heard the tone if anyone had—and she hadn't heard him moving around.

Nothing strange in that, she supposed, except she had somehow expected him to be an early riser. Why? Because he'd been in the navy? Not everyone in the navy worked days and slept nights. She knew that much. Maybe he'd had some kind of night duty. Which got her to wondering what kind of work he'd done, and how he'd gotten enough medals to paper a wall, according to Gage.

Well, she could always try asking him, but she doubted he would answer. And how could she complain about that when she kept her own secrets?

It was a lovely summer morning, and she could have walked to Maude's but uneasiness made her take the Suburban anyway. Besides, she told herself, trying to pretend she wasn't acting only out of over-heightened fear, if Marsha really did want to get a big dog, the Suburban might be the best way to get it home.

Marsha was already there at a table with coffee in front of her. Hardly had Cory slid into a seat facing her when Maude stomped by, slamming a mug down and filling it. A little bowl of creamer cups already sat in the middle of the table.

Cory actually felt a smile twitch at the corners of her mouth. In a year she'd never bought anything here except coffee, and Maude had apparently given up on talking her into anything else. Once in a blue moon, a piece of pie would be slapped down in front of her but never show up on the bill. Interesting woman, Maude. Cory was quite sure she had never met anyone like her.

Marsha smiled at her, but the expression didn't reach her eyes. She looked exhausted, and Cory suspected they had both spent nights filled with nightmares and restlessness.

"I'm glad that you told me a bunch of women got the same call," Marsha said.

"I don't know how many, but Gage indicated there were a few of us. That's why he thinks it's a prank."

"Makes sense." Marsha opened another little cup of

half-and-half and lightened her coffee even more. "And I guess if a few reported the calls, there were probably more like me who never called him at all."

"Probably," Cory agreed. "You look like you slept about as well as I did."

Marsha's laugh was short and hollow. "Yeah, we look like a pair of zombies, don't we? I just couldn't stop thinking about Jack all night, about all the things he threatened to do to me. But it's been almost a year, so he probably never wanted to come after me. He just wanted to scare me."

And Marsha had plenty of reason to be scared, considering the things her ex had done to her. Cory wanted to say something reassuring, but couldn't. How could she reassure anyone when she was living with a similar terror herself? Her pursuers might have more reason to try to track her, since she could help identify one of them as a murderer, but did that mean Marsha's ex was necessarily less determined?

"Are you still going to get a dog?"

Marsha nodded. "I called the vet before I came here. He says he has a couple of dogs I might like and that they're naturally protective breeds."

"That sounds good."

"I told him I wanted a big dog, but he recommended against it."

"Really?"

Marsha gave a small, tired laugh. "He asked me how much I wanted to walk it, and did I want to be able to hold it in my lap…" Her voice broke, then steadied. "Sorry. I'm just tired. But anyway, the idea of a dog that would curl up on my lap sounded good, and with the hours we work, I couldn't walk a dog at the same time of day every day…" She trailed off, sighed and looked down into her coffee.

All of a sudden, Cory felt something she hadn't felt in far too long: a desire to protect someone besides herself. The urge rose fiercely, and burned away some of the fear.

Those men had stolen her life, but for the last year she'd let them steal her, too. She'd let them turn her into a quivering, frightened recluse whose only concern was surviving each day.

How much more twisted could she get? How could she let them keep doing this to her? She wasn't the only person on this planet with fears and needs. Look at Marsha. What had she ever done except marry the wrong man? Yet, she, too, had been driven into a hole in the ground.

Angry, Cory couldn't sit still another moment. She slapped some bills on the table, to cover both their coffees, and stood. "Let's go get your dog. You need a reason to smile."

Marsha appeared startled, but then began to grin. "Yeah," she said. "Let's go get that dog."

"Cute and cuddly," Cory said. "The cutest, cuddliest one we can find."

Because there still had to be something good in life, and a dog was as good a start as anything else.

Conard County wasn't a heavily populated place, so it had a limited tax base and had to cut some corners. Hence the vet and animal control shared property and kennels, and the vet, Dr. Mike Windwalker, was on retainer to care for the impounded animals. Like most small-town vets, he handled everything from horses to the occasional reptile.

A handsome man in his mid-thirties, he'd replaced the former vet five years ago and seemed to enjoy his broad-spectrum practice. He had one assistant, though he could probably have used more.

"You picked a good day to do this," he remarked as he

led Marsha and Cory back through his office toward the kennels. "I'm not very busy so I'll have time to help you make a good match."

As they approached the wire gate beyond which lay the sheltered kennels, the sounds of dogs barking started to build.

"They know we're coming," the vet said with a smile. "But before we go in…" He turned to Marsha. "I want to know a bit more about why you want a dog. Just for protection? Or would you like a companion? And can you afford much dog food?"

Marsha bit her lip, then admitted, "I'm tired of being alone so much. Yes, I want a dog that can alert me when someone comes, but I think I'd like to have one to love, too. And play with. I'd love to play with a dog. As for food—" she wrinkled her nose "—I probably shouldn't have a dog with a huge appetite."

At that Mike Windwalker smiled. "Then I have a couple of good ones for you. Love and protection can come in small sizes as well as large."

Cory stayed back a bit, watching as Mike introduced Marsha to various small dogs. She didn't want to get too interested in the process because when Wade left, unless she got a better job or more hours at her current one, she simply wouldn't be able to take care of a pet. Nor, when she thought about it, could she have one running around at night with the motion detectors on.

But it was so hard to resist all the puppy-dog eyes. It would have been entirely too easy to choose one for herself, and she had to remind herself again and again that she couldn't afford it.

But she felt a definite stab of envy when Marsha eventually settled on a Pomeranian. "Definitely loyal," the vet said approvingly. "She'll let you know any time anyone approaches the house and these dogs can be relied on to fight for their owners if necessary." He shook his head. "People often underestimate the protectiveness of the small breeds. There are ways to get around a dog, any dog, but these small guys have hearts like lions."

Marsha definitely looked as if she'd fallen in love. And while she naturally had a cheerful nature, it was often eclipsed behind spurts of worry. Right now, she looked as if she didn't have a worry in the world.

"Just one caveat," the vet said. "I offer obedience classes for free, and with this one you'd be wise to take them."

"I will."

"I'm starting a new class Saturday morning at nine."

Marsha beamed at him. "I'll be there."

When she drove back home a short while later, Cory felt she'd managed to accomplish at least one good deed, small as it was. And it had been small. She hadn't been able to give Marsha the dog, or even help her decide which one was best, but she suspected Martha might not have acted so quickly on her own, simply because living in fear had a way of paralyzing you. Even small decisions sometimes seemed too big to make.

And that had to stop, she told herself sternly. It had to stop now. For too long now she'd been little more than a wasted lump of human flesh.

Wade must have heard her pull up, because he was waiting for her at the foot of the stairs. Apparently he'd been sleeping because his hair had that tousled look, and his blue sport shirt hung open over his jeans.

Cory couldn't help herself. She stopped dead and stared. That was some chest, smoothly muscled, bronzed and just begging for a touch. Oh, man, as if she needed this now.

With effort she dragged her gaze upward and then wished she hadn't, because she saw in his obsidian eyes that he hadn't missed her look. He revealed nothing about his reaction to it, though, nor did he make any attempt to button his shirt.

"Did Marsha get her dog?" he asked before the silence got long enough that she wouldn't be able to pretend he hadn't noticed what she'd been noticing.

"Yes. A Pomeranian."

"I had a buddy who had one. He called it his pocket piranha."

The remark was utterly unexpected, and it bypassed every short circuit the past year had put in Cory's brain. She giggled. Actually giggled.

A faint smile leavened Wade's face. "He liked to bite my ankles."

That seemed even funnier. "Such a stupid dog." She giggled again.

"Stupid?"

"Taking on someone your size? That's stupid."

Wade's smile widened just a hair more. "He knew I wouldn't hurt him. Dogs have good instincts."

She laughed again, still amused by the image. Then it struck her that he seemed to have been waiting for her. "Is there something you need?"

"Well, actually…" He hesitated. "I know the deal was I would eat out. But I was wondering, would you mind if I bought groceries and cooked for myself? I'll leave things squared away so you won't even notice I was in there."

For some reason she liked the idea that he wouldn't be leaving her alone three times a day to hunt up a meal. Amazing how far she had come in less than a day. What had initially seemed like a threat now seemed like a bulwark. Nor was this a matter she wanted to take issue over.

"I don't mind." Although she was a little surprised that he'd felt it necessary to say she wouldn't even know he'd been in the kitchen. Most people wouldn't have bothered to mention it, unless asked.

She drew a sharp breath, and all of a sudden her heart tugged. She'd heard promises like that before, unsolicited ones. *You'll never notice I was in there.*

A few faces floated before her eyes, youngsters all, former students all. And she knew what phrases like that really meant. Could this big, powerful man with all his medals still carry scars like that? After all this time?

But she couldn't ask.

"Is something wrong?"

His question shook her back to the moment. "No. Really. My mind just wanders sometimes. I think I spend too much time alone." Her laugh this time carried no mirth, but was more of an apology.

"I'll just go get some groceries then."

She shook her head. "It may go against your grain to look for help, but you shouldn't try to carry groceries home when I can drive you. Just let me get a glass of water, and then I'll take you."

For an instant she thought he would argue. Something about him said that he didn't relinquish autonomy easily, or accept help easily, at least not from virtual strangers. But then he nodded. "Take your time. Obviously I'm in no rush."

Wow, she thought as she headed toward the kitchen, at this rate they might even start to converse in whole paragraphs. She took her time drinking her water because she heard him climb the stairs again, probably to brush his hair, button his shirt and pull on some shoes.

Sure enough, five minutes later she heard him descend again. She finished her water and went out to the foyer. "Ready?" she asked, though it was clear that he was. His boots had given way to some comfortable and battered deck shoes, and he'd buttoned and brushed.

"If you are," he replied.

She grabbed her purse and keys, saying, "Let's go then."

"You're sure you don't mind?"

There it was again, a niggle. A hint. She looked at him, wishing she could just come right out and ask. But that might be a mistake, because he'd probably just get angry at her prying, and rightfully so. He hadn't poked into her life, so she should give him the same respect.

"I don't mind at all," she assured him, and summoned a smile. Aware now of what might lurk in his past, she felt old lessons rising up to guide her. And the thought that she might, through her training, help this man feel a bit more comfortable made her feel better than she had in a long time. She might not be able to teach anymore, but it would be so good to help.

Always assuming, of course, that she wasn't totally wrong about him.

The drive to the store was silent, but she was getting used to that with him, and didn't feel as uncomfortable as she had just yesterday.

When she pulled into a parking slot, though, he spoke. "You don't have to wait for me," he said. "If there's something you need to do."

She shook her head. "Not a thing. Maybe I'll check and see if they can give me any extra hours."

She climbed out and locked the car. Another car pulled in nearby, and the driver, a man, appeared to be fussing through some papers. Probably lost his shopping list, Cory thought with a small sense of amusement.

Wade waited for her, then walked beside her across the parking lot, measuring his stride to hers.

"You work here?" he asked.

"Yes." Then she volunteered, "We all had our hours cut back a couple of weeks ago."

"That hurts. No wonder you need a roomer. How's Marsha managing?"

"Somewhat better. She gets an alimony check."

He paused just after they stepped through the automatic doors and looked at her. "Then her ex knows where she is."

"Theoretically not. The court sends the checks and is supposed to keep her address private."

He nodded. "Good thing."

She headed for the manager's office at the customer service desk while he got a cart and started down the aisles. Interesting that he'd expressed concern for Marsha, she thought. Apparently a real heart beat behind the stone.

The manager, Betsy Sorens, greeted her with her usual wide smile. "Sorry, Cory. No extra hours. Not yet anyway. You're at the top of my list though when we can start adding them."

Cory felt almost embarrassed. "Why should I be at the top of the list? That doesn't seem right, Betsy. So many others need hours, too."

"We all need hours, some more than the rest. You're self-supporting. A lot of the other employees have other sources of income."

Cory felt her cheeks color a bit. "Still…"

Betsy shook her head. "You're a good employee. If I can do a little something for you, I will."

A customer came then with a complaint, so Cory smiled, waved and left. Wandering around the store with nothing to buy and nothing to do felt odd. Almost without thinking, she paused occasionally to straighten the stock on the shelves.

She hated to have time hanging on her hands, and she'd certainly had too much of that in the past year. She'd once been busy almost every second of the day, between Jim and her job. Now she had endless hours of free time, and that meant too many hours to think.

Hours to think about the past, about that phone call yesterday, hours to let her fear and anxiety build when there was no real reason for it. Certainly they would have found her by now if they were going to.

She met Wade in one of the aisles and glanced into his cart. There wasn't much there yet.

"Having trouble?" she asked.

One corner of his mouth lifted. "You might say that."

"What's wrong?"

"I've been mostly eating in mess halls or eating out of boxes for years. I know the basics about cooking, but shopping for one person isn't as easy as I thought."

That was a whole lot of syllables, she thought, and for some reason that made her smile. "I have an idea."

"What's that?"

"I hate cooking just for myself. Why don't we take turns cooking for each other?" she suggested.

"Are you sure? You could be taking an awful gamble."

"On your cooking?"

"What else would I mean?" he asked.

"I'm willing to take it. And if it doesn't work out, well, I could teach you to cook. Or you could just let me do it."

He shook his head. "No way am I going to let you cook for me every night. That wasn't part of the deal."

She could almost see him closing down again, as if the idea that he might lean on her concerned him. "Okay then, cooking lessons if you need them."

That seemed to satisfy him. Armed with the idea that they'd take turns cooking seemed to loosen him up though. He started tossing more items into the cart.

"I should go buy some more groceries," she said suddenly. "I just realized, I only bought enough for myself for a couple of days."

"Let me," he said. "It'll cover the cooking lessons I'll probably need."

She opened her mouth to argue, but then shut it. This man absolutely needed to feel as if he wasn't a burden. That much was clear to her so she endured it as he spent money on foods she would have ignored because of the price.

But the thought of cooking some of the dishes she had once loved to cook and eat soon had her thinking of ingredients she should buy.

"I don't know what's needed to cook some of this stuff," Wade said. "Grab whatever you need." It was enough to get her going.

Along the way she saw the man from the parking lot again. He was pushing a cart and carrying a piece of paper, and nodded when he saw her. She managed to smile back. Evidently he'd found his list.

Before they even reached the checkout, two more people had smiled and nodded at her. She was used to that when she was working and in uniform, but for the first time it struck her that folks around here might be friendly as a matter of course. Maybe she ought to make a bigger effort.

By the time they left the store with another four bags of groceries, she was looking forward to dinner.

And how long had it been since she'd last felt that way? No, she wasn't going there, not when she was actually feeling good, feeling almost normal, for the first time in a year. There was absolutely nothing wrong with feeling good, she reminded herself. Nothing at all. Jim wouldn't have wanted her to become the woman she had been during the past year.

The shadow that hovered over all her days tried to return when she had to deal with the alarm, but she refused to let it. No more of that, she told herself, as if something as simple as a command to herself could change her entire outlook and banish the fear that never quite deserted her.

But at least she was making an effort, and when she looked over the past day, she felt glad those kids had made that stupid call. Yes, it had thrown her into a tizzy, and yes, it had upset Marsha just as much, but in the course of reacting to it, she had helped Marsha a little bit. Now she could at least help Wade learn to cook.

Little things, but more purposeful than almost anything since that awful night. Time to cherish her tiny victories.

"When do you usually like to eat dinner?" she asked as they worked together to put things away. She stopped a moment to look at her refrigerator. It hadn't been that full while she lived here, ever. And now it held an embarrassment of riches.

He paused, a box of cornstarch in hand, and looked at her. "Ma'am, you're talking to a SEAL. I learned to eat when the food was there."

"Oh." She bit her lip. "A SEAL? Really?"

"Really."

That would explain at least some of it, she thought, how he could look so hard and dangerous at times. It might even explain his lack of expression and his disinclination to talk. Hesitantly she said, "I can't imagine what it must have been like."

"No."

And that closed the subject. Well, it would if she let it. How much did she want to risk now that they'd found some common ground? But the silence seemed heavy in some way, no longer comfortable. With one word he'd fixed an image of himself in her mind and she didn't know how to absorb it. Nor did she know why she wanted to cross the barrier he had set so firmly in place with that one word.

Recklessly, she didn't take the warning. "I've seen programs about SEALs," she offered.

"A lot of people have." He started folding her cotton grocery bags neatly.

"The training looks terribly hard."

"It is."

Volumes of information. She almost sighed. "I saw another program about an operation where the SEALs had to board a ship at sea to remove a container of plutonium that could have been used to make a bomb."

"Yes."

"It's amazing what you guys can do."

"Most people have no idea what we do." With that he put the folded bags in a neat stack on her counter and walked from the kitchen.

She listened to him climb the stairs, listened to the creak as he went into his room.

And with him departed the little bit of positive purpose she'd found just today.

# CHAPTER FOUR

CORY FELT BAD. For the first time in forever, she had felt positive, felt ready to reach out, however tentatively. And she'd blown it.

She had pressed Wade, even when her instincts had warned her that might be a mistake. Apparently her skills had atrophied over the past year. There'd been a time when she would have handled that approach a whole lot better.

Or would she? How could she even know anymore? For so long she'd been curled inward in a tight ball around her own fear and pain. Maybe she would have flubbed the conversational attempt even back then. Wade, after all, was a grown man, not one of her kids. His barriers had to be even higher, even more deeply ingrained.

Regardless, she wished she'd just kept her mouth shut, because it had been surprisingly nice to do ordinary, routine tasks with someone else, even a someone she didn't know, and could barely talk with. Just the rhythm of it had probably been one of the most soothing experiences she could remember in a while.

Worse, she was brooding about what surely had to be the most minor of trespasses. It wasn't as if she'd demanded personal war stories or anything. Far from it.

Let it go, she told herself. Good advice except that perhaps the worst change in her over the past year was the way she could seldom just dismiss things. Like that phone call last night.

In her previous life, she wouldn't have given it a second thought. Once upon a time, even if it had disturbed her, she'd have been able to shake it off in relatively short order.

Events had changed her. Worry had burrowed mole holes in her mind, ever ready to grant easy access to the next concern that showed up. The stupidest things could run in circles for hours or days, and she could no longer shake them.

But today, thanks to Marsha and then Wade, she'd managed to put that call out of her mind. To put it in its proper place.

But it was still there, ready to pounce the instant she allowed it to. If she sat here too much longer brooding, the fear would steal back in and soon she'd be like a dog gnawing at a bone, unable to let it go.

Finally she stood up, deciding the best thing in the world would be to take a walk. She'd spent too many hours hiding in this house over the past year, and that had turned her into an even worse mess.

She wondered if she had failed to heal because fear had taken over to a paralyzing degree. Which was more ridiculous when she considered the entire weight of the federal government had thrown itself behind making her disappear.

Yes, she was still grieving, but somehow grief and fear had become so intertwined she no longer knew which was which. The one was a healthy thing, the other not.

Today she seemed to have taken two successful baby steps in the right direction. It was time, she decided, to step back out into the sunlight, to start living again the way most other people lived: without the constant expectation of the terrible happening.

Nobody got a guarantee, after all.

Grabbing her keys, leaving her purse behind, she

slipped into her jogging shoes then turned off the alarm. She had to turn it off, because once it was set and had been on more than forty seconds, opening and closing the door without triggering the alarm sequence became impossible. Failure to turn off the alarm within forty seconds meant that the police would be called.

So she punched in the code to turn it off, listening to the near-squeal it made. As soon as it was disarmed, she could reset it and safely leave.

But she didn't get to the rearming part.

"Where are you going?"

She turned and saw Wade at the top of the stairs. A spark of annoyance flared, a welcome change from the steady diet of fear she'd been living with. "Out. What business is it of yours?"

"None." His shirt was unbuttoned again, but he still wore his jeans and deck shoes. This time she noticed more than the broad expanse of his chest. She noted his flat belly, the fact that he had the coveted "six-pack" of abdominal ripples, though not overdeveloped. She had to drag her gaze away, back to his face. He started down the stairs. "I'll go with you."

Her jaw dropped a little, and her annoyance grew. "Why? I'm just going to walk around the block."

"I'd like a walk."

But he didn't have to take it with her. She almost said so, quite sharply, and then realized something. Her fear hadn't just dissipated on its own today. No, he had driven it back.

Now what? Would she insist she go on the walk alone? When she might well get scared again halfway around the block? Was she going to take the offered crutch?

She ought to say no, for her own good. It was high time she started conquering her fears. But then remembering how she had felt when she'd made him leave the room earlier, she decided she didn't want to needlessly offend him again.

It was as good an excuse as any, she supposed, because now that she actually thought about it, she wasn't sure she yet had the courage to take that walk alone. Especially after that phone call last night.

"Damn!" she swore.

He was now at the foot of the stairs, buttoning his shirt, and looked at her. "What?"

"I'm so confused I can't stand it."

"About what?"

She hesitated.

"You don't have to tell me. Walking helps quite a bit."

Giving her emotional space, but not physical space. She looked at him, and for the first time got past the sheer impact of his solidity and strength to notice that he was a handsome man. Very handsome, in a rugged, healthy way.

She sighed. Not now. Please. But it was a simple fact that the frisson he made her feel was not fear for her life, but fear of dangerous sexual attraction. With a man as closed off as Wade Kendrick, there could only be pain on that path.

But she was still young enough and healthy enough to feel those urges. Well, maybe that was a good thing. Another part of her coming back to life.

"Are we taking that walk?"

"Uh, yeah." She punched in the codes again and together they stepped out onto the small porch. She set out purposefully in the direction of the town park, thinking it would do her some good to see kids at play again. Among the many things she had avoided in the past year was children, because they reminded her of things lost. But she might be ready to let them remind her of some of the goodness in life.

Once again he measured his pace to hers, as if it came automatically. And once again, he said nothing.

The summer afternoon was warm, the sun as brilliant as it could get this far north. And without warning she found herself talking, although she had to catch herself frequently so she didn't reveal too much.

"I used to live in…down south. Almost in the tropics, actually. I notice the difference in the sun here."

"It is different," he agreed.

"The days are longer in the summer, but the sun never gets as high or bright. And the winter nights are so long here."

"Yeah."

"But at least I don't burn as easily." She managed a small laugh. "In the summer down there you can get a tan walking across a parking lot."

It was his turn to give a small laugh, as if he, too, were trying. "I've been in all kinds of climates."

Well, that was a positive step, she thought. "I imagine so." She was careful not to question. Instead she chose to talk a little more about herself. "I've had a lot to adjust to, and I haven't been doing a very good job of it."

For a few paces he didn't say anything. Then, "I guess it's harder to adjust when you're afraid."

"It's that obvious, huh?"

"Like I said, only to someone who would know fear."

"I don't know whether that's a compliment or a criticism."

"Neither. Just an observation."

"Do you ever get afraid?" As soon as the words were out she realized she might have trespassed too far again, but it was too late to snatch them back. She almost held her breath, wondering if he would turn and walk away.

Instead, he astonished her by answering. "I'm human."

Sideways, but still an answer. She relaxed a bit and looked around, taking in the old trees that lined the street, their leaves rustling ceaselessly in the summer breeze. Nobody else seemed to be out and about, but that wasn't unusual. Here, as everywhere, most couples both needed to work.

"In the evenings," she remarked, "there will often be people sitting out on their front porches. Different from where I used to live. Most of the neighborhoods around me back home were built relatively recently, when it was important to have a privacy-fenced backyard. You'd almost never see anyone out front unless they were doing yard work."

"In most places in the world where I've been, a house is where you sleep or shelter from the elements. The rest of life happens in common areas, on the street, in front of the house. Not for everyone, of course. There are always some who want to keep the unwashed masses away. And in some cultures an enclosed courtyard is considered necessary, but given that several generations of a family live together, it's not exactly isolation."

That was practically half an encyclopedia coming from this man. "Do you think we're losing something with those fenced backyards?"

"Depends on what you want out of life. But once you build that fence, if you're having a barbecue you're not going to have a neighbor who might drop over for a chat and bring a six-pack, and wind up staying on for dinner."

"True." She turned that around for a few seconds. "I don't really know how different it feels to live in a place like this," she finally admitted. "Basically, when I come home from work I pass all these probably very nice people on their front porches and go inside and lock myself in."

"Maybe you have good reason."

Maybe she did. Or maybe she'd been acting like a wounded animal that wanted to be left alone in its burrow. The whole point of the Marshals moving her here had been so that she didn't have to live this way. Another sigh escaped her.

"I thought," she said reluctantly, "that I was breaking out of the cycle earlier today. I even told myself to go take a walk."

"But?"

"But then I realized that I'd just been distracted. That despite everything, I'm still worried at some level because of that call last night. Oh, I can't even explain it to myself."

They reached the park and found a bench not far from the sidewalk. Nobody else was there, so Cory's hope for distraction was disappointed.

Wade let the silence flow around them with the breeze for a few minutes before he spoke again. "Sometimes," he said quietly, "we get confused because we're changing."

That made her look at him, and for an instant she wished she hadn't because she felt again that unexpected, unwanted attraction. What was going on with her? Why did she suddenly have the worst urge to put her head on the shoulder of a stranger? To feel his arms close around her?

She jumped up from the bench and headed home. Walking it off seemed like the only sane course available to her. "We need to start dinner," she said, the sole explanation she could offer for her behavior. Because there was no way she could tell him that the feelings he awakened in her were nearly as frightening as that phone call had been.

Despite her sudden takeoff, he fell in step beside her before she had made two full strides. Glued to her side. Part of her wanted to resent that, and part of her was grateful for it. Confusion? She had it in spades. At least her fear and grief had been clear, so very clear. No questions there.

Now the questions were surfacing, the conflicting feelings, all the stuff she'd avoided for so long. She forced herself to slow her pace to an easier walk. She'd been running again, she realized. Had she forgotten every other mode of existence?

"Darn," she said under her breath. All of a sudden it was as if someone had held up a mirror, and painful or not she had to look at herself. She wasn't seeing a whole lot that she liked, either.

"Something wrong?" Wade asked mildly.

She stopped midstride and looked at him. Mistake, because the truth burst out of her and she wasn't sure she wanted it to. What did she know about this guy after all? "Has something ever made you stop and take a good look at yourself?"

"Yes."

"What if you don't like what you see?" She didn't wait for an answer, just started walking again. She didn't expect an answer, frankly. It wasn't the kind of question anyone else could answer.

But he surprised her. "You make up your mind to change."

"Easier said than done."

"Always."

Some inner tension uncoiled just a bit. Change? Why not? After all, she'd allowed herself to be changed by life, had just rolled along like a victim. That did not make her feel proud. "Sometimes," she said more to herself than him, "you just have to grab the rudder." She hadn't done that at all since the shooting. Not at all.

"Grabbing the rudder is easier to do when the seas aren't stormy."

She glanced at him again. Oh, there was a story there, and she wished she knew what it was, but she didn't dare ask. This man could disappear even in plain sight, and she didn't want him to disappear again. At least not yet.

For some reason the invader had ceased to be an invader. Maybe just his presence had reminded her that she still had a life to live. Maybe his obvious protectiveness had made her feel just a little safer. Or maybe the attraction she felt was overcoming all the walls she'd slammed into place.

Because she had slammed those walls into place. She hadn't built them brick by brick. No, she'd put up the steel barricades almost instantly in the aftermath. Huge parts of her had simply withdrawn from life, no longer willing to take even small risks, like making a friend.

She stole another glance at Wade and wondered at herself. If ever a guy looked like a bad risk for even something as simple as friendship, he was it. Yet for some reason she was opening up to him. Not much, but enough that she could get herself into trouble if she didn't watch her step.

She ought to be afraid of him, the way she was afraid of everything else. Instead all she could do was notice how attractive he was. Wonder if that hard line of his mouth would feel as hard if he kissed her. What that hard body would feel like against her soft curves.

Ah, she was losing her mind. For real. It had finally snapped. After a year of inability to feel anything but grief and anguish, she had finally broken. Now she was looking at a virtual stranger as a sex object.

*Way to go, Cory. Very sensible.* Clearly she couldn't trust herself at all anymore.

Two cars came down the street toward them as they rounded the corner right before her house. She lifted her hand to wave, deciding it was about time to make a friendly gesture. The woman in the first car smiled and waved back. The man in the second car didn't even glance at them.

They reached the door and went inside, resetting the alarm. Without a word, he followed her into the kitchen, evidently ready to get his first cooking lesson. She started pulling things out, preparing to make a dish with Italian sausage and pasta and fresh vegetables. The recipe was one that had emerged one day from a scramble through the cupboards and the realization that the only way she could put together dinner was the stone-soup method.

"I can't trust myself anymore," she muttered, at first unaware that she was thinking out loud. When you lived alone long enough, having conversations with yourself often moved from the mind to the mouth. "Everything's been so screwed up for so long. But then how do I know my thinking wasn't screwed up before? I was living in some kind of enchanted universe before. A place where bad things didn't happen."

She turned from pulling a package of frozen Italian sausage from the freezer and saw Wade standing there, arms folded, watching. And that's when she realized her muttering hadn't been private. Her cheeks heated a bit. "Sorry, sometimes I talk to myself. Bad habit."

"Don't mind me."

"Well, you don't want to hear it. And I'm not sure I want anyone else to hear the mess that's going on inside my head."

"I can go upstairs if you like."

She shook her head. "Stay. I promised to teach you some cooking, and this is a great dish to start with." She passed him the package of frozen sausage. "Microwave, hit the defrost button twice, please."

He took the sausage and did as she asked. Soon the familiar hum filled the kitchen. Green peppers and tomatoes were next, a true luxury these days, washed in the sink and readied for cubing. "Do you like onions?"

"Very much."

So she pulled one out of the metal hanging basket and peeled it swiftly before setting it beside the other vegetables. As soon as she reached for the chef's knife, though, Wade stepped forward. "I can slice and dice. How do you want it?"

"Pieces about one-inch square." She passed him the knife and as their hands brushed she felt the warmth of his skin. All of a sudden she had to close her eyes, had to batter down the almost forgotten pleasure of skin on skin. Such a simple, innocent touch, and it reminded her of one of the forms of human contact she absolutely missed most: touch. Even simple touches. She almost never let anyone get that close anymore, certainly not a man.

A flood tide of forgotten yearnings pierced her, and she drew a sharp breath.

"What's wrong?"

He was so near she felt his breath on her cheek. Warm and clean. A shiver rippled through her as she fought the unwanted feelings, and forced her eyes open, ready to deny anything and everything.

But the instant her gaze met his, she knew she could deny nothing. His obsidian eyes darkened even more, and she heard him inhale deeply as he recognized the storm inside her. There was a clatter as the knife fell to the counter, and the next thing she knew she was wrapped in his powerful arms.

He lifted her right off the floor and set her on the counter, moving in between her legs until she could feel his heat in places that had been too cold and too empty for so long. This was not a man who hesitated, nor one who finessed the moment.

He swooped in like a hawk and claimed her mouth as if it were rightfully his. An instant later she learned that thin mouth could be both soft and demanding. That his hard chest felt every bit as hard as it looked, and felt even better as it crushed her breasts. His arms were tight and steely, and she should have been afraid of their power, afraid of what he could do to her whether she wanted it or not.

But all she could feel was the singing in her body as it responded to needs more primal than any she had ever imagined. Somehow the dissenting, cautious voices in her head fell silent. Somehow she lifted her arms and wrapped them around his neck, holding on for dear life.

Because this was life. Here and now. Like Sleeping Beauty awakening from a nightmare, she discovered she could want something besides freedom from terror and pain, and that good things were still to be had despite all.

Her body responded to life's call as her mind no longer seemed able to. His tongue passed the first gate of her teeth, finding hers in a rhythm as strong as her heartbeat, a thrusting that echoed like a shout in a canyon until it reached all the way to her very core and came back to her in a powerful throbbing.

A gasp escaped her between one kiss and the next. Her legs lifted, trying to wrap around his narrow hips, trying to bring her center right up against his hardness, trying to find an answer to the ache that overpowered her. Any brain she had left gave way before the demands of her body for more and deeper touches. Her physical being leaped the barriers that had existed only in her mind.

He moved against her, mimicking the ultimate act, not enough to satisfy, but enough to promise. She wanted every bit of that promise. Every bit.

He drew a ragged breath as he released her mouth, but he didn't leave her. No, he trailed those lips across her cheek, down the side of her throat, making her shiver with even more longing, causing her to make a small cry and arch against him. One of her hands slipped upward, finding the back of his head, pressing him closer yet. She wanted to take this journey as never before.

Then the microwave dinged.

All of a sudden, reality returned with a crash. He pulled away just a couple of inches and looked at her, his eyes darker than night. She stared back, hardly aware that she was panting, suddenly and acutely aware of how she had exposed herself.

As if he read her awareness on her face, he stepped back a little farther. The absence of pressure between her thighs made her ache even more, made some part of her want to cry out in loss. But with the return of awareness came a bit of sense.

He didn't pull completely away, as if he knew how sensitive this could become. How dangerous for her, and maybe for him.

Instead, even as she let her legs fall away, he reached out to gently brush her hair with his hand.

"You're enchanting," he said huskily.

Enchanting? No one had ever called her that. She remained mute, unable to speak, knowing that her eyes, her face, her breathing must be telling a truth she didn't want to hear herself say. Not yet, maybe never.

"I forgot myself."

He wasn't the only one. She didn't know what to say, could only stare at him, torn between yearning, loss and the returning shreds of common sense.

He leaned forward, giving her the lightest of kisses on her lips. "I think," he said, "that I'd better cut those vegetables."

She managed a nod, awhirl with so many conflicting feelings she doubted she could ever sort them out. He turned to pick up the knife, and moved down the counter about a foot to the cutting board and vegetables.

"You don't have to be afraid of me," he said, his voice still a little thick. "I'll behave."

Another odd choice of words. As she fought her way back from the frustration of awakened, unmet desires, she tucked that away for future consideration. Right now, the thing she most needed was some equilibrium. Thinking could come later.

Wade, just about to start slicing the vegetables, put the knife down and turned toward her. He gripped her around the waist and set her back on her feet. "Sorry," he said. "Should have thought of that."

She could have slid off the counter on her own, but hadn't because she still felt so shaky. Unable to tell him that, she mumbled her thanks and turned desperately in another direction, away from him, seeking something to keep busy with. This was a simple meal, and he was about to do the major part of the work.

Finally she measured out the penne into a bowl, then walked around him to get the sausage from the microwave. *Just act as if it never happened,* she told herself. Maybe it never had.

But her traitorous body said otherwise. Oh, it had happened all right, and she suspected the internal earthquakes had just begun. Even the light brush of her own clothing over her skin, especially between her legs, reminded her that something primal had awakened.

She coated the bottom of a frying pan with olive oil, then began to slowly cook and brown the sausage on medium heat. Her hands still shook a little when she pulled out the stockpot she used for cooking pasta. A cheap pot, it wouldn't have served well for anything that wasn't mostly liquid, and she found herself pausing, suddenly locked in the most ridiculous memory of her previous pasta cooker, an expensive pot with a built-in colander and a smaller insert for steaming vegetables.

It was an odd memory, coming out of nowhere. She had long since ceased to care about the things she had lost during her transition to this new life, but for no reason she could almost feel the weight of that pot in her hands and with it the tearing edge of memories, ordinary memories, the simple kinds of things that should hold no threat whatever. It wasn't a memory of Jim, of their life together. It was just a memory of a damn pot, one she had bought long before she married Jim. Nothing but a memory from the life of a woman who had once slowly built up a kitchen full of all the best cooking utensils because she loved to cook, and part of that expression was using the best of everything.

On a teacher's salary, many of those items had truly been an indulgence. She had scrimped to buy them, until she had had a kitchen that would have pleased a world-class chef.

And now she was using a five-dollar aluminum stockpot and a chef's knife she'd bought on sale at the grocery store.

How odd, she thought, looking at the pot. How very odd what had once seemed important to her. And how little she usually missed those things now that they were gone. In fact, even had she been able to afford them, she doubted she would have replaced them.

They didn't matter any longer. Who had that woman been, anyway? Had she ever known? She certainly didn't know who she was now.

A faint sigh escaped her, and she put the pot in the sink to fill it with water. Indulgences. Her past life had been full of them, her new life was empty of them. In the midst of the storm, all she could say about it was that she had never known who she was? Had no idea who she had become?

When she started to lift the heavy pot full of water, Wade stepped in and lifted it for her. "Don't call me a pig," he said. "I've just been trained to act a certain way."

She arched a brow at him. "So a woman can't lift anything heavy?"

"Why should she when I'm standing right here?"

Once again she was left wondering how to take him. But this time she asked, emboldened, perhaps, by the fact that he had called her enchanting. "What exactly do you mean? That I'm too weak to do it?"

He shook his head. "No."

That awful answer again, the one that told her nothing. "Then what?" she insisted, refusing to let him get away with it.

He put the pot on the stove. "Would it make you feel better if we had an argument?"

That yanked her up short and hard. Was that what she was doing? Trying to get angry so she could forget the other things he made her feel? Or was this some kind of insistence on independence that actually made no sense? She bit her lip.

He faced her again. "It's my training. It's my background. Call it a simple courtesy."

And he'd done it even though he'd expected her to object. In fact, he'd tried to deflect the objection before it occurred. Would she have even thought he was being chauvinistic if he had not shot that defense out there to begin with?

"You're a very difficult man to understand," she said finally. "Not that you try to make it any easier."

"No. I don't."

"Thank you for lifting the pot."

"You're welcome."

Feeling a bit stiff and awkward now, she returned to cooking. Maybe she should never have agreed to this whole cooking thing. Maybe she should have kept him at a distance, as a roomer she hardly saw.

Because right now she felt too much confusion for comfort.

Confusion and fear. Great companions.

## CHAPTER FIVE

WADE WENT TO ground for the night. He had no problem staying out of the way upstairs until sometime in the morning. He had a finely honed instinct that warned him when it was time to become part of the background. Wallpaper. Just another tree in a forest. Now was such a time.

The hours ticked by as he read a novel he'd bought during his bus trip but had never really started. He had plenty to think about anyway as the hours slipped toward dawn. The past he still needed to deal with, the future he needed to create out of whole cloth and finally because he could avoid it no longer, a woman who slept downstairs.

Not quite two days ago, he'd met Cory Farland for the first time. There had been no mistaking that she lived in a constant state of fear, though he didn't know why. Now, in an extremely short space of time, she had made several attempts to break out of that fear, to become proactive, to take charge of even little things. And she had come perilously close to having sex with a total stranger.

He recognized the signs of someone emerging from a terrible emotional trauma. Her actions were a little off center, her reactions misaligned. He didn't even have to try to imagine the kind of confusion she must be experiencing within herself because he'd lived through it.

He wanted to kick himself, though, for giving in to the sexual desire that had been so plainly written on her face in the kitchen. Yeah, she was a helluva sexy woman, but she wasn't a one-night-stand kind of woman. If he'd pursued the matter any further, he might have given her another wound to add to the seemingly heavy scars she already carried.

His own actions had taken him by surprise, though. He usually had much better self-control, and he couldn't imagine why she'd gone to his head so fast. Yeah, it had been a long time, but that was a poor excuse. He'd quit enjoying pointless sexual encounters many years ago. Lots of women were eager to hop into bed with a SEAL, and there'd been a time when he had been glad to oblige.

Not anymore. Not for a long time now. The hero worship, the sense that he was another notch on a belt, had palled ages ago. Nor did he have the least desire for notches of his own.

What he wanted was a connection. And he knew he couldn't make them. As he'd already told Cory, he didn't make them at all. Couldn't afford them, sure. But couldn't make them, either. And he'd long since given up trying to pretend he could. Best to just hold the world at a distance.

But trying to hold the world at a distance didn't mean he could ignore that fact that Cory might need his protection. She seemed afraid in a way that suggested the threat, whatever it was, still lurked somewhere, that she had found no resolution.

It also fascinated him that while she had shared Marsha's story of an abusive husband, she had shared nothing at all about why that phone call had terrified her so. Secrets meant something. And in this case, since her first call had been to the sheriff, he doubted she was on the run from a legal problem.

Which left...what?

And then something clicked together in his brain.

He sat up a little straighter as the circumstances he

had so far observed came into focus. Moved here about a year ago, deliberately censored her speech when she spoke about where she came from. Her silences were more revealing than her speech. No offered comparison of her situation to Marsha's. High-tech alarm system when she had little money. And terrible, terrible fear. Collapsing because some anonymous person had said, "I know where you are."

WITSEC. Witness Protection.

He knew the protocols, had been part of WITSEC teams abroad. Usually the protected person was in some kind of trouble up to his neck, and was being protected because he'd agreed to inform against his own cohort.

But he'd bet his jump wings that this woman had never done anything more illegal in her life than speed on the highway. Which meant she had been an innocent witness to a crime and her life was in danger because of it. A crime that had yet to be solved. Nothing else would put her in the protection program. And nothing else would have caused the Marshals to spend so much money on that alarm system. Your average confessing criminal didn't get that kind of care.

He swore under his breath and stared at the closed door of his bedroom. Every instinct and every bit of his training rushed back to front and center.

No wonder that call had terrified her. No wonder she seemed as jumpy as a cat on a hot stove. No wonder she hadn't been able to create a life for herself here.

Then he remembered something from their walk home that afternoon, and gave himself a huge mental kick in the butt.

Without a thought, he jumped to his feet, dressed in his darkest clothes and his favorite boots. Then he switched off the motion sensors, wishing there was some way to silence the squeal, and headed downstairs. Six months of trying to be normal vanished in an instant.

HE BARELY REACHED the foot of the stairs before Cory came staggering from her bedroom, her eyes heavy-lidded with sleep, a blue terry-cloth robe held tightly around her with her arms.

"Sorry," he said. "I just needed to move around." Check the perimeter. "I didn't think it would do much good for your sleep if I clomped around upstairs."

Her brown eyes regarded him groggily. "What time is it?" she asked finally, smothering a yawn.

He glanced at the highly complex dive chronometer on his arm. He hadn't worn it in months, but for some reason he'd put it on during the night. As if something had niggled at him, saying it was time to go on duty. "A little past five," he answered.

"Good enough time to start the coffee," she said, yawning again.

"I can do it. Why don't you go back to bed?"

"I'm one of those people. Once I'm awake…" She gave a shrug and shuffled toward the kitchen.

"I'm just going to walk around the block," he said.

"Fine." She didn't even look back, just waved a hand.

So he turned off the alarm and turned it back on again so he could slip out the door. He was going to hate that alarm before long. It hampered him. He should have been able to do this without waking her at all.

On the other hand, he was glad he didn't have to leave her unprotected in there. Outside the sun was rising already, casting a rosy light over the world. He walked around the house, then set out to jog around the block.

He should have noticed it sooner, but the guy who had parked beside them at the store, then met them in the aisle had been the very same man who had driven past them on Cory's street in a different car. Evidently he'd relaxed more over the past six months than he'd realized, because he never would have failed to notice that immediately when he was on the job. Now that he'd made the connection, he had to know if they were still being watched. Had to make up for lost time.

But neither the mystery man nor either of his cars showed up.

Which of course meant nothing except that if the guy was indeed shadowing Cory, his prey was in for the night. Reaching the house again, his breath hardly quickened by his fast jog over such a short distance, he stepped inside once more, tended the squealing, annoying alarm and made his way to the kitchen.

Cory sat at the table, chin in her hands, eyes half-closed as she waited for the coffeemaker to finish.

"Do you ever hate that alarm?" he asked as he pulled mugs out of the cupboard and put one of them in front of her.

"Sometimes." She gave him a wan smile. "I never love it, that's a fact."

"I'll get used to it," he said as he reached for the coffee carafe and filled both their mugs. Then he got the half gallon of milk out of the fridge for her and placed it beside the carafe on the table.

"Thank you. You do get used to it."

"Sorry I woke you," he said again. "But I just couldn't sit still another moment." Not exactly as simple as that, but just as true.

"No need to apologize. I may not get back to sleep now, but I usually can manage a nap in the afternoon if I need it. I'll be fine." She poured maybe half a teaspoon of milk into her coffee, then raised the mug to her lips and breathed the aroma in through her nose. "Fresh coffee is one of the greatest smells in the world."

"It is," he agreed. He pulled out the chair across from her, but looked at her before he sat. "Do you mind?"

Something crossed her face, some hint of concern, but it was gone fast and he couldn't make out what it meant. She waved toward the chair. "Help yourself."

He turned the chair so he could straddle it, then sat facing her. "Looks like it's going to be a nice day out there."

"Probably. I miss the rain, though."

"Rain?"

She covered her mouth, stifling another yawn. "Back in…back where I used to live, this time of year we'd be having afternoon thunderstorms almost every day. I miss them."

"But you get some here, too, right?"

"Sometimes. Not nearly every day, though. In a way, they're prettier here."

"How so?"

"You can see so far you can almost watch them build out of nothing. Sometimes anyway." She gave a little shake of her head. "No trees to get in the way if you drive out of town."

"True."

"But there's not as much lightning with them. I used to love the lightning shows in—" Again a sharp break. An impatient sound. "We used to watch them some nights. One storm in particular, there must have been a lightning bolt every second or so. And when they'd hit the ground, you could see a green glow spread out from them and rise into the sky. I only saw it in that one storm, but I was fascinated enough to research it."

"What was it?"

"Corona discharge. It's actually quite common in electrical discharges, but often we don't even see it. The air around gets ionized as the charge dissipates. Most corona discharges aren't dangerous, but when lightning is involved, it can be."

She sipped her coffee, then held the cup in both hands with her elbows on the table. "You must have seen storms all over the world."

"I have. Monsoons, hurricanes, typhoons and then just the regular buggers, which can be bad enough."

"Yes, they can. There's so much power in a thunderstorm. Incredible power. I used to te—" Another break. She looked down, effectively hiding her face behind her mug.

Teach? he wondered. Deliberately, he let it pass. The last thing he wanted to do was cause her fear because she'd revealed something she felt she shouldn't. Not yet anyway. It wouldn't serve any useful purpose to make her more afraid.

He fell silent, enjoying his coffee while his mind turned over the things he should do, and might do, to help protect her. Maybe one of the first things he should do was find a way to speak to the sheriff. But given WITSEC procedures, he doubted Dalton would give him anything useful. No, he guessed he was on his own with this, at least until he had something more than suspicion.

But he was fairly decent on his own. And he was intimately acquainted with his own abilities and weaknesses. After all, he'd spent twenty years honing those abilities and weeding out those weaknesses.

So the question now was how much he should share with Cory. Should he let her know what had coalesced everything for him? Or should he let it ride to avoid making her any more frightened? That was always a difficult question in WITSEC ops. You needed your protectee to

be as cooperative as possible, as helpful as possible, but
you didn't want to scare him or her needlessly because
that could result in actions born of fear that could endanger the entire operation.

Cory still had her head down, her face concealed. He
studied her, trying to see her as a mission, not as a woman
who had stirred some long-buried feelings in him.

He needed to gain her confidence, sufficiently that she
would trust him if he told her to do something. That was
primary. But how? This was no ordinary operation where
being bulked-up in body armor and armed to the teeth
would do the job.

Well, he couldn't let her know how much she had betrayed by her silences. That would scare her into wondering if she'd left a crumb trail for someone to follow.

Yet, he feared someone had found her. That phone call,
he was now certain, had been no innocent prank. Someone
was sounding out women who fit a certain profile. Waiting to see if something changed after the call. He could
explain it no other way. Certainly you wouldn't warn your
intended target if you were certain you had the right one.
Instead, and he had done this on an operation or two, you
would try to precipitate revealing action.

The person or persons who hunted Cory might still
be wondering. That would depend on how many changes
the other women who got those calls made. Marsha had
adopted a dog, making no secret of the fact that she wanted
it for protection.

But what had Cory done?

The rest of the picture slammed into place. She'd taken
in a boarder. One who could easily look like a bodyguard.

Cripes. Was he himself the link that had led the hunter
to her? That would depend on whether the hunter learned

of him before or after the phone call, and for security purposes, he had to assume the worst.

The thought sickened him.

But still, sitting right before him was the woman whose trust he needed, a woman who knew nothing about him, and was likely to know nothing about him unless he started opening up the coffins of his past enough that she felt she knew him.

He swore silently, and poured more coffee into his mug. He needed to go totally against his own nature here. Needed to expose himself in ways he never did.

In that regard, this was a very different type of operation. But where to begin?

He cleared his throat, trying to find words. She looked at him immediately, which didn't really help at all. But he had to take the plunge, sort of like jumping out of a helicopter into a stormy sea and falling sixty or more feet into water that had turned into bricks.

Her eyes looked more alert now, pretty brown eyes, naturally soft and warm, especially right now when fear hadn't tightened them.

"I, um, told you I'm not good at making connections."

She nodded, but didn't try to say anything.

"Truth is, I feel like an alien."

Her eyebrows lifted, but her eyes remained warm, and even gentled a bit. "How so?"

Well now, that was hard to explain. But he'd been the one who brought it up. "Because I've been places ordinary people don't go."

She gave another nod, a slow one. "I take it you don't mean geographically."

"No." And leaving it there wasn't going to get this part of his mission done. He could almost hear the vault doors creak as he opened the crypt of feelings he didn't care to share. "I've done things, seen things, survived things most people can't even imagine. I know what I'm capable of in ways most people never will, thank God. And I can't talk about it. Partly because most of it is classified, but partly because no one will understand anyway."

"I can see that."

"The only people who truly understand are the people I served with. And we all have that sense of alienation. Some are proud of it. Maybe even most. But there's a cost."

"I would imagine so."

"So we can't make connections. We try. Then we watch it all go up in smoke. Our wives leave us because we can't talk, our kids feel like we're strangers who just show up from time to time, even parents look at us like they don't know who we are. And they don't. We pretend, try to appear ordinary, but nothing inside us is ever ordinary again. And finally we realize the only people we can truly connect with anymore are our fellow team members."

He watched her eyes glaze with thought as she absorbed what he was saying. "I guess," she said slowly, "I can identify with that just a little bit."

He waited to see if she would volunteer anything more, but she didn't. So he decided to forge ahead. "I'm not saying this out of self-pity."

"I didn't think you were."

"I'm just trying to explain why I'm so difficult to talk with. Over the years, between secrets I couldn't discuss, and realities I shouldn't discuss, I got so I didn't talk much at all."

She nodded once more. "Did you have a wife? Kids?"

"I was lucky. I watched too many marriages fall apart before I ever felt the urge. That's one closet without skeletons."

"And now your only support group, the rest of your team, has been taken away from you."

He hadn't thought of it that way before, but he realized she was right. "I guess so."

"So what do you do now?"

"I'm trying to work my way into a life without all that, but I'll be honest, I'm having trouble envisioning it."

"I'm…" She hesitated. "I guess I'm having the same kind of problem, generally speaking. I can't seem to figure out where I want to go, either."

He waited, hoping she'd offer more, but she said nothing else, merely sipped her coffee. So he tried a little indirect prompting. "Big changes can do that. You'd think, though, that since I knew I was going to retire I could have planned better."

A perfect opportunity to say her changes had come without time to plan, or even any choices, but she didn't say anything. Which left him to try to find another way in.

For the first time, it occurred to him that talking to him must be as frustrating for others as talking to Cory was for him. Okay, regardless of his reasons for preferring silence, that wasn't going to work this time. If he was right, and he was rarely wrong about things like this, she had to learn to trust him.

But he'd never had to win anyone's trust in this way before. Oh, he'd gained the trust of his team members in training, during operations and eventually even some of it by reputation. But none of those tools were available to him here. A whole new method was needed and he didn't have the foggiest idea how to go about finding it.

Nor, if he was right, did they have months to get to that point.

Maybe he had to keep talking. He sure as hell couldn't think of any other way. The problem was that most of the past twenty years of his life contained so much classified information, and so much that he couldn't share with the uninitiated, that his own memory might as well have been stamped Top Secret. And what did you talk about besides the weather if you couldn't refer to your memories?

But then Cory herself opened the door to a place that wasn't classified but that he wished could be. She asked, "Do you have any family?"

His usual answer to that was a flat no. But given his task here, he bit the bullet. "None that I speak to."

"Oh. Why?"

"It was a long time ago." Which meant he ought to be able to elaborate. It had nothing to do any longer with who he was. In fact, he'd removed them almost as cleanly as an amputation.

Then she totally floored him. Before he could decide what to tell her, and what to omit, she said gently, "You were abused, weren't you?"

Little had the power to stun him any longer, but that simple statement did. "What, am I wearing a mark on my forehead?"

She shook her head. "I don't mean to pry. But just a couple of things you've said... Well, they reminded me of some...people I worked with."

Still hedging her way around her past, while asking about his. The tables had turned, and he'd helped her do it. Didn't mean he had to like it.

"Well, yes," he finally said. "What things did I say?"

"It doesn't matter, really. You're not that child any longer, but there were just some echoes of things I've heard before. Most people wouldn't even notice."

The way most people wouldn't notice her omissions. His estimate of her kicked up quite a few notches. In her own way, she was as observant as he.

She reached for the carafe between them, and poured a little more coffee into her mug. Then she added just a tiny bit of milk. "Sometimes," she said, "I guess things stay with us, even when they've been left far in the past."

"I guess." How could he deny it when she had picked up on something he'd buried a long, long time ago? "Yeah, they were abusive."

"Physically as well as emotionally?"

"Yeah."

"I'm sorry." Her brown eyes practically turned liquid with warmth and concern. "Did that play a part in you becoming a SEAL?"

He was about to deny it, because he had, after all, been out of the house for nearly a year before he joined the navy. But then he realized something, and saw how it dovetailed into what was going on here, and he made a conscious decision to breach a barrier so old and so strong that he was hardly aware of it any longer.

"Yes," he said finally. "In a way I suppose it did."

"How so?"

Well, he'd opened the vault. "After I got out of high school, I couldn't shake them off fast enough. I worked my way through a few jobs, feeling at loose ends. Confused."

"Confused?" She repeated the word, and he could tell she felt the connection to her own situation. He could have waited for her to add something, but he suspected she wouldn't.

"Confused," he said again flatly. "I'd lived most of my life with one goal, to survive and to get away from them. And once I was away, I didn't have a goal anymore. I felt like a stranger to myself. I finally realized that the way I was drifting I wasn't going to get anywhere, so one morning I walked into a recruiter's office. Then I had a goal again, something more than merely surviving. They gave me one."

She nodded. "I can understand that. I really can. I'd like to have a goal again."

He took a gamble, sharing a little more of himself. "When you've lived for so long thinking of yourself in one way, looking at life in one way, and then something dramatic changes, it's like the earth vanishes from beneath your mental feet. Your whole identity can vanish."

"That's exactly how it feels." Her face reflected pain.

"Especially when everything you thought you were was a reflection of the life you were living."

He heard her draw a small, sharp breath. So he plunged on, laying himself out there. "For so long I'd identified myself in opposition to my parents, partly by denying all they told me I was, and partly in reaction against them and everything they did and believed. And all of a sudden I didn't have anything to push against anymore. Any goal to fight for. Well, I'm kind of there again."

Her head jerked up and she looked straight at him. "Because you retired?"

He nodded. "For twenty years, the navy gave me an identity and a goal. Now it's all gone again."

"Oh, Wade," she said quietly. "I know how hard that is."

"Somehow," he said pointedly, "I think you do."

Her eyes widened a shade. Then she confided something for the very first time. "I was…my husband died a little over a year ago. Before I came here. Everything went up in smoke."

Still evasive, but at last a nugget of the truth. He waited, hoping she would say more, but she didn't. And he'd said about all he could stand about himself. Admitted more to her than he had really wanted to about himself. Voiced out loud the struggle he'd been facing for six months now without any success.

God, he felt exposed. And life had taught him that when you exposed yourself this way, all you did was give someone ammunition to use against you.

He could have used a ten-mile run right then, but he fought down the urge to get up and walk away. Only two things stopped him: this woman might be at risk, and he realized he couldn't keep running from himself any longer.

He'd been running an awful long time. All the way back to the age of four. Running inside his head, running with his career, always running.

One of these days he needed to stop, and apparently today was going to be the day.

## CHAPTER SIX

WADE EXCUSED HIMSELF to go shower. Cory placed the coffee carafe back on the warmer, put the milk away and washed their mugs. She smothered another yawn, considered getting dressed, then discarded the idea. It was just too early to bother, especially when she didn't have anywhere to go.

But she did have a lot to think about. Wandering into her living room, she curled up on one end of the couch, tucking her robe around her legs, and put her chin in her hand thinking over all Wade had shared with her that morning.

She wished she knew what had unlocked his silence but she had to admit it was good to know something about him even if it wasn't a whole lot.

But she wasn't at all surprised to find out he'd been an abused child. Nor did it surprise her to learn that the navy had given him what he needed. Often abused children needed order in their lives, clear-cut rules to follow, after being subjected to the unpredictable whims of mean adults. The regimented lifestyle took away the fear of never knowing what would bring retribution down on their heads.

And apparently he'd needed to take charge at the same time, or he never would have gone into the SEALs. Maybe there'd even been an element of nobody's ever going to get away with treating me that way again.

She didn't consider herself an expert, but in eight years of teaching she'd certainly seen enough kids fighting these same battles, and few enough who were willing to talk about it. It was sad how they became coconspirators with their abusers, protecting their tormentors with silence and even outright lies.

And often, even when she thought she had enough to report it to the authorities, nothing came from it. Without physical evidence, as long as the child denied it, there was little enough anyone could do.

The thing that had always struck her, though, was the incalculable emotional damage that must come from being so mistreated by the very people a child by rights ought to be able to trust.

Well, she'd always wondered about that, and now she was looking at it. He seemed to blame his job for his inability to make connections, and perhaps it was responsible in large measure, but she suspected the seeds of the problem lay in his childhood. If you couldn't trust your own parents, who could you trust?

She closed her eyes, chin still in her hand. As always, when confronted with something like this, she wanted to help, but in this case she didn't see how she possibly could. This was a man who must be what? Thirty-eight? Thirty-nine? She couldn't just step in like some delivering angel. He wouldn't want it, and honestly, she didn't know enough to be much help. The best she could do was listen when he was willing to talk.

He had turned out to be a good case for not judging a book by its cover, though. If her ears hadn't become properly tuned through teaching, she probably would have thought all along that he was a hard, harsh man, sufficient unto himself, needing no one and nothing. That's certainly what he had tried to become, and the image he tried to perpetuate.

And she had to admit she felt a lot more comfortable

now knowing that he wasn't the stone monolith he had first seemed.

Listening to him had also made her think about her own situation, and doing so made her squirm a bit. Yes, terrible things had happened to her, and her entire life had changed as a result, but how could she truly excuse her waste of the past year? Terror and trauma could explain only so much. The woman she had once believed herself to be had turned out to be a weakling and a coward.

She gave herself no quarter on that one. Some of it could be excused, but not all of it. After all, look what Wade had managed to achieve out of his own trauma as a child. He may have drifted for nearly a year, but then he'd taken a stand to make something of himself.

She hadn't even tried.

But even as she sat there trying to beat herself up in the hopes that she might regain some sense of purpose or direction, she found herself remembering that episode in the kitchen yesterday, when he had lifted her onto the counter and kissed her.

Oh, man, that had started some kind of internal snow-ball rolling. Just the memory of those all-too-brief moments was enough to make her clamp her thighs together as the throbbing ache reawakened. She had thought that part of her dead and buried for good, only to discover it could come back to life at the merest touch.

Like a daffodil determined to bloom even though snow still lay on the ground in an icy blanket, her body responded to the memory as surely as the touch. She could only imagine what it might feel like to be claimed by such a man, one so powerful and strong, one so confident in his own desire. Sex with Jim had been good: loving and tender. She couldn't help but feel that the entire experience would be different with Wade: hot and hard.

And maybe that's what she needed now, someone to push her past all the invisible lines she had drawn around herself, someone to knock her off center enough to emerge from her cocoon.

Because she sure as hell needed some kind of kick.

Wade returned downstairs eventually, waking her from a half doze where dreams of hot kisses had collided with inchoate fears, the kind of feeling that something was chasing her, but she couldn't escape it, and the kisses felt like both protection and trap.

Freshly shaven, smelling of soap even from several feet away, he sat facing her. "Sorry, woke you again."

"I didn't want to doze off. If you want some, the coffee should still be hot." The memory of her odd half dream made her cheeks equally hot. She hoped he couldn't see and thought he probably couldn't since she kept the curtains closed, and the early daylight out.

It was time to start opening those curtains. Time to allow the sunlight into her house, something she hadn't yet done in all this time.

She rose at once and went to the pull cord. The instant her hand touched it, Wade barked, "Don't."

With that single command, he drove all her resolutions out of her head and brought the crippling fear back in a rush.

She froze, feeling her knees soften beneath her. She wanted some anger, even just one little flare of it, but it failed to come. Instead she reached for the wall beside the curtain, propping herself against it and closing her eyes.

When her voice emerged, it was weak. "Why?"

"I'm sorry." As if he sensed the storm that had just torn through her, leaving her once again gutted by fear, he came to her, slipping his arm around her waist, and guiding her back to the couch. "I'm sorry," he said again as he helped her sit, and sat beside her. He kept her hand, holding it between both of his, rubbing it with surprising gentleness.

This had to stop, Cory thought. This had to stop. One way or another, she had to find a way to get rid of this fear. Else how was she ever going to do anything again? "I can't keep doing this," she said to Wade, her voice thin. "I can't."

"Keep doing what?"

"Being afraid all the time. And I was just starting to do things to fight it back. Like letting you move in here. Like helping Marsha yesterday. Like opening the damn curtains for the first time in a year! And you told me to stop. Why? Why?"

At least she didn't dissolve into tears, but she felt on the brink of it. Ever since that phone call, she'd been teetering as she hadn't teetered in a long time. Before that she'd lived in a steady state at least, even if it was one of grief and fear.

Wade surprised her by drawing her into his arms and holding her. "I'm sorry," he murmured, and stroked her hair gently. "I'm sorry."

"After...after..." The thought fled before a renewed rush of terror as something struck her. "What do you know?" she asked on a whisper. "What do you know that I don't?"

His hand hesitated, then resumed stroking her hair. "I'm not sure I know anything."

"Tell me!" Her hands balled into fists, and she pounded one of them against his chest, not hard, but enough to make a point. That chest yielded to her fist about as much as cement.

He sighed, tightening his arms around her.

"Wade, don't do this to me. You either know something or you don't."

When his answer seemed slow in coming, she stiffened, ready to pull away. "You can't do this," she said, anger beginning to replace fear, and weakness with strength. "You can't! You can't just waltz into my life and then do things to make me afraid all over again. Not without a reason. I won't stand for it."

"All right. Just keep in mind this may be meaningless."

"Just tell me."

"That man we met at the store yesterday morning? The one we ran into later in the aisle?"

"Yes? What about him?"

"Early this morning I realized he was driving the car behind the woman who waved to us as we were walking back to the house."

She hardly remembered the incident and had to make herself think back. Yes, a man had driven past them, right after that woman. She tipped her head back, trying to look at him. "But it was a different car."

"Yes, it was. But it was the same man. Maybe he just owns two cars."

No matter how hard she tried, she couldn't remember the face of the man in the car during their walk. "How can you be sure? I can't even remember what he looked like."

"Training. If I hadn't gotten so lazy over the last six months, I'd have picked up on it right away. And he might just have two cars. A lot of folks do."

He looked down at her at last, his obsidian eyes like chips of stone. "I can't ignore it. Coincidence or not, I cannot ignore it."

She bit her lip, then said, "That's what made you come down so early this morning. Why you went out to jog. You were looking for him."

He nodded. "I didn't find him."

"So it could be coincidence."

"Maybe."

She shook her head a little, trying to sort through a

bunch of conflicting thoughts. Finally she came up with one question. "That phone call couldn't be part of it, could it? I mean…" She wanted to believe it was all random chance, but the phone call kept rearing up in her mind, some part of her insisting it was no prank. "It doesn't make sense. Why call me if you know where I am?"

"Because maybe you don't know exactly which of a handful of women is your target."

"And how would that prove a damn thing?"

He loosened his hold on her, giving her space, but she didn't move away. She didn't want to. Odd considering that he was busy ripping her newfound courage to shreds. Not that it had been much to begin with.

He spoke finally. "Sometimes the only way to identify a target is to do something that makes them take a revealing action."

She searched his face, but it remained unreadable. "You've done that?"

"A couple of times."

"It works?"

"It did for me."

"But I haven't done anything since the call! So that can't be what's going on."

"Maybe. Maybe not."

"Stop being so elliptical. Just tell me what you're thinking. Please!"

"I moved in here right before you got the call. What if the person trying to locate you saw me only after the call?"

Her stomach sank, and right along with it her heart. "Bodyguard," she whispered. Then she had another horrifying thought. "Marsha got a dog."

"If I were them, I doubt I'd pay much attention to a dog."

She was feeling sicker by the second. "No. Especially

not when they could trace her back if they want to. If they can."

"Can they?"

In that question she heard the million unanswered questions her own life had become. She had as good as admitted what was going on here. And he had apparently figured out plenty on his own. Now what? Tell the truth, or leave the lies hanging out there. The omissions. The secrets.

Then she had another thought. "What if…" This one really sickened her. So much so she wrenched away from him and jumped up from the couch. She backed away, wrapping her arms around herself, staring at him, feeling horror start to grow.

"What if I'm the one hunting you?" he asked. "Good question. Call the sheriff right now. Tell him to come get me. Tell him whatever you want."

"And then what?"

"And then I'll leave. I'll be gone from this county as fast as I can pack my duffel."

Did she want that? No…no… Not if he was who he was really supposed to be. "You know too much about me."

"Lady, I know nothing about you. I've guessed some things, but you sure as hell haven't told me anything."

"What did you guess?"

He passed a hand over his face. "Will it scare you if I get up and pace? I'm not really good at holding still unless I have to."

She waved a hand, indicating permission. God, when he stood he seemed to fill the entire room.

He started pacing, but slowly, taking care not to come too close to her. "You know I noticed how afraid you are."

"Yes."

"Well, I noticed some other things, too, and last night it just all kind of came together for me. The way when you talk about things from your past you hesitate and then skip anything that might actually give away where you lived before. I also noticed that when you got scared by the phone call you turned to the sheriff."

"What does that tell you?"

He looked at her. "That you're scared and on the run from some threat that still haunts you. But you're not running from the law, or your first response wouldn't have been to call Gage Dalton."

She nodded stiffly. "Okay."

"I noticed the security system. You can't afford it."

"No," she admitted.

"I've been involved in WITSEC ops overseas."

"WITSEC?"

"Witness security. Witness protection."

"Oh…my…God…" She sank onto the rocking chair, arms still tightly wrapped around her.

"All the signs are there for someone who can read them. Which most people can't. It took me more than a day to figure it out, so don't worry that you've tipped off everyone in the county. I'm sure you haven't. But it's the only picture that fits. Am I wrong?"

She shook her head stiffly. "It was that easy?"

"Actually, you made it very hard. Like I said, I didn't glom on to it immediately. But when I put a few things together, it was the only explanation I could think of. The alternative was to think you're just crazy, and you're not crazy, Cory."

She felt numb, almost out of her own body, with shock. This man had figured her out so fast, and yet he said it had taken him too long. How did that add up?

But if he'd figured it out, how many others had? No one, he said. But could she safely believe it?

"Trust me," he said, "it wouldn't occur to anyone not familiar with the protocols. You don't give anything away."

"I...find that hard to believe, now."

"Well, believe it. WITSEC is not the first thing that would occur to anyone about you. It would probably be the last."

"Why?"

"Because no one would suspect you of being a criminal, even if they suspect you have some secrets."

"I'm not a criminal!"

"I know that. It's obvious. And since everyone thinks that only criminals get witness protection, you're even more covered. Very well covered."

Her eyes burned and she felt hollow as she looked at him. "What now?" she asked, a bare whisper.

"Well, all I have is a suspicion. But you can choose how to act on it. Call the sheriff, I'll tell him everything I noticed about the guy. Call the Marshals and they'll move you again. Or...I can try to protect you until we get something solid."

She'd already made up her mind she didn't want to move again. Once was enough. What few tenuous connections she had managed to make here were more than she wanted to sacrifice. She couldn't face another blank slate in a blank town, couldn't face having to start all over again, small though her start here had really been. After all, there was Emma, Marsha, Gage, Nate and Marge Tate. While she hadn't exactly gotten close, she had come to know them a bit. And she discovered she wanted to know them even better.

She raised her eyes to his, resolve steadying her. "I'm not running again."

He nodded. "I kind of decided the same thing this morning."

She nodded slowly. "I guess you did." Her decision made, her muscles began to uncoil slowly, one by one. "I guess I need to tell you the story."

"Cory, you don't have to tell me a damned thing. I can work this without knowing. Your secrets can remain your secrets. But I gather, since you didn't recognize the guy at the store, that he's not someone you're afraid of."

"No. Actually...I saw only one man. The man who killed my husband and shot me."

"Shot you?" He stopped short.

She nodded, and for some reason she didn't understand, she opened her robe and tugged her pajama top up enough to reveal the scar across her midriff. "He killed my baby, too."

He swore, a word she wasn't used to hearing, and the next thing she knew he'd gathered her up off the chair and was carrying her through the house toward her bedroom. There he laid her down on the queen-size bed, and stretched out beside her. Without another word, he drew her into a close embrace, as if he wanted to surround her with the shield of his body. As if he wanted to shelter her from it all.

But nothing could. She stared blindly at his chin as her head rested on his upper arm, feeling as if a wind had blown through her and left her empty in every way, empty of her past, empty of her hopes and dreams, empty of feeling.

Something in her had died all over again.

In the hollowness that seemed to engulf her, she heard her own voice. It sounded dreamy, disconnected, as if it belonged to someone else and she wasn't in control. And maybe she wasn't.

"I didn't really grieve about the baby," she heard her-

self say. "I'd just found out that morning. Not enough time
for it to become real."

"Mmm." A sound to let her know he was listening, indicating no reaction whatever. She didn't want a reaction.
She couldn't have handled one just then.

"What was real was that when I woke up from surgery
they told me that the only part of Jim I had left was gone,
too. I miscarried because of the trauma."

"I'm sorry."

"I was…I was at the best and brightest point of my life
that night. The happiest. I had Jim, we were going to have
a baby. Maybe no one is entitled to that much happiness."

"Everyone is entitled to that kind of happiness."

"Really? Even you?"

He didn't answer, his silence speaking volumes.

"We went out for dinner to celebrate the news, came
home and…made love. I was so happy I couldn't even
sleep. And then some son of a bitch came through our door
and took it all away with a gun."

He murmured something, but she didn't try to make
it out. She didn't care. Numbness still wrapped her like
cotton wool.

"I saw the man. They couldn't find him, though,
couldn't identify him. We think…they think…he was
working for a drug gang that Jim was about to bring in
indictments against. A hired gun, probably. They put me
in protection from the instant I got to the hospital. They
wouldn't even let me go to Jim's funeral."

His arms tightened a bit, but he said nothing.

"Then, after three months in a safe house, they told
me I had to relocate because the word on the street was
there was a contract on me because I could identify Jim's
murderer."

"Not penny-ante criminals then."

"No. Sometimes I think they were bigger fish than even Jim realized."

"Maybe so."

"There wasn't even a threat beforehand. No warning of any kind. The grand-jury testimony was sealed, the indictments were going to be sealed until they'd rounded everyone up. Maybe there was a leak from somewhere. No one seemed to know. I'll probably never know."

"So three months in a safe house, and then the beginning of the journey to nowhere."

"First, first they did a little plastic surgery. I had a nose job. Just enough to make me look different if anyone had a photo of me. My hair…I have to color it. I wear it differently now. Not big changes."

"Big enough changes. The nose especially. Minimal change, maximum impact."

"That's what they said. Change a nose and you change the whole face."

"That must have been hard for you."

"Even now I sometimes jump when I look in a mirror. Anyway, they moved me through three towns before the nose job. After that, it was another six towns. We'd stay for a while, then they'd pack me up and move me again. They said they were making sure nobody could follow me."

"That's right."

"So you've done that part, too?"

"I've done it all, from the moving to the safe-house protection. Of course, I had the disadvantage of having to protect a couple of really bad guys. Sometimes it seems hardly worth the trouble."

"But it is, right?"

"If they have enough information, yes. In your case, it would have been an honor."

She reached up with one hand and touched his chin. At once he tipped his head to look at her. "I hated it."

"I imagine so."

"But they were really doing everything they possibly could for me. Even while I hated it, I understood it. They went out of their way for me."

"Because you were innocent."

"Because my husband was an assistant U.S. attorney. Because he was one of theirs. I don't kid myself that I would have gotten the same kind of care except for Jim. The only man I could put behind bars is the man who killed a federal prosecutor."

Something in his dark eyes seemed to soften just a hair, but he didn't argue with her, probably because he knew she was right.

"Those kinds of resources," she said, "don't get spent on just anybody. I could have witnessed almost any other murder, been the only one able to identify the killer, and I'd have been on my own before long."

"Seems like you're kind of on your own now."

"That's the way it works."

He nodded. "Most of the time. Are you angry about that?"

"That I got first class instead of coach? How could I be angry about that? What I'm angry about is that every single thing I cared about was stripped away from me. My family, my friends, my career. Sometimes I get angry at myself for letting them take me away."

"Be sensible. What good would it possibly have done to get yourself killed?"

"It might have spared me the limbo I've been living in."

He sighed and cupped her cheek with his warm hand. "Now that's crazy talk. Somehow we'll get this guy and then you can get on with your life."

"Can I? I'm not so sure of that. I was supposed to be safe ever since I got here, but I haven't spent one hour of one day without looking over my shoulder."

"All I can tell you is that things may be coming to a head finally. And that I'm trained for this kind of stuff. And that the last year...Cory, think about all you went through. Of course you couldn't get your bearings, especially when you had good reason to be terrified."

"Apparently so, since I seem to have been found."

He fell silent for a half minute, then said, "You're going to hate me for this."

"For what?"

"Maybe it's a good thing you've been found. Maybe we can deal with this mess for once and for all. Maybe we can get your life back."

"I don't exactly have a life to get back anymore."

"Maybe you could even go home and resume your career."

"I don't know about that. I'm not sure I want to." She was sorry then, sorry because the numbness wore off suddenly and she started feeling again.

And what she felt was a pain deeper and wider than the Grand Canyon. When she started to cry, he just gathered her closer.

As if that would help. As if anything could help.

## CHAPTER SEVEN

HE WIPED HER tears gently away when she finally quieted. For a long time he just held her, but finally he spoke. "We have to talk about how to deal with this."

"What can we possibly do?

"Well, I'll have to think about that some, but we've still got to talk. We have to sort through your options and my options, and see what we can come up with. There's a lot I can do, but I don't usually plan entire operations by myself."

"Teamwork?"

"Yes. And you're my team. And the sheriff, too. We've got to talk this all over with him."

"I don't want to! What if he calls the Marshals? I don't want to do that again."

"Easy now. I'm sure we can convince Gage not to do that. But as good as I may be, I'm still just one man, Cory. We're going to need some help."

She pressed her face into his shoulder, hating all of this, from the fear that tingled along her spine to the sense of being trapped in a nightmare. Why couldn't she have even an hour of forgetfulness? Was that so much to ask?

Then he shifted her, so that she lay even closer to him. His hand began to run over her back, in steady, soothing circles. At least she thought he meant them to be soothing, but after a few minutes they had a totally different effect. Their passionate kiss yesterday had made her aware of her own needs again, and it didn't take long for her body to remind her that there was still something good in life, something that could be hers for the asking. Something that would make her forget.

But forgetfulness quickly took a backseat to a slowly building heat. Even if her mind and heart quailed, her body wanted to spring back to life, to grasp it with both hands and revel in it.

The softest of sighs escaped her, and she tried to wiggle closer, to say with her body what she could not with words.

His hand paused. As soon as she realized he must have received her silent message, she caught and held her breath, torn between an impulse to pull away and hide, and an almost excruciating hope that he wouldn't turn her away.

She should run. Now. Because she couldn't handle the rejection. Not now. Not after all she had exposed about herself.

*Turn away now, don't give him the chance to say no.*

But her body refused to obey her brain. It wanted something primal, something more elemental, an affirmation of life that bypassed all those messed-up circuits in her brain.

His hand left her back. She tensed in expectation of the rejection. But instead he caught her chin and turned her face up so they were looking at one another, only inches apart. His dark eyes searched hers, then moved over her face, as if seeking an answer to some question.

Then he swooped in like a bird of prey and took her mouth in a kiss that stunned her with its intensity, as if he wanted to draw her very soul out of her.

Oh, he knew how to kiss. His tongue mated with hers in a rhythm that exactly matched the pulsing it set off in her body. Fireworks sparkled along her nerve endings, making every inch of her so sensitive that the merest brush of clothing against her skin seemed overwhelmingly sensual and sexual.

He shifted, tugging both her legs between his, so they were locked together and her throbbing center was out of reach even as it grew heavy and aching with need.

All from a kiss.

Her body wanted to fight the imprisonment until she felt his hardness against her belly. She understood then. He wanted her every bit as much as she wanted him, but he would make her wait, slow her down, force patience where she felt none.

And that understanding made her relax into his arms, and let him have his way. No need to rush. No need at all. Somehow that freed her in a way desire alone couldn't have.

He continued to hold her close with one arm as he kissed her, but his other hand began to wander. He slipped it under her robe, leaving only her pajamas in the way, and stroked her side from breast to thigh, to the point where his leg trapped hers, then swept it up again, slowly...oh, so slowly.

And as it returned upward, it slid beneath her pajama top, and she gasped. She arched a little, breaking the kiss as she felt his callused palm touch her bare skin. He stayed there for a while, drawing slow, lazy circles on her middle while his mouth claimed hers again, this time more gently, echoing the touch of his fingers.

Impatience started to build in her again, causing her to squirm a bit against his bondage, but he didn't release her. Her breasts ached for a touch, a kiss, until she thought she would go out of her mind from the longing.

Yet still he withheld it.

Tearing her mouth from his, she gasped for air, then reached with one hand to undo the buttons of his shirt. If he wasn't going to give her more, she would take more.

He didn't stop her when she pulled open his shirt and pressed her palm at last to his chest. She thought she even heard a deep sound of pleasure escape him as she began to trace the contours of those hard muscles, glorying in the smoothness of his skin, in the ripples across his belly, in the small points of his nipples. Exquisite. Perfect. As much a feast for her hands as he had been for her eyes.

Then without warning, his hands gripped her around her waist, he freed her from the prison of his legs and, leaving her almost dizzy, he lifted her over him, so that she straddled his hips.

A groan escaped her as he tugged her down until her moist yearning depths met his hardness through layers of denim and cotton. What was he doing? She needed to get rid of the clothing that interfered.

But when she reached for the snap of his jeans, he stopped her and murmured roughly, "Just ride me, Cory."

She didn't know what he meant until his hands gripped her hips again and he moved her against him. All of a sudden those layers of fabric didn't seem to matter. Her hips helplessly rocked against him, demanding a solution to the problem of need.

And as she rocked, he slipped his hands up under her nightshirt and cupped her breasts, rubbing his thumbs over her nipples.

He might as well have plugged her into an electric socket. Shocks zinged through her, setting her alight, then zipped to her center, creating an ache that made her forget everything, everything except her need.

"That's the way…" He groaned the words, urging her on, tormenting her even as he encouraged her to ride the cresting wave. And somehow, by keeping them both clothed, he had set her free in an unexpected way.

Set her free to take what she wanted as she rubbed

herself against him over and over. Set her free to give in to her need without thought of anything or anyone other than herself.

Free to be.

Free to ride the crest of the wave all the way until she tumbled wildly into the warm waters below.

And knew peace.

She lay on Wade's chest, his arms around her as aftershocks made her tremble. Her legs sprawled on either side of him, leaving her open, and each aftershock caused her to tighten them just a bit against his hips.

She felt more safe, more secure and more relaxed than she had since…the shooting. And she couldn't even rustle up a smidgen of guilt about it.

Well, except that she didn't know if Wade had enjoyed it quite as much as she had, didn't know if he'd found completion himself. And had no way to ask.

Silly, after what they had just shared, an experience all the more exhilarating because of the way he had brought it about, that she should feel a bit shy. But there it was.

But oh, she never would have believed that having sex while fully clothed could actually enhance the experience, could arouse her so much, could give her such a sense of primitive freedom. In a way, she supposed, it had been an updated version of dragging her away to a cave by her hair. Little finesse, a lot of hunger, and bam!

He'd lingered just long enough for her inhibitions to weaken, and then he'd forced her to shed them all. Quick, hot and ready.

And damn, it felt good.

He moved at last, just a bit, lifting a hand to stroke the back of her head, then wind a strand of her hair around his finger.

"You okay?" he asked gruffly.

"I'm fine," she murmured. "You?"

"Pretty amazed, actually."

At that she lifted her head and looked at him. His hard face looked softer now, and even his obsidian eyes seemed less like rock and more like deep waters. "How so?"

"I couldn't begin to explain."

She laid her cheek on his chest again. "Some things beggar words, I guess."

"Maybe so." He released the strand of her hair, and ran a fingertip along the curve of her jaw. "Were you a teacher, before?"

This man had a gift for putting a few pieces together into complete a puzzle, so she guessed it shouldn't have surprised her that he had figured that out. "Why do you ask?"

"Something you said. Well, actually, something you started to say and never finished. You caught yourself just as you started to say the word."

"And you finished it."

"I do that sometimes."

"God, you're incredible. It's like you read minds."

"I'm just observant. You don't have to tell me."

"No, it's okay. I was a teacher. Maybe I'll teach again someday."

"Was there a reason they didn't just get you a certificate here?"

"They felt it would leave too much of a trail." And here was reality, intruding again. She almost wanted to beat her fist on something.

"Sorry, guess I'm ruining the moment."

She must have grown tenser, she thought. In some way he'd picked up on her reaction. He was amazing. In so many ways. Jim had been a sensitive guy, but not this sensitive. "No, I can't hide for long from reality. Not now," she admitted finally. "Not when there may be a threat."

"No." A word of agreement.

Her stomach chose that moment to growl loudly. No more breaks for her today, she thought almost ruefully.

"I think," Wade said after a moment, "that you ought to take a shower while I go make us some breakfast."

"You're going to do the cooking?"

"I told you I know some basics. I may not be able to turn out that pasta thing you managed last night, but I can make a mean scrambled egg, and I can cook it with anything from sunlight, to a flameless ration heater, to a candle to a stove."

"I recommend the stove."

"Since it's available."

She lifted her head and looked at him again. "How do you cook with sunlight?"

"We carry mirrors for signaling. All you have to do is set it up right."

She nodded. "Someday you'll have to show me."

He rolled then, dumping her off him onto the bed. He smiled, actually smiled down at her as he raised himself on one elbow. "Shower," he repeated. "I'll go make some edible scrambled eggs."

Then he gave her a quick hard kiss and was gone.

FOR THE FIRST time in forever, Cory thought about what she was putting on. Ordinarily she grabbed a uniform from her closet, or just a shirt and jeans, not caring which. But this morning she dithered over whether she should wear a denim skirt, the brown plaid shirt with the piped yoke or a plainer polo shirt.

Finally she told herself to stop being ridiculous, pulled on fresh jeans—in Florida jeans were rarely worn except when it was cool, but here everyone wore them even if it was hot—and the gold polo shirt. She even added a bit of lipstick and mascara, from among the few personal possessions she'd been able to bring with her: nothing that wouldn't fit into a suitcase.

Good smells reached her as soon as she opened her bedroom door. Apparently Wade had added some bacon to the menu from the groceries he had bought yesterday, and from the aroma she could tell he'd brewed fresh coffee. Not only a second cup today, but a second pot. Now that was an extravagance she hadn't enjoyed in far too long.

When she entered the kitchen, she found the table already set. The bacon was draining on a paper towel over a plate on the table, and a stack of toast stood on the counter beside the toaster, already buttered.

"You can cook," she said with surprise.

"Told you. What do you think happens when we're at some small firebase on our own? We take turns, and God help the guy who can't even make a decent breakfast."

A little laugh escaped her.

"And here it's easy. You even have a toaster. Take a seat. I'll bring you coffee."

She sat, saying, "I thought you guys had prepackaged meals. What are they called?"

"MREs. Meals, Ready-to-Eat. Three lies in three letters. I won't give you any of the slang names for them."

"But you cooked anyway?"

"When we move, we move fast and travel light. Try to live off the land. Besides, what you eat affects how you smell, so it's best to eat local diet as much as possible."

She noticed his consistent use of the present tense, and wondered if he really found it that hard to put his years as a SEAL in the past, or if the present situation had just put him back in the mental mode as if he'd never left.

"I never would have thought of that," she said as he joined her at the table with the toast and eggs.

The eggs were perfectly cooked, not too dry or moist, though he evidently hadn't whipped them. But why would that occur to him, considering he had done most of his cooking in the field? He'd spiced them with just a hint of cayenne, too, making them more savory.

"Perfect," she said, complimenting him.

One corner of his mouth lifted in a smile. "Thanks. I hate overdone eggs. I'll eat them, but I won't like it."

For a man who said he didn't know how to converse, he was doing a darn good job of it. Maybe something in him had begun to open up, too, as it had inside her.

Almost as soon as she had the thought, he clammed up again. They ate breakfast in silence and hardly said a word as they washed up afterward.

But then, after they moved back into the shadowed living room, he said, "I'm going to call the sheriff."

And ugly reality came crashing back down.

WADE CALLED GAGE then excused himself to jog around the block. He didn't say why he was going, but Cory figured it out without having to ask: he was going to make sure the guy he'd noticed yesterday wasn't hovering around. She spent the time pretending to tidy up the house, although all she really needed to do was some dusting. She'd done all her major housework just a few days ago, and while the dust hadn't really built up since then, it gave her an excuse to keep moving, and moving seemed like a good way to hold her fears at bay. Barely.

Wade returned to the house at the same time Gage arrived. They entered together, Gage in civvies, and joined Cory in the living room. Before she could even greet Gage or put down her dustrag, Wade said, "I didn't see him."

Cory wasn't sure that eased her mind at all, given what Wade suspected. She dropped the rag on the table, brushed her hand quickly against her jeans, then shook Gage's hand and invited him to sit. "Coffee?"

He shook his head. "I'm fine. Thanks, Cory. So let's cut to the chase. Wade said next to nothing except you needed to see me."

Cory nodded, then sank slowly onto the Boston rocker. Gage took the easy chair again, and Wade the end of the couch nearest to her. She looked at Wade. "You explain. Please."

"Okay." Wade leaned forward, resting his elbows on his splayed knees, and folded his hands. "I knew from the outset Cory had something to be afraid of. I was here when she got that call, after all, the one she called you about."

Gage nodded. Cory noted he wasn't giving a thing away. He wasn't likely to speak a word until he was certain who knew what, and what they thought was going on. Protecting her secrets.

"Anyway, I won't bore you with all the irrelevant details, unless you think you need them. I've been on WIT-SEC operations overseas, and by early this morning I realized that Cory must be in Witness Protection."

Gage immediately stiffened. "I don't think…"

"Relax," Wade said. "No one else would guess. I figured it out because I was here, I could see the fear, and some of her omissions were glaring, to say the least."

Gage swore and looked at Cory. "I'm sorry. I never would have brought Wade here if I'd ever thought someone would figure this out."

"It's okay," Cory said. "I'm not upset that he knows. Far from it. And honestly, I think he's right when he says no one else would guess. He figured it out because he had the experience to put the pieces together."

"I hope so," Gage said flatly. Right now he wasn't looking too friendly.

Wade appeared untroubled by the reaction. Or maybe he had just gone back to his inner fortress. Cory surprised herself by hoping like hell that he hadn't. She didn't want him to go back to that. She kind of liked the man he'd revealed himself to be, even though he had as yet revealed little.

"Anyway," Wade continued with little expression, "I also figured out why someone might have made that phone call, and I remembered something I would have caught on to immediately if I hadn't spent the last six months trying to lose most of what I learned as a SEAL."

"And that is?"

"First let me explain a method we used a time or two in operations. You don't always have a clear idea of who your target is. Sometimes you don't have a photo, or even a decent description. So what we would do was try to scare a group of potential targets, then watch who took the most revealing action."

Gage nodded slowly. "So you're saying you don't think that phone call was a prank."

"It might well not be. And the reason I'm suspicious is because we saw the same guy at two different places yesterday. He followed us into the parking lot at the grocery, then we ran into him again in the aisle."

"That doesn't mean anything."

"That alone wouldn't. However, when we were walking home from the park together yesterday afternoon, I saw the guy again. Driving a different car down the street out front."

"Hell." Gage scratched his head almost irritably.

"I realize, of course, that some people have more than one car. I realize that call may indeed have been a prank.

But when you put it all together with Cory's being in protection because she's the only person who can identify the man who murdered her husband, it doesn't pay to ignore coincidence."

"No. No, it doesn't. But what would you say is the revealing action Cory took? Because I don't see that she did a thing."

"Except take me in. And the guy who's watching might not have seen me arrive before the call. Actually no reason he should have, because he wouldn't have been looking for telltales until after the call…and I arrived basically right before it."

Gage nodded slowly. "It's possible."

"The thing is," Wade continued, "if you assume he's got his eye on, oh, say half a dozen women who've moved here sometime over the last year, and he has to watch all of them, he's going to be looking around at one after another to see who did what after the phone call. And after the call he sees two things: Cory and her friend Marsha go to the pound and pick out a dog for Marsha. That might have been enough to point a finger at Marsha except that then Cory comes home and a very short time later she emerges to go to the grocery store with me."

"And you could easily look like a bodyguard."

Cory spoke. "I think Wade is right, Gage. Especially when you consider that I not only suddenly have Wade living here, but we went shopping together. Ordinarily when people do that, they have a long-term relationship of some kind. But Wade wasn't in my life until the day before yesterday. In fact, when I look back at it, it could easily have appeared that I was doing the shopping and Wade was just there."

"Okay," Gage said. "And then you saw him again in the afternoon. In a different car."

"And he didn't even glance at us," Wade remarked, "while the woman in the car ahead of him smiled and waved."

"Most folks in Conard County smile and wave. We're pretty sure someone is an outsider when they don't." He rubbed his chin then looked at Cory.

"But you can't identify him as the man who killed your husband?"

"No, he didn't look anything like that man. I'd have noticed instantly if he had."

Gage cocked one eyebrow and looked at them both. "You know how thin this is?"

"Very," Wade said immediately.

"But it's still not something I can overlook. Give me a minute to think."

For an instant, crazily, Cory heard the *Jeopardy* music in her head. Where had that come from? She looked at Wade and saw a man who was infinitely capable of waiting when necessary, one who might prefer to be moving, but one who could also sit as still as a statue when he chose. He chose to be a statue right now.

Finally Gage spoke. "Okay. The way I see it is that while we can't be sure, Wade is making a good point about revealing actions. The guy who is after Cory may not know her appearance has been changed. They don't often do that in Witness Protection, but given that he can't find anyone who matches her appearance exactly, that kind of provocation would make sense, assuming he somehow found out where she is. And the only way I can think that he would have learned that is if he got the info from someone who works for the Marshals."

Cory's heart skipped a beat then climbed right into her throat. "I didn't even think of that," she whispered hoarsely.

Gage's dark eyes turned her way. "It's been a year, Cory, so it's obvious the Marshals succeeded in making sure no one followed you. So the only way this guy could have any idea you're here is if someone in the program talked. Some kind of leak."

"My God," she whispered. Her skin started to crawl with fear and anxiety again. "What else might he know?"

Gage shook his head. "I don't know, but if Wade is right about that call, then he didn't manage to find out your new name. So whatever someone leaked, it was minimal, or this guy would have your name and address."

"Yes, that's true."

"And it would be my guess that you didn't follow the usual protocol of using the same first name you had before, along with a last name that starts with the same initial, or he'd just as good as have your new name and address."

"No, they told me that's what most people do but one of the Marshals..." Her voice broke, then steadied. "One of the Marshals was a good friend of my husband's. He seemed more worried than the rest, and he was the one who suggested I come up with a totally different name."

"Did you?" Wade asked suddenly. "Totally different? Or could there be a link between your name now and your past?"

Cory bit her lip. "My mother's name was Cory. And her maiden name was McFarland."

Wade looked at Gage. "He could find that out, now that he thinks he might have located her."

Gage nodded. "All too easily. Assuming he bothers to look."

"Why wouldn't he look?" Cory asked, her heart still beating a nervous tattoo.

"Because, assuming this guy does indeed know where you are, he may feel he's already got all the information he needs. I can't read his mind, Cory. I just know we have to take steps."

"What kind of steps? Are you going to call the Marshals?"

Gage shook his head. "Why in the name of all that's holy would I call them? If this isn't just some kind of weird coincidence, then we're dealing with an organization that has already leaked information about you. They're the last ones I'm going to call now. Unless that's what you want me to do."

Cory shook her head quickly. "No. No. I don't want to run again. I can't do that again." Her entire soul seemed to be screaming that another round of running and hiding would break her forever. Clenching her fists, she said again, "No."

Gage's face gentled. "Not even to save your life?"

"What life? If I don't make a stand now, I'll never have one. I'm tired of always being frightened, of always looking over my shoulder. This guy is a killer and I'm the only one who can put him behind bars. If he's found me, then I want to finish it now. I can't…I can't keep living this way. I just can't."

"All right then." Gage stood. "I won't even call the Marshals for a sketch of the murderer. I'm going to send an artist over here to do one just for us. I'd also like a sketch of the guy Wade thinks was following you. Are you up to that, Cory?"

"Definitely." The decision was made. She would stand her ground.

And amazingly, that decision calmed her. The calm probably wouldn't last, but for now it felt wonderful to have finally made the choice. "I'm through letting that guy ruin my life," she said, looking from Gage to Wade.

"And frankly, the way I've been living is no life at all. So let's finish it, one way or another."

THE POLICE SKETCH artist turned out to be nothing like Cory had imagined. Esther Nighthawk was a beautiful redhead who wore a long skirt and leaned heavily on a cane. Under one arm, she carried a sketchbook.

"Oh, I just do this to help out," Esther said as Cory invited her into the kitchen so she'd have a table to work on. "I'm a full-time watercolorist, but I enjoy the challenge of doing these sketches for the sheriff."

She settled on the chair facing Cory, and opened her sketchpad to a blank page. Then she pulled a box of drawing pencils from the large woven bag she carried. "I'm sorry we haven't met before. My husband and I live on a ranch—he raises sheep—and I only get to town every couple of weeks for shopping. Or when one of the children needs to come in for something."

"That sounds like a nice life," Cory said almost wistfully.

"It is." Esther's gaze softened a bit. "My life sure changed radically after I met Craig. Before then I spent most of my time hiding."

"From what?"

"Life. I had myself convinced that my art was all that mattered, but basically I was just afraid of a whole bunch of things. Neurotic would probably be a good word."

"And now?"

"Now I love every minute of every day." Esther smiled. "So, you're going to help me draw a picture of a man Gage seems to be worried about?"

"Yes. I'll try, anyway."

"You talk, I'll draw."

So Cory closed her eyes for a minute, and tried to summon her memory of the man who killed Jim. "It's hard," she said after a moment. "You know how faces seem to skate away when you concentrate on them?"

"I know. That's why you're not going to concentrate. You're going to give me one detail to start with. I'll draw it, and you watch. As you watch me, tell me what's right and what's not. It'll work. Trust me."

So that's what Cory did. She started with the general shape of the guy's head, and after a few erasures she decided it was correct. Then a nose, and that needed only three iterations. Little by little, the image built, and Esther was right, it was easier to say when something was wrong than to give an exact description of what was right.

A half hour later and she was looking at an eerily familiar face, one she couldn't have pulled out of her memory any other way.

"That's him," she said. "You couldn't possibly get any closer."

Esther nodded, smiling. "It's never as hard as people think it will be."

"Only because you're such a good artist."

Wade joined them, and together he and Cory helped create a sketch of the man they had met at the grocery.

"This is truly amazing," Cory remarked again as she looked at the second sketch. "I thought I'd forgotten him entirely, but this is him."

"You're very gifted," Wade told Esther. "Very gifted."

Esther laughed. "Keep stroking my ego. More is always better." She began to pack up her materials. "Listen, why don't you come out to the ranch for dinner some night? I'd like a chance to get to know you better, and maybe someday you can tell me what this is all about."

"I'd love that," Cory said immediately, realizing she would. The urge to put down roots here had become almost compulsive since just a few days ago. It was as if warning flags had started to pop up in her psyche, telling her that if she continued on her current course she might as well die.

And along with all those warning flags, a desire to start making connections again, a real life again, pushed her.

Possibly into a very dangerous place, the dangerous place she'd spent more than a year hiding from.

Cory said goodbye to Esther at the door, then stepped back away from the opening as Wade ushered the woman to her car.

"Lock up and set the alarm after me," he murmured as he passed. "I'm going to scout a bit before I come back."

She did as told, then went to sit in the living room and wait. How had she survived the past year living this way? Waiting for a doom that never came, too afraid to lead any real kind of life, trying to be invisible even at her job.

With absolute certainty, she knew she couldn't return to that way of life. She'd been dying by inches for too long. She couldn't do it anymore. No way.

And if that meant possibly sticking her head into a noose, then that was what she would do.

Wade returned about twenty minutes later, quieting then resetting the alarm before he joined her.

"You're going to go crazy," she said when he sat beside her.

"I am? Why?"

"Because I just looked in the mirror."

"Meaning?"

She gave a little shake of her head. "Inside this house is limbo. I sit here doing next to nothing, worrying, grieving, afraid. You're going to go nuts locked in here with me."

"I see." He drummed his fingers briefly on the arm of the couch. "I won't go crazy. I've been known to sit in hides for days on end waiting for the right moment, or the target, to appear. I can do it."

"Well, I'm tired of it. I was just sitting here wondering how I'd managed to do nothing for so long."

"Aww, Cory," he said quietly. "Give yourself a break. You went through a terrible trauma, and then you got dumped on a foreign shore where almost nothing was familiar anymore. You needed time. You took it."

"You're very generous."

"Just calling it the way I see it. If you'd lost your husband but been allowed to remain with your friends and family, to keep your job, you could have coped with your grief better. If you hadn't lost your husband but had simply been obliged to move, you would have coped with that, too."

"So sure?"

"I've watched your transformation over the last two days. I'm sure. What's more, I think you need to cut yourself some slack because you experienced two major traumas, both of them stressful to the extreme. And then you had a killer to fear. Most people would have dug a hole and pulled it in after themselves."

"That's basically what I did."

"But look at you now. For whatever reason, you've reached the point where you're ready to take action. But that doesn't mean the time you took to hide and lick your wounds was wrong."

She would never have imagined this man could be so kind. Or that he would be willing to put himself out there the way he had today. He'd seemed so self-contained, so impervious, so...rocklike. Yet while she still felt the almost insurmountable strength in him, she had found a kindness and understanding that seemed like a gift.

It was likely that if she'd ever put herself out there over

the past year, she might have found that kind of kindness and understanding from other sources, but she'd been terrified into silence not only by the fact that a killer might be hunting her, but also by all the strictures the Marshals had placed on her. All the warnings. They had meant well, she was sure, but how do you pick up a life that had been so completely and totally interrupted?

"It was like they wanted me to erase myself and start out like a baby all over again."

He nodded. "From their point of view, that seems like the best way to handle it. But it also leaves you without much of a starting point for anything."

"Others are probably more resilient."

"Most of those others didn't see their husbands murdered and lose their baby at the same time."

The stark truth of that bowed her head. She drew a shaky breath, hoping she wouldn't dissolve into tears again.

He slipped his arm around her shoulders and squeezed gently. "Just grant that you've been doing the best you can."

"I want to do better."

"You've made that clear." He paused for a moment, then said, "The way you need to think about the last year or so is that you were wounded. And it takes time to heal. So while you're recovering, there are lots of things your body won't let you do. Or in your case, your mind and emotions. Things that need to rest will rest."

"I hardly think being totally terrified was much of a rest."

"How can you know?"

"What do you mean?" She turned her head to look at him.

"Maybe the fear was a rest from things that were even harder for you to bear."

That drew her up short. She hadn't thought of it that

way before, not at all. "Maybe," she said finally. "I know how it's been feeling, though."

"How's that?"

"Like I've been stuck in a quagmire of awful feelings with no way out."

"And now?"

"I see a door. I don't like what might be on the other side. It scares me. But, like I said, I've got to crawl out of this swamp or I'm going to die anyway."

"We'll get you out."

He sounded so confident. She wished she could be as sure. But life offered absolutely no guarantees, and if she had just accepted that months ago, she might have already started to construct a new life.

Of course, if she had done that, she'd still be sitting here worried that the killer might have found her. Would it have made it any easier for her if she'd allowed herself to put down all those roots she was thinking of now? Not one bit.

In fact, it might have become even scarier. And this was already going to be scary enough.

# CHAPTER EIGHT

SHE TRIED TO pass the time reading a book, but that didn't work at all. Wade prowled the house from time to time only to return to the living room and sit for a while. She had no idea if he was peering out windows or what. Maybe he just couldn't hold still.

She could barely stand it herself. Finally she closed the book and looked at him. "Are we supposed to just sit here indefinitely like bumps on a log?"

One corner of Wade's mouth lifted and he came to sit beside her on the sofa. "What would you ordinarily do?"

"Exactly this," she admitted. "Only now I'm too antsy."

"Well, I don't think we should do anything until Gage tells us he has his ducks in a row. Waiting is always the hardest part."

She pursed her lips, trying to find some way to anticipate what might come next. "This guy, this killer, he wasn't afraid to come to our house in the dead of night, knock on the door and shoot everything that moved."

"Apparently not."

"So what's to keep him from doing the same thing here?"

"Nothing, except that I'm an unknown in the equation. That won't hold him back indefinitely, but I'm sure it's giving him pause."

"What kind of pause?"

"He's probably wondering just what kind of protection

I can provide. Whether there's a way he can separate us. All of which is based on the assumption that he's really found you."

She sighed. "I wish I knew for certain."

"There are times when you can act, and times when you simply have to react. This is one of those times that we have to wait to react. Because we don't know anything for certain."

She felt a crooked smile twist her lips. "Listen to me. I spent more than a year just letting myself be pushed one way or another and now all of a sudden I want to do something. Anything."

"I know that feeling."

"You probably do." She looked down at the book she was still holding. "I still can't understand what they thought they'd accomplish by killing Jim. It's not like they could erase the grand-jury testimony, or prevent indictments from being handed down."

"I don't know. Maybe they thought that if they removed one prosecutor, the government would have a hard time finding someone else to take over. Intimidation is the only reason I can see."

"I doubt it worked."

"But you don't know?"

She shook her head. "Jim didn't talk about his cases with me. He couldn't. So even if I tried to check newspaper stories or court records, I couldn't tell which case was his."

"But you knew he was after a drug gang."

"That was all I knew. And I'm sure he wasn't the only prosecutor working on a case like that. In a way it's hard not knowing if all his work put those guys in jail. But at the same time…" She shrugged. "What difference does it really make? It won't change anything. Not for me, or Jim, or our baby."

He turned her a little, cupping her chin with his hand, and kissed her gently. "I'm so sorry."

If he meant the kiss to be comforting, it went beyond that. Way beyond that. She wished she knew how his kiss could drive everything else from her mind in a flash. And this one hadn't even attempted to be sexy.

She searched his dark eyes and caught her breath as she saw the heat there. She wasn't alone in her sudden desire, not alone at all. Yet he didn't press her, didn't even try to tip her in that direction.

His hunger for her went straight to her head, lifting her out of herself so that she forgot everything except this man and the heaviness growing between her thighs, a heaviness that demanded an answer.

There was something incredible in arousing a man so powerful and self-contained so easily and quickly. Maybe it was the only way he felt he could truly connect anymore. Maybe he would have responded that way to any woman.

She didn't care. She knew what she wanted, and it was right in front of her. In his eyes she could see that he wanted it, too.

Her fingers moved before she realized it, reaching for the buttons of his shirt. He waited, letting her unfasten them, watching her face intently the whole time. When the last button was undone, she looked down at this chest and sighed.

"You're beautiful," she said, meaning it. Pressing her palms to that wonderful, warm skin, she ran her hands over him, feeling the rocks and rills of honed muscle, glorying in the sensations and in the way he indulged her exploration.

A slightly ragged breath escaped him. "Are you sure?" he murmured. "Very sure?"

"Yes." The word came out on the last puff of air in her

lungs, and hardly had it escaped her, than he scooped her up in his powerful arms and carried her back toward her bedroom.

"I won't stop this time," he warned her. "No half measures."

"I don't want half measures." The truest words she had spoken in a long, long time.

"No quarter," he said.

She wasn't sure what he meant by that, but she was eager to take this ride all the way to the end. Not only did she want this, she needed this. All of it.

He laid her on the bed in her half-darkened room and stood over her like a hero of myth, so big, so hard, almost unreal in his strength and power.

He shrugged off his shirt, then made it clear what was coming when he reached for his belt and the snap of his jeans.

Was she sure? Oh, yes. She watched with hungry fascination, hearing each tooth in the zipper as he drew it slowly down. It was the sexiest sound she had ever heard.

"Stop me now," he said, pausing. "Now."

"No." His own word flung back at him.

She dragged her gaze up from where his hands rested against his fly and saw a lazy smile start to curve his mouth. His eyelids drooped a little with passion, but the rest of his face hardened with hunger.

He kicked off his shoes, then in one smooth movement shoved his pants down and discarded his socks. When he straightened, he was naked to her gaze, and what a breathtaking sight he was.

Michelangelo had never carved a more perfect male body. Nor had anyone to her knowledge ever carved a statue with an erection like that. He was big, he was hard and he was ready.

And the sight of his readiness made her damp, so damp she might have been embarrassed if she weren't already in thrall to her needs. And his. For his need excited her even more than her own.

He bent over her, his fingers pausing just briefly as he once again warned her. "Last chance."

She had begun to pant with the hunger he had already stoked in her, and it was hard to say one word, just one word: "Yesss…"

He stripped her clothes away impatiently, tossing each piece across the room until she lay naked. He paused a moment, drinking her with his eyes, leaving her feeling at once utterly vulnerable and utterly beautiful. No one had ever looked at her like that before, not even Jim, as if she were the most desirable woman he had ever seen. Just that look was enough to make her nipples harden and her center throb so hard it almost hurt.

In that instant, she became woman primal. Everything else vanished entirely. Nothing mattered except this man and this moment. She hardly noticed that he used the few seconds to don protection, because she watched his eyes as they traveled over her like a caress.

Lying over her, his leg pinning hers, his arms holding her tight, he plundered her mouth with a kiss so hungry and needful it echoed all the pain inside her. His hands began to knead her flesh with a heat and longing that just missed being painful. She didn't care. Each touch made her feel so wanted, and oh, heavens, how much she needed to feel wanted.

His mouth closed on her nipple, sending spears of longing straight to her womb. His hand stroked the smooth skin of her hip, and then dived impatiently between her thighs, seeking her heat, her moisture, her life-giving core. She was caught in a storm, with no desire to escape. Whatever he took seemed rightfully his.

Raising his head, he muttered guttural words of encouragement as his touch lifted her higher and higher. Too fast, she thought dizzily, but even that objection drifted away as he took her closer and closer to the brink she dimly sensed was waiting.

"So sweet," he muttered in her ear, and yet another river of excitement poured through her. "Come on, Cory, that's the way."

When her hands clawed at him and the sheets, needing something to hang on to, he grabbed them and moved them upward, wrapping her fingers around the spindles of her headboard. "Hang on," he muttered roughly. "Don't let go." Then he settled between her legs.

Gasping for air, clinging so tightly to the headboard that she dimly felt her hands aching, she opened her eyes and looked up at him. He loomed over her in the dim room, huge and powerful, so strong. She had never imagined, never dreamed, that anything could be as overwhelming as these moments. Every cell in her body was begging for him, begging for completion, for the answer to the screaming ache he had awakened in her body.

He touched her, gently. He found that delicate knot of nerves, then rubbed so carefully, lifting her higher and higher until she hung suspended in exquisite agony and nearly screamed his name.

"Now," he demanded. Slipping an arm beneath her hips, he lifted her to him and took her in one swift, deep thrust, filling an emptiness she had forgotten could exist.

The precipice was close, so close, and his every movement drove her nearer the edge. Letting go of the headboard, she grabbed his shoulders, digging her fingers into smooth, muscled flesh, drawing him down, needing his weight on her as she had seldom needed anything. Needing him.

"Let it happen," he growled in her ear. "Damn it, let it happen!"

Then, with a single, long, deep thrust of his hips, he pushed her over the edge. Moments later his face contorted and he followed her over.

Cory thought the explosion inside her would never end.

THEY LAY TANGLED together, sweaty and exhausted. Too weary and sated, Cory thought, to work up even a smidgen of fear. The best medicine in the world.

When Wade tried to lever himself off her, she grabbed his shoulders, afraid he might leave.

"I'm not going anywhere," he murmured. He slid off her, to lie beside her on his back, still breathing heavily.

The air felt cool against her hot, damp skin, another delicious contrast. Yes, they needed to cool down, but she hated not feeling the touch of his skin. When she blindly reached out with her hand, his was there to grip hers and hold it. When she gave his fingers a little squeeze, he squeezed back.

"Why can't life always be like this?" she asked softly. As soon as the question emerged, she knew reality was returning, and there was no way to hold it off.

"If life were always like this, we'd never do anything else." He surprised her with a note of humor in his voice.

She turned on her side and smiled at him, a smile that felt easier than any she'd tried to frame in fifteen months. "Would that be so bad?"

A small chuckle escaped him. "No way."

Reaching out, she trailed a finger over his still-damp chest and downward to his hip bone. His manhood responded with a small leap. "Mmm, I could get used to this."

"Used to what?" he asked.

"Having you at my mercy."

"Ah!" In one swift movement, so fast it caught her utterly by surprise, he pushed her on her back and leaned over her, his leg imprisoning hers, his dark eyes holding her. "Who is at whose mercy?"

A truly silly smile rose to her lips. "I like it either way."

"Good." Now he ran a fingertip over her, tracing circles around her breasts and down to her belly, causing her to shiver. "We'll take turns."

"Soon?" she asked hopefully.

"Soon," he said, one corner of his mouth lifting. "But maybe not right now."

She sighed. "Okay."

He lowered his head and brushed a light kiss on her lips. "I'd like nothing better, Cory. But Gage will probably call soon."

She couldn't argue with that, though she wanted to push back the dark shadows that edged into the corners of her mind. Yes, there were things they had to face, maybe had to face soon, but she felt a huge tide of resentment, something she'd never felt before. Before it had always been the fear and grief, leaving room for little else.

"I resent this," she announced, then instantly regretted her words as she saw him pull back a little. Of course he would misunderstand. "Not you," she hastily said. "I just hate that I'm feeling good for the first time in forever and now I have to think of...of..."

"I understand." His infinitesimal withdrawal vanished as he moved closer, and dropped another light kiss on her mouth.

"How bad was it?" she asked, stroking his short hair as he laid his cheek on her breast.

"What?"

"Your childhood."

He stiffened a bit, and said nothing. Time seemed to drag as she held her breath, wondering if she had pushed too far into tender territory. It really was none of her business, and she suspected this was a man who didn't like admitting his vulnerability, despite what he had tried to share with her over coffee in the wee hours.

"It was bad," he said finally. "I spent a lot of time locked in closets. My dad was fond of whipping me with the buckle end of his belt."

"My God!"

"I survived."

"But…"

He reached up and laid a finger over her mouth. "I survived," he said firmly. "What doesn't kill you makes you stronger."

"You really believe that?"

"Yes."

Perhaps, she thought. Perhaps. But surviving didn't necessarily mean the scars were gone, either emotionally or physically. She had sensed the emotional ones quickly, in some of his almost apologetic statements. As if he felt a need to erase himself. Another thought occurred to her.

"Do you feel like a fish out of water now, away from the SEALs, I mean?"

At that he lifted his head. "Lady, if you're going to ask a man to bare his soul, it might be best to let him choose the time and place."

She felt hurt. Unreasonably so, she tried to tell herself, but it didn't quite erase the pang. Logically she knew that women were more likely to become emotionally attached through the act of lovemaking than men, and logically she realized the experience they had just shared had probably made her feel a whole lot closer to him than it had made him feel to her. They were strangers, after all, brought together by a coincidence, and now held together by a threat. He undoubtedly planned to move on as soon as he sorted out whatever it was he had come here to deal with.

And she would be left alone again. Common sense dictated that she not allow herself to grow close to this man. She needed to think of their lovemaking as merely a way to affirm life, and not one thing more.

She ought to know better, and clutching at straws just because a man was decent enough not to leave her in the lurch with this mess was dangerous. She didn't think she could take another loss, so why set herself up for one?

She tried to smile at him, but her face felt pinched. "I need to get dressed. Gage might call at any minute."

"Ah, hell," he said and rolled onto his back.

She looked at him and saw he was staring at the ceiling now. "What?"

"I just hurt you, and I really didn't want to do that."

She felt another pang, this time for him. "No. Really. It's just a girl thing, expecting confidences at a time like this. I know better."

He turned his head to look at her. "I should know better, too. I'm sorry."

Then he jackknifed up off the bed and started hunting up clothes. Hers he dropped beside her on the bed. He climbed into his own swiftly, and left the room before he even finished buttoning and zipping.

One hot tear rolled down Cory's face. She had tried to reach out, and had reached out in exactly the wrong way at the wrong time.

Why would any man want her anyway? She had become

a terrified husk of a woman, with nothing left inside her that anyone else would want.

She definitely ought to know better.

WADE STOOD IN the kitchen, filled with self-loathing. He had started another pot of coffee brewing, because coffee had fueled him through some of the most difficult times in his life and had become a habit he clung to the way some people clung to a cup of tea or a blanket for comfort.

He'd drunk it instant, mixed with water barely safe for drinking. He'd sucked it down hot and thick on shipboard. He'd guzzled it thin and watery when what few grounds he had needed to be reused. It didn't much matter how it tasted as much as it mattered that he could cradle a cup in his hands and take comfort in one of life's small habits.

Despite warning himself, he'd taken the step: he'd made love to the woman. And despite warning her and himself that he couldn't make connections, he'd taken the one action most likely to create a connection. You didn't make love to a woman like that and expect her to treat it as a form of entertainment.

So he'd taken that all-too-critical step, he'd started forming a connection, a connection he absolutely believed himself incapable of sustaining. If he had an ounce of common sense, he'd rupture it right now, pack his bags and get out of here before he did some real harm.

He couldn't do that, not with the threat he believed to be lurking. Yes, he knew the sheriff and his entire department would be keeping an eye on Cory. No, he didn't have an inflated sense of his own importance.

But he did know how the best net in the world remained a sieve simply because you couldn't plug every hole, and unless Gage meant to assign someone round the clock to stick to Cory's side—and he doubted that because this was a small county and probably had a force just big enough for the ordinary tasks it faced—then someone had to be pinned to Cory's side. Someone who knew how to handle threats like this.

That left him.

Even if others had such training hereabouts, he doubted it was as fresh as his own. He doubted their reflexes remained so honed that the merest glimpse of something moving out of the corner of their eyes could shift them instantly into hyperdrive.

It was true that you never forgot your training, but you could slow down. Hell, hadn't he come here intending to do just that?

So that likely made him the meanest, fastest SOB around here right now. Walking away was not an option.

What to do about Cory? She'd naturally felt their love-making had brought them closer, and to be fair, he kind of felt it, too. Not like with the women who'd just wanted to sleep with a SEAL. This was different. Different kind of woman, different kind of experience.

Hell, he wasn't even proud of the way he'd made love to her, so rough and ready, without any of the hearts-and-flowers-type stuff she deserved.

He'd been strung out on need in a way he'd never felt before, and all the self-control he owned seemed to have been focused on giving her a chance to say no. When she hadn't, his self-control had vanished.

And then, after his caveman routine, all she had wanted was to feel closer to him. To know that she hadn't been used like some plastic fantastic lover.

Cripes. He leaned his forehead against the cabinet, waiting for the coffee, and asked himself how he had just managed to mess up two people with one thoughtless act.

But that was him, wasn't it? The whole relationship

thing was beyond him, always had been. The relationships he had managed over the years had been built on shared experience and trust within the boundaries of his job. With Cory he had no rules, no guidelines, no purpose other than making sure she survived until they figured out what was going on here.

And he didn't know how to handle it. The only thing he knew for certain was that Cory was as fragile as fine glass emotionally, and he'd probably just added a ding, if not a crack.

He ought to be hanged.

"Wade?"

Her tentative voice reached him from the kitchen entryway. He screwed his eyes shut and tried to get a grip on his self-disgust. "Yeah?"

"I'm sorry. I shouldn't have asked."

He whirled about to find her standing there, clothed once again, her eyes pinched and lost-looking. She was apologizing when he'd put that look back on her face.

"Goddamn it," he said.

Her head jerked. "I'll just leave you alone."

"No."

She hesitated, wrapping her arms around herself as if she needed to hold something in, or hold herself together. "No?" she repeated.

"No. Grab a seat. Stay."

Still she hesitated, but then, after what seemed an eternity, she moved to the table and sat. She kept on hugging herself though, a sure indicator that all was not right in the world of Cory Farland.

He turned his back to her. "I stink at this," he said. Once again he pressed his forehead to the cabinet, glad the coffee hadn't finished yet because it gave him time not to look at her.

"Stink at what?"

"I told you. Connections. Relationships. Whatever the current terminology is. I'm the guy sitting alone at the back of the bar with a beer while the others shoot the breeze. I don't talk about much that isn't mission specific. Nobody really knows me, and I like it that way."

"Because you can't be hurt."

An impatient sound escaped him. "Don't give me the psychobabble. Even if it is true."

"Okay."

The coffee finished, and his excuse was gone. He pulled two mugs from the cupboard and filled them before he carried them to the table. Then he got her milk for her and put it in front of her.

He straddled the chair facing her, but didn't look at her. He didn't want to see that pinched expression again.

"I'm a minefield," he said finally. "Loaded with emotional trip wires. Yeah, I was abused as a kid. So were lots of other people, so don't give me any special passes because of it. I got away as soon as I could, and I promised myself I'd never get into that position again, a position where anyone could beat me up like that. The navy picked me up out of the mud, basically, restored my self-confidence, gave me a purpose and a goal. But they couldn't take away the trip wires. So I learned to keep them buried because they're absolutely useless. What the hell good does it do to keep reacting to things that happened twenty, thirty years ago when they're not still happening?"

She made a little sound but he couldn't tell if she was agreeing.

"What matters," he said finally, "is who I am now. What I became over the years. Unfortunately, I never got around to the part about dealing with people I didn't have a professional relationship with. So I stink at it."

"Mmm." Totally noncommittal. Well, what did he expect when he'd basically told her to shut up while he spewed?

Finally he raised his eyes and looked at her. At least she didn't look ready to shatter any longer. If anything, her face had grown calmer.

"I don't want to talk about when I was a kid," he said. "I don't need to talk about it. I got past it the day I realized that if my old man ever came at me like that again I could snap him in two."

She gave a little nod.

"I got past the fear. I got past most of the anger. I got past the feeling of helplessness."

"Good." She lifted her cup and sipped her coffee. "Good."

"Anything that's left is my own fault, not theirs in any way."

"Really."

"Really." And he didn't want to argue about this. "Anything I'm dealing with now is baggage I picked up all on my own."

"Such as?"

"Things I saw, things I did, things I chose not to do. If there's one thing I learned from being in the service, it's that ultimately I'm responsible for myself. The past is past, and it's useless except as a lesson for doing it better next time."

She drew a long breath. "You really believe that?"

"Yes. I do. And I'm quite capable of looking at the things I chose not to do over the years and taking responsibility for them. I chose to let my professional life consume me, I chose not to try to branch out into some kind of normal life. Admittedly, watching my buddies, I eventually concluded it wasn't worth the trouble. At least not while I was still on the job. So it's my fault and nobody else's that I chose not to learn how to build day-to-day relationships apart from the job."

"So you take that whole burden on yourself?"

"Of course. I made the decisions."

"That's a pretty heavy load. Most of us at least accept that our pasts played a role in making us who we are."

"I'm not saying it didn't play a role. But I'm the one, in the end, who says how much and what kind of a role. I'm not arguing that I'm not a product of my past, I'm arguing that I'm a product of the decisions I made in my past."

She nodded slowly, and his gut clenched a bit when he saw her face tightening up. "What?" he asked. "What did I say?"

Her lips tightened. "I'm just thinking about what you said. So you don't even think that as a child you were a victim?"

He shook his head impatiently. "I'm not saying that. When I was a kid, I handled what was dished out to me the best way I could figure out. Every kid does. And when we're kids, we don't have the breadth of experience that comes later, so we're easy to victimize. But later…no. Which is not to say no one is ever a victim. I'm not saying that at all."

"Then what are you saying?" she asked, her voice stretched tight.

"I'm saying that it's what we choose to do with it that puts us in control. It's the choices we make, and the lessons we choose to take. And I made some god-awful choices, and maybe I took some of the wrong lessons. That's what I'm saying, and I'm not going to blame any of it on the kid I used to be, because I was a man when I made a lot of these decisions."

She gave a single, jerky nod.

"Cory...what? Am I hurting you? Crap, I don't want to do that."

"No...no. You're making me think."

Oh, hell. He suddenly realized how she could be taking this. "I'm not criticizing you. I'm not saying you weren't a victim."

"I know that. I get that. It's just that..."

He waited, and when she didn't speak, he finally prodded. "Just that what?"

"Just that you're right. I've kind of been thinking along the same lines over the past couple of days. That bastard stole my husband, my baby, my old life. But I'm still breathing. So what did I do? I crawled into a hole in the ground and stopped living. I chose to let him take away even my hope."

"Aw, hell." He couldn't take any more of this. He rose from the table, knocking over the chair and ignoring it. He rounded to her and scooped her right up out of her chair, carrying her to the living room where he sat with her in his lap.

"You don't get it," he whispered, hugging her close. "You didn't do anything wrong. Everyone needs time to heal before they can get going again. You needed the time. You needed it. I keep telling you that. What if you'd had your leg blown off? Do you think you could skip surgery and rehab? Of course not. All I'm trying to tell you is that I take responsibility for the fact that I chose not to learn basic life skills. Like how to talk to a lady. Like how to reach out. Like how to share myself."

"Actually," she said brokenly, "I think you're doing a damn fine job of it right now."

"Not good enough. I've hurt you twice in the past half hour. I'm ham-fisted at this."

Her hand gripped his shirt, balling it. "Listen to yourself. Just listen. You'll make all kinds of excuses for me, but none for yourself. Think about that, Wade. The people who used to beat you up are gone from your life. So what do you do? You beat yourself up for them."

He grew so still and silent that she almost panicked. Had she done it again? Pushed him to places he was unwilling to go, to even look at? She tensed herself, in expectation that he'd toss her off his lap and walk out the door never to be seen again.

But then, finally, she felt him relax. His hand covered hers, where it knotted his shirt, and held it.

"Maybe you're right," he said gruffly.

"Maybe you think you can't make connections, but have you ever tried? You're doing just fine with me."

"But I hurt you."

"So? That's part of any relationship. People hurt each other. When it's unintentional, it's okay. I don't think you want to hurt me. Do you?"

"Hell no."

"Then okay. It happens." She sighed. "Do you think my marriage to Jim was pure perfection? We had our fights. We hurt each other sometimes. The important thing is forgiving and forgetting when the hurt wasn't intentional. That's how you make a relationship that works."

He turned that around in his mind, giving her credit for being far more adult in some ways than he was. "With me a person would need the patience of a saint."

"Same here." She squirmed a little on his lap, reminding him that he still wanted her like hell on fire, then rested her head against his shoulder. "We've all got trip wires, Wade. Fact of life. And when those wires get laid by terrible emotional experiences, they're hard to get rid of."

"Well, I laid a lot more of them over the years." He didn't have to look very far back to see where they'd come from. "Combat vets get lots of them. A sound. A sight. A smell. Even a word. I told you I can't hold still. That's not purely my training at work. It's my learning."

"Learning?"

"How long do you think you can live on the edge before living on the edge becomes the only way to live? You think you can unwind just because you're home, out of the zone? Too many of us drink too much because it's the only way to wind down. Others of us just live with the constant skin-crawling feeling that something is about to happen, that we can't relax for even a minute."

She nodded against his shoulder, just a small movement. "I've lived that way for a little over a year. You've lived that way your whole life. Insecure, sure something bad is always just around the corner."

"Yeah. It makes me explosive, like a bomb." He sighed, not sure where he wanted to take this, not sure why he was spilling his guts like this. Maybe he was hoping that his warning would get through, that she'd back away. Or maybe he was hoping that the next time he did or said something wrong she'd understand he didn't mean to hurt her.

But regardless of what she understood, he would hurt her. He'd slam an emotional door in her face, or retreat behind his personal drawbridge. In one way or another, he'd go into self-protection mode, and once he got into that mode, he might well stage a preemptive attack.

"You've got to understand," he said roughly. "You have to."

"Understand what?"

"That protecting myself is automatic. Regardless of the kind of threat."

She tipped her head against his shoulder and he knew she was looking up at him. He refused to look back at her.

Let her read what she could from his chin; he wouldn't give her any more than that. Not right now. Maybe never.

"Okay," she said finally. "You protect yourself. I understand that."

A frustrated sound escaped him. "Do you understand what that might mean?"

"Maybe not in every detail. But I get the general picture."

He envied the note of confidence in her voice, but he didn't believe it. Whatever this woman had been through in her life, and the little she had told him had been bad enough, he didn't think it could possibly prepare her for what he could dish out. She had absolutely no idea of all that he was capable of.

But he did. That was the curse of so many years in Special ops. You knew what your limits were, and worse, you discovered you didn't have a whole lot of them. Whatever the mission required. And sometimes the mission was your own self-protection.

That didn't mean he was ashamed of himself, because he wasn't. But it did mean he knew himself in ways most people never faced. Most people never needed to look into the darkest parts of human nature. And people like him were the reason they never had to. But those who had looked…well, they lived in an uncomfortable world with all the rosy tint stripped away.

It was a sad fact of life that someone needed to visit those black places, that someone needed to come face-to-face with the ugliest things in the human heart and soul.

But those who went there remained apart and different because once you'd looked into the abyss, it became part of you.

She thought she understood, God bless her. She thought because she had seen the terrible thing the night the killer came to her house, that she had some idea. But she had no idea at all, because seeing was not the same as doing. Sometimes a person like Cory glimpsed the abyss. But folks like him not only glimpsed it. They walked into it. They melded with it.

And when they returned they were forever changed in ways only someone who had trod the path with them could imagine.

So how the hell did you get around that?

# CHAPTER NINE

GAGE CALLED DURING the early afternoon. Cory got the cord-less-extension phone from her bedroom so they could both listen to him and talk as necessary.

"Okay," Gage said. "I've got both pictures going out to all deputies. They're not being told anything about you, Cory, just that I want these guys hauled in on sight for questioning in a possible homicide case. They're to be treated as armed and dangerous."

Cory caught her breath inaudibly at the description, then wondered why. It wasn't as if she didn't already know how dangerous these guys were. But somehow hearing it from Gage's lips made the threat seem more imminent. He had removed it from the realm of speculation and put it out there as reality.

Only as she felt her heart slam in response did she realize just how much denial she had been living with. Yes, she'd been afraid, maybe even ridiculously afraid all this time, but at some level she had desperately believed this moment would never come. And even now a part of her brain insisted on saying, *We don't know for sure.*

And that was true. They were acting on little more than suspicion and a confluence of coincidences. As Jim had so often said of such things, "It won't stand up in court."

Gage knew that, surely. Yet he was moving forward as if a real threat had been made.

And maybe it had, in that phone call. It had certainly

been made a year ago when the Marshals decided they had to put her into permanent protection. After all, it wasn't as if they were manufacturing a paranoid conspiracy out of whole cloth.

She barely listened to the discussion the two men were having. It was as if a switch had been thrown at the instant she had faced the naked threat yet again. Once again she felt numb, utterly numb, perhaps even hollow. Yet there seemed to be no place left inside her for the fear, or even anger. In fact, even the spark of hope that had ignited in her over the past couple of days had deserted her.

There was nothing, could be nothing for her ever, unless she got this threat off her back for good.

Sitting there, hardly hearing as the two men talked, she faced the dismal reality of what her life had become and what it would remain as long as that killer was after her.

There would be no recovery, no hope, no future. That was what that man and his vendetta had done to her. He might as well have finished her off with a bullet to the head.

She couldn't go back to the woman she had been just a few days ago. Because over the past few days, she had tasted hope and life again, however briefly. She might have found just the illusion of it in Wade's arms, but it was enough to make her realize she could not go back. Whatever the cost.

Into the emptiness crept a steely resolve unlike anything she had ever felt before. Death, she knew in her heart, was infinitely preferable to the way she had been existing. She could not, would not, go back to that.

Nor did she pin her hopes for a future on Wade. She understood that he was a troubled, complex, complicated man who had come here seeking some kind of release, but he would have to find that on his own. Just as she would have to find her own resolve to live again, for herself.

No crutches, for they were unreliable, and temporary at best. So, she thought, as ice seemed to settle over her, she would deal with this mess. Then she would look for the woman she wanted to become. The woman who had once loved being a teacher. The woman who had enjoyed cooking as if her own kitchen was part of the finest restaurant.

And perhaps she'd discover other parts of herself in the process, parts she'd never had a chance to find before because she'd been too preoccupied with her goals, and then with Jim.

She was, she resolved, going to find her own two feet.

And the first step was getting rid of this threat. Allowing it to steal not one more day of her life.

She hung up the phone before the two men even finished their conversation. The details of what they planned really didn't matter.

All that mattered was that she was going to face down her husband's killer or die trying.

It DIDN'T TAKE Wade long to notice the change in her. She sensed him start watching her more closely a couple of hours later. She didn't care. He could watch her all he wanted. If she'd had a psychological break of some kind, it was a beneficial one.

She had had enough.

If that meant turning into an ice queen until this was over, then that was fine by her. Remembering how she had collapsed only two days ago after that phone call, she looked at herself and decided ice was infinitely preferable to that. Death was infinitely preferable to that. She had paid the price for someone else's criminal act long enough.

She started dinner at her usual time. Wade joined her,

but didn't say anything. Nor did she have much to say, except to give him directions, since he seemed determined to help. Nothing personal. Nothing emotive. Just dry, flat instructions.

She felt no particular desire to eat, recognizing her hunger only as a sign she needed fuel. She didn't even allow herself to enjoy the tasks in the kitchen. Not now. No way.

Not even in the littlest way did she want to feel regret for what was gone. No room for that now.

Finally, over dinner, he asked, "What's going on?"

"What do you mean?"

"You've got a thousand-yard stare."

That at least caught her interest. "What's that?"

"It's the way men look coming out of battle. Distant. Shut down."

She forked some salad and ate it, pondering the comment as an intellectual exercise, having no other reaction to it. "I guess that would about cover it," she finally said.

"Did something happen?"

She barely glanced at him. "I've had enough. That's all. This gets finished if I have to hunt that man myself."

"I see."

He probably did. She returned to eating.

He resumed eating, too. But after a few minutes he spoke. "I get worried when I see that look."

"Oh? Why?"

"Because when I see it, it means someone really has had enough. That the only way they can keep from breaking is to totally withdraw. It's usually a sign of post-traumatic stress disorder."

"Hmm. Well, I probably have that, too."

"Probably."

Again silence fell. Then, "Cory?"

"What?"

"It's not good."

She raised her gaze from her plate. "What's not good? That I've decided enough is enough? That I've decided I'm going to get my life back or die trying?"

He shook his head. "That's not what I mean."

"Then what do you mean?"

"Shutting down. Not caring. That's dangerous. I've seen men do stupid things and get themselves killed when they have that look in their eyes."

She simply looked at him, then resumed eating. Go back to what she had felt before? No way. This was infinitely preferable to feeling.

Wade didn't say any more as they finished the meal. She barely tasted it. Fuel, nothing more. He joined her in the washing up, so it didn't take long.

Then there was nothing to do except wait. The thing was, she didn't want to wait. Not anymore. The Sword of Damocles no longer frightened her, but it was still hanging over her head.

"I'm going to take a walk," she announced.

"Not without me."

"I didn't say I was going alone."

"Okay," he said. "Okay."


OH, HE DIDN'T like that look in her eyes at all. He pulled on his boots, lacing them tightly, readying himself. He even went so far as to put his sheathed knife on his belt, then let his shirttails hang out over it. He could throw that knife with as much accuracy over short distances as he could hit a target with a gun from seven hundred yards. These were some of the skills he'd learned, used and had to live with.

And since he couldn't carry a rifle with him on the streets, the knife would have to do. As would the garrote he stuck into his pocket, and the three plastic ties that could double as handcuffs.

Even if he went to prison for the rest of his life for it, he would allow nothing to harm Cory. Nothing. The certainty settled into his heart with entirely too much familiarity. It was not a new feeling, and he knew to the nth degree what he could do when he felt like this.

He supposed he was now wearing his own thousand-yard stare. The calm of imminent battle had settled over him.

The feeling was as familiar as a well-broken pair of boots, like those he had just donned. Comfortable, but that didn't mean he liked it. He'd been in enough battles to know better. Even success seldom left a good taste in his mouth. Or a totally quiet conscience.

Even less did he like the way the skin on the back of his neck crawled. It was back, all of it, just like that: everything he'd tried to shed and untangle over the past six months resurrected as if it had never gone away.

The man he wanted to leave behind took over now, emerging front and center almost mockingly. It didn't matter, though. This was the man he had chosen to become over many years, and now he needed to be that man again. For Cory's sake.

Whatever it took. Mission-specific goals became paramount, pushing everything else into the background. The man he had hoped he might become would just have to wait for another day.

Even in battle mode, however, he wished Cory wouldn't take this walk. It would create unnecessary, uncontrolled exposure. Things like this should be planned in advance, contingencies reviewed.

But much as he wished she wouldn't do this, he could see that nothing was going to stop her short of breaking the law and keeping her a prisoner in her own home. As he had said, when he saw that look in someone's eye, he knew they were capable of doing something stupid.

All he could do was call Gage and tell him what he and Cory were about to do.

"Are you out of your minds?" Gage asked.

"I can't stop her short of imprisoning her. You want to come argue?"

"Hell. All right, I'll see if I can get some people in the vicinity fast."

After he hung up the phone, he went to meet Cory at the front door. Her eyes remained flat and empty, but her body was moving impatiently. God, he knew that feeling all too well.

"I can't talk you out of this?" he asked quietly.

She just looked at him and switched off the alarm. He was the one who had to punch it to reset it before they slipped out the door.

This was definitely not good.

She paused on the front porch as if deciding which direction to take.

"You need to think," he said.

"I am thinking."

"No, you're trying to take the bull by the horns without any adequate preparation. You should stay inside and let me scout first."

"I want my life back. And I'm through waiting for that bastard to give it back."

He could understand that. He could even identify with it. What worried him was the flatness of her statement. If she'd been angry or upset, he'd have had a chance to reason with her. But in this state, there would be no reasoning.

She turned away from the park. He took it as a good sign. She might be utterly reckless with her own safety, but not even in her present mood was she prepared to risk the families and children who might be in the park.

She walked briskly, as if she had somewhere to go. That was fine by him. His own senses went on high alert, his field of vision widening as he slipped into the mode where his brain paid as much attention to his peripheral vision as to his central field. Maybe more. For most people that happened only with an adrenaline rush. For him it happened from long practice.

The same thing with his hearing. The brain usually filtered most sounds, prioritizing and even making people unaware of background noise at a conscious level. But like a person who'd been hard of hearing for a while and had just gotten his first hearing aid, when he went into this mode every sound became equally important, and none were dismissed as mere distraction.

Hyperaware, hyperalert. All without a whisper of adrenaline. Unfortunately, Cory had none of his training, and in her current state, she most likely wouldn't have adrenaline to sharpen her senses.

Which made her a liability.

Cripes, he hoped she walked off this mood. It wasn't that he wanted her to be terrified, but a reasonable caution would be nice. A person couldn't make good decisions without even a modicum of fear in a dangerous situation.

Which was what he had been trying to tell her a little while ago. And she just plain wasn't listening.

Well, it wasn't as if he hadn't seen this before. Hadn't dealt with it before. It could happen to a man at any time: after his first battle, after a particularly nasty or long-lasting fight, or for no discernible reason at all. It just happened. Some cog slipped and everything shut down.

He supposed it was a form of self-protection and probably had its uses as long as it didn't go on too long, or start happening inappropriately.

They took a power walk, as he'd heard some describe it. Not quite running or jogging, but it would have been impossible to move any faster and still call it walking. When he glanced at Cory, he saw her face was still set in a blank expression, and perspiration had begun to give her skin a dewy look.

But he didn't look at her often. With his senses stretched he was trying to take in and process every sight, sound and smell within reach.

And he memorized the layout of the area for several miles around Cory's house. It pleased him about as much as the mountains of Afghanistan had. This might not be mountains with boulders and caves to hide behind at every turn, but the houses, garages, cars, trees and shrubs served the same purpose, and like many older towns, the houses nearly hugged each other. The people who had originally built this area had been looking for comfort in numbers, not privacy by lawns.

He wondered if she had any idea that pacing up and down every street as she did was a good recon. Probably not. Such things were undoubtedly far from her mind.

And as they walked, he noticed an increasing number of patrol cars. Nothing truly obvious, but probably more of a show of force than this neighborhood routinely saw.

He honestly didn't know if that was good. Scaring these guys off temporarily would only delay the problem. But one thing he was sure of by the time they marched back up onto Cory's porch was that he'd caught no sight of the man, or either of his cars, that had set off his internal alarms.

What did that mean? He could think of answers both good and bad.

Inside the house, once he reset the alarm, he watched

Cory march down the hallway to her bedroom, then he heard her shower come on.

Damn, this house was stuffy. It held the day's warmth close, and the smells of their meal still filled the air. Imagine having lived like this for the past year, afraid to even open a window.

On impulse, he switched off the alarm, and opened a window in the living room, and another in her kitchen, allowing the freshening evening breeze to blow through. He could keep an eye on both while she showered, and the breeze would clear out the downstairs in only a few minutes.

Then it occurred to him that by shutting down the alarm system, he had left every window in the house unprotected against intrusion.

Well, hell. Sighing impatiently, he went back to the keypad and looked through all the warnings it gave him and finally got to the question about bypassing zones. He hesitated only a moment, taking time to scan the list of zones on the plastic card behind the keypad. Okay. He could switch off the living room and kitchen, and leave the rest of the house online.

He hit the bypass for each zone, then re-enabled the alarm. Now all he had to do was keep an eye out and wait to see what emerged from the shower. A woman who had collected herself, or one who remained withdrawn.

She did emerge finally, wearing a scanty tank top and shorts. He spared a moment to notice those lovely legs and graceful arms. She seemed not to notice he had opened the windows, nor to care, although she probably would shortly. The dry air held heat poorly, and as the sun sank the breeze had just begun to take on a chill.

Cory seemed oblivious, however, going to the living

room and sitting on the couch, staring at nothing in particular.

He decided he needed to try to engage her again. Try to draw her out of that netherworld where the brain and emotions went when they felt overwhelmed.

"Cory?"

She barely glanced at him.

"What happened?"

"What do you mean?"

At least she was answering him. "I mean what made you…" He hesitated, not wanting to use the word snap. A person in this state could switch from withdrawal to rage in an instant. "What pushed you over the edge?" he said finally, realizing there was no delicate way to phrase this.

"All of it."

"Well, yes." This was like walking through a minefield. "But something particular happened to put that look in your eye."

The slightest movement of her shoulder suggested a shrug. "You and Gage were talking on the phone. That's when I realized that I don't want to live this way anymore. I refuse to live this way any longer. I'm done with it."

Good. She was talking. "That's understandable."

"There's no point in living if I have to live this way. So I just won't do it anymore."

And that was where the danger lay. That came awfully close to suicidal thoughts. He sought a way to get through the cloak of detachment that shrouded her. "Making up your mind that you've had enough shouldn't lead you to act rashly."

"Why not?" Her hollow eyes regarded him unblinkingly. "Why should I put up with this one day, one hour, longer than necessary?"

"Because once we deal with this, it would be nice for you to be around to try building a new life."

"What am I supposed to build a new life with? That bastard took everything that mattered to me, directly or indirectly. Survival is not enough."

"Then what is?"

Finally he saw a spark of life in her gaze. Just a spark. "I don't know. I don't care anymore."

"Yes, you do."

She looked away, saying nothing.

"Admit it, Cory. In the past couple of days you've started to feel a little hope again. A little pleasure. You've tasted the idea that life could be good again."

"No." She turned to face him, and now she was angry. Good and angry. Part of the reaction, but in its own way as difficult to deal with as the distancing.

"Do you really think," she said, "that sex with you is enough to make life good again? Do you really think a hasty tumble in the hay is all I need to make things better? God, even a man should know better than that."

He didn't argue. She was right. Even if it stung.

"For the love of heaven," she said, jumping to her feet. "I'm living in a prison! I got a couple of hours of parole but that's all I got. And then I asked myself why I should start hoping again. What makes me think this mess is going to get any better? That there'll be anything left for me except ashes even if we do catch this guy."

She rounded on him. "The Marshals haven't caught him in all these months. Fifteen months the Marshals and FBI have been hunting this man and they can't find him. In fact, I bet if I checked with them, I'd find out he's moved down their priority list to a level below some escaped felon or some bank robber. Just another ice-cold case."

He remained silent, letting her rant however she needed to.

"If they ever find this guy, it's going to be because he comes after me. And now you and Gage even suspect that somebody must have revealed my location. Some protection. All they did was take away the little I had left. They should have just let me go home to my blood-soaked condo. At least I wouldn't have had to endure a year of this!"

She wrapped her arms around herself and began pacing the small living room. "What they did was put me in solitary confinement. You say you can't make connections? I haven't been able to because getting too close to someone increased the possibility that I'd say something I shouldn't. Look at how fast you picked up on it from things I didn't say. They told me I'd be safe once they moved me, but I never believed it. How could I believe it when they couldn't catch the gunman and I was the only one who could identify him? How could I believe it when that monster who killed my husband put a contract on me?"

"I don't know," he said quietly, mostly to show that he was listening.

"You know what I think?" she demanded.

"No."

"I think they put me into Witness Protection because I was an ongoing embarrassment. They couldn't catch the bad guy, they couldn't send me back to my life for fear I'd become a front-page scandal if I turned up dead. So they sent me away. Far away. And once they got me settled in this run-down house with a minimum-wage job, they handed me a couple of business cards and never looked back. Problem solved."

"You believe that?"

"What else am I supposed to believe? Here I am, a year

after they dumped me, and that killer may be after me because of them. He may have found me because of them."

"We don't know that."

"How else would he have found me here? Look around you, Wade. Does this look like the kind of place you try to hide a witness? Newcomers here stick out. So why the hell did they pick this place? Why not some major city where I'd be just one of millions?"

It was a good question and had already occurred to him. "Maybe they thought no one would ever look in a place like this."

"Clearly they may have been wrong. Regardless, here I am, all alone, facing the thing they said they were protecting me from."

He lowered his voice even more. "You're not alone."

"Not now. Because you just happened to land here looking for peace. Bet they didn't count on that."

Uneasiness began to creep through him. "Do you know what you're saying?"

"Yes!"

"There's just one problem with that. A phone call."

She threw up a hand. "So? Like you said, the guy needed to figure out which of a number of women who moved here in the last year was the right one. But if you're at all right about that call, and that guy we ran into, someone put him on my tail. And the only people aside from Gage who are supposed to know where I am are the Marshals."

He didn't speak, just turned her paranoia around in his mind, testing it for validity.

"I mean, how am I supposed to know that Seth Hardin sent you here? Because Gage said so? Because Gage said you've got a wall full of medals and you check out? That doesn't mean you didn't come here for some other purpose.

I can't even trust you. You're a trained killer yourself and you figured out my situation pretty darn fast."

At that, everything inside him went still, cold and silent. Everything she said was true, insofar as it went. But it was twisted through the lens of fear and paranoia and trauma. Regardless, he never again was going to let anyone kick him this way. Bad enough he had to live with what he was, without someone using it against him to claim he was untrustworthy.

He stood. "I'll leave."

She didn't answer, just continued to stand there hugging herself and glaring.

"But let me make one thing clear to you, lady. I don't lie, and good men in far worse situations than this have trusted me. I never betray a trust."

He turned, then remembered the windows. Without a word, he slammed the living room window shut and locked it. Then he went to do the same in the kitchen and came back to reset the alarm. Cory suddenly appeared beside him.

"I'll be gone in less than thirty minutes," he said tautly.

"Wade…"

"No, Cory. Not another word. Nobody talks to me that way."

He was halfway up the stairs when he heard her start sobbing.

## CHAPTER TEN

OH, GOD, WHAT had she done? The numbness that had sheltered her most of the afternoon and evening had vanished, first leaving her furious, then filling her with despair as she heard her own words about Wade play back in her mind.

As she started sobbing, he just kept climbing the stairs, never looking back. And she couldn't blame him, she could only blame herself. Where had that ugliness come from, all that suspicion? How could such words have passed her lips? How could such thoughts have entered her mind, especially when she knew something of Wade's background.

It was as if an evil genie had taken over her tongue, spewing vile words as if they had some basis in truth.

But they had none. Only moments after having said those things, she had realized she didn't believe them. Not about Wade. And now she couldn't call those words back.

She returned to the living room and curled up in a ball on the couch, letting the tears flow. Facing the fact that she had become some kind of emotional cripple. Nothing worked right anymore. Nothing. Her whole psyche was so messed up that the normalcy she'd been pining for over the past few days would probably escape her forever.

If she survived this. And the really scary thing was that she didn't even care anymore if she did. She just wanted to be done with it.

So what had she done? She'd struck out at the one person who had managed to make her want to live again. That was the real threat he posed: that he had made her want to move past this nightmare into a future of some kind. That he had made her want to start looking forward again, rather than back.

And she had struck at him in the way she had guessed would hurt him the most: attacking his honor.

What kind of person had she become? She didn't like herself at all anymore, not one little bit. Turning over, she buried her face in a throw pillow and wondered if she'd ever again be able to justify the space she took up on this planet. Because right now she had to face the fact she was a waste of life. A mean waste of life.

These weren't the lessons she should take from what had happened to her. My God, she'd been a teacher. How many times had she tried to help students learn to grow from their bad experiences? How many times had she painted object lessons in how even a bad experience could be turned to something good?

Now look at her. She couldn't even take her own advice.

Finally the tears stopped, simply because there were none left. The storm had moved through, but this time it hadn't left her feeling totally numb. No, she still hurt, and she despised herself. No convenient, comfortable numbness now.

She sat up finally to find the house dark. Even more surprising, however, was that she saw Wade sitting in the recliner across from her, a bulky shadow among shadows.

"I thought you were leaving."

"I don't abandon my post."

Totally neutral. As if he had put his own feelings away in a vault somewhere, as she had for hours today.

"I'm sorry," she said. "I can't tell you how sorry. I don't know where that ugliness came from."

"Doesn't matter." Indifferent. Unrevealing. The way he had seemed when he first arrived.

She had done that, she admitted. She had driven him back into that place where the walls were high and the battlements well guarded. And there was no way she could call back those words. "I'm sorry," she said again, useless words once the wounds had been inflicted. "I didn't even mean it. I don't know what I was thinking."

"You weren't thinking."

"Obviously. I was acting like an animal, striking out at everything indiscriminately."

"Maybe so."

Oh, he was giving her nothing, not one little thing. Could she blame him? "I was afraid."

"No, you were angry."

"They come from the same thing."

"Mmm."

God, it was like talking to a brick wall again. And now it was not just annoying or disturbing. Now it hurt. It was almost enough to make her mad again, that he could hurt her this way.

She sat silently for a while, scrubbing the dried tears from her face. Finally she decided the only way to get past his walls was to lower her own. Her heart accelerated a bit at the danger in exposing herself this way. But she owed it to him, especially since after what she had said he was still in this house, still ready to protect her even with his life. Didn't such a man deserve the truth?

"I was…I was striking out because you made me start to hope again. I was afraid because you made me feel that a normal life might be possible for me. And I don't believe that anymore. I can't believe that. Look at me. I'm damaged goods. I'll never be normal again."

"It's unlikely."

Damn! She couldn't believe she had done this to him, and it was too late to rip out her own tongue.

Then, finally, in the dark so she couldn't even attempt to read his face, he began to speak. His tone was measured, his words slow.

"Nobody," he said, "who has seen and experienced what you and I have seen and experienced will ever be so-called normal again. It's an impossible thing to ask."

"I guess so." A hot, stray tear trickled down her cheek and she dashed it away.

"There will always be scars," he continued. "Things will never look the way they used to before violence entered our lives."

"No." Now she sounded like him.

A few seconds ticked by. Then, "But just because we carry scars, just because we've lived through things a lot of other people don't, doesn't mean there's anything wrong with us. Far too many people in this world have experienced violence in one form or another. Maybe that makes us more normal than those who haven't."

"What an awful thought." One that caused her a pang, not only for all the others of whom he spoke, but because it reminded her just how much self-pity she'd indulged, maybe was still indulging. He was right, and she knew it. One only had to turn on the news to see what millions of others suffered, many on a daily basis.

"Maybe. Still true. I've seen a lot of the world, and violence touches more lives than you can imagine. I'm not saying that's right, I'm just saying it is."

"You're right." Her voice broke a little. "I was protected from it all my life."

"Some people are. Some of us are lucky enough not to live in war zones, or among thugs. But an awful lot of us, sooner or later, taste the ugliest side of human nature.

Unfortunately, you didn't even have a support group of friends and family who shared your experience. Maybe that's the worst thing WITSEC did to you. It protected you physically, but left you with no help to heal emotionally."

She caught her breath. "Maybe," she agreed.

"Most of us are luckier than you. We have all kinds of social support."

"You didn't, when you were a child."

"No, but I sure as hell did after I grew up. But the scars are still there. All of them. Unlike you, I've had decades to deal with my crap. You haven't. And you can see what a stellar example of healing I am."

"Don't knock yourself. I already did that, and unfairly, too."

"I'm just trying to make a point. You can have a life again. It's just that sometimes you're going to hurt. Always."

"I guess so."

"With time the hurting comes less often. But it never entirely vanishes. Sorry, but I can't offer more than that."

"It should be enough."

"It's life. Whether it's enough is something only you can decide."

"I'd almost decided. Then…well, you saw what happened."

"Yeah." He was silent a moment, then with a surprising note of humor he added, "You tried to build your walls back up with dynamite."

She winced, because the description was so apt. And the only person who'd been hurt by her explosion was him. She'd had no idea she could turn so ugly, and the knowledge didn't comfort her at all. "My explosion didn't work very well. I'm sorry."

"It's okay," he said finally. "I understand, believe me.

I've seen it plenty of times, even done it myself a few times. That's what I meant about trip wires. You just start thinking you might reach for the brass ring, and then everything inside you starts shrieking warnings. Hell, you probably don't even believe you're entitled to live a normal life."

She honestly hadn't looked at it that way before, but the sinking in her stomach acknowledged the truth of his words. "That's a place I haven't gone."

"Not yet, maybe. You will. At some point, if it hasn't already, survivor guilt will give you a rough ride. If it does, and I'm around, talk to me about it. Been there, done that."

If he was around. That word caused her another sharp pang. "God, I'm a mess."

"No more so than anyone else in your shoes. Try to find some comfort in that."

"I can't believe you're trying to make me feel better after the way I treated you. You're being awfully generous." And that made him a truly remarkable person, in anyone's book.

"Don't beat yourself up." His tone had grown softer, kinder than when they had begun this conversation, and that only made her feel worse.

"But the things I said!"

"I don't blame you for them. After I got upstairs and cooled off a bit, I realized you touched one of my trip wires. At least one. I overreacted."

"I don't think you did." She was still aching over the things she had said and implied about him. "You offered to protect me when you didn't need to do a thing. You deserve better from me."

"You didn't say anything so god-awful, in the circumstances. Just let it go. I have."

But had he? He might say so, but given the way he had responded, she knew full well her angry words must have cut him to the quick in the places that mattered most to him, like his sense of duty and honor. Ideals to which he'd devoted his entire adult life. Maybe he wasn't proud of everything he'd had to do. She could scarcely imagine the kinds of jobs SEALs must be sent on. Maybe some of those things even stuck in his craw. But she was fairly certain he'd never betrayed one of his buddies, and had never failed in his duty. And she'd made him sound like nothing better than a hired gun.

God, she wished she could erase the memory of her words.

"Ah, damn, lady," he said on a sigh, "just let it go. Don't you think you already have enough baggage?"

"Maybe, but that doesn't give me the right to hand out more of it to anyone."

"You didn't hand me any baggage. Period."

Of course not. She didn't matter enough to him to be able to hurt him that way. In one sense she felt relieved that her shrewing hadn't hurt him in any lasting way. In another, awfully selfish way, she didn't like that she mattered so little to him. But why should she? Two days did not a relationship make. Not even good sex could make up for lack of time.

And, as he had told her more than once, he didn't make those kinds of connections anyway. So maybe she shouldn't feel bad about what she had said, at least as far as hurting him went. He didn't allow himself that kind of vulnerability.

Judging by the way he had initially reacted to her rant, she supposed he wasn't totally impervious. At least not at that moment in time, although she would guess she had sent him back to that place where he let nothing touch him.

But there was more at issue here than whether she had

hurt him. She had behaved deplorably, according to her own standards whether she had wounded him or not.

He surprised her then by rising and crossing the room to stand in front of her. It was still dark, the room illuminated only by the faintest light from outside streetlamps that managed to creep around cracks in the corner.

"I want you," he said baldly.

Her heart leaped instantly. Something about her loved the way he was so open and honest about his needs, the way he voiced them without varnish or hesitation. Best of all, without embarrassment. That freed her from all those things, too.

She lifted a hand to take his. "Just don't carry me."

"Why not?"

"Because just once I'd like to get into bed with you under my own steam."

At that he laughed. "It's a deal. Sorry, I guess I've been picking you up a lot."

"Only a few times." She answered the gentle tug of his hand and rose to her feet. "Why do you do that?"

"I don't know." He said nothing for a few seconds, still holding her hand. "Maybe," he said finally, almost breaking her heart in the process, "it's the only way I know to keep you close."

Ah, God, that was such a revealing thing for him to say, as if he had stripped his mind and emotions bare. It was one thing to say you wanted someone sexually. It was entirely another to admit you wanted to keep them close but didn't know how. Her throat tightened so that she couldn't even speak.

All she could do was stare starkly at the fact that they were both wounded souls, each in their own broken way trying to make some kind of connection again, regardless of what either of them might claim. He sought physical

connections because he didn't know how to make the other
kind. She fought emotional connections because they hurt
too much, and found the same solace he did in the physical.

Was that wrong? No, it wasn't. And maybe it was the
first step on a much longer path they both needed to walk,
whether together or separately. She squeezed his fingers
to show her understanding, then cleared her throat, finding her voice again.

"I, um, guess it's okay if you carry me then."

A little laugh escaped him. "Oddly, I think I'd prefer
it a whole lot more if you came with me, Cory. Come lie
with me, lady."

He couldn't have chosen words more likely to ignite her
desire, though she couldn't have said why. Heat spiraled
through her to her very core, making her feel heavy with
longing. Already her body ached for his touches, for his
weight, for the fullness of feeling him inside her. She'd felt
desire before in her life, but never this hot and this fast.

And he did that with simple words. Somehow that come
lie with me affected her more viscerally than, let's make
love, or many of the other affectionate or teasing sugges-
tions she used to hear from Jim. Come lie with me.

The words made her nerves hum, and she had no desire to analyze any further. She was tired of being under
a microscope, his or her own. Wade offered her the freedom to be, just be, in this moment and no other. And she
reached out with both hands for the gift.

This time he evidently felt no desire for the rough-and-
ready matings they'd had before. This time he stood beside
the bed with her, and began to remove her clothing slowly,
almost as if he were unwrapping a present and wanted to
savor the anticipation a little longer. To draw out each moment of expectation.

He took his time even with things that should have

happened quickly, like lifting her tank top over her head. Trailing his fingers up her sides as he did so sent ripples of longing through her for more. Oh, she felt so greedy, and he made her feel that way.

Then he followed the movement all the way up as he lifted the top, tracing the most sensitive parts of her inner arms all the way to her fingertips. When he at last tossed the top aside, she felt almost worshipped.

Nor did he stop there. He cast aside his own shirt, and the darkness in the room added to the mystery of all that was happening inside her. When his hands gently gripped her waist and pulled her close, there was something inexplicably exquisite about the feeling of his skin against her belly, except for her breasts, still shrouded by her bra. Then he bent and took her mouth in a kiss that stole her breath, and seemed to touch her very soul. His tongue mated slowly with hers as his fingertips drew gentle patterns on her back and sides, promising so much, taking nothing at all. He merely ignited her cells one by one until she felt alive with fire.

Then his mouth left hers, trailing slowly down her neck, causing her to arch and moan softly with delight.

"You are so sexy," he murmured against her neck, his breath hot and moist. A shiver rippled through her. Had anything ever felt this exquisite?

On a wisp of breath she answered, "You make me feel so sexy."

"Good. Good." His mouth trailed lower, lips and tongue outlining the cups of her bra, promising but not giving. Not yet. She shivered again and lifted her arms, looping them loosely around him in offering. When she felt his muscles bunching beneath her palms, she stroked them, following hard curves and hollows down toward the small of his back, where she marveled over a new discovery. In the dip there, she felt a soft, thin tuft of fur, so masculine, so perfect.

He trembled a bit as she stroked him there, then dipped one finger beneath the waistband of his jeans.

He mumbled something against the upper curve of her breast, and then with a quick movement, he released the clasp of her bra, allowing her to tumble free.

The throbbing at her center reached new heights as lightning seemed to zing along her nerves, every new sensation headed toward her core as if it was all that existed.

The air grew thin in the room, and she panted helplessly, her head falling back, her eyes closing, giving herself to the moment and to him as she had seldom given herself before: mindlessly, helplessly. If any part of her didn't ache in that throbbing, primal rhythm, she had long since ceased to be aware of it.

Here and now. Everything else vanished.

WADE FELT THE moment when she left the world behind, her entire consciousness focused on what was happening inside her. He wasn't far behind, but he struggled against his own hardening body, the pounding demands of his own needs.

Because he wanted to be sure to give it all to her, everything. He couldn't explain it, maybe didn't want to look too closely. All he knew was that he wanted to brand himself on this woman, right here and now in a way she would never forget.

So when she reached for the clasp of his jeans, moaning softly, he stopped her. Instead he reached for her shorts and panties, and tugged them down with one hand just as his mouth found her pebbled nipple and drew it deeply inside. He sucked gently at first, but as she pressed herself harder against him, he threw gentleness to the wind and sucked on her as if he could draw her right inside him.

The groan that escaped her fueled his own needs, and he had to push them back. If this woman remembered nothing else about him, she was going to remember this night, these hours.

Something even more primal than need for satisfaction drove him. This was a claiming of some kind, a claim he had never tried to make before. And for some reason, that need to claim added to his passion, making him almost as desperate as he was hungry.

The damn shorts and panties flew away at last, tugged off her ankles as he swept her up in one arm, his mouth still latched to her breast, each movement of his tongue and lips sending a fresh quiver through her.

She was clinging to him now, clinging as tightly as she could manage to his back, and the feel of her arms hanging on to him was surely the most wonderful thing he had ever felt. More wonderful even than the acts to come.

He'd have gone to the stake before he would ever admit how long it had been since someone's arms had been around him, or how good it felt, or how much he needed it.

He almost didn't want to lower her to the bed.

But his body had already made promises to her, and he was going to keep every one of them.

He laid her down, cast aside the rest of his clothing, pausing only to tug some protection from his pocket. He hadn't anticipated this, hadn't anticipated any sexual relationship at all, but the military had taught him well. He always carried protection, and for the first time he was truly grateful for it because it would ensure no harm came to Cory from him.

He tossed the packets on the bedside table. Then he wrapped his arms around the naked beauty beside him, and felt her arms wrap around him, and had the craziest feeling that he could stay right here, right now forever.

Their bodies met, warm smooth skin against warm smooth skin, their legs tangled, working for even greater closeness.

But he had promises to keep. With mouth and hands he began to explore her, every inch of her, stealing all her secrets even as he lifted her to moaning heights of passion. Then his mouth followed his hands, across her belly, her hips, down the insides of her thighs to the delicate arches of her feet.

He could think of no better way to worship her than by kissing her every inch.

The pounding in his loins now hammered in his brain. Slowly he slipped up over her, smelling her wonderful musky scent, then dipping his mouth and tongue into her most private places.

Claiming. Branding. Possessing.

Causing her to arch upward with a soft scream as he touched the delicate knot of nerves that gave so much pleasure-pain. She tasted good. So good. This was something he had almost never shared, it seemed so intimate to him, and he knew just the barest moment of fear he might not be doing it right, but her body immediately answered as if it had heard his question.

Oh, it was so right. So good. He licked, nibbled, tasted, even plunged his tongue deep into her, and felt a smile stretch his lips when her hands grabbed his head, pressing him closer still, then clawed at his shoulders as if she could barely stand the pleasure.

He felt the ripping shudder as an orgasm took her, listened to her moan helplessly, then before the riptide had fully passed, he pulled on a condom and moved up over her, staking his claim completely as he slid into her warm, welcoming depths.

"Wade!" Half sigh, half cry, and never had his name sounded so beautiful. Triumph filled him in that moment, because she was his, all his.

Then the throbbing in his body demanded more, her hands tugged at him, trying to move him, and when at last he began to thrust, she sighed his name again, wrapped her arms around his back and her legs around his hips.

Holding him. Hugging him with her entire being. Making him welcome in every way as she carried him with her to the stars.

For that little while, he even allowed himself to believe he could belong.

## CHAPTER ELEVEN

THEY LAY TOGETHER for a long time, just cuddling. That was something new to him, too. And he liked it. Finally he decided to tell her so, even though he was aware it could make her dislike him, to know how casually he had treated sex in his past. But for some odd reason, he was telling Cory lots of things he'd never told anyone else. Maybe because she always seemed to understand.

"This is the first time," he said slowly.

He felt a ripple pass through her and when he peered at her face in the nearly total dark, he thought he saw a smile. "What's so funny?"

"Turn on a light," she suggested. "I want to see your face, too."

Exposure. Confidences were easier in the dark, as he'd learned sitting in an awful lot of hides in alien lands. But he obliged her, turning on the small lamp beside the bed. It was dim, just enough light to read by.

She was smiling at him with puffy lips and puffy eyes, and he had to admit she looked happier than he'd yet seen her. "Nothing's funny," she said in answer to his question. "I just don't think this is the first time you've made love to a woman."

"Oh. That isn't what I meant." And now he half wished he hadn't mentioned it at all.

"Then what?" Her smile slipped away, her gaze grew gentle.

He hesitated. "First time I ever cuddled after."

Her eyes widened, and for an instant she looked as if she didn't understand. But when she did, something happened on her face that seemed to reach out and touch his heart.

"Oh, Wade," she said softly, and all of a sudden her arms wound around him, hanging on tightly, so tightly, and giving him that feeling again. "Oh, Wade, I think that's the saddest thing I've ever heard."

"No...no, don't be sad. Be happy. I am."

She burrowed her face into his shoulder, and he felt her kiss him there. "You," she whispered, "are more special than you know."

"So are you."

She didn't answer, just tightened her hold on him even more.

He would have liked to stay there forever, and maybe if he'd been an ordinary guy, he could have done so. But he was a former SEAL, and coded into him now was a mission clock, one that wouldn't stop ticking. He couldn't forget reality for long, couldn't forget there might be a killer out there circling in even now. Couldn't forget that even alarm systems were little protection against a determined assassin. He ought to know: he'd disabled more than one.

So finally, feeling as if he were ripping off his own skin, he gave in to the demands of reality. "Let's take a shower," he said. A gentle way to ease them back. To stay as they were left them with few defenses. He might not be at a total disadvantage naked, but he couldn't say the same for Cory. And if they got distracted again—a very tempting possibility—they could miss something important.

So they showered together, playing games with a bar of soap and a nylon puff that neither had been designed for, but that made them both grin, and elicited some pleasurable sighs.

He helped towel her dry, then slipped from the bathroom while she worked a bit at her hair. His internal clock and other triggers were beginning to drive him nuts. He'd allowed himself to be off duty for too long.

A quick check of the alarm showed him nothing amiss, but he crept through the house anyway, once again putting his knife on his belt, donning boots because protecting the feet was so essential. He skipped the shirt, though, as the house was warm enough. Cory would just have to live with the sight of the knife.

When he was sure the house was still secure, he followed the glow of light to the kitchen and found Cory making coffee. He glanced at the clock. "A little late for coffee. Or maybe awfully early, depending."

She shook her head, and when she faced him, he could tell that reality had settled in once again for her, too. All the softness was gone, except, perhaps, for her eyes when they brushed over him.

Until they came to rest on the knife.

"I see," was all she said, and turned her back again, waiting for the coffee. "I didn't think we'd get much sleep. One way or the other."

"No," he admitted. "Cory, I'm sorry."

"Stop apologizing, damn it. It's not your fault all this is happening. It's not your fault I'm such a mess. So we took a vacation. At least I did. For a little while I felt normal, I'm not going to apologize for it, and okay, now we face the real world again."

"You are normal."

"Oh, let's not get back on that again. Look at what I did today. I freaked out, basically. I totally shut down. Then I took it out on you."

Turning, she grabbed two mugs and put them on the

table. Then she got out the milk. A burst of steam announced the coffeemaker was pretty much done.

He watched, feeling an unaccustomed pain in his chest. A few minutes later, when they sat at the table, he spoke again. "Quit feeling bad about what you said to me."

"Why shouldn't I feel bad? I was horrid. I'm surprised you could even want to make love to me after that."

This was not good. He didn't want her to feel this way about herself. Not at all. Not ever. How could he make it clear to her that he really had forgotten what she had said?

Finally he chose his words with care. "I've had a lot of time to develop confidence in myself and who I am. The names don't stick anymore. I've been called far worse. I'm not saying I'm perfect. God knows, that's the last thing I'd say about myself. But I have had time to build and internalize a lot of confidence over the last twenty years. You haven't. You got stripped of everything, and now you've got a bunch of broken pieces to work with. Of course you're going to strike out sometimes. But you'll do just fine. You'll find a new version of yourself. If anything, I hope you do it better than I did."

"Meaning?"

"Maybe you can get rid of some of the trip wires."

At that she laughed unsteadily. "I don't even know where any of mine are."

"Sure you do. You know what makes you uneasy, you know what scares you. You even told me what made you feel threatened."

"I did?"

"Hope," he said simply. "You're terrified to hope."

LONG MINUTES PASSED in silence as Cory faced what he was saying. It was as if his simple statement had stripped away everything else and forced her to look at what might be the deepest wound of all. And it hurt. She finally covered her lower face with her hand and closed her eyes. "I used to take hope for granted."

"I know. You will again."

He sounded so sure, but considering how long she'd been living without it, and how much its reemergence scared her, she wasn't sure about that. What did she have to hope for, after all? That one morning she'd wake up and discover that her life was free of threat, that she could then take up the strands of the woman she had once been?

She'd never be that woman again. Ever. And in the murkiness of now, she couldn't even imagine who she might become if the threat was removed.

"First," he said, "it's little things. Immediate things. Little hopes. Just seeds."

"Do you hope?"

"Hell yeah. I hope for lots of things, some big, some small."

"Such as?"

"I hope I can settle into civilian life at least enough that I'm not a ticking time bomb just waiting to be startled. I hope someday I get past this edginess and stop seeing every shadow as a place of concealment. I hope that I can sleep without waking in a cold sweat from nightmares."

"You do that, too?"

"All the time. Not as much as even a few months ago, but yeah."

"Me, too. For a long time I was afraid to sleep."

"I can imagine."

"For a long time I nearly jumped out of my skin at the sound of a knock."

"But it's better now?"

"Yes. It is."

"You see?" He spread his hands. "Baby steps, Cory.

You've already started to take them. It's been my experience, though, that you'll take a few backward steps along the way."

"I think I took a big one today."

"No."

"No? What do you call what I did? That...that thousand-yard stare you called it. That numbness. That recklessness. Then yelling at you."

"The yelling was you coming back. I've seen guys go a lot deeper and stay there a lot longer. You actually had a pretty fast turnaround."

"And that's good?"

"You bet. There's a lot of life left in you, Cory. You're starting to kick the traces of fear and despair. It'll be rough for a while, but I believe you'll do it."

"I hope so." Then a little laugh slipped out of her. "I hope so. Listen to me."

"Sounds good." He stirred in the chair, and he seemed to lean forward, toward her. "You may have gone through more healing in the last year than you really realize. I don't know. I'm no shrink. I can only tell you what I've seen, and what I've learned from my own experience."

"I'm tired of being such a mess all the time."

"Tell me about it. But look at you. You're still here. You're still trying to deal. You could have quit a long time ago."

"I don't know."

"No way I can judge. But ask yourself, have you been living in terror every single minute of the last year you've been here?"

She started to say yes, then realized that wasn't entirely true. Her heart skipped a beat with the understanding, for it surprised her. Maybe what she thought of herself wasn't exactly true. "At first, yes. But then only when something happened to worry me. I can't say I spent the whole year in shaking terror."

"No, I'd bet most of the time you let it slide to the back of your mind. When nothing threatened you directly, when you were working."

She nodded slowly. "That's true."

"So the idea that you spent a year doing nothing but living in terror is your perception. Basically it was the story you told yourself, but maybe not exactly what you were doing."

"No, it's true," she said, straightening a little. "I'd forget about it. Maybe not for too long at one time, but I did. I had to."

"Of course you did. So give yourself a little credit here, Cory. In some pretty awful circumstances, having lost everything that meant anything to you, you managed to function. To hold a job, pay the bills, read books, maybe go to a movie. You kept going. You were probably doing a whole lot better than you thought."

"No. No, I wasn't." She still remembered all too vividly her many failures. And there were scores of them. Things undone, things unsaid. If she sat down and made a list, she'd hate herself.

"So sure? You didn't quit. A lot of people would have. Granted, healing probably would have been easier, maybe even happened faster, if you hadn't been cut off from everything. But that only makes what you've achieved all the more admirable."

"I haven't achieved anything!"

"Getting through the past year on your own is a huge achievement. Why don't you count your strengths instead of your weaknesses for a change?"

That comment drew her up short. Her strengths? She'd been looking at herself for a year as a quivering blob of fear, incapable of answering her own door without peeking out first to see who was there.

"You went to work, didn't you? You went to the bank, and the grocery store. You even made a few friends."

"Not really. I couldn't let anyone get too close."

"But was that a failing or a reasonable caution given what you went through?"

She almost wanted to protest that he didn't know her well enough to guess what she had been like for the past year. And yet, she found herself drawn up short by awareness, a shift of perspective on her own actions and behavior. Yes, she had lived with fear, but not enough fear that it had prevented her from functioning. Not enough that it had kept her locked in this house.

Going to work hadn't caused her a nervous breakdown, although she'd never dropped her guard about what she said. Yes, answering her door had been difficult, but considering what had come through her door that night fifteen months ago, maybe it was surprising she could answer a door at all. She'd had dinner a few times with Nate and Marge Tate, with Gage and Emma Dalton. She went to the library regularly, and never considered avoiding it, at least not since the first few weeks.

Maybe she was confusing heightened caution with terror, at least later. There was no question she had been terrified right after Jim was killed. No question she had been terrified when she had finally been dropped here on her own. But of course she had been. For the first time in months she didn't have a Marshal at her elbow, had to venture out on her own, pick up the threads of the basic necessities of life.

And she had done it. Unhappily, with her heart so broken it sometimes seemed too painful to draw a breath, hating it and fearing the unknown that loomed before her as much as the past that might try to follow her. But she had done it.

"You see?" he said, almost as if he sensed the shift in her. "What happened today has probably happened to you a number of times since your husband was killed. You disconnected because it was too much. The past, the present, all of it converged on you again when you listened to Gage and me talking. So you shut down. That's an important protective thing. Sometimes it's the only way we can deal."

"You do it, too?"

"I thought I said so. And God knows I've seen enough people do it. You see it in survivors all the time. Survivors of battle, survivors of natural disasters. That's the thing. It's like the brain gets so overloaded it just says enough. It can't deal, so it basically removes you as far as it can. It's not a failing. It's not something wrong with a person. It's survival. It's only a bad thing when it takes over for too long and too completely."

"But you said post-traumatic stress disorder. Isn't that an illness?"

"But that's not what I saw today, Cory. PTSD, yes, but the useful, coping kind. I guess what I'm trying to get at is that after watching you, especially today, I don't think you're as bad off as you think."

She sighed, letting his words sink in slowly, rearranging her mental and emotional furniture, trying to see herself in a more positive light. The change left her feeling uneasy. Then a new thought occurred to her, one that caused her a pang.

"Maybe you're right about survivor guilt."

He stirred again. "What do you mean?"

"It hasn't been just fear and grief. Maybe I've been punishing myself with both of them." Even as she could accept the emotional logic of that, she didn't like the idea much. She almost hoped he would deny it.

"Could be, I suppose. But now you're getting into shrink territory, and I've probably already ventured too far that way. I'm just talking from what I've seen and experienced over the years."

She turned the idea around in her head, though, weighing it against her emotional response. The Marshals had tried to give her everything she needed to move forward in a safe life. If she looked at the past year honestly, they had succeeded. But she had refused to fully accept the gift. Grieving had been one thing. Even some initial fear at being on her own. But at some point had she started using fear as a way to flagellate herself and limit her options because she was still alive when Jim and her baby were not?

It was as if doors were finally opening in her mind, giving her a different view than the box she had tried to paint around herself during the past year.

Plenty of food for thought, and plenty to leave her feeling adrift inside herself. Who was she, actually? And what had she really been doing with herself over the past year? She suspected these new ideas of herself might be closer to the mark than the abbreviated form she had adopted previously. Grief and fear did not begin to explain it all.

She sighed. "I've got a lot of thinking to do. But I'd appreciate it if you would accept my apology for what I said earlier. I'm horrified at myself."

"I thought I already had. Apology accepted."

"You're a very kind man."

He said nothing for a while, and she wondered if she had offended him somehow. Then he said, an almost rueful note of humor in his voice, "I think I need to learn how to accept a compliment."

"Does it bother you that I said you're kind?" How awful

if it did, because he had certainly been kind to her, kinder than she had any right to expect.

He answered, still sounding rueful. "My mind is trying to remind me of all the times I wasn't kind."

At that a forlorn little laugh escaped her. "Yeah, the way I'm sitting here remembering all the ways I wasted the last year. All the things I could have done but didn't."

"I'll cut myself some slack if you will."

"Deal." But was it? Could she really see herself through his eyes, rather than her own? He certainly made a compelling case for a Cory who had acted the way most people would after what she had been through, rather than the Cory she had talked herself into thinking she was.

Then she asked a question that she knew was freighted with baggage. But it was a question that needed an answer because it might help her plant one of those seeds of hope he had talked about, give her something to hang on to.

"Wade?"

"Yes?"

"Tell me just one little hope you have right now. Just one little thing, not the big things."

She watched as his face started to freeze, but before he could turn completely to stone again, she watched him relax his expression muscle by muscle. For a full minute, he didn't say anything.

"Wade?"

"I hope that you'll hug me again sometime," he said finally.

He couldn't have sent a surer shaft straight into her heart. Aching for him, for his isolation and loneliness, she rose and rounded the table. He pushed back as if to rise, but before he could she slid onto his lap and wrapped her arms around him tightly.

"I hope," she whispered tremulously, "that you'll let me hug you again lots of times. It feels so good to me."

He wrapped his arms snugly around her in answer. "Anytime, Cory. Anytime."

THE SKIN-CRAWLING SENSATION came back, possibly because he'd gone AWOL for a few hours. Or it returned because he sensed something internally. Some inner clock was ticking, counting out the minutes and hours it would take for the killer to respond if he had identified Cory.

The sensation had never failed him when there was danger, had rarely been wrong about danger that didn't exist.

The sun would rise in less than an hour. This was the time of attack, when darkness still provided a cloak and most humans were at their weakest. This was the hour when many a guard lost his alertness, when sleep stole awareness no matter how hard one tried to stay awake.

The hour before dawn.

Maybe that's all it was. But he counted back through his mind, first the phone call, then the stranger who drove two different cars. Maybe he was to be the killer himself. Or he was merely the assassin's lookout, an unidentifiable face that should have passed unnoticed while collecting information.

Damn, he wished he knew.

He had at last persuaded Cory to doze on the couch, promising he would be right there and awake. But he wished he could slip out and sweep the perimeter, because no matter how well the sheriff's deputies did the job, he could do it better himself.

He checked the alarm more than once, making sure it hadn't been disconnected. No warnings showed on the status display.

The phone rang. He grabbed it immediately, hoping the

single ring wouldn't disturb Cory. She sighed but remained asleep, exhausted and trusting him.

God, he hoped he was worthy of that trust.

He slipped into the kitchen with it, after the barest of greetings, and heard Gage's voice. Through the kitchen curtains, he could see the pale light of dawn.

"We identified the guy you saw with the two different cars," Gage said. He sounded barely awake himself.

"Yeah? Who?"

"A private detective out of Denver."

"Hell."

"Exactly. I've got the Denver P.D. going to roust him and find out who he was working for."

"Like I can't imagine."

"This could be good. At least we'll know exactly what info he passed on, and who he passed it to."

"Yeah. Maybe we can even use him." Wade's brain slipped into high gear and he refilled his coffee mug. The more he thought about it, the better he liked this setup.

"That was my thought," Gage said. "If it's not too late. But first I have to question him. He'll be cooperative if he wants to keep his license."

"How long is that going to take?"

"I'm going to start with a phone interview once Denver picks him up. I'll let you know. Don't let her out of the house for now."

"I won't. Listen, Gage?"

"Yeah?"

"I gotta get some sleep, man. Four hours."

"I'll send Sara Ironheart over in mufti. Like for coffee. Give me an hour. I can also put eyes on the house, but that might take a little longer so we don't give the game away."

"Absolutely don't give the game away. We've got to end this."

"I agree. Can you make it another hour?"

"I'm fine. But I'll be better on a little sleep."

He hung up and rubbed his eyes. A private dick, huh? Someone who wouldn't know the story, could be fed a line of bull. Someone unrelated to the case who could be sent here to find Cory without setting off alarms. In theory, anyway.

This killer was no tyro at this. No tyro at all. The palms of his hands started itching as he thought of all the things he'd like to do to the assassin. Things he knew he'd never do because he was an ordinary citizen now.

But there were hundreds of ways a man could die, and in his experience few of them were quick or merciful.

With a shake of his head, he pushed the thoughts away. He wasn't that man anymore. In fact, he was trying to become a very different man. One who might actually be worthy of breathing the same air as a woman like Cory Farland.

One thing he did know for certain. He would do whatever it took to keep Cory safe. Even if it meant spending the rest of his life in hell.

## CHAPTER TWELVE

SARA IRONHEART ARRIVED with the gentlest of taps on the window beside the front door. She wore a heavy jacket, overshirt and jeans, and from its concealment flashed her badge. He also caught a glimpse of a 9mm semiautomatic in a shoulder holster.

Cringing because it would undoubtedly wake Cory, Wade turned off the alarm and let her in. Then he turned the alarm on as quickly as possible, hating that damn beep.

"Wade?" Cory called drowsily.

"I'm here," he called back. "Everything's fine. Get some more sleep."

She mumbled something, and from the doorway he watched her turn a bit on the couch and slip back into slumber. This woman, he thought, wasn't anywhere near the scared kitten she thought herself.

He motioned Sara to follow him into the kitchen, and closed the door on the hallway so their conversation wouldn't disturb Cory more.

"Thanks for coming."

"Least I can do." A beautiful woman with raven-black hair that was highlighted by just a few threads of silver, she gave him a half smile. "Gage filled me in. You go to sleep."

"Coffee's over there, mugs in the cupboard above."

"Thanks."

"Four hours max," he cautioned her.

She nodded. "I'll wake you."

Then, sentry in place, he went back to the living room
and made himself as comfortable as he could on the recliner.

An adrenaline jolt tried to keep him from sleeping, but
this was a battle he'd fought and won many times. A man
couldn't survive his job without learning to sleep anytime,
anywhere, even standing bolt upright. And the recliner was
a hell of an improvement over that.

A couple of minutes later he'd quieted his body, and
sleep slipped over him. A light sleep.

For even as he dozed, his ears never quit working, cata-
loging every sound as either normal or not.

It was another one of those survival things.

CORY AWOKE, A warm, lovely dream giving way to instant
panic. Someone was in the house.

"Shh," a voice said quietly, and she opened her eyes
to see Sara Ironheart squatting beside her. "It's okay. I'm
spelling Wade."

Cory drew a shuddering breath, managing a nod as
her racing heart started to settle from a terrified gallop to
something closer to normal.

"Coffee?" Sara whispered.

Cory nodded and pushed herself upright. When she
saw Wade dozing in the recliner, everything inside her
turned warm and soft. The gifts he had given her during
the night hours seemed to have settled in and taken root.
She felt good, despite the reminder of the threat that Sara
represented.

She rose as quietly as she could and followed Sara to
the kitchen.

"He sleeps lightly," Sara remarked. "Reminds me of
my cat. His ears almost twitch at every sound, even when
his eyes don't open."

Cory smiled. "He's amazing."

"I could tell you were starting to wake, getting restless. I didn't mean to scare you, but I didn't want you to realize someone else was here without knowing immediately who I was."

"Thanks. I appreciate that." She filled her own mug and topped Sara's. They sat together at the kitchen table. "So what's going on?"

"Wade said he needed to catch some sleep, so Gage sent me over. That's all."

"Yeah, he was up all night." She didn't explain her part in that, but she supposed Sara could put the pieces together.

Then another thought struck her. "If he didn't feel comfortable sleeping without someone here on guard, something must have happened."

"I honestly don't know." Sara smiled ruefully. "My brother-in-law—you've met Micah?"

"I've seen him around."

"Well, he used to be special forces, and I've seen him get antsy at times, as if he senses something but doesn't quite know what. Even after all these years he'll still go into a hypervigilant mode at times. Don't ask me to explain what gets them going. It's like they have some kind of internal radar for when something is off-kilter. Or gathering."

"Is he often right?"

"Let's just say I've been glad more than once to have him on my team, as well as a member of the family."

Cory nodded slowly. "It must be hard on them, though."

"I can't say. It's been my experience they don't talk a whole lot about it." Sara's smile was almost wry. "Sometimes I think they get hooked into some kind of mystical cosmic-information highway. Like when my son broke his arm. Micah started getting worked up the day before

Sage fell out of the tree. Said he could feel something was going to happen."

"Wow." Cory tried to imagine it.

"Other times, on the job mostly, he's tried to explain it as some kind of internal countdown clock. If X happened, then Y should happen within a certain time frame." Sara shrugged. "I don't know. I'm just a cop, but I guess I have my own form of the same thing. Hunches. Little niggles. The feeling that something isn't right."

"Good intuition."

"Whatever you call it." Sara glanced at the clock. "Wade made me promise four hours and not a second longer. So I'll wake him a little after ten."

"He could sleep longer," Cory protested. They were still keeping their voices low, so it was hard to put enough emphasis into the words. "He needs it."

"When a man like that says four hours, he means it. I'm not going there."

Nor, Cory decided, would she. Wade could be determined about some things, and she had already nearly made him walk out with some nasty words. Who knew how he'd respond to direct defiance, even a little one like this.

Only he probably wouldn't see it as little. He had undertaken to protect her, and she supposed he would have good reason to get hopping mad if she broke his rules.

And she'd be foolish not to cooperate with her protector, even over something so small.

A sigh escaped her, and she began to feel a bit as she had when the Marshals had kept her in the safe house those three months. Trapped, watched, with no volition. At least this time she had moved past mourning. Mostly.

But events roused the old memories, and she sat there with her hands wrapped around her coffee mug, forcing herself to sort through them.

The loss of Jim and the baby still ached, but more like a tooth that had been treated than one that had a raging infection. It would probably always hurt. But as Wade had showed her, she could live again, if she committed to it. Committed to moving on and taking whatever little joys came her way, instead of feeling guilty about them.

Once she got this killer off her back.

Even that, she realized, was a choice she was making. Would she let that man's desire to protect himself keep her always one step removed from truly living? Or would she take charge of her own life again?

Because nobody, nobody, had a promise that they would see tomorrow. She surely ought to have learned that the hard way. She was here now only because a gunshot had failed to kill her, too.

Borrowed time? Maybe. Or maybe this was just life and it was time to stand up and participate again.

A HALF HOUR later, Cory went in to wake Wade. It was the first time she had seen him wake, and she was fascinated. At first his eyes snapped open and he tensed, as if ready to spring, but the instant he saw her, his face softened. "Everything okay?" he asked.

"Everything's fine. Sara's getting ready to go."

"Okay." He passed his hand over his face and sat up. Then he wrapped his arms around her hips and pressed his face to her belly. Instantly warm tingles awoke in her center. Reaching out, she ran her hand over his short hair.

"One of these days," he muttered.

"One of these days what?"

He sighed, then tipped his head back and smiled at her. "One of these days we're going to have all the time we want alone together."

She smiled, liking the sound of that. "I'll hold you to it."

"Good."

But then he let go of her, and the guardian returned, flattening his face, steeling his eyes. He pushed out of the chair and went with her to the kitchen, where Sara was donning her jacket to conceal her gun. She looked like just anyone, nothing giving away that she was a deputy.

"Okay, then," she said with a smile. "I'll be off."

At that moment there was a knock at the door. They all stiffened. Cory's heart slammed. That sound would probably always make her heart slam.

"Let me get it," Wade said.

But Sara was right on his heels, gun magically appearing. She stood back, holding the pistol in a two-handed grip, waiting, while Wade looked out the window beside the door. Cory peered around the edge of the kitchen door, gripping the frame so tightly her knuckles turned white.

"Gage," Wade said.

He opened the door to the sheriff, and Cory almost gasped in amazement. Gage didn't look anything like himself. No, he looked like a man who could have lived on the streets undercover for DEA, as he once had: utterly disreputable in a worn leather jacket, stained jeans and a ball cap rather than his usual Stetson.

"Hi," he said as he stepped inside. "Sorry, but I didn't want it to look like the sheriff was stopping in."

"You sure don't," Cory managed.

Gage chuckled. "Good. Okay, we've got plenty to talk about now."

Sara spoke. "Want me to stay?"

"Oh, yeah. We've got some planning to do."

The living room was the only place where they could all sit. Gage took the recliner, Sara the rocker, leaving the couch for Cory and Wade.

Cory's heart had begun to beat a little nervously, knowing Gage wouldn't be here unless he had learned something.

"Okay," he said. "I told Wade earlier, and I don't know if he had a chance to tell you, Cory, but the guy he saw who he thought might be tailing you was a private detective from Denver." Reaching into one of his pockets, he pulled out a notebook and flipped it open. "I'll try to stick to just what you need to know."

"Okay." Her heart skipped then beat a bit faster. Her mouth started to dry with anticipated fear.

"His client, who is going by the name of Vincent Ordano, hired him to find you under the pretext that you had embezzled a huge sum of money from him. He claimed he could track you only as far as this county, that you seemed to have changed your appearance and name, and the only way to flush you out was to make you think you'd been found. Just as Wade suggested might be the strategy."

Cory felt her stomach turn over, and she covered her mouth with her hand, as if that could somehow help.

"Anyway, as Wade suspected, again, the investigator, Moran, scoped out women of a certain age group who had moved here within the last year. He found eight of you, and since Ordano couldn't be sure which of you it was, Moran made the phone call and watched the reactions. He settled on you and your friend Marsha, for exactly the reasons Wade suspected. Moran saw that Marsha got a dog, but he was far more concerned about Wade appearing out of nowhere in your life. That struck him as a whole lot odder than buying a dog. My apologies."

"There's nothing to apologize for," Cory said.

"No? Maybe not. None of us thought you taking a roomer would be pulling some kind of trigger. Regardless, Moran then started some background checking. Marsha, of course, had a trail he could follow all the way back.

Yours was sketchy enough to make him think you might be the one hiding."

A soft sound of distress escaped Cory. Wade immediately took her hand, but at the moment it proved to be scant comfort. "It was that easy?"

"Only because someone, somewhere, pointed Ordano to this county," Gage reminded her. "And that's something we are definitely going to deal with as soon as we get Ordano."

"How are we going to do that?"

"That's what we're going to discuss. But let me finish up here, because there's actually some good news in this morass."

Cory managed a nod, and tightened her grip on Wade's hand.

"Moran hasn't reported back yet to Ordano that he's sure you're the woman Ordano wants. He only finished his background checks late last night, and we caught him this morning before he even got to his office. To say the guy is appalled would be an understatement, so we have his full cooperation."

"But if he knows where Ordano is…"

"He doesn't. Their communications have all been by phone and email, and services were paid for with a credit card by phone. We assume Ordano must be nearby, but we don't know exactly where. I'm tracing activity on the credit card Moran was given, but the information may well be out-of-date by the time we get it. If there is any. He might not be using that card anymore, or any other cards under that name. Hell, we don't know that he really is Vincent Ordano. I've got folks researching him, but they may well come up empty-handed."

Cory tried to swallow but her mouth was too dry.

"And I am not, I repeat not, going to call the Marshals on this." Gage's frown was deep and dark. "I don't know who talked, but someone evidently did, and until I find out, this stays here, in this county, among my people."

"I agree," Wade said flatly. "The least little slip could start the clock ticking again. I don't want Cory having to live any longer in fear."

"Absolute agreement here," Gage said. "We take care of our own in this county, and Cory has been through more than enough."

Cory actually felt her throat tighten. She was part of this county now, this place she had tried not to connect with. An unexpected homecoming in the midst of this mess. Yes, she wanted to stay here, and she would do whatever was necessary.

"For the moment," Gage continued, "we have an advantage. Moran hasn't identified Cory to Ordano. That means we can arrange an ambush and substitute a stand-in."

"No." The word came out Cory's mouth almost before she was aware of it.

Everyone looked at her.

"No one is going to risk their life for me. Absolutely not."

"Cory," Wade started to say.

"No." The determination that filled her now was unshakable. "Don't you see? I have enough to live with. I couldn't live with it if someone was hurt or killed in my place. What's more, I think I need to do this. I need to face this guy. I'll never be free of fear again unless I do this." She wondered if she could even convey how strongly she felt that this was something she had to do to lay to rest some of her demons for good. How could you explain that you had run long enough, and now it was time to stand your ground?

But instead of endless argument, she was surprised because all three of them seemed to understand what she was trying to say.

"Okay," Gage said, and Wade nodded, albeit with obvious reluctance. "We'll set up an ambush. Since I want Cory in armor, we need to set it up to occur at night when she can reasonably wear a jacket to conceal the armor. I'm thinking the supermarket parking lot. It would be reasonable for Cory to leave work a half hour or so after the store is closed, and to leave apparently alone. Yet there are plenty of places around where we can conceal ourselves. There are always cars out there overnight for example. A Dumpster. Some trees. Rooftops. The trick will be making sure we don't pick a hiding place that Ordano would choose."

Wade spoke. "Give me a thousand-yard sight line, and I won't miss."

Gage's head tilted a bit. "Are you asking me to deputize you?"

"If it'll make this work better. At least make sure I'm on a roof somewhere with an unhindered sight line. In case."

Cory shuddered helplessly at what he was proposing. She didn't want him to have that on his conscience because of her. She didn't think she could stand it.

Sara spoke. "Micah's a trained sniper, too."

"So put both of us out there. It'll reduce the number of people you need on the ground, and thus reduce the number of people who might give us away."

Gage nodded slowly. "Okay. I like it. I'll go set it up, and give Moran his story to pass along. I'll see if I can't get him to do it in a way that'll push Ordano to move quickly. We can't afford to give him a lot of time to plan."

Cory spoke through stiff lips. "If what happened that night he came after my husband is any indication, he's not one for a lot of planning. He may be good at covering his tracks, but there were so many other times he could have gotten Jim when he was alone…" Her voice broke. "He didn't have to come into the condo when we were both there."

"Good point," Wade said, squeezing her hand gently. "The guy's an opportunist, and a bit careless. He chose an easy way to get at your husband at a time when escape would also be easy, with no one out and about to notice him. And he didn't care about collateral damage, obviously."

He paused a moment, then added, "This Ordano may think of himself as an assassin, but I'd give him low marks. My bet is he's an ordinary thug who took the job for money, and that he doesn't have a whole lot of experience."

Cory looked at him. "How could you know that?"

"Because I would have done it cleaner, and you wouldn't have been around."

The words chilled Cory, but she looked into those dark eyes of his, and she saw a whisper of the pain he felt because he had been required to do such things in his past. She ached for him, for the burdens he carried in silence, for the duty that had scarred him. It raised him even higher in her estimation that he couldn't shrug off such things, that she could see the ghosts in his gaze.

"All right," she said, as if everything had been settled. "Just tell me where to be, and when, and exactly what you want me to do. But let me make it perfectly clear, I will not let anyone take the risk in my place. I cannot live with that. I will not live with that."

Gage sighed and nodded. "I get it, Cory. And sometimes we have to face our demons head-on. It's the only way to be free."

That was it in a nutshell. It didn't mean that she'd sleep

any better until this was over. It didn't mean her heart would stop galloping.

But she had to stand up for herself. Now. This time. No matter the cost.

GAGE AND SARA left like a couple, arms linked, heads bowed together and talking as they walked down the street a little way to Sara's battered pickup. Keeping up the pretense, just in case.

Just in case.

The words seemed to hang in her mind like smoke long after a fire has burned out. They had to assume that Moran was Ordano's only information source, but they had to assume at the same time that he was not. No chances, no unnecessary risks.

And Cory felt as if the house were closing in on her, just as those safe houses had a year ago. Only now that she had lost it completely did she realize just how much freedom she had exercised in the past year despite her fear. Freedom to run to the store. Freedom to sit in her backyard on a warm evening. Simple things, but huge in their absence.

"We'll take care of this soon," Wade told her. They were both pacing like caged animals, which might have amused her at another time. Right now it wasn't even remotely funny.

"What if he gets away?"

"He won't."

She faced him. "You can't promise that."

He stilled, becoming as motionless as a statue. "If he gets away, I promise you I will hunt him to the ends of the earth. He will not escape me."

Her chest tightened and began to ache. She reached out and seized his hand, clutching it between both of hers. "No,

Wade. Promise me you won't do that. I couldn't stand it. I couldn't bear you to turn into that kind of hunter for me."

His gaze remained hard. "It wouldn't be the first time."

"Maybe not. But you've already done it for the last time. Promise me you won't do that for me. You've already served your time and done your duty. Now…now is for building, not destroying. Promise me, please."

His gaze never wavered. "I can't."

Then he turned from her and resumed his pacing.

Oh, God! She stood still, watching him, knowing there was not a thing she could say or do. This man would do his duty, however he perceived it, and that was that.

The only question was if she would accept it. Accept him. As he was. As he had been. As he might have to become again.

And somewhere deep inside, she knew she already had.

# CHAPTER THIRTEEN

WADE FIGURED AT most two days. His reasoning was straightforward. If Ordano was anywhere in the vicinity, he would move fast. Probably the very next night when Cory went to work. If he was halfway across the country, he might take another day.

"But no longer," he said. "This guy wants the threat removed, the faster the better."

Gage agreed.

Cory went to work at her usual time. Her shift seemed to drag. Gage had talked to her boss, so arrangements had been made so that Cory would leave the locked store alone at about a half hour past closing, while others remained inside, out of sight.

Even though she worried about the other employees, Cory was grateful that she would not have to spend that hour alone in an empty store, locked though it would be. Gage felt the presence of the other employees would prevent Ordano from trying to break in and take her out inside the store.

They were doing everything they could to ensure the attack happened in the parking lot. And all they wanted her to do was go in the back room, put on the body armor, pull her jacket over it, then leave the store. And if she saw Ordano, all they asked was that she drop to the ground and roll. Making herself small. Getting herself out of the way.

Walking bait. Exposing herself completely. Her skin

crawled in anticipation, and as the hour grew closer, her heart accelerated and her stomach filled with nervous butterflies. She must have made a dozen trips to the fountain to ease the dryness in her mouth, but it only returned minutes later.

She knew the deputies were out there. She knew Wade was on some rooftop, deputized at least for a few days.

But worst of all was the way Wade had withdrawn again, turning into the stony man she had first met. No smile lightened his dark eyes. No unnecessary word passed his lips. He was gone from her as surely as if he had left town.

That hurt. It hurt so much that she now would have new baggage to deal with if she survived the next few days: the baggage of having fallen in love with a man who could shut her out as surely as if he had closed a door and locked it.

And she hurt for him, for the places this must be taking him back to, for all the memories it must be evoking. Right or wrong, duty or not, no soldier survived without scars. And every single one of his must have been ripped open by having to once again slip into the role he had chosen to protect her: Sniper. Killer. Hunter.

God, she almost wished Ordano had found her before Wade ever appeared. She couldn't stand the thought of what he must be dealing with now.

The hour came at last. Her heart climbed into her throat as she looked at Betsy, her manager. The woman nodded, her face conveying fear and sorrow.

"Be careful."

Cory nodded. She went to the back room, climbed into the body armor and jacket then headed for the front door.

Betsy had given her a key so she could lock the door as she left. Gage didn't want to risk anyone else being vis-

ible through all that glass, because Ordano had proved he
didn't care who he shot in addition to taking out his target.

The hair on the back of her neck was standing on end
as Cory stepped out into a night that seemed strangely
chilly for summer. Her entire back prickled with the sense
of being watched as she turned and locked the front door
from the outside.

But of course there were a dozen eyes on her right now,
at the very least. Wade and Micah on the rooftops somewhere. Other deputies hiding in cars or elsewhere. Gage
hadn't shared the details, nor did she especially want to
know them.

Maybe those were deputies she spied sitting on the sidewalk in front of the pizza place four doors down, looking
like two drunks sharing a bottle, totally ragged and sharing a torn blanket. How would she know?

They certainly sounded drunk, and argued over who
had drunk the most of the bottle they passed between them.

Slowly she began to cross the parking lot. Per direction,
she had left her car at the farthest end so she would have a
longer walk. Giving Ordano more opportunity.

There were a half dozen other cars in the lot. Some
probably occupied by deputies. All appearing empty. She'd
been ordered to avoid walking anywhere near any of them.
Stay in the open. Stay away from those places of concealment.

Step after step she walked, her legs feeling like lead, her
heart beating so loud she couldn't hear much else. Wandering a little to avoid the cars. Making loose shopping
carts her excuse for the meandering walk, giving the at-
tacker more opportunity to approach. Trying to make it
necessary for him to leave his vehicle. If he was in one.

She glanced around again, but could see no heads in any
of the cars. And of course, there was her own Suburban, a

threat in itself, although she was sure it had been watched continuously since her arrival. She doubted anyone could have managed to hide himself in or around it.

At least, she had to believe that.

Another step. Grabbing another cart and shoving it toward a corral. Annoy the man, Gage had said. Make him impatient.

Well, there were certainly enough forgotten carts out here to help her do that.

She began to shiver, though she couldn't possibly be cold. Her legs went from lead to rubber, and she began to wonder if she would be able to make it all the way to her car.

Another cart. Turn around and walk it back. She clung to it for support even as she pushed it.

How had Wade lived like this for so long? She didn't think she could stand it for another ten minutes.

Maybe it wouldn't happen tonight. She was getting closer to her car, farther from the two guys sitting out in front of the pizza place. More isolated with every step.

"There you are."

She didn't recognize the voice. She froze, her fear ratcheting up to full-blown terror. Stiffly, she turned.

She recognized the face the instant she saw it. It was him. And he was pointing a gun at her from within the confines of a loose jacket. "You!" She gasped the word as she looked into a face that had haunted her nightmares.

"We're going to take a ride," he said. "A nice little ride, just the two of us."

That gun was pointed straight at her. Fear clouded her brain for a few seconds. Paralyzing her, making her forget what she was supposed to do.

"Move it," he said, his voice low and threatening.

But she couldn't move. Then, almost automatically, like any person faced with a gun, she started to obey.

No! The word shrieked in her brain. Drop and roll away. Drop and roll away.

For a few seconds she didn't think she'd be able to. It was as if her body had become a statue. But she might be blocking the sight line they had warned her about. And how would they know this was the guy if she didn't drop and roll? That was their signal that this was the one.

All of a sudden Wade's face popped into her mind. Somehow, thinking of him reminded her that she was capable. Not merely a frightened mouse, but a capable woman.

FROM HIS ROOFTOP, Wade watched the encounter. He couldn't tell from the way Cory was acting if this was the guy, or just somebody who wanted to ask for directions. She stood there, still but yet standing, not doing the one thing they had told her to do.

Looking through the scope on the sniper rifle Gage had given him, he couldn't see enough. Cory blocked part of his view. And he couldn't shoot unless he was sure.

Damn!

He held his breath, hoping he didn't watch her get murdered while he dithered about whether the target might not be the right guy. But he couldn't shoot until he was sure.

He glanced across the way to another rooftop where Micah lay, triangulating on the parking lot. The man seemed undecided, too.

Not enough info. He looked through his scope again, focusing, trying to see some defining detail. Only long experience kept him calm, his heartbeat steady. *Forget it's Cory,* he told himself. *Don't let emotions get involved.*

*Stay calm. Steady breaths, finger on trigger, waiting. Become ice.*

Then the two deputies in front of the pizza place started arguing loudly, in slurred voices. The man facing Cory turned just a bit. And Cory dropped to the ground.

It was him.

He held his breath and began to squeeze. But before he got off his shot, the loud pop of Micah's rifle pierced the night.

The guy dropped like a marionette whose strings had been cut. Wade waited, keeping a bead on him as the two "drunks" dropped bottle and blanket and charged across the lot toward Cory.

Only when they got there, and he could see through his scope that they kicked the guy's gun away and bent to cuff him, did Wade ease off on the trigger.

An explosive breath escaped him and he rolled over on his back, staring up at the star-studded heavens.

Thank God. Thank God.

Then the night erupted with colored lights and the sounds of sirens.

He could only lie there drained, thanking God. But a minute later, the adrenaline hit and he was up. He had to get to Cory. Now.

CORY WAS ON her feet by the time Wade came charging up. Shaking from head to foot, she was staring down at the man who had killed her husband. It seemed he was still alive. She didn't know how she felt about that.

But then Wade's arms closed around her, and she was sure she had never felt anything more wonderful in her life. She sagged into his embrace and said his name over and over.

"Are you okay?" he demanded, clutching the back of her head and pressing her tightly to his chest.

She managed a nod.

Gage's voice reached her. "Take her home, Wade. We'll talk after I take care of this creep."

There wasn't an ounce of protest in her, and this time she didn't at all mind when Wade scooped her off her feet and carried her to her car. She hated it only when he let go of her after putting her in the passenger seat and buckling her in.

But when he climbed in beside her, and had turned over the ignition and shifted into gear, he reached over and grabbed her hand as if he were afraid it might slip away.

He carried her into the house, too. And this time when he turned off the alarm, he didn't turn it back on. No need now. From somewhere deep inside, a smile nearly rose to her lips. No more living in fear.

Wade stripped her of her jacket and the armor, then wrapped her chilled body in a blanket and settled her on the couch. "You need something hot to drink. Coffee? Something to eat?"

She doubted she could eat a thing. She still felt adrift, apart, as if she didn't quite belong in the here and now. "Coffee," she managed.

He went to start a pot, but came back immediately to sit beside her, wrap her in his powerful arms and rub her to stimulate circulation. "Do you feel dizzy? Weak? Maybe you're in shock."

"I'm fine." Slowly, but surely, she realized she was. By the time the coffee was ready and he returned with two mugs, she actually smiled at him.

"I did it," she said.

And slowly, slowly, he smiled back, leaving the stony Wade behind, maybe for good. "You certainly did."

And for that moment, it was enough.

THEY CUDDLED THROUGHOUT the night. First on the couch, then in her bed. Not making love, just cuddling and hugging. Little talking even, but as dawn began to lighten the world beyond the windows, Cory felt something she hadn't felt in a long time.

Pride. And exhilaration. She had done it. She had faced the killer. She had helped catch him.

It was her final act for Jim and their baby. The best memorial she could give them. But it was also the first act in her new life.

She bounded out of bed, and headed for the kitchen to make a huge breakfast, feeling hungry for food, but also hungry for life.

Wade followed, muttering something about a woman who didn't know when she had it good in a warm bed, but she laughed at his grumpiness until he laughed, too.

Oh, it was so good to hear him laugh. So good to feel like laughing.

She made mounds of scrambled eggs and hash browns, poured tall glasses of orange juice. And when they sat to eat, Wade said something that made her feel as light as a helium balloon.

"I'm so proud of you."

From him, that meant a whole lot. "I'm pretty proud of me, too."

"You should be."

She grinned at him and was thrilled when he grinned back.

"You make a mean hash brown, lady."

"Anytime." It felt good to cook for him, good to be doing something for someone else again. At the back of her mind lurked a little rain cloud, warning that there was no permanence here, that Wade would inevitably move on once he had settled whatever he had come here to settle with himself. But she didn't want to think about that now.

No, she was willing to toss her heart over the moon, and

take the pain later, because it felt so good to be truly alive again, and life was nothing at all if you wouldn't take risks. A lesson she had learned all too well over the past year.

After they cleaned up, they took a walk together, and for the first time in forever, Cory noticed all the beauty around her, from the birdsong to the ceaseless breeze that whispered through the old tress lining the street. For the first time in a long time, she noticed that life was all around her.

Later they dozed for a while on the couch, for they'd been up most of the night, but then Gage dropped by, and the first of many questions got answered.

"Ordano is in the hospital under guard. The Marshals arrived this morning and the FBI will be here in a little while. The guy started talking as soon as he came out of anesthesia. If you care, Cory, we now know who hired him to kill your husband. And we know who gave you away."

"Who?"

"A secretary in the Marshals' office. All it took was some sweet-talking, some wine and a few dinners to convince her she was in love with the creep. She managed to find out where you'd been placed and passed the information to him, but nothing else. She didn't have access to begin with so she shouldn't have even been able to learn that much."

"Wow," said Cory. "The things people do for love."

"Or when they think it's love. Anyway, she's been arrested, and procedures are going to be changed, or so I've been promised, although that's not going to be a problem for you anymore."

Cory smiled at him. "No, I guess it isn't."

Gage smiled back. "You'll still have to make a sworn statement for the FBI, and identify Ordano as the man who killed your husband. And there are going to be some other charges related to what happened last night. But one thing for absolute certain, you are never going to have to worry about that man again."

She couldn't stop smiling. "It's a wonderful feeling. I can't tell you how wonderful."

"I think I can imagine." Then Gage looked at Wade. "We've got a place for you as a deputy if you decide you want to hang around. Just think about it."

Rising, he picked up his hat and nodded to them both. "I'll call when we need your statement. It'll probably be later today or early tomorrow."

"I'm free." Free. At last. And how good it felt.

When Gage left, however, other thoughts tried to crowd in. Feeling suddenly nervous, and not sure she even wanted to hear the answer, but needing to know how many possibilities might lie before her, she said to Wade, "Will you take the job with the sheriff?"

"I don't know. I'll think about it. I guess it depends."

Her heart slammed uncomfortably. "Depends on what?"

Wade turned toward her, looking suddenly remote. Or was it something else she saw in his dark eyes. Concern? Unease? She couldn't quite read him.

"On whether you want me to hang around."

She caught her breath and her mouth went dry. Speech seemed impossible. But as she remained silent, she saw his face start to harden into stone again, and near panic struck her. She couldn't let him do that. No matter how hard it was for her to make herself utterly vulnerable to the wound he could inflict on her heart.

"I want you to hang around," she said almost breathlessly.

At once his face began to thaw. "Do you mean that?"

She took her newfound courage in her hands. "I mean I never want you to leave."

"Ever? You hardly know me."

"I know you well enough to know I don't want to give you up. Maybe you don't believe in love at first sight. I'm not sure I used to. It took me a while to fall in love with Jim. But with you…" She hesitated. "Wade, I've been in love before. I know what it is. All of it, good and bad. And I know for certain that I am in love with you."

For a moment he remained perfectly still. Her heart began to beat a nervous tattoo, for fear she had tried to claim something he wasn't prepared to let anyone claim. After all, he'd said he couldn't make connections.

"I think…I think I'm in love with you, too," he said. "I never felt this way before, so I'm not sure of anything except…I always want to be with you. Nobody's ever made me feel what you make me feel. I never knew a hug could mean so much or feel so good. I never knew I could get so intensely preoccupied with another person that I hang on to every word, every look, every gesture. I want to make you happy, if you'll just show me how. I want never to hurt you. Is that love?"

She leaned toward him and wrapped her arms around him. A moment later his closed around hers. "I want this forever," she whispered.

"Me, too." A sigh escaped him. "I want to marry you. I want to know that you want to marry me. For the first time in my life, Cory, I want the ring and the promises. Do you?"

She tilted her head up and looked at him, hoping her heart was in her eyes. "I want them, too, Wade, and I thought I'd never want them again. But I want them with you."

"So will you marry me?"

She watched the sun dawn on his face as she answered, simply, "Yes."

Then he pulled her onto his lap and kissed her, making this deepest of connections in the best way he knew how.

And with that kiss, they ushered in the dawn.

* * * * *

We hope you enjoyed the

# MILITARY HEROES
# COLLECTION.

If you liked these stories, then you'll love
**Harlequin® Romantic Suspense** stories!

You want sparks to fly!
**Harlequin® Romantic Suspense** stories deliver
with strong and adventurous women, brave and
powerful men and the life-and-death situations
that bring them together!

Enjoy four *new* stories from
**Harlequin® Romantic Suspense** every month!

SPECIAL EXCERPT FROM

 **HARLEQUIN**

## ROMANTIC suspense

When Drew offers to marry his brother's widow and care for her son, he never expects to fall for Alyssa. But when the child is kidnapped, Drew will do whatever it takes to make his family whole again.

Read on for a sneak peek at

# OPERATION UNLEASHED

by Justine Davis, available June 2014 from Harlequin® Romantic Suspense.

"We did this."

Her voice was soft, almost a whisper from behind him. He spun around. She'd gone up with Luke to get him warm and dry, and set him up with his current favorite book. He was already reading well for his age, on to third-grade level readers, and Drew knew that was thanks to Alyssa. "Yes," he said, his voice nearly as quiet as hers. "We did."

"It has to stop, Drew."

"Yes."

"What can I do to make that easier?"

God, he hated this. She was being so reasonable, so understanding. And he felt like a fool because the only answer he had was "Stop loving my brother."

"I'm not Luke," he said, not quite snapping. "Don't treat me like a six-year-old."

"Luke," she said sweetly, "is leaving temper tantrums behind."

He drew back sharply. Opened his mouth, ready to truly snap this time. And stopped.

"Okay," he said after a moment, "I had that one coming."

"Yes."

In an odd way, her dig pleased him. Not because it was accurate, he sheepishly admitted, but because she felt confident enough to do it. She'd been so weak, sick and scared when he'd found her four years ago, going toe-to-toe with him like this would have been impossible. But she was strong now, poised and self-assured. And he took a tiny bit of credit for that.

"You've come a long way," he said quietly.

"Because I don't cower anymore?"

He frowned. "I never made you cower."

For an instant she looked startled. "I never said you did. You saved us, Drew, don't think I don't know that, or will ever forget it. I have come a long way, and it's in large part because you made it possible."

It was a pretty little speech, a sentiment she'd expressed more than once. And not so long ago it had been enough. More than enough. It had told him he'd done exactly what he'd intended. That he'd accomplished his goal. That she was stable now, strong, and he'd had a hand in that.

And it wasn't her fault that wasn't enough for him anymore.

**Don't miss
OPERATION UNLEASHED
by Justine Davis,
available June 2014 from
Harlequin® Romantic Suspense.**

HRSEXP0514

# ROMANTIC suspense
## *LONE STAR REDEMPTION*
## by Colleen Thompson

### *Rusted Spur, Texas...*
### *where passion meets suspense!*

Desperate to reunite her missing twin with her dying
mother, Jessie Layton arrives at the Rayford ranch with
all the questions a good journalist would ask—plus
three more: Why is Zach, the extremely handsome
son, defending his mother's obvious lies?
Who is the "miracle child" they dote on?
And why is Zach so hostile?

But even as they spar, the reporter and the rancher
fight a growing attraction, intensified by the lethal
danger following Jessie. Together they risk their lives
confronting secrets that could destroy Zach's family...
if he chooses to tell the truth and do right by the
headstrong woman who's corralled him!

Look for *LONE STAR REDEMPTION*
by Colleen Thompson in June 2014.
Available wherever books and ebooks are sold.

*Heart-racing romance, high-stakes suspense!*

www.Harlequin.com

HRS27876

**Two classic stories from the *New York Times* bestselling queen of romantic suspense**

# LISA JACKSON

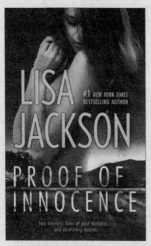

### Yesterday's Lies

It's been five years since Trask McFadden betrayed Tory's trust, landing her father behind bars. She'd hoped Trask was out of her life forever, but now he's returned to the Lazy W Ranch, claiming to have discovered a clue that might prove her father's innocence. For the sake of her family, Tory's trying to forgive, but she's finding it much harder to forget when Trask's presence begins to stir up feelings she'd thought were long gone....

### Devil's Gambit

Tiffany Rhodes's horse farm was in trouble long before she met Zane Sheridan, a breeder with a shady reputation. Yet she can't help but feel relieved when Zane offers to buy her out. Though Tiffany doesn't trust him, she's drawn to him like a magnet. What does this mysterious man want from her...and can she contain her desire long enough to find out?

## Available wherever books are sold!

### Be sure to connect with us at:

Harlequin.com/Newsletters

Facebook.com/HarlequinBooks

Twitter.com/HarlequinBooks

**HARLEQUIN® HQN™**

™ www.Harlequin.com

PHLJ877